CONTACT

'*Contact* [deals] with issues . . . worth pondering . . . The range and depth of ideas is quite uncommon' – *The New York Times Book Review*

'Imaginative flair . . . The Sagan wit is on full display . . . *Contact* jabs at commercial civilisation, nationalism, sexism . . .' – *The Wall Street Journal*

'Dazzling. . . . *Contact* becomes the greatest adventure of all time' – *Associated Press*

'A masterly piece of work blending adroit characterisation and flights of scientific fancy that spring from today's fact' – *Belfast Telegraph*

'A feast of marvels' – *San Francisco Chronicle*

'Who could be better qualified than the author of the highly successful *Cosmos* to turn the possibility of extra-terrestrial intelligence, and humankind's first contact with it, into imaginative reality? This is precisely what Sagan does in this eagerly awaited and, as it turns out, engrossing first novel . . . Sagan's informed and dramatically enacted speculations into the mysteries of the universe . . . make *Contact* an exciting adventure' – *Publishers Weekly*

'Like a good mystery, *Contact* keeps us curious to the end . . . Ingenious and satisfying' – *Newsweek*

'A splendid story whose appeal is universal' – *Yorkshire Post*

CONTACT

A Novel

Carl Sagan

www.orbitbooks.net

ORBIT

First published in Great Britain by
Century Hutchinson Limited in 1986
Arrow edition 1986
Legend edition 1988
This edition published by Orbit in 1997
Reprinted 1998 (twice), 2000, 2002, 2005, 2007 (twice)

A CIP catalogue record for this book
is available from the British Library.

ISBN 978-1-85723-580-7

Papers used by Orbit are natural, recyclable products made from
wood grown in sustainable forests and certified in accordance with
the rules of the Forest Stewardship Council.

Printed and bound in Great Britain by Clays Ltd, St Ives plc
Paper supplied by Hellefoss AS, Norway

Orbit
An imprint of
Little, Brown Book Group
100 Victoria Embankment
London EC4Y 0DY

An Hachette Livre UK Company

www.orbitbooks.net

For Alexandra,
who comes of age
with the Millennium.
May we leave your generation a world
better than the one we were given.

Contents

Part I

THE MESSAGE

My heart trembles like a poor leaf.
The planets whirl in my dreams.
The stars press against my window.
I rotate in my sleep.
My bed is a warm planet.

— MARVIN MERCER
    PS 153, Fifth Grade, Harlem
    New York City, NY (1981)

1
Transcendental Numbers

> Little fly,
> Thy summer's play
> My thoughtless hand
> Has brushed away.
>
> Am not I
> A fly like thee?
> Or art not thou
> A man like me?
>
> For I dance
> And drink and sing,
> Till some blind hand
> Shall brush my wing.
>
> — WILLIAM BLAKE
> *Songs of Experience*
> 'The Fly,' Stanzas 1–3
> (1795)

By human standards it could not possibly have been artificial: It was the size of a world. But it was so oddly and intricately shaped, so clearly intended for some complex purpose that it could only have been the expression of an idea. Gliding in polar orbit about the great blue-white star, it resembled some immense, imperfect polyhedron, encrusted with millions of bowl-shaped barnacles. Every bowl was aimed at a particular part of the sky. Every constellation was being attended to. The polyhedral world had been performing its enigmatic function for eons. It was very patient. It could afford to wait forever.

When they pulled her out, she was not crying at all. Her tiny brow was wrinkled, and then her eyes grew wide.

She looked at the bright lights, the white- and green-clad figures, the woman lying on the table below her. Somehow familiar sounds washed over her. On her face was an odd expression for a newborn – puzzlement perhaps.

When she was two years old, she would lift her hands over her head and say very sweetly, 'Dada, up.' His friends expressed surprise. The baby was polite. 'It's not politeness,' her father told them. 'She used to scream when she wanted to be picked up. So once I said to her, "Ellie, you don't have to scream. Just say, 'Daddy, up'"' Kids are smart. Right, Presh?'

So now she was *up* all right, at a giddy altitude, perched on her father's shoulders and clutching his thinning hair. Life was better up here, far safer than crawling through a forest of legs. Somebody could step on you down there. You could get lost. She tightened her grip.

Leaving the monkeys, they turned a corner and came upon a great spindly-legged, long-necked dappled beast with tiny horns on its head. It towered over them. 'Their necks are so long, the talk can't get out,' her father said. She felt sorry for the poor creature, condemned to silence. But she also felt a joy in its existence, a delight that such wonders might be.

'Go ahead, Ellie,' her mother gently urged her. There was a lilt in the familiar voice. 'Read it.' Her mother's sister had not believed that Ellie, age three, could read. The nursery stories, the aunt was convinced, had been memorized. Now they were strolling down State Street on a brisk March day and had stopped before a store window. Inside, a burgundy-red stone was glistening in the sunlight. 'Jeweler,' Ellie read slowly, pronouncing three syllables.

Guiltily, she let herself into the spare room. The old Motorola radio was on the shelf where she remembered it. It was very big and heavy and, hugging it to her chest, she almost dropped it. On the back were the words 'Danger. Do Not Remove.' But she knew that if it wasn't plugged in, there was no danger in it. With her tongue between her lips, she removed the screws and exposed the innards. As she had suspected, there were no tiny orchestras and miniature announcers quietly living out their small lives in anticipation of the moment when the toggle switch would be clicked to 'on.' Instead there were beautiful glass tubes, a little like light bulbs. Some resembled the churches of Moscow she had seen pictured in a book. The prongs at their bases were perfectly designed for the receptacles they were fitted into. With the back off and the switch 'on,' she plugged the set into a nearby wall socket. If she didn't touch it, if she went nowhere near it, how could it hurt her?

After a few moments, tubes began to glow warmly, but no sound came. The radio was 'broken,' and had been retired some years before in favor of a more modern variety. One tube was not glowing. She unplugged the set and pried the uncooperative tube out of its receptacle. There was a metallic square inside, attached to tiny wires. The electricity runs along the wires, she thought vaguely. But first it has to get into the tube. One of the prongs seemed bent, and she was able after a little work to straighten it. Reinserting the tube and plugging the set in again, she was delighted to see it begin to glow, and an ocean of static arose around her. Glancing toward the closed door with a start, she lowered the volume. She turned the dial marked 'frequency,' and came upon a voice talking excitedly – as far as she could understand, about a Russian machine that was in the sky, endlessly circling the Earth. Endlessly, she thought. She turned the dial again, seeking other stations. After a while, fearful of being discovered, she unplugged the set, screwed the back on loosely, and with still more difficulty lifted the radio and placed it back on the shelf.

As she left the spare room, a little out of breath, her mother came upon her and she started once more.

'Is everything all right, Ellie?'

'Yes, Mom.'

She affected a casual air, but her heart was beating, her palms were sweating. She settled down in a favorite spot in the small backyard and, her knees drawn up to her chin, thought about the inside of the radio. Are all those tubes really necessary? What would happen if you removed them one at a time? Her father had once called them vacuum tubes. What was happening inside a vacuum tube? Was there really no air in there? How did the music of the orchestras and the voices of the announcers get *in* the radio? They liked to say, 'On the air.' Was radio carried by the air? What happens inside the radio set when you change stations? What was 'frequency'? Why do you have to plug it in for it to work? Could you make a kind of map showing how the electricity runs through the radio? Could you take it apart without hurting yourself? Could you put it back together again?

'Ellie, what have you been up to?' asked her mother, walking by with laundry for the clothesline.

'Nothing, Mom. Just thinking.'

In her tenth summer, she was taken on vacation to visit two cousins she detested at a cluster of cabins along a lake in the Northern Peninsula of Michigan. Why people who lived on a lake in Wisconsin would spend five hours driving all the way to a lake in Michigan was beyond her. Especially to see two mean and babyish boys. Only ten and eleven. Real jerks. How could her father, so sensitive to her in other respects, want her to play day in and day out with twerps? She spent the summer avoiding them.

One sultry moonless night after dinner she walked down alone to the wooden pier. A motorboat had just gone by, and her uncle's rowboat tethered to the dock was softly bobbing in the starlit water. Apart from distant cicadas and an almost subliminal shout echoing across the lake, it was perfectly still. She looked up at the brilliant spangled sky and found her heart racing.

14

Without looking down, with only her outstretched hand to guide her, she found a soft patch of grass and laid herself down. The sky was blazing with stars. There were thousands of them, most twinkling, a few bright and steady. If you looked carefully you could see faint differences in color. That bright one there, wasn't it bluish?

She felt again for the ground beneath her; it was solid, steady . . . reassuring. Cautiously she sat up and looked left and right, up and down the long reach of lakefront. She could see both sides of the water. The world only looks flat, she thought to herself. Really it's round. This is all a big ball . . . turning in the middle of the sky . . . once a day. She tried to imagine it spinning, with millions of people glued to it, talking different languages, wearing funny clothes, all stuck to the same ball.

She stretched out again and tried to sense the spin. Maybe she could feel it just a little. Across the lake, a bright star was twinkling between the topmost branches. If you squinted your eyes you could make rays of light dance out of it. Squint a little more, and the rays would obediently change their length and shape. Was she just imagining it, or . . . the star was now definitely above the trees. Just a few minutes ago it had been poking in and out of the branches. Now it was higher, no doubt about it. That's what they meant when they said a star was rising, she told herself. The Earth was turning in the other direction. At one end of the sky the stars were rising. That way was called East. At the other end of the sky, behind her, beyond the cabins, the stars were setting. That way was called West. Once every day the Earth would spin completely around, and the same stars would rise again in the same place.

But if something as big as the Earth turned once a day, it had to be moving ridiculously fast. Everyone she knew must be whirling at an unbelievable speed. She thought she could now actually feel the Earth turn – not just imagine it in her head, but really feel it in the pit of her

15

stomach. It was like descending in a fast elevator. She craned her neck back further, so her field of view was uncontaminated by anything on Earth, until she could see nothing but black sky and bright stars. Gratifyingly, she was overtaken by the giddy sense that she had better clutch the clumps of grass on either side of her and hold on for dear life, or else fall up into the sky, her tiny tumbling body dwarfed by the huge darkened sphere below.

She actually cried out before she managed to stifle the scream with her wrist. That was how her cousins were able to find her. Scrambling down the slope, they discovered on her face an uncommon mix of embarrassment and surprise, which they readily assimilated, eager to find some small indiscretion to carry back and offer to her parents.

The book was better than the movie. For one thing, there was a lot more in it. And some of the pictures were awfully different from the movie. But in both, Pinocchio – a life-sized wooden boy who magically is roused to life – wore a kind of halter, and there seemed to be dowels in his joints. When Geppetto is just finishing the construction of Pinocchio, he turns his back on the puppet and is promptly sent flying by a well-placed kick. At that instant the carpenter's friend arrives and asks him what he is doing sprawled on the floor. 'I am teaching,' Geppetto replies with dignity, 'the alphabet to the ants.'

This seemed to Ellie extremely witty, and she delighted in recounting it to her friends. But each time she quoted it there was an unspoken question lingering at the edge of her consciousness: *Could* you teach the alphabet to the ants? And would you want to? Down there with hundreds of scurrying insects who might crawl all over your skin, or even sting you? What could ants know, anyway?

★

Sometimes she would get up in the middle of the night to go to the bathroom and find her father there in his pajama bottoms, his neck craned up, a kind of patrician disdain accompanying the shaving cream on his upper lip. 'Hi, Presh,' he would say. It was short for 'precious,' and she loved him to call her that. Why was he shaving at night, when no one would know if he had a beard? 'Because' – he smiled – 'your mother will know.' Years later, she discovered that she had understood this cheerful remark only incompletely. Her parents had been in love.

After school, she had ridden her bicycle to a little park on the lake. From a saddlebag she produced *The Radio Amateur's Handbook* and *A Connecticut Yankee in King Arthur's Court*. After a moment's consideration, she decided on the latter. Twain's hero had been conked on the head and awakened in Arthurian England. Maybe it was all a dream or a delusion. But maybe it was real. Was it possible to travel backwards in time? Her chin on her knees, she scouted for a favorite passage. It was when Twain's hero is first collected by a man dressed in armor who he takes to be an escapee from a local booby hatch. As they reach the crest of the hill they see a city laid out before them:

' "Bridgeport?" said I . . .
' "Camelot," said he.'

She stared out into the blue lake, trying to imagine a city which could pass as both nineteenth-century Bridgeport and sixth-century Camelot, when her mother rushed up to her.

'I've looked for you everywhere. Why aren't you where I can find you? Oh, Ellie,' she whispered, 'something awful's happened.'

In the seventh grade they were studying 'pi.' It was a Greek letter that looked like the architecture at Stonehenge, in England: two vertical pillars with a crossbar at top – π. If you measured the circumference of a

17

circle and then divided it by the diameter of the circle, that was pi. At home, Ellie took the top of a mayonnaise jar, wrapped a string around it, straightened the string out, and with a ruler measured the circle's circumference. She did the same with the diameter, and by long division divided the one number by the other. She got 3.21. That seemed simple enough.

The next day the teacher, Mr Weisbrod, said that π was about 22/7, about 3.1416. But actually, if you wanted to be exact, it was a decimal that went on and on forever without repeating the pattern of numbers. Forever, Ellie thought. She raised her hand. It was the beginning of the school year and she had not asked any questions in this class.

'How could anybody know that the decimals go on and on forever?'

'That's just the way it is,' said the teacher with some asperity.

'But why? How do you know? How can you count decimals forever?'

'Miss Arroway' – he was consulting his class list – 'this is a stupid question. You're wasting the class's time.'

No one had ever called Ellie stupid before, and she found herself bursting into tears. Billy Horstman, who sat next to her, gently reached out and placed his hand over hers. His father had recently been indicted for tampering with the odometers on the used cars he sold, so Billy was sensitive to public humiliation. Ellie ran out of the class sobbing.

After school she bicycled to the library at the nearby college to look through books on mathematics. As nearly as she could figure out from what she read, her question wasn't all that stupid. According to the Bible, the ancient Hebrews had apparently thought that π was exactly equal to three. The Greeks and Romans, who knew lots of things about mathematics, had no idea that the digits in π went on forever without repeating. It was a fact that had been discovered only about 250 years ago. How was she expected to know if she couldn't ask questions? But Mr Weisbrod had been right about the first few digits. Pi wasn't 3.21. Maybe the mayonnaise lid had been a little squashed, not a perfect circle. Or maybe she'd been sloppy in measuring the string. Even if she'd been much more careful, though, they couldn't expect her to measure an infinite number of decimals.

There was another possibility, though. You could *calculate* pi as accurately as you wanted. If you knew something called calculus, you could prove formulas for π that would let you calculate it to as many decimals as you had time for. The book listed formulas for pi divided by four. Some of them she couldn't understand at all. But there were some that dazzled her: $\pi/4$, the book said, was the same as $1 - \frac{1}{3} + \frac{1}{5} - \frac{1}{7} + \ldots$, with the fractions continuing on forever. Quickly she tried to work it out, adding and subtracting the fractions alternately. The sum would bounce from being bigger than $\pi/4$ to being smaller than $\pi/4$, but after a while you could see that this series of numbers was on a beeline for the right answer. You could never get there exactly, but you could get as close as you wanted if you were very patient. It seemed to her a miracle that the shape of every circle in the world was connected with this series of fractions. How could circles know about fractions? She was determined to learn calculus.

The book said something else: π was called a 'transcendental' number. There was no equation with ordinary numbers in it that could give you π unless it was infinitely long. She had already taught herself a little algebra and understood what this meant. And π wasn't the only transcendental number. In fact there was an infinity of transcendental numbers. More than that, there were infinitely more transcendental numbers than ordinary numbers, even though π was the only one of them she had ever heard of. In more ways than one, π was tied to infinity.

She had caught a glimpse of something majestic.

Hiding between all the ordinary numbers was an infinity of transcendental numbers whose presence you would never have guessed unless you looked deeply into mathematics. Every now and then one of them, like π, would pop up unexpectedly in everyday life. But most of them, an infinite number of them, she reminded herself— were hiding, minding their own business, almost certainly unglimpsed by the irritable Mr Weisbrod.

She saw through John Staughton from the first. How her mother could even *con*template marrying him – never mind that it was only two years after her father's death – was an impenetrable mystery. He was nice enough looking, and he could pretend, when he put his mind to it, that he really cared about you. But he was a martinet. He made his students come over weekends to weed and garden at the new house they had moved into, and then made fun of them after they left. He told Ellie that she was just beginning high school and was not to look twice at any of his bright young men. He was puffed up with imaginary self-importance. She was sure that as a professor he secretly despised her dead father, who had been only a shopkeeper. Staughton had made it clear that an interest in radio and electronics was unseemly for a girl, that it would not catch her a husband, that understanding physics was for her a foolish and aberrational notion. 'Pretentious,' he called it. She just didn't have the ability. This was an objective fact that she might as well get used to. He was telling her this for her own good. She'd thank him for it in later life. He was, after all, an associate professor of physics. He knew what it took. These homilies would always infuriate her, even though she had never before – despite Staughton's refusal to believe it – considered a career in science.

He was not a gentle man, as her father had been, and he had no idea what a sense of humor was. When anyone assumed that she was Staughton's daughter, she would be outraged. Her mother and stepfather never suggested that she change her name to Staughton; they knew what her response would be.

Occasionally there was a little warmth in the man, as when, in her hospital room just after her tonsillectomy, he had brought her a splendid kaleidoscope.

'When are they going to do the operation,' she had asked, a little sleepily.

'They've already done it,' Staughton had answered. 'You're going to be fine.' She found it disquieting that whole blocks of time could be stolen without her knowledge, and blamed him. She knew at the time it was childish.

That her mother could truly love him was inconceivable. She must have remarried out of loneliness, out of weakness. She needed someone to take care of her. Ellie vowed she would never accept a position of dependence. Ellie's father had died, her mother had grown distant, and Ellie felt herself exiled to the house of a tyrant. There was no one to call her Presh any more.

She longed to escape.

'"Bridgeport?" said I.

'"Camelot," said he.'

2
Coherent Light

Since I first gained the use of reason my inclination toward learning has been so violent and strong that neither the scoldings of other people . . . nor my own reflections . . . have been able to stop me from following this natural impulse that God gave me. He alone must know why; and He knows too that I have begged Him to take away the light of my understanding, leaving only enough for me to keep His law, for anything else is excessive in a woman, according to some people. And others say it is even harmful.

> — Juana Ines de la Cruz
> *Reply to the Bishop of Puebla* (1691), who had attacked her scholarly work as inappropriate for her sex

I wish to propose for the reader's favourable consideration a doctrine which may, I fear, appear wildly paradoxical and subversive. The doctrine in question is this: that it is undesirable to believe a proposition when there is no ground whatever for supposing it true. I must, of course, admit that if such an opinion became common it would completely transform our social life and our political system; since both are at present faultless, this must weigh against it.

> — Bertrand Russell
> *Skeptical Essays*, I (1928)

Surrounding the blue-white star in its equatorial plane was a vast ring of orbiting debris – rocks and ice, metals and organics – reddish at the periphery and bluish closer to the star. The world-sized polyhedron plummeted through a gap in the rings and emerged out the other side. In the ring plane, it had been intermittently shadowed by icy boulders and tumbling mountains. But now, carried along its trajectory toward a point above the opposite pole of the star, the sunlight gleamed off its millions of bowl-shaped appendages. If you looked very carefully you might have seen one of them make a slight pointing adjustment. You would not have seen the burst of radio waves washing out from it into the depths of space.

For all the tenure of humans on earth, the night sky had been a companion and an inspiration. The stars were comforting. They seemed to demonstrate that the heavens were created for the benefit and instruction of humans. This pathetic conceit became the conventional wisdom worldwide. No culture was free of it. Some people found in the skies an aperture to the religious sensibility. Many were awestruck and humbled by the glory and scale of the cosmos. Others were stimulated to the most extravagant flights of fancy.

At the very moment that humans discovered the scale of the universe and found that their most unconstrained fancies were in fact dwarfed by the true dimensions of even the Milky Way Galaxy, they took steps that ensured that their descendants would be unable to see the stars at all. For a million years humans had grown up with a personal daily knowledge of the vault of heaven. In the last few thousand years they began building and emigrating to the cities. In the last few decades, a major fraction of the human population had abandoned a rustic way of life. As technology developed and the cities were polluted, the nights became starless. New generations grew to maturity wholly ignorant of the sky that had transfixed their ancestors and that had stimulated the modern age of science and technology. Without even noticing, just as astronomy entered a golden age most people cut themselves off from the sky, a cosmic isolationism that ended only with the dawn of space exploration.

Ellie would look up at Venus and imagine it was a world something like the Earth – populated by plants and animals and civilizations, but each of them different from the kinds we have here. On the outskirts of town, just after sunset, she would examine the night sky and scrutinize that unflickering bright point of light. By comparison with nearby clouds, just above her, still illuminated by the Sun, it seemed a little yellow. She tried to imagine what was going on there. She would stand on tiptoe and stare the planet down. Sometimes, she could almost convince herself that she could really see it; a swirl of yellow fog would suddenly clear, and a vast jeweled city would briefly be revealed. Air cars sped among the crystal spires. Sometimes she would imagine peering into one of those vehicles and glimpsing one of *them*. Or she would imagine a young one, glancing up at a bright blue point of light in *its* sky, standing on tiptoe and wondering about the inhabitants of Earth. It was an irresistible notion: a sultry, tropical planet brimming over with intelligent life, and just next door.

She consented to rote memorization, but knew that it was at best the hollow shell of an education. She did the minimum work necessary to do well in her courses, and pursued other matters. She arranged to spend free periods and occasional hours after school in what was called 'shop' – a dingy and cramped small factory established when the school devoted more effort to 'vocational education' than was now fashionable. 'Vocational education' meant, more than anything else, working with your hands. There were lathes, drill presses, and other machine tools which she was forbidden to approach, because no matter how capable she might be, she was still 'a girl.' Reluctantly, they granted her permission to pursue her own projects in

24

the electronics area of the 'shop.' She built radios more or less from scratch, and then went on to something more interesting.

She built an encrypting machine. It was rudimentary, but it worked. It could take any English-language message and transform it by a simple substitution cipher into something that looked like gibberish. Building a machine that would do the reverse – converting an ecrypted message into clear when you didn't know the substitution convention – that was much harder. You could have the machine run through all the possible substitutions (A stands for B, A stands for C, A stands for D . . .), or you could remember that some letters in English were used more often than others. You could get some idea of the frequency of letters by looking at the sizes of the bins for each letter of type in the print shop next door. 'ETAOIN SHRDLU,' the boys in print shop would say, giving pretty closely the order of the twelve most frequently used letters in English. In decoding a long message, the letter that was most common probably stood for an E. Certain consonants tended to go together, she discovered; vowels distributed themselves more or less at random. The most common three-letter word in the language was 'the.' If within a word there was a letter standing between a T and an E, it was almost certainly H. If not, you could bet on R or a vowel. She deduced other rules and spent long hours counting up the frequency of letters in various schoolbooks before she discovered that such frequency tables had already been compiled and published. Her decrypting machine was only for her own enjoyment. She did not use it to convey secret messages to friends. She was unsure to whom she might safely confide these electronic and cryptographic interests; the boys became jittery or boisterous, and the girls looked at her strangely.

Soldiers of the United States were fighting in a distant place called Vietnam. Every month, it seemed, more young men were being scooped off the street or the farm and packed off to Vietnam. The more she learned about the origins of the war, and the more she listened to the public pronouncements of national leaders, the more outraged she became. The President and the Congress were lying and killing, she thought to herself, and almost everyone else was mutely assenting. The fact that her stepfather embraced official positions on treaty obligations, dominoes, and naked Communist aggression only strengthened her resolve. She began attending meetings and rallies at the college nearby. The people she met there seemed much brighter, friendlier, more *alive* than her awkward and lusterless high school companions. John Staughton first cautioned her and then forbade her to spend time with college students. They would not respect her, he said. They would take advantage of her. She was pretending to a sophistication she did not have and never would. Her style of dress was deteriorating. Military fatigues were inappropriate for a girl and a travesty, a hypocrisy, for someone who claimed to oppose the American intervention in Southeast Asia.

Beyond pious exhortations to Ellie and Staughton not to 'fight,' her mother participated little in these discussions. Privately she would plead with Ellie to obey her stepfather, to be 'nice.' Ellie now suspected Staughton of marrying her mother for her father's life insurance – why else? He certainly showed no signs of loving her – and *he* was not predisposed to be 'nice.' One day, in some agitation, her mother asked her to do something for all their sakes: attend Bible class. While her father, a skeptic on revealed religions, had been alive, there was no talk of Bible class. How could her mother have married Staughton? The question welled up in her for the thousandth time. Bible class, her mother continued, would help instill the conventional virtues; but even more important, it would show Staughton that Ellie was willing to make some accommodation. Out of love and pity for her mother, she acquiesced.

So every Sunday for most of one school year Ellie went to a regular discussion group at a nearby church. It was one of the respectable Protestant denominations, untainted by disorderly evangelism. There were a few high school students, a number of adults, mainly middle-aged women, and the instructor, the minister's wife. Ellie had never seriously read the Bible before and had been inclined to accept her father's perhaps ungenerous judgment that it was 'half barbarian history, half fairy tales.' So over the weekend preceding her first class, she read through what seemed to be the important parts of the Old Testament, trying to keep an open mind. She at once recognized that there were two different and mutually contradictory stories of Creation in the first two chapters of Genesis. She did not see how there could be light and days before the Sun was made, and had trouble figuring out exactly who it was that Cain had married. In the stories of Lot and his daughters, of Abraham and Sarah in Egypt, of the betrothal of Dinah, of Jacob and Esau, she found herself amazed. She understood that cowardice might occur in the real world – that sons might deceive and defraud an aged father, that a man might give craven consent to the seduction of his wife by the King, or even encourage the rape of his daughters. But in this holy book there was not a word of protest against such outrages. Instead, it seemed, the crimes were approved, even praised.

When class began, she was eager for a discussion of these vexing inconsistencies, for an unburdening illumination of God's Purpose, or at least for an explanation of why these crimes were not condemned by the author or Author. But in this she was to be disappointed. The minister's wife blandly temporized. Somehow these stories never surfaced in subsequent discussion. When Ellie inquired how it was possible for the maidservants of the daughter of Pharaoh to tell just by looking that the baby in the bullrushes was Hebrew, the teacher blushed deeply and asked Ellie not to raise

27

unseemly questions. (The answer dawned on Ellie at that moment.)

When they came to the New Testament, Ellie's agitation increased. Matthew and Luke traced the ancestral line of Jesus back to King David. But for Matthew there were twenty-eight generations between David and Jesus; for Luke forty-three. There were almost no names common to the two lists. How could both Matthew and Luke be the Word of God? The contradictory genealogies seemed to Ellie a transparent attempt to fit the Isaianic prophecy after the event – cooking the data, it was called in chemistry lab. She was deeply moved by the Sermon on the Mount, deeply disappointed by the admonition to render unto Caesar what is Caesar's, and reduced to shouts and tears after the instructor twice sidestepped her questions on the meaning of 'I bring not peace but the sword.' She told her despairing mother that she had done her best, but wild horses wouldn't drag her to another Bible class.

She was lying on her bed. It was a hot summer's night. Elvis was singing, 'One night with you, that's what I'm beggin' for.' The boys at the high school seemed painfully immature, and it was difficult – especially with her stepfather's strictures and curfews – to establish much of a relationship with the young college men she met at lectures and rallies. John Staughton was right, she reluctantly admitted to herself, at least about this: The young men, almost without exception, had a penchant for sexual exploitation. At the same time, they seemed much more emotionally vulnerable than she had expected. Perhaps the one caused the other.

She had half expected not to attend college, although she was determined to leave home. Staughton would not pay for her to go elsewhere, and her mother's meek intercessions were unavailing. But Ellie had done spectacularly well on the standardized college entrance examinations and found to her surprise her teachers telling her that she was likely to be offered scholarships by well-known universities. She had guessed on a number of multiple-choice questions and considered her performance a fluke. If you know very little, only enough to exclude all but the two most likely answers, and if you then guess at ten straight questions, there is about one chance in a thousand, she explained to herself, that you'll get all ten correct. For twenty straight questions, the odds were one in a million. But something like a million kids probably took this test. *Someone* had to get lucky.

Cambridge, Massachusetts, seemed far enough away to elude John Staughton's influence, but close enough to return from on vacation to visit her mother – who viewed the arrangement as a difficult compromise between abandoning her daughter and incrementally irritating her husband. Ellie surprised herself by choosing Harvard over the Massachusetts Institute of Technology.

She arrived for orientation period, a pretty dark-haired young woman of middling height with a lopsided smile and an eagerness to learn everything. She set out to broaden her education, to take as many courses as possible apart from her central interests in mathematics, physics, and engineering. But there was a problem with her central interests. She found it difficult to discuss physics, much less debate it, with her predominantly male classmates. At first they paid a kind of selective inattention to her remarks. There would be a slight pause, and then they would go on as if she had not spoken. Occasionally they would acknowledge her remark, even praise it, and then again continue undeflected. She was reasonably sure her remarks were not entirely foolish, and did not wish to be ignored, much less ignored and patronized alternately. Part of it – but only a part – she knew was due to the softness of her voice. So she developed a physics voice, a professional voice: clear, competent, and many decibels above conversational. With such a voice it was important to be right. She had to pick her moments. It was hard to continue long in such a voice, because she

29

was sometimes in danger of bursting out laughing. So she found herself leaning toward quick, sometimes cutting, interventions, usually enough to capture their attention; then she could go on for a while in a more usual tone of voice. Every time she found herself in a new group she would have to fight her way through again, just to dip her oar into the discussion. The boys were uniformly unaware even that there was a problem.

Sometimes she would be engaged in a laboratory exercise or a seminar when the instructor would say, 'Gentlemen, let's proceed,' and sensing Ellie's frown would add, 'Sorry, Miss Arroway, but I think of you as one of the boys.' The highest compliment they were capable of paying was that in their minds she was not overtly female.

She had to fight against developing too combative a personality or becoming altogether a misanthrope. She suddenly caught herself. 'Misanthrope' is someone who dislikes everybody, not just men. And they certainly had a word for someone who hates women: 'misogynist.' But the male lexicographers had somehow neglected to coin a word for the dislike of men. They were almost entirely men themselves, she thought, and had been unable to imagine a market for such a word.

More than many others, she had been encumbered with parental proscriptions. Her newfound freedoms – intellectual, social, sexual – were exhilarating. At a time when many of her contemporaries were moving toward shapeless clothing that minimized the distinctions between the sexes, she aspired to an elegance and simplicity in dress and makeup that strained her limited budget. There were more effective ways to make political statements, she thought. She cultivated a few close friends and made a number of casual enemies, who disliked her for her dress, for her political and religious views, or for the vigor with which she defended her opinions. Her competence and delight in science were taken as rebukes by many otherwise capable young women. But a few looked on her as what mathematicians call an existence theorem – a demonstration that a woman could, sure enough, excel in science – or even as a role model.

At the height of the sexual revolution, she experimented with gradually increasing enthusiasm, but found she was intimidating her would-be lovers. Her relationships tended to last a few months or less. The alternative seemed to be to disguise her interests and stifle her opinions, something she had resolutely refused to do in high school. The image of her mother, condemned to a resigned and placatory imprisonment, haunted Ellie. She began wondering about men unconnected with the academic and scientific life.

Some women, it seemed, were entirely without guile and bestowed their affections with hardly a moment's conscious thought. Others set out to implement a campaign of military thoroughness, with branched contingency trees and fallback positions, all to 'catch' a desirable man. The word 'desirable' was the giveaway, she thought. The poor jerk wasn't actually desired, only 'desirable' – a plausible object of desire in the opinion of those others on whose account this whole sorry charade was performed. Most women, she thought, were somewhere in the middle, seeking to reconcile their passions with their perceived long-term advantage. Perhaps there were occasional communications between love and self-interest that escaped the notice of the conscious mind. But the whole idea of calculated entrapment made her shiver. In this matter, she decided, she was a devotee of the spontaneous. That was when she met Jesse.

Her date had taken her to a cellar bar off Kenmore Square. Jesse was singing rhythm and blues and playing lead guitar. The way he sang and the way he moved made clear what she had been missing. The next night she returned alone. She seated herself at the nearest table and locked eyes with him through both his sets. Two months later they were living together.

31

It was only when his bookings took him to Hartford or Bangor that she got any work done at all. She would spend her days with the other students: boys with the final generation of slide rules hanging like trophies from their belts; boys with plastic pencil holders in their breast pockets; precise, stilted boys with nervous laughs; serious boys spending all their waking moments becoming scientists. Absorbed in training themselves to plumb the depths of nature, they were almost helpless in ordinary human affairs, where, for all their knowledge, they seemed pathetic and shallow. Perhaps the dedicated pursuit of science was so consuming, so competitive, that no time was left to become a well-rounded human being. Or perhaps their social disabilities had led them to fields where the want would not be noticed. Except for science itself, she did not find them good company.

At night there was Jesse, leaping and wailing, a kind of force of nature that had taken over her life. In the year they spent together, she could not recall a single night when he proposed they go to sleep. He knew nothing of physics or mathematics, but he was wide awake inside the universe, and for a time so was she.

She dreamed of reconciling her two worlds. She had fantasies of musicians and physicists in harmonious social concert. But the evenings she organized were awkward and ended early.

One day he told her he wanted a baby. He would be serious, he'd settle down, he'd get a regular job. He might even consider marriage.

'A baby?' she asked him. 'But I'd have to leave school. I have years more before I'm done. If I had a baby, I might never go back to school.'

'Yeah,' he said, 'but we'd have a baby. You wouldn't have school, but you'd have something else.'

'Jesse, I *need* school,' she told him.

He shrugged, and she could feel their lives together slip off his shoulders and away. It lasted another few months, but it all had really been settled in that brief exchange. They kissed each other goodbye and he went off to California. She never heard his voice again.

In the late 1960s, the Soviet Union succeeded in landing space vehicles on the surface of Venus. They were the first spacecraft of the human species to set down in working order on another planet. Over a decade earlier, American radio astronomers, confined to Earth, had discovered that Venus was an intense source of radio emission. The most popular explanation had been that the massive atmosphere of Venus trapped the heat through a planetary greenhouse effect. In this view, the surface of the planet was stifling hot, much too hot for crystal cities and wondering Venusians. Ellie longed for some other explanation, and tried unsuccessfully to imagine ways in which the radio emission could come from high above a clement Venus surface. Some astronomers at Harvard and MIT claimed that none of the alternatives to a broiling Venus could explain the radio data. The idea of so massive a greenhouse effect seemed to her unlikely and somehow distasteful, a plant that had let itself go. But when the *Venera* spacecraft landed and in effect stuck out a thermometer, the temperature measured was high enough to melt tin or lead. She imagined the crystal cities liquifying (although Venus wasn't quite *that* hot), the surface awash in silicate tears. She was a romantic. She had known it for years.

But at the same time she had to admire how powerful radio astronomy was. The astronomers had sat home, pointed their radio telescopes at Venus, and measured the surface temperature just about as accurately as the *Venera* probes did thirteen years later. She had been fascinated with electricity and electronics as long as she could remember. But this was the first time she had been deeply impressed by radio astronomy. You stay safely on your own planet and point your telescope with its associated electronics. Information about other worlds then

33

comes fluttering down through the feeds. She marveled at the notion.

Ellie began to visit the university's modest radio telescope in nearby Harvard, Massachusetts, eventually getting an invitation to help with the observations and the data analysis. She was accepted as a paid summer assistant at the National Radio Astronomy Observatory in Green Bank, West Virginia, and upon arrival, gazed in some rapture at Grote Reber's original radio telescope, constructed in his backyard in Wheaton, Illinois, in 1938, and now serving as a reminder of what a dedicated amateur can accomplish. Reber had been able to detect the radio emission from the center of the Galaxy when no one nearby happened to be starting up the car and the diathermy machine down the street was not in operation. The Galactic Center was much more powerful, but the diathermy machine was a lot closer.

The atmosphere of patient inquiry and the occasional rewards of modest discovery were agreeable to her. They were trying to measure how the number of distant extragalactic radio sources increased as they looked deeper into space. She began to think about better ways of detecting faint radio signals. In due course, she graduated cum laude from Harvard and went on for graduate work in radio astronomy at the other end of the country, at the California Institute of Technology.

For a year, she apprenticed herself to David Drumlin. He had a worldwide reputation for brilliance and for not suffering fools gladly, but was at heart one of those men you can find at the top of every profession who are in a state of unrelieved anxiety that someone, somewhere, might prove smarter than they. Drumlin taught Ellie some of the real heart of the subject, especially its theoretical underpinnings. Although he was inexplicably rumored to be attractive to women, Ellie found him frequently combative and unremittingly self-involved. She was too romantic, he would say. The universe is

34

strictly ordered according to its own rules. The idea is to think as the universe does, not to foist our romantic predispositions (and girlish longings, he once said) on the universe. Everything not forbidden by the laws of nature, he assured her – quoting a colleague down the hall – is mandatory. But, he went on, almost everything is forbidden. She gazed at him as he lectured, trying to divine this odd combination of personality traits. She saw a man in excellent physical condition: prematurely gray hair, sardonic smile, half-moon reading glasses perched toward the end of his nose, bow tie, square jaw, and remnants of a Montana twang.

His idea of a good time was to invite the graduate students and junior faculty over for dinner (unlike her stepfather, who enjoyed a student entourage but considered having them to dinner an extravagance). Drumlin would exhibit an extreme intellectual territoriality, steering the conversation to topics in which he was the acknowledged expert and then swiftly dispatching contrary opinions. After dinner he would often subject them to a slide show of Dr D. scuba diving in Cozumel or Tobago or the Great Barrier Reef. He was often smiling into the camera and waving, even in the underwater images. Sometimes there would be a submarine vista of his scientific colleague, Dr Helga Bork. (Drumlin's wife would always object to these particular slides, on the reasonable grounds that most of the audience had already seen them at previous dinner parties. In truth, the audience had already seen all the slides. Drumlin would respond by extolling the virtues of the athletic Dr Bork, and his wife's humiliation increased.) Many of the students gamely went along, seeking some novelty they had previously missed among the brain corals and the spiny sea urchins. A few would writhe in embarrassment or become absorbed in the avocado dip.

A stimulating afternoon for his graduate students would be for them to be invited over, in twos or threes, to drive him to the edge of a favorite cliff near Pacific

Palisades. Casually attached to his hang glider, he would leap off the precipice toward the tranquil ocean a few hundred feet below. Their job was to drive down the coast road and retrieve him. He would swoop down upon them, beaming exultantly. Others were invited to join him, but few accepted. He had, and delighted in, the competitive advantage. It was quite a performance. Others looked on graduate students as resources for the future, as their intellectual torchbearers to the next generation. But Drumlin, she felt, had quite a different view. For him graduate students were gunslingers. There was no telling which of them might at any moment challenge him for the reigning title of 'Fastest Gun in the West.' They were to be kept in their places. He never made a pass at her, but sooner or later, she was certain, he was bound to try.

In her second year at Cal Tech, Peter Valerian returned to campus from his sabbatical year abroad. He was a gentle and unprepossessing man. No one, least of all he himself, considered him especially brilliant. Yet he had a steady record of significant accomplishment in radio astronomy because, he explained when pressed, he 'kept at it.' There was one slightly disreputable aspect of his scientific career: He was fascinated by the possibility of extraterrestrial intelligence. Each faculty member, it seemed, was allowed one foible: Drumlin had hang gliding and Valerian had life on others worlds. Others had topless bars, or carnivorous plants, or something called transcendental meditation. Valerian had thought about extraterrestrial intelligence, abbreviated ETI, longer and harder – and in many cases more carefully – than anyone else. As she grew to know him better, it seemed that ETI provided a fascination, a romance, that was in dramatic contrast with the humdrum business of his personal life. This thinking about extraterrestrial intelligence was not work for him, but play. His imagination soared.

Ellie loved to listen to him. It was like entering

Wonderland or the Emerald City. Actually, it was better, because at the end of all his ruminations there was the thought that maybe this could really be true, could really happen. Someday, she mused, there might in fact and not just in fantasy be a message received by one of the great radio telescopes. But in a way it was worse, because Valerian, like Drumlin on other subjects, repeatedly stressed that speculation must be confronted with sober physical reality. It was a kind of sieve that separated the rare useful speculation from torrents of nonsense. The extraterrestrials and their technology had to conform strictly to the laws of nature, a fact that severely crimped many a charming prospect. But what emerged from this sieve, and survived the most skeptical physical and astronomical analysis, might even be true. You couldn't be sure, of course. There were bound to be possibilities that you had missed, that people cleverer than you would one day figure out.

Valerian would emphasize how we are trapped by our time and our culture and our biology, how limited we are, by definition, in imagining fundamentally different creatures or civilizations. And separately evolved on very different worlds, they would *have* to be very different from us. It was possible that beings much more advanced than we might have unimaginable technologies – this was, in fact, almost guaranteed – and even new laws of physics. It was hopelessly narrow-minded, he would say as they walked past a succession of stucco arches as in a De Chirico painting, to imagine that all significant laws of physics had been discovered at the moment our generation began contemplating the problem. There would be a twenty-first-century physics and a twenty-second-century physics, and even a Fourth-Millennium physics. We might be laughably far off in guessing how a very different technical civilization would communicate.

But then, he always reassured himself, the extraterrestrials would have to know how backward we were. If we were any more advanced, they would know about

37

us already. Here we were, just beginning to stand up on our two feet, discovering fire last Wednesday, and only yesterday stumbling on Newtonian dynamics, Maxwell's equations, radio telescopes, and hints of Super-unification of the laws of physics. Valerian was sure they wouldn't make it hard for us. They would try to make it easy, because if they wanted to communicate with dummies they would have to make allowances for the dummies. That's why, he thought, he'd have a fighting chance if a message ever came. His lack of brilliance was in fact his strength. He knew, he was confident, what dummies knew.

As a topic for her doctoral thesis, Ellie chose, with the concurrence of the faculty, the development of an improvement in the sensitive receivers employed on radio telescopes. It made use of her talents in electronics, freed her from the mainly theoretical Drumlin, and permitted her to continue her discussions with Valerian – but without taking the professionally dangerous step of working with him on extraterrestrial intelligence. It was too speculative a subject for a doctoral dissertation. Her stepfather had taken to denouncing her various interests as unrealistically ambitious or occasionally as deadeningly trivial. When he heard of her thesis topic through the grapevine (by now, she was not talking to him at all), he dismissed it as pedestrian.

She was working on the ruby maser. A ruby is made mainly of alumina, which is almost perfectly transparent. The red color derives from a small chromium impurity distributed through the alumina crystal. When a strong magnetic field is impressed on the ruby, the chromium atoms increase their energy or, as physicists like to say, are raised to an excited state. She loved the image of all the little chromium atoms called to feverish activity in each amplifier, frenzied in a good practical cause – amplifying a weak radio signal. The stronger the magnetic field, the more excited the chromium atoms became. Thus the maser could be tuned so that it was particularly sensitive to a selected radio frequency. She found a way to make rubies with lanthanide impurities in addition to the chromium atoms, so a maser could be tuned to a narrower frequency range and could detect a much weaker signal than previous masers. Her detector had to be immersed in liquid helium. She then installed her new instrument on one of Cal Tech's radio telescopes in Owens Valley and detected, at entirely new frequencies, what astronomers call the three-degree black-body background radiation – the remnant in the radio spectrum of the immense explosion that began this universe, the Big Bang.

'Let's see if I've got this right,' she would say to herself. 'I've taken an inert gas that's in the air, made it into a liquid, put some impurities into a ruby, attached a magnet, and detected the fires of creation.'

She would then shake her head in amazement. To anyone ignorant of the underlying physics, it might seem the most arrogant and pretentious necromancy. How would you explain this to the best scientists of a thousand years ago, who knew about air and rubies and lodestones, but not about liquid helium, stimulated emission, and superconducting flux pumps? In fact, she reminded herself, they did not have even the foggiest notion about the radio spectrum. Or even the idea of a spectrum – except vaguely, from contemplating the rainbow. They did not know that light was waves. How could we hope to understand the science of a civilization a thousand years ahead of us?

It was necessary to make rubies in large batches, because only a few would have the requisite properties. None were quite of gemstone quality, and most were tiny. But she took to wearing a few of the larger remnants. They matched her dark coloring well. Even if it was carefully cut, you could recognize some anomaly in the stone set in a ring or a brooch: the odd way, for example, that it caught the light at certain angles from an abrupt internal reflection, or a peach-colored blemish inside the ruby red. She would explain to nonscientist friends that she liked rubies but couldn't afford them. It was a little like the scientist who first discovered the biochemical pathway of green plant photosynthesis, and who forever after wore pine needles or a sprig of parsley in his lapel. Colleagues, their respect for her growing, considered it a minor idiosyncrasy.

The great radio telescopes of the world are constructed in remote locations for the same reason Paul Gauguin sailed to Tahiti: For them to work well, they must be far from civilization. As civilian and military radio traffic has increased, radio telescopes have had to hide – sequestered in an obscure valley in Puerto Rico, say, or exiled to vast scrub desert in New Mexico or Kazakhstan. As radio interference continues to grow, it makes increasing sense to build the telescopes off the Earth altogether. The scientists who work at these isolated observatories tend to be dogged and determined. Spouses abandon them, children leave home at the first opportunity, but the astronomers stick it out. Rarely do they think of themselves as dreamers. The permanent scientific staff in remote observatories tend to be the practical ones, the experimentalists, the experts who know a great deal about antenna design and data analysis, and much less about quasars or pulsars. Generally speaking, they had not longed for the stars in childhood; they had been too busy repairing the carburetor in the family car.

After receiving her doctorate, Ellie accepted an appointment as research associate at the Arecibo Observatory, a great bowl 305 meters across, fixed to the floor of a karst valley in the foothills of northwestern Puerto Rico. With the largest radio telescope on the planet, she was eager to employ her maser detector to look at as many different astronomical objects as she could – nearby planets and stars, the center of the Galaxy, pulsars and quasars. As a full-time member of the

Observatory staff, she would be assigned a significant amount of observing time. Access to the great radio telescopes is keenly competitive, there being many more worthwhile research projects than can possibly be accommodated. So reserved telescope time for the resident staff is a perquisite beyond price. For many of the astronomers, it was the only reason they would consent to live in such godforsaken places.

She also hoped to examine a few nearby stars for possible signals of intelligent origin. With her detector system it would be possible to hear the radio leakage from a plant like Earth even if it was a few light-years away. And an advanced society, intending to communicate with us, would doubtless be capable of much greater power transmissions than we were. If Arecibo, used as a radar telescope, was capable of transmitting one megawatt of power to a specific locale in space, then a civilization only a little bit in advance of ours might, she thought, be capable of transmitting a hundred megawatts or more. If they were intentionally transmitting to the Earth with a telescope as large as Arecibo but with a hundred-megawatt transmitter, Arecibo should be able to detect them virtually anywhere in the Milky Way Galaxy. When she thought carefully about it, she was surprised that, in the search for extraterrestrial intelligence, what *could* be done was so far ahead of what *had* been done. The resources that had been devoted to this question were trifling, she thought. She was hard pressed to name a more important scientific problem.

The Arecibo facility was known to the locals as 'El Radar.' Its function was generally obscure, but it provided more than a hundred badly needed jobs. The indigenous young women were sequestered from the male astronomers, some of whom could be viewed at almost any time of day or night, full of nervous energy, jogging along the circumferential track that surrounded the dish. As a result, the attentions directed at Ellie upon her arrival, while not entirely unwelcome, soon became a distraction from her research.

The physical beauty of the place was considerable. At twilight, she would look out the control windows and see storm clouds hovering over the other lip of the valley, just beyond one of the three immense pylons from which the feed horns and her newly installed maser system were suspended. At the top of each pylon, a red light would flash to warn off any airplanes that had improbably strayed upon this remote vista. At 4 A.M., she would step outside for a breath of air and puzzle to understand a massed chorus of thousands of local land frogs, called 'coquis' in imitation of their plaintive cry.

Some astronomers lived near the Observatory, but the isolation, compounded by ignorance of Spanish and inexperience with any other culture, tended to drive them and their wives toward loneliness and anomie. Some had decided to live at Ramey Air Force Base, which boasted the only English-language school in the vicinity. But the ninety-minute drive also heightened their sense of isolation. Repeated threats by Puerto Rican separatists, convinced erroneously that the Observatory played some significant military function, increased the sense of subdued hysteria, of circumstances barely under control.

Many months later, Valerian came to visit. Nominally he was there to give a lecture, but she knew that part of his purpose was to check up on how she was doing and provide some semblance of psychological support. Her research had gone very well. She had discovered what seemed to be a new interstellar molecular cloud complex, and had obtained some very fine high time-resolution data on the pulsar at the center of the Crab Nebula. She had even completed the most sensitive search yet performed for signals from a few dozen nearby stars, but with no positive results. There had been one or two suspicious regularities. She observed the stars in question again and could find nothing out of the ordinary. Look at

42

enough stars, and sooner or later terrestrial interference or the concatenation of random noise will produce a pattern that for a moment makes your heart palpitate. You calm down and check it out. If it doesn't repeat itself, you consider it spurious. This discipline was essential if she was to preserve some emotional equilibrium in the face of what she was seeking. She was determined to be as tough-minded as possible, without abandoning the sense of wonder that was driving her in the first place.

From her scant supply in the community refrigerator, she had made a rudimentary picnic lunch, and Valerian sat with her along the very periphery of the bowl-shaped dish. Workmen repairing or replacing the panels could be seen in the distance, walking on special snowshoes so they did not tear the aluminum sheets and plunge through to the ground below. Valerian was delighted with her progress. They exchanged bits of gossip and current scientific tidbits. The conversation turned to SETI, as the search for extraterrestrial intelligence was beginning to be called.

'Have you ever thought about doing it full time, Ellie?' he asked.

'I haven't thought about it much. But it's not really possible, is it? There's no major facility devoted to SETI full time anywhere in the world, as far as I know.'

'No, but there might be. There's a chance that dozens of additional dishes might be added to the Very Large Array, and make it into a dedicated SETI observatory. They'd do some of the usual kind of radio astronomy also, of course. It would be a superb interferometer. It's only a possibility, it's expensive, it needs real political will, and it's years away at best. Just something to think about.'

'Peter, I've just examined some forty-odd nearby stars of roughly solar spectral type. I've looked in the twenty-one centimeter hydrogen line, which everybody says is the obvious beacon frequency – because hydrogen is the most abundant atom in the universe, and so on. And I've

43

done it with the highest sensitivity ever tried. There's not a hint of a signal. Maybe there's no one out there. Maybe the whole business is a waste of time.'

'Like life on Venus? That's just disillusionment talking. Venus is a hellhole of a world; it's just one planet. But there's hundreds of billions of stars in the Galaxy. You've looked at only a handful. Wouldn't you say it's a little premature to give up? You've done one-billionth of the problem. Probably much less than that, if you consider other frequencies.'

'I know, I know. But don't you have the sense that if they're anywhere, they're everywhere? If really advanced guys live a thousand light-years away, shouldn't they have an outpost in our backyard? You could do the SETI thing forever, you know, and never convince yourself that you'd completed the search.'

'Oh, you're beginning to sound like Dave Drumlin. If we can't find them in his lifetime, he's not interested. We're just beginning SETI. You *know* how many possibilities there are. This is the time to leave every option open. This is the time to be optimistic. If we lived in any previous time in human history, we could wonder about this all our lives, and we couldn't do a thing to find the answer. But this time is unique. This is the first time when *any*body's been able to look for extraterrestrial intelligence. You've made the detector to look for civilizations on the planets of millions of other stars. Nobody's guaranteeing success. But can you think of a more important question? Imagine them out there sending us signals, and nobody on Earth is listening. That would be a joke, a travesty. Wouldn't you be ashamed of your civilization if we were able to listen and didn't have the gumption to do it?'

Two hundred fifty-six images of the left world swam by on the left. Two hundred fifty-six images of the right world glided by on the right. She integrated all 512 images into a wraparound view of her surroundings. She

44

was deep in a forest of great waving blades, some green, some etiolated, almost all larger than she. But she had no difficulty clambering up and over, occasionally balancing precariously on a bent blade, falling to the gentle cushion of horizontal blades below, and then continuing unerringly on her journey. She could tell she was centered on the trail. It was tantalizingly fresh. She would think nothing, if that's where the trail led, of scaling an obstacle a hundred or a thousand times as tall as she was. She needed no pitons or ropes; she was already equipped. The ground immediately before her was redolent with a marked odor left recently, it must be, by another scout of her clan. It would lead to food; it almost always did. The food would spontaneously appear. Scouts would find it and mark the trail. She and her fellows would bring it back. Sometimes the food was a creature rather like herself; other times it was only an amorphous or crystalline lump. Occasionally it was so large that many of her clan would be required, working together, heaving and shoving it over the folded blades, to carry it home. She smacked her mandibles in anticipation.

'What worries me the most,' she continued, 'is the opposite, the possibility that *they're* not trying. They could communicate with us, all right, but they're not doing it because they don't see any point to it. It's like . . .' – she glanced down at the edge of the tablecloth they had spread over the grass – 'like the ants. They occupy the same landscape that we do. They have plenty to do, things to occupy themselves. On some level they're very well aware of their environment. But we don't try to communicate with them. So I don't think they have the foggiest notion that we exist.'

A large ant, more enterprising than his fellows, had ventured onto the tablecloth and was briskly marching along the diagonal of one of the red and white squares. Suppressing a small twinge of revulsion, she gingerly flicked it back onto the grass – where it belonged.

3

White Noise

Heard melodies are sweet, but those unheard
Are sweeter.

— JOHN KEATS
'Ode on a Grecian Urn' (1820)

The cruelest lies are often told in silence.

— ROBERT LOUIS STEVENSON
Virginibus Puerisque
(1881)

The pulses had been journeying for years through the great dark between the stars. Occasionally, they would intercept an irregular cloud of gas and dust, and a little of the energy would be absorbed or scattered. The remainder continued in the original direction. Ahead of them was a faint yellow glow, slowly increasing in brightness among the other unvarying lights. Now, although to human eyes it would still be a point, it was by far the brightest object in the black sky. The pulses were encountering a horde of giant snowballs.

Entering the Argus administration building was a willowy woman in her late thirties. Her eyes, large and set far apart, served to soften the angular bone structure of her face. Her long dark hair was loosely gathered by a tortoise barette at the nape of her neck. Casually dressed in a knit T-shirt and khaki skirt, she strolled along a hallway on the first floor and entered a door marked 'E. Arroway, Director.' As she removed her thumb from the fingerprint deadlock, an observer might have noticed a ring on her right hand with an oddly milky red stone unprofessionally set in it. Turning on a desk lamp, she rummaged through a drawer, finally producing a pair of earphones. Briefly illuminated on the wall beside her desk was a quotation from the *Parables* of Franz Kafka:

> Now the Sirens have a still more fatal weapon
>   than their song, namely their silence . . .
> Someone might possibly have escaped from
>   their singing;
> but from their silence, certainly never.

Extinguishing the light with a wave of her hand, she made for the door in the semidarkness.

In the control room she quickly reassured herself that all was in order. Through the window she could see a few of the 131 radio telescopes that stretched for tens of kilometers across the New Mexico scrub desert like some strange species of mechanical flower straining toward the sky. It was early afternoon and she had been up late the night before. Radio astronomy can be performed during daylight, because the air does not scatter radio waves from the Sun as it does ordinary visible light. To a radio telescope pointing anywhere but very close to the Sun, the sky is pitch black. Except for the radio sources.

Beyond the Earth's atmosphere, on the other side of the sky, is a universe teeming with radio emission. By studying radio waves you can learn about planets and stars and galaxies, about the composition of great clouds of organic molecules that drift between the stars, about the origin and evolution and fate of the universe. But all these radio emissions are natural – caused by physical processes, electrons spiraling in the galactic magnetic field, or interstellar molecules colliding with one another, or the remote echoes of the Big Bang red-shifted from gamma rays at the origin of the universe to the tame and chill radio waves that fill all of space in our epoch.

In the scant few decades in which humans have pursued radio astronomy, there has never been a real signal from the depths of space, something manufactured, something artificial, something contrived by an alien mind. There have been false alarms. The regular time variation of the radio emission from quasars and, especially, pulsars had at first been thought, tentatively, tremulously, to be a kind of announcement signal from someone else, or perhaps a radio navigation beacon for exotic ships that plied the spaces between the stars. But they had turned out to be something else – equally exotic, perhaps, as a signal from beings in the night sky. Quasars seemed to be stupendous sources of energy, perhaps connected with massive black holes at the centers of galaxies, many of them observed more than halfway back in time to the origin of the universe. Pulsars are rapidly spinning atomic nuclei the size of a city. And there had been other rich and mysterious messages that had turned out to be intelligent after a fashion but not very extraterrestrial. The skies were now peppered with secret military radar systems and radio communication satellites that were beyond the entreaty of a few civilian radio astronomers. Sometimes they were real outlaws, ignoring international telecommunications agreements. There were no recourses and no penalties. Occasionally, all nations denied responsibility. But there had never been a clear-cut alien signal.

And yet the origin of life now seemed to be so easy – and there were so many planetary systems, so many worlds and so many billions of years available for biological evolution – that it was hard to believe the Galaxy was not teeming with life and intelligence. Project Argus was the largest facility in the world dedicated to the radio search for extraterrestrial intelligence. Radio waves traveled with the speed of light, faster than which nothing, it seemed, could go. They were easy to generate and easy to detect. Even very backward technological civilizations, like that on Earth, would stumble on radio early in their exploration of the physical world. Even with the rudimentary radio technology available – now, only a few decades after the invention of the radio telescope – it was nearly possible to communicate with an identical civilization at the center of the Galaxy. But there were so many places in the sky to examine, and so many frequencies on which an alien civilization might be broadcasting, that it required a systematic and patient observing program. Argus had been in full operation for more than four years. There had been glitches, bogeys, intimations, false alarms. But no message.

'Afternoon, Dr Arroway.'

The lone engineer smiled pleasantly at her, and she nodded back. All 131 telescopes of Project Argus were controlled by computers. The system slowly scanned the sky on its own, checking that there were no mechanical or electronic breakdowns, comparing the data from different elements of the array of telescopes. She glanced at the billion-channel analyzer, a bank of electronics covering a whole wall, and at the visual display of the spectrometer.

There was not really very much for the astronomers and technicians to do as the telescope array over the years slowly scanned the sky. If it detected something of interest, it would automatically sound an alarm, alerting project scientists in their beds at night if need be. Then Arroway would go into high gear to determine if this one was an instrumental failure or some American or Soviet space bogey. Together with the engineering staff, she would devise ways of improving the sensitivity of the equipment. Was there any pattern, any regularity in the emission? She would delegate some of the radio telescopes to examine exotic astronomical objects that had been recently detected by other observatories. She would help staff members and visitors with projects unrelated to SETI. She would fly to Washington to keep interest high at the funding agency, the National Science Foundation. She would give a few public talks on Project Argus – at the Rotary Club in Socorro or the University of New Mexico in Albuquerque – and occasionally greet an enterprising reporter who would arrive, sometimes un-announced, in remotest New Mexico.

Ellie had to take care that the tedium did not engulf her. Her co-workers were pleasant enough, but – even apart from the impropriety of a close personal rela-tionship with a nominal subordinate – she did not find herself tempted into any real intimacies. There had been a few brief, torrid but fundamentally casual relationships with local men unconnected with the Argus project. In this area of her life, too, a kind of ennui, a lassitude, had settled over her.

She sat down before one of the consoles and plugged in the earphones. It was futile, she knew, a conceit, to think that she, listening on one or two channels, would detect a pattern when the vast computer system monitoring a billion channels had not. But it gave her a modest illusion of utility. She leaned back, eyes half closed, an almost dreamy expression enveloping the contours of her face. She's really quite lovely, the technician permitted himself to think.

She heard, as always, a kind of static, a continuous echoing random noise. Once, when listening to a part of the sky that included the star $AC + 79\,3888$ in Cassiopeia, she felt she heard a kind of singing, fading tantalizingly in and out, lying just beyond her ability to convince herself that there was something really there. This was the star toward which the *Voyager 1* spacecraft, now in the vicinity of the orbit of Neptune, would ultimately travel. The spacecraft carried a golden phonograph record on which were impressed greetings, pictures, and songs from Earth. Could they be sending us their music at the speed of light, while we are sending ours to them only one ten-thousandth as fast? At other times, like now, when the static was clearly patternless, she would remind herself of Shannon's famous dictum in information theory, that the most efficiently coded message was indistinguishable from noise, unless you had the key to the encoding beforehand. Rapidly she pressed a few keys on the console before her and played two of the narrow-band frequencies against each other, one in each earphone. Nothing. She listened to the two planes of polarization of the radio waves, and then to the contrast between linear and circular polarization. There were a billion channels to choose from. You could spend your life trying to out-guess the computer, listening with pathetically limited human ears and brains, seeking a pattern.

Humans are good, she knew, at discerning subtle patterns that are really there, but equally so at imagining them when they are altogether absent. There would be some sequence of pulses, some configuration of the static, that would for an instant give a syncopated beat or a brief melody. She switched to a pair of radio telescopes that were listening to a known galactic radio source. She heard a glissando down the radio frequencies, a 'whistler' due to the scattering of radio waves by electrons in the tenuous interstellar gas between the radio source and the Earth. The more pronounced the glissando, the more electrons were in the way, and the further the source was from the Earth. She had done this so often that she was able, just from hearing a radio whistler for the first time, to make an accurate judgment of its distance. This one, she estimated, was about a thousand light-years away – far beyond the local neighborhood of stars, but still well within the great Milky Way Galaxy.

Ellie returned to the sky-survey mode of Project Argus. Again no pattern. It was like a musician listening to the rumble of a distant thunderstorm. The occasional small patches of pattern would pursue her and intrude themselves into her memory with such insistence that sometimes she was forced to go back to the tapes of a particular observing run to see if there was something her mind had caught and the computers had missed.

All her life, dreams had been her friends. Her dreams were unusually detailed, well-structured, colorful. She was able to peer closely at her father's face, say, or the

51

back of an old radio set, and the dream would oblige with full visual details. She had always been able to recall her dreams, down to the fine details – except for the times when she had been under extreme pressure, as before her Ph.D. oral exam, or when she and Jesse were breaking up. But now she was having difficulty recalling the images in her dreams. And, disconcertingly, she began to dream sounds – as people do who are blind from birth. In the early morning hours her unconscious mind would generate some theme or ditty she had never heard before. She would wake up, give an audible command to the light on her night table, pick up the pen she had put there for the purpose, draw a staff, and commit the music to paper. Sometimes after a long day she would play it on her recorder and wonder if she had heard it in Ophiuchus or Capricorn. She was, she would admit to herself ruefully, being haunted by the electrons and the moving holes that inhabit receivers and amplifiers, and by the charged particles and magnetic fields of the cold thin gas between the flickering distant stars.

It was a repeated single note, high-pitched and raucous around the edges. It took her a moment to recognize it. Then she was sure she hadn't heard it in thirty-five years. It was the metal pulley on the clothesline that would complain each time her mother gave a tug and put out another freshly washed smock to dry in the Sun. As a little girl, she had loved the army of marching clothes-pins; and when no one was about, would bury her face in the newly dried sheets. The smell, at once sweet and pungent, enchanted her. Could that be a whiff of it now? She could remember herself laughing, toddling away from the sheets, when her mother in one graceful motion swooped her up – to the sky it seemed – and carried her away in the crook of her arm, as if she herself were just a little bundle of clothes to be neatly arranged in the chest of drawers in her parents' bedroom.

*

'Dr Arroway? Dr Arroway?' The technician looked down on her fluttering eyelids and shallow breathing. She blinked twice, removed the headphones, and gave him a small apologetic smile. Sometimes her colleagues had to talk very loudly if they wished to be heard above the amplified cosmic radio noise. She would in turn compensate for the volume of the noise – she was loath to remove the earphones for brief conversations – by shouting back. When she was sufficiently preoccupied, a casual or even convivial exchange of pleasantries would seem to an inexperienced observer like a fragment of a fierce and unprovoked argument unexpectedly generated amidst the quiet of the vast radio facility. But now she only said, 'Sorry. I must have drifted off.'

'It's Dr Drumlin on the phone. He's in Jack's office and says he has an appointment with you.'

'Holy Toledo, I forgot.'

As the years had passed, Drumlin's brilliance had remained undiminished, but there were a number of additional personal idiosyncrasies that had not been in evidence when she had served briefly as his graduate student at Cal Tech. For example, he had the disconcerting habit now of checking, when he thought himself unobserved, whether his fly was open. He had over the years become increasingly convinced that extraterrestrials did not exist, or at least that they were too rare, too distant to be detected. He had come to Argus to give the weekly scientific colloquium. But, she found, he had come for another purpose as well. He had written a letter to the National Science Foundation urging that Argus terminate its search for extraterrestrial intelligence and devote itself full time to more conventional radio astronomy. He produced it from an inside pocket and insisted that she read it.

'But we've only been at it four and a half years. We've looked at less than a third of the northern sky. This is the first survey that can do the entire radio noise minimum at optimum bandpasses. Why would you want to stop now?'

'No, Ellie, this is endless. After a dozen years you'll find no sign of anything. You'll argue that another Argus facility has to be built at a cost of hundreds of millions of dollars in Australia or Argentina to observe the southern sky. And when that fails, you'll talk about building some paraboloid with a free-flying feed in Earth orbit so you can get millimeter waves. You'll always be able to think of some kind of observation that hasn't been done. You'll always invent some explanation about why the extraterrestrials like to broadcast where we haven't looked.'

'Oh, Dave, we've been through this a hundred times. If we fail, we learn something of the rarity of intelligent life – or at least intelligent life that thinks like we do and wants to communicate with backward civilizations like us. And if we succeed, we hit the cosmic jackpot. There's no greater discovery you can imagine.'

'There are first-rate projects that aren't finding tele-scope time. There's work on quasar evolution, binary pulsars, the chromospheres of nearby stars, even those crazy interstellar proteins. These projects are waiting in line because this facility – by far the best-phased array in the world – is being used almost entirely for SETI.'

'Seventy-five percent for SETI, Dave, twenty-five percent for routine radio astronomy.'

'Don't call it routine. We've got the opportunity to look back to the time that the galaxies were being formed, or maybe even earlier than that. We can examine the cores of giant molecular clouds and the black holes at the centers of galaxies. There's a revolution in astronomy about to happen, and you're standing in the way.'

'Dave, try not to personalize this. Argus would never have been built if there wasn't public support for SETI. The idea for Argus isn't mine. You know they picked me as director when the last forty dishes were still under construction. The NSF is entirely behind –'

54

'Not entirely, and not if I have anything to say about it. This is grandstanding. This is pandering to UFO kooks and comic strips and weak-minded adolescents.'

By now Drumlin was fairly shouting, and Ellie felt an irresistible temptation to tune him out. Because of the nature of her work and her comparative eminence, she was constantly thrown into situations where she was the only woman present, except for those serving coffee or making a stenotypic transcript. Despite what seemed like a lifetime of effort on her part, there was still a host of male scientists who only talked to each other, insisted on interrupting her, and ignored, when they could, what she had to say. Occasionally there were those like Drumlin who showed a positive antipathy. But at least he was treating her as he did many men. He was evenhanded in his outbursts, visiting them equally on scientists of both sexes. There were a rare few of her male colleagues who did not exhibit awkward personality changes in her presence. She ought to spend more time with them, she thought. People like Kenneth der Heer, the molecular biologist from the Salk Institute who had recently been appointed Presidential Science Adviser. And Peter Valerian, of course.

Drumlin's impatience with Argus, she knew, was shared by many astronomers. After the first two years a kind of melancholy had pervaded the facility. There were passionate debates in the commissary or during the long and undemanding watches about the intentions of the putative extraterrestrials. We could not guess how different from us they might be. It was hard enough to guess the intentions of our elected representatives in Washington. What would the intentions be of fundamentally different kinds of beings on physically different worlds hundreds or thousands of light-years away. Some believed that the signal would not be transmitted in the radio spectrum at all but in the infrared or the visible or somewhere among the gamma rays. Or perhaps the extraterrestrials were signaling avidly but with a technology we would not invent for a thousand years.

Astronomers at other institutions were making extraordinary discoveries among the stars and galaxies, picking out those objects which, by whatever mechanism, generated intense radio waves. Other radio astronomers published scientific papers, attended meetings, were uplifted by a sense of progress and purpose. The Argus astronomers tended not to publish and were usually ignored when the call went out for invited papers at the annual meeting of the American Astronomical Society or the triennial symposia and plenary sessions of the International Astronomical Union. So in consultation with the National Science Foundation, the leadership at Argus had reserved 25 percent of the observing time for projects unconnected with the search for extraterrestrial intelligence. Some important discoveries had been made – on the extragalactic objects that seemed, paradoxically, to be moving faster than light; on the surface temperature of Neptune's big moon, Triton; and on the dark matter in the outer reaches of nearby galaxies where no stars could be seen. Morale began to improve. The Argus staff felt they were making a contribution at the cutting edge of astronomical discovery. The time to complete a full search of the sky had been lengthened, it was true. But now their professional careers had some safety net. They might not succeed in finding signs of other intelligent beings, but they might pluck other secrets from the treasury of nature.

The search for extraterrestrial intelligence – everywhere abbreviated SETI, except by those who talked somewhat more optimistically about communication with extraterrestrial intelligence (CETI) – was essentially an observing routine, the dull staple for which most of the facility had been built. But a quarter of the time you could be assured of using the most powerful array of radio telescopes on Earth for other projects. You had only to get through the boring part. A small amount of time had also been reserved for astronomers from other institutions. While the morale had improved noticeably, there were many who agreed with Drumlin; they glanced longingly at the technological miracle that Argus' 131 radio telescopes represented and imagined using them for their own, doubtless meritorious, programs. She was alternately conciliatory and argumentative with Dave, but none of it did any good. He was not in an amiable mood.

Drumlin's colloquium was in part an attempt to demonstrate that there were no extraterrestrials anywhere. If we had accomplished so much in only a few thousand years of high technology, what must a truly advanced species, he asked, be capable of? They should be able to move stars about, to reconfigure galaxies. And yet, in all of astronomy there was no sign of a phenomenon that could not be understood by natural processes, for which an appeal to extraterrestrial intelligence had to be made. Why hadn't Argus detected a radio signal by now? Did they imagine just one radio transmitter in all of the sky? Did they realize how many billions of stars they had examined already? The experiment was a worthy one, but now it was over. They didn't have to examine the rest of the sky. The answer was in. Neither in deepest space nor near the Earth was there any sign of extraterrestrials. They did not exist.

In the question period, one of the Argus astronomers asked about the Zoo Hypothesis, the contention that the extraterrestrials were out there all right, but chose not to make their presence known, in order to conceal from humans the fact that there were other intelligent beings in the cosmos – in the same sense that a specialist in primate behavior might wish to observe a troop of chimpanzees in the bush but not interfere with their activities. In reply, Drumlin asked a different question: Is it likely that with a million civilizations in the galaxy – the sort of number he said was 'bandied about' at Argus – there would not be a single poacher? How does it come about that every civilization in the galaxy abides by an ethic of noninterference? Is it probable that not one of them would be poking around on the Earth?

'But on Earth,' Ellie replied, 'poachers and game wardens have roughly equal levels of technology. If the game warden is a major step ahead – with radar and helicopters, say – then the poachers are out of business.'

The remark was greeted warmly by some of the Argus staff, but Drumlin only said, 'You're reaching, Ellie. You're reaching.'

To clear her head it was her practice to go for long solo drives in her one extravagance, a carefully maintained 1958 Thunderbird with removable hardtop and little glass portholes flanking the rear seat. Often she would leave the top at home and speed through the scrub desert at night, with the windows down and her dark hair streaming behind her. Over the years, it seemed, she had gotten to know every small impoverished town, every butte and mesa, and every state highway patrolman in southwestern New Mexico. After a night observing run, she would love to zoom past the Argus guard station (that was before the cyclone fencing went up), rapidly changing gears, and drive north. Around Santa Fe, the faintest glimmerings of dawn might be seen above the Sangre de Cristo Mountains. (Why should a religion, she asked herself, name its places after the blood and body, heart and pancreas of its most revered figure? And why not the brain, among other prominent but uncommemorated organs?)

This time she drove southeast, toward the Sacramento Mountains. Could Dave be right? Could SETI and Argus be a kind of collective delusion of a few insufficiently hard-nosed astronomers? Was it true that no matter how many years went by without the receipt of a message, the project would continue, always inventing a new strategy for the transmitting civilization, continually devising novel and expensive instrumentation? What *would* be a convincing sign of failure? When would she be willing to give up and turn to something safer, something more guaranteed of results? The Nobeyama Observatory in Japan had just announced the discovery of adenosine, a complex organic molecule, a building block of DNA, sitting out there in a dense molecular cloud. She could certainly busy herself usefully in looking for life-related molecules in space, even if she gave up searching for extraterrestrial intelligence.

On the high mountain road, she glanced at the southern horizon and caught a glimpse of the constellation Centaurus. In that pattern of stars the ancient Greeks had seen a chimerical creature, half man, half horse, who had taught Zeus wisdom. But Ellie could never make out any pattern remotely like a centaur. It was Alpha Centauri, the brightest star in the constellation, that she delighted in. It was the nearest star, only four and a quarter light-years away. Actually, Alpha Centauri was a triple system, two suns tightly orbiting one another, and a third, more remote, circling them both. From Earth, the three stars blended together to form a solitary point of light. On particularly clear nights, like this one, she could sometimes see it hovering somewhere over Mexico. Sometimes, when the air had been laden with desert grit after several consecutive days of sand storms, she would drive up into the mountains to gain a little altitude and atmospheric transparency, get out of the car, and stare at the nearest star system. Planets were possible there, although very hard to detect. Some might be closely orbiting any one of the triple suns. A more interesting orbit, with some fair celestial mechanical stability, was a figure eight, which wrapped itself around the two inner suns. What would it be like, she wondered, to live on a world with three suns in the sky? Probably even hotter than New Mexico.

The two-lane blacktop highway, Ellie noticed with a pleasant little tremor, was lined with rabbits. She had seen them before, especially when her drives had taken her as far as West Texas. They were on all fours by the shoulders of the road; but as each would be momentarily illuminated by the Thunderbird's new quartz headlights, it would stand on its hind legs, its forelimbs hanging limply, transfixed. For miles there was an honor guard of desert coneys saluting her, so it seemed, as she roared through the night. They would look up, a thousand pink noses twitching, two thousand bright eyes shining in the dark, as this apparition hurtled toward them.

Maybe it's a kind of religious experience, she thought. They seemed to be mostly young rabbits. Maybe they had never seen automobile headlights. To think of it, it was pretty amazing, the two intense beams of light speeding along at 130 kilometers an hour. Despite the thousands of rabbits lining the road, there never seemed to be even one in the middle, near the lane marker, never a confused scurrying out of the way, never a forlorn dead body, the ears stretched out along the pavement. Why were they aligned along the pavement at all? Maybe it had to do with the temperature of the asphalt, she thought. Or maybe they were only foraging in the scrub vegetation nearby and curious about the oncoming bright lights. But was it reasonable that none of them ever took a few short hops to visit his cousins across the road? What did they imagine the highway was? An alien presence in their midst, its function unfathomable, built by creatures that most of them had never seen? She doubted that any of them wondered about it at all.

The whine of her tires on the highway was a kind of white noise, and she found that involuntarily she was – here, too – listening for a pattern. She had taken to listening closely to many sources of white noise: the motor of the refrigerator starting up in the middle of the night; the water running for her bath; the washing machine when she would do her clothes in the little laundry room off her kitchen; the roar of the ocean during a brief scuba-diving trip to the island of Cozumel off Yucatan, which she had cut short because of her impatience to get back to work. She would listen to these everyday sources of random noise and try to determine whether there were fewer apparent patterns in them than in the interstellar static.

She had been to New York City the previous August for a meeting of URSI (the French abbreviation for the International Scientific Radio Union). The subways were dangerous, she had been told, but the white noise was irresistible. In the *clacka-clacka* of this underground railway she had thought she heard a clue, and resolutely skipped half a day of meetings – traveling from 34th Street to Coney Island, back to midtown Manhattan, and then on a different line, out to remotest Queens. She changed trains at a station in Jamaica, and then returned a little flushed and breathless – it was, after all, a hot day in August, she told herself – to the convention hotel. Sometimes, when the subway train was banking around a steep curve, the interior bulbs would go out and she could see a regular succession of lights, glowing in electric blue, speeding by as if she were in some impossible hyper-relativistic interstellar spacecraft, hurtling through a cluster of young blue supergiant stars. Then, as the train entered a straightaway, the interior lights would come on again and she would become aware once again of the acrid smell, the jostling of nearby straphangers, the miniature television surveillance cameras (locked in protective cages and subsequently spray-painted blind), the stylized multicolored map showing the complete underground transportation system of the City of New York, and the high-frequency screech of the brakes as they pulled into the stations.

This was a little eccentric, she knew. But she had always had an active fantasy life. All right, so she was a little compulsive about listening to noise. It did no harm that she could see. Nobody seemed to notice much. Anyway, it was job-related. If she had been so minded, she could probably have deducted the expense of her trip to Cozumel from her income tax because of the sound of the breakers. Well, maybe she *was* becoming obsessive.

She realized with a start that she had arrived at the Rockefeller Center station. As she quickly stepped out through an accumulation of daily newspapers abandoned on the floor of the subway car, a headline of the *News-Post* had caught her eye: GUERRILLAS CAPTURE JOBURG RADIO. If we like them, they're freedom fighters, she thought. If we don't like them, they're terrorists. In the unlikely case we can't make up our minds, they're temporarily only guerrillas. On an adjacent scrap of newspaper was a large photo of a florid, confident man with the headline: HOW THE WORLD WILL END. EXCERPTS FROM THE REV. BILLY JO RANKIN'S NEW BOOK. EXCLUSIVELY THIS WEEK IN THE *NEWS-POST*. She had taken the headlines in at a glance and tried promptly to forget them. Moving through the bustling crowds to the meeting hotel, she hoped she was in time to hear Fujita's paper on homomorphic radio telescope design.

Superposed on the whine of the tires was a periodic thump at the joins of swathes of pavement, which had been resurfaced by different New Mexico road crews in different epochs. What if an interstellar message were being received by Project Argus, but very slowly – one bit of information every hour, say, or every week, or every decade? What if there were very old, very patient murmurs of some transmitting civilization, which had no way of knowing that we get tired of pattern recognition after seconds or minutes? Suppose they lived for tens of thousands of years. And *taaaaalked verrrry slooooowwwwly*. Argus would never know. Could such long-lived creatures exist? Would there have been enough time in the history of the universe for creatures who reproduced very slowly to evolve to high intelligence? Wouldn't the statistical breakdown of chemical bonds, the deterioration of their bodies according to the Second Law of Thermodynamics, force them to reproduce about as often as human beings do? And to have lifespans like ours? Or might they reside on some old and frigid world, where even molecular collisions occur in extreme slow motion, maybe only a frame a day. She idly imagined a radio transmitter of recognizable and familiar design sitting on a cliff of methane ice, feebly illuminated by a distant red dwarf sun, while far below waves of an ammonia ocean beat relentlessly against the shore – incidentally generating a white noise indistinguishable from that of the surf at Cozumel.

The opposite was possible as well: the fast talkers, manic little creatures perhaps, moving with quick and jerky motions, who transmitted a complete radio message – the equivalent of hundreds of pages of English text – in a nanosecond. Of course, if you had a very narrow bandpass to your receiver, so you were listening only to a tiny range of frequencies, you were forced to accept the long time-constant. You would never be able to detect a rapid modulation. It was a simple consequence of the Fourier Integral Theorem, and closely related to the Heisenberg Uncertainty Principle. So, for example, if you had a bandpass of a kilohertz, you couldn't make out a signal that was modulated at faster than a millisecond. It would be a kind of sonic blur. The Argus bandpasses were narrower than a hertz, so to be detected the transmitters must be modulating very slowly, slower than one bit of information a second. Still slower modulations – longer than hours, say – could be detected easily, provided you were willing to point a telescope at the source for that length of time, provided you were exceptionally patient. There were so many pieces of the sky to look at, so many hundreds of billions of stars to search out. You couldn't spend all your time on only a few of them. She was troubled that in their haste to do a full sky survey in less than a human lifetime, to listen to all of the sky at a billion frequencies, they had abandoned both the frantic talkers and the laconic plodders.

But surely, she thought, they would know better than

we what modulation frequencies were acceptable. They would have had previous experience with interstellar communication and newly emerging civilizations. If there was a broad range of likely pulse rates that the receiving civilization would adopt, the transmitting civilization would utilize such a range. Modulate at microseconds, modulate at hours. What would it cost them? They would, almost all of them, have superior engineering and enormous power resources by Earth standards. If they wanted to communicate with us, they would make it easy for us. They would send signals at many different frequencies. They would use many different modulation timescales. They would know how backward we are, and would have pity.

So why had we received no signal? Could Dave possibly be right? No extraterrestrial civilizations anywhere? All those billions of worlds going to waste, lifeless, barren? Intelligent beings growing up only in this obscure corner of an incomprehensibly vast universe? No matter how valiantly she tried, Ellie couldn't make herself take such a possibility seriously. It dovetailed perfectly with human fears and pretentions, with unproved doctrines about life-after-death, with such pseudosciences as astrology. It was the modern incarnation of the geocentric solipsism, the conceit that had captured our ancestors, the notion that *we* were the center of the universe. Drumlin's argument was suspect on these grounds alone. We wanted to believe it too badly.

Wait a minute, she thought. We haven't even examined the northern skies once with the Argus system. In another seven or eight years, if we've still heard nothing, that'll be the time to start worrying. This is the first moment in human history when it's possible to search for the inhabitants of other worlds. If we fail, we've calibrated something of the rarity and preciousness of life on our planet – a fact, if it is one, very much worth knowing. And if we succeed, we'll have changed the history of our species, broken the shackles of provincial-

64

ism. With the stakes this high, you have to be willing to take some small professional risks, she told herself. She pulled off the side of the road and did a shallow racing turn, changed gears twice, and accelerated back toward the Argus facility. The rabbits, still lining the roadside, but now pinked by dawn, craned their necks to follow her departure.

4

Prime Numbers

Are there no Moravians in the Moon, that not a missionary has yet visited this poor pagan planet of ours to civilize civilization and Christianize Christendom?

> – HERMAN MELVILLE
> *White Jacket* (1850)

Silence alone is great; all else is weakness.

> – ALFRED DEVIGNY
> *La Mort du Loup*
> (1864)

The cold black vacuum had been left behind. The pulses were now approaching an ordinary yellow dwarf star and had already begun spilling over the retinue of worlds in this obscure system. They had fluttered by planets of hydrogen gas, penetrated into moons of ice, breached the organic clouds of a frigid world on which the precursors of life were stirring, and swept across a planet a billion years past its prime. Now the pulses were washing against a warm world, blue and white, spinning against the backdrop of the stars.

There was life on this world, extravagant in its numbers and variety. There were jumping spiders at the chilly tops of the highest mountains and sulfur-eating worms in hot vents gushing up through ridges on the ocean floors. There were beings that could live only in concentrated sulfuric acid, and beings that were destroyed by concentrated sulfuric acid; organisms that were poisoned by oxygen, and organisms that could survive only in oxygen, that actually breathed the stuff.

A particular lifeform, with a modicum of intelligence, had recently spread across the planet. They had outposts on the ocean floors and in low-altitude orbit. They had swarmed to every nook and cranny of their small world. The boundary that marked the transition of night into day was sweeping westward, and following its motion millions of these beings ritually performed their morning ablutions. They donned greatcoats and dhotis; drank brews of coffee, tea, or dandelion; drove bicycles, automobiles, or oxen; and briefly contemplated school assignments, prospects for spring planting, and the fate of the world.

The first pulses in the train of radio waves insinuated themselves through the atmosphere and clouds, struck the landscape and were partially reflected back to space. As the Earth turned beneath them, successive pulses arrived, engulfing not just this one planet but the entire system. Very little of the energy was intercepted by any of the worlds. Most of it passed effortlessly onward – as the yellow star and its attendant worlds plunged, in an altogether different direction, into the inky dark.

Wearing a Dacron jacket displaying the word 'Marauders' above a stylized felt volleyball, the duty officer, beginning the night shift, approached the control building. A klatch of radio astronomers was just leaving for dinner.

'How long have you guys been looking for little green men? It's more than five years, isn't it now, Willie?'

They chided him good-naturedly, but he could detect an edge to their banter.

'Give us a break, Willie,' another of them said. 'The quasar luminosity program is going great guns. But it's gonna take forever if we only have two percent of the telescope time.'

'Sure, Jack, sure.'

'Willie, we're looking back toward the origin of the universe. There's a big stake in our program, too – and we *know* there's a universe out there; you don't know there's a single little green man.'

'Take it up with Dr Arroway. I'm sure she'll be glad to hear your opinion,' he replied a little sourly.

The duty officer entered the control area. He made a quick survey of dozens of television screens monitoring the progress of the radio search. They had just finished examining the constellation Hercules. They had peered into the heart of a great swarm of galaxies far beyond the Milky Way, the Hercules Cluster – a hundred million light-years away; they had tuned in on M-13, a swarm of 300,000 stars, give or take a few, gravitationally bound together, moving in orbit around the Milky Way Galaxy 26,000 light-years away; they had examined Ras Algethi, a double system, and Zeta and Lambda Herculis – some stars different from the Sun, some similar to it, all nearby. Most of the stars you can see with the naked eye are less than a few hundred light-years away. They had carefully monitored hundreds of little sectors of the sky within the constellation Hercules at a billion separate frequencies, and they had heard nothing. In previous years they had searched the constellations immediately west of Hercules – Serpens, Corona Borealis, Boötes, Canes Venatici . . . and there also they had heard nothing.

A few of the telescopes, the duty officer could see, were devoted to picking up some missed data in Hercules. The remainder were aiming, boresighted, at an adjacent patch of sky, the next constellation east of Hercules. To people in the eastern Mediterranean a few thousand years ago, it had resembled a stringed musical instrument and was associated with the Greek culture hero Orpheus. It was a constellation named Lyra, the Lyre.

The computers turned the telescopes to follow the stars in Lyra from starrise to starset, accumulated the radio photons, monitored the health of the telescopes, and processed the data in a format convenient for their human operators. Even *one* duty officer was something of an indulgence. Walking by a bottle of hard candies, a coffee machine, a sentence in elvish runes out of Tolkien by the Artificial Intelligence Laboratory at Stanford, and a bumper sticker reading BLACK HOLES ARE OUT OF SIGHT, Willie approached the command console. He nodded pleasantly to the afternoon duty officer, now collecting his notes and preparing to leave for dinner. Because the day's data were conveniently summarized in amber on the master display, there was no need for Willie to inquire about the progress of the preceding hours.

'As you can see, nothing much. There was a pointing glitch – at least that's what it looked like – in forty-nine,' he said, waving vaguely toward the window. 'The quasar bunch freed up the one-tens and one-twenties about an hour ago. They seem to be getting very good data.'

'Yeah, I heard. They don't understand . . .'

His voice trailed off as an alarm light flashed decorously on the console in front of them. On a display marked 'Intensity vs. Frequency' a sharp vertical spike was rising.

'Hey, look, it's a monochromatic signal.'

Another display, labeled 'Intensity vs. Time,' showed a set of pulses moving left to right and then off the screen.

'Those are numbers,' Willie said faintly. 'Somebody's broadcasting numbers.'

'It's probably some Air Force interference. I saw an AWACS, probably from Kirtland, about sixteen hundred hours. Maybe they're spoofing us for fun.'

There had been solemn agreements to safeguard at least some radio frequencies for astronomy. But precisely because these frequencies represented a clear channel, the military found them occasionally irresistible. If global war ever came, perhaps the radio astronomers would be the first to know, their windows to the cosmos overflowing with orders to battle-management and damage-assessment satellites in geosynchronous orbit, and with the transmission of coded launch commands to distant strategic outposts. Even with no military traffic, in listening to a billion frequencies at once the astronomers had to expect some disruption. Lightning, automobile ignitions, direct broadcast satellites were all sources of radio interference. But the computers had their number, knew their characteristics and systematically ignored them. To signals that were more ambiguous the computer would listen with greater care and make sure they matched no inventory of data it was programmed to understand. Every now and then an electronic intelligence aircraft on a training mission – sometimes with a radar dish coyly disguised as a flying saucer camped on its haunches – would fly by, and Argus would suddenly detect unmistakable signatures of intelligent life. But it would always turn out to be life of a peculiar and melancholy sort, intelligent to a degree, extraterrestrial just barely. A few months before, an F-29E with state-of-the-art electronic countermeasures passed overhead at 80,000 feet and sounded the alarms on all 131 telescopes. To the unmilitary eyes of the astronomers, the radio signature had been complex enough to be a plausible first message from an extraterrestrial civilization. But they found the westernmost radio telescope had received the signal a full minute before the easternmost, and it soon became clear that it was an object streaking through the thin envelope of air surrounding the Earth rather than a broadcast from some unimaginably different civilization in the depths of space. Almost certainly this one was the same thing.

The fingers of her right hand were inserted into five evenly spaced receptacles in a low box on her desk. Since the invention of this device, she was able to save half an hour a week. But there hadn't really been a great deal to do with that extra half hour.

'And I was telling Mrs Yarborough all about it. She's the one in the next bed, now that Mrs Wertheimer passed on. I don't mean to toot my own horn, but I take a lot of credit for what you've done.'

'Yes, Mother.'

She examined the gloss on her fingernails and decided that they needed another minute, maybe a minute-thirty.

'I was thinking about that time in fourth grade –

70

remember? When it was pouring and you didn't want to go to school? You wanted me to write a note the next day saying you'd been out because you were sick. And I wouldn't do it. I said, "Ellie, apart from being beautiful, the most important thing in the world is an education. You can't do much about being beautiful, but you can do something about an education. Go to school. You never know what you might learn today." Isn't that right?'

'Yes, Mother.'

'But, I mean, isn't that what I told you then?'

'Yes, I remember, Mom.'

The gloss on her four fingers was perfect, but her thumb still had a dull matte appearance.

'So I got your galoshes and your raincoat – it was one of those yellow slickers, you looked cute as a button in it – and scooted you off to school. And that's the day you couldn't answer a question in Mr Weisbrod's mathematics class? And you got so furious you marched down to the college library and read up on it till you knew more about it than Mr Weisbrod. He was impressed. He told me.'

'He told you? I didn't know that. When did you talk to Mr Weisbrod?'

'It was a parent-teacher meeting. He said to me, "That girl of yours, she's a spunky one." Or words to that effect. "She got so mad at me, she became a real expert on it." "Expert." That's what he said. I know I told you about it.'

Her feet were propped up on a desk drawer as she reclined in the swivel chair; she was stabilized only by her fingers in the varnish machine. She felt the buzzer almost before she heard it, and abruptly sat up.

'Mom, I gotta go.'

'I'm *sure* I've told you this story before. You just never pay attention to what I'm saying. Mr Weisbrod, he was a nice man. You never could see his good side.'

'Mom, really, I've gotta go. We've caught some kind of bogey.'

71

'Bogey?'

'You know, Mom, something that might be a signal. We've talked about it.'

'There we are, both of us thinking the other one isn't listening. Like mother, like daughter.'

'Bye, Mom.'

'I'll let you go if you promise to call me right after.'

'Okay, Mom. I promise.'

Through the whole conversation, her mother's need and loneliness had elicited in Ellie a wish to end the conversation, to run away. She hated herself for that.

Briskly she entered the control area and approached the main console.

'Evening, Willie, Steve. Let's see the data. Good. Now where did you tuck away the amplitude plot? Good. Do you have the interferometric position? Okay. Now let's see if there's any nearby star in that field of view. Oh my, we're looking at Vega. That's a pretty near neighbor.'

Her fingers were punching away at a keyboard as she talked.

'Look, it's only twenty-six light-years away. It's been observed before, always with negative results. I looked at it myself in my first Arecibo survey. What's the absolute intensity? Holy Toledo. That's hundreds of janskys. You could practically pick that up on your FM radio.

'Okay. So we have a bogey very near to Vega in the plane of the sky. It's at a frequency around 9.2 gigahertz, not very monochromatic: The bandwidth is a few hundred hertz. It's linearly polarized and it's transmitting a set of moving pulses restricted to two different amplitudes.'

In response to her typed commands the screen now displayed the disposition of all the radio telescopes.

'It's being received by 116 individual telescopes. Clearly it's not a malfunction in one or two of them. Okay, now we should have plenty of time baseline. Is it

72

moving with the stars? Or could it be some ELINT satellite or aircraft?'

'I can confirm sidereal motion, Dr Arroway.'

'Okay, that's pretty convincing. It's not down here on Earth, and it probably isn't from an artificial satellite in a Molniya orbit, although we should check that. When you get a chance, Willie, call up NORAD and see what they say about the satellite possibility. If we can exclude satellites, that will leave two possibilities: It's a hoax, or somebody has finally gotten around to sending us a message. Steve, do a manual override. Check a few individual radio telescopes – the signal strength is certainly large enough – and see if there's any chance this is a hoax; you know, a practical joke by someone who wishes to teach us the error of our ways.'

A handful of other scientists and technicians, alerted on their buzzers by the Argus computer, had gathered around the command console. There were half smiles on their faces. None of them was thinking seriously of a message from another world quite yet, but there was a sense of no-school-today, a break in the tedious routine to which they had become accustomed, and perhaps a faint air of expectation.

'If any of you can think of any other explanation besides extraterrestrial intelligence, I want to hear about it,' she said, acknowledging their presence.

'There's no way it could be Vega, Dr Arroway. The system's only a few hundred million years old. Its planets are still in the process of forming. There isn't time for intelligent life to have developed there. It has to be some background star. Or galaxy.'

'But then the transmitter power has to be ridiculously large,' responded a member of the quasar group who had returned to see what was happening. 'We need to get going right away on a sensitive proper motion study, so we can see if the radio source moves with Vega.'

'Of course, you're right about the proper motion, Jack,' she said. 'But there's another possibility. Maybe

73

they didn't grow up in the Vega system. Maybe they're just visiting.'

'That's no good either. The system is full of debris. It's a failed solar system or a solar system still in its early stages of development. If they stay very long, their spacecraft'll be clobbered.'

'So they only arrived recently. Or they vaporize incoming meteorites. Or they take evasive action if there's a piece of debris on a collision trajectory. Or they're not in the ring plane but in polar orbit, so they minimize their encounters with the debris. There's a million possibilities. But you're absolutely right; we don't have to guess whether the source is in the Vega system. We can actually find out. How long will that proper motion study take? By the way, Steve, this isn't your shift. At least tell Consuela you're going to be late for dinner.'

Willie, who had been talking on the phone at an adjacent console, was displaying a wan smile. 'Well, I got through to a Major Braintree at NORAD. He swears up and down they have nothing that'll give this signal, especially not at nine gigahertz. 'Course, they tell us that every time we call. Anyway, he says they haven't detected any spacecraft at the right ascension and declination of Vega.'

'What about darks?'

By this time there were many 'dark' satellites with low radar cross sections, designed to orbit the Earth unannounced and undetected until an hour of need. Then they would serve as backups for launch detection or communications in a nuclear war, in case the first-line military satellites dedicated to these purposes were suddenly missing in action. Occasionally a dark would be detected by one of the major astronomical radar systems. All nations would deny that the object belonged to them, and breathless speculation would erupt that an extraterrestrial spacecraft had been detected in Earth orbit. As the Millennium approached, the UFO cults were thriving again.

'Interferometry now rules out a Molniya-type orbit, Dr Arroway.'

'Better and better. Now let's take a closer look at those moving pulses. Assuming that this is binary arithmetic, has anybody converted it into base ten? Do we know what the sequence of numbers is? Okay, here, we can do it in our heads . . . fifty-nine, sixty-one, sixty-seven . . . seventy-one . . . Aren't these all prime numbers?'

A little buzz of excitement circulated through the control room. Ellie's own face momentarily revealed a flutter of something deeply felt, but this was quickly replaced by a sobriety, a fear of being carried away, an apprehension about appearing foolish, unscientific.

'Okay, let's see if I can do another quick summary. I'll do it in the simplest language. Please check if I've missed anything. We have an extremely strong, not very monochromatic signal. Immediately outside the band-pass of this signal there are no other frequencies reporting anything besides noise. The signal is linearly polarized, as if it's being broadcast by a radio telescope. The signal is around nine gigahertz, near the minimum in the galactic radio noise background. It's the right kind of frequency for anyone who wants to be heard over a big distance. We've confirmed sidereal motion of the source, so it's moving as if it's up there among the stars and not from some local transmitter. NORAD tells us that they don't detect any satellites – ours or anybody else's – that match the position of this source. Interferometry excludes a source in Earth orbit anyway.

'Steve has now looked at the data outside the auto-mated mode, and it doesn't seem to be a program that somebody with a warped sense of humor put into the computer. The region of the sky we're looking at in-cludes Vega, which is an A-zero main sequence dwarf star. It's not exactly like the Sun, but it's only twenty-six light-years away, and it has the prototype stellar debris ring. There are no known planets, but there certainly could be planets we don't know anything about around

Vega. We're setting up a proper motion study to see if the source is well behind our line of sight to Vega, and we should have an answer in – what? – a few weeks if we're restricted on our own, a few hours if we do some long-baseline interferometry.

'Finally, what's being sent seems to be a long sequence of prime numbers, integers that can't be divided by any other number except themselves and one. No astrophysical process is likely to generate prime numbers. So I'd say – we want to be cautious, of course – but I'd say that by every criterion we can lay our hands on, this looks like the real thing.

'But there's a problem with the idea that this is a message from guys who evolved on some planet around Vega, because they would have had to evolve very fast. The entire lifetime of the star is only about four hundred million years. It's an unlikely place for the nearest civilization. So the proper motion study is very important. But I sure would like to check out that hoax possibility some more.'

'Look,' said one of the quasar survey astronomers who had been hovering in the back. He inclined his jaw to the western horizon where a faint pink aura showed unmistakably where the Sun had set. 'Vega is going to set in another couple of hours. It's probably already risen in Australia. Can't we call Sydney and get them looking at the same time that we're still seeing it?'

'Good idea. It's only middle afternoon there. And together we'll have enough baseline for the proper motion study. Give me that summary printout, and I'll telefax it to Australia from my office.'

With deliberate composure, Ellie left the assembled group crowded around the consoles and returned to her office. She closed the door very carefully behind her.

'Holy shit!' she whispered.

'Ian Broderick, please. Yes. This is Eleanor Arroway at Project Argus. It's something of an emergency. Thanks,

76

I'll hold on. . . . Hello, Ian? It's probably nothing, but we have a bogey here and wonder if you could just check it out for us. It's around nine gigahertz, with a few hundred hertz bandpass. I'm telefaxing the parameters now. . . . You have a feed good at nine gigahertz already on the dish? That's a bit of luck. . . . Yes, Vega is smack in the middle of the field of view. And we're getting what looks like prime number pulses. . . . Really. Okay, I'll hold on.'

She considered again how backward the world astronomical community still was. A joint computer data-basing system was still not on-line. Its value for asynchronous telenetting alone would . . .

'Listen, Ian, while the telescope finishes slewing, could you set up to look at an amplitude-time plot? Let's call the low-amplitude pulses dots and the high-amplitude pulses dashes. We're getting . . . Yes, that's just the pattern we've been seeing for the last half hour. . . . Maybe. Well, it's the best candidate in five years, but I keep remembering how badly the Soviets got fooled with that Big Bird satellite incident around '74. Well, the way I understand it, it was a US radar altimetry survey of the Soviet Union for cruise missile guidance. . . . Yes, a terrain mapper. And the Soviets were picking it up on omnidirectional antennas. They couldn't tell where in the sky the signals was coming from. All they knew was they were getting the same sequence of pulses from the sky at about the same time every morning. Their people assured them it wasn't a military transmission, so naturally they thought it was extraterrestrial. . . . No, we've excluded a satellite transmission already.

'Ian, could we trouble you to follow it for as long as it's in your sky? I'll talk to you about VLBI later. I'm going to see if I can't get other radio observatories, distributed pretty evenly in longitude, to follow it until it reappears back here. . . . Yes, but I don't know if it's easy to make a direct phone call to China. I'm thinking of sending an IAU telegram. . . . Fine. Many thanks, Ian.'

Ellie paused in the doorway of the control room – they called it that with conscious irony, because it was the computers, in another room, that by and large did the controlling – to admire the small group of scientists who were talking with great animation, scrutinizing the data being displayed, and engaging in mild badinage on the nature of the signal. These were not stylish people, she thought. They were not conventionally good-looking. But there was something unmistakably attractive about them. They were excellent at what they did and, especially in the discovery process, were utterly absorbed in their work. As she approached, they fell silent and looked at her expectantly. The numerals were now being converted automatically from base 2 to base 10 . . . 881, 883, 887, 907 . . . each one confirmed as a prime number.

'Willie, get me a world map. And please get me Mark Auerbach in Cambridge, Mass. He'll probably be at home. Give him this message for an IAU telegram to all observatories, but especially to all large radio observatories. And see if he'll check our telephone number for the Beijing Radio Observatory. Then get me the President's Science Adviser.'

'You're going to bypass the National Science Foundation?'

'After Auerbach, get me the President's Science Adviser.'

In her mind she thought she could hear one joyous shout amidst a clamor of other voices.

By bicycle, small truck, perambulatory mailman, or telephone, the single paragraph was delivered to astronomical centers all over the world. In a few major radio observatories – in China, India, the Soviet Union, and Holland, for example – the message was delivered by teletype. As it chattered in, it was scanned by a security officer or some passing astronomer, torn off, and with a look of some curiosity carried into an adjacent office. It read:

78

ANOMALOUS INTERMITTENT RADIO SOURCE AT RIGHT ASCENSION 18h 34m, DECLINATION PLUS 38 DEGREES 41 MINUTES, DISCOVERED BY ARGUS SYSTEMATIC SKY SURVEY. FREQUENCY 9.24176684 GIGAHERTZ, BANDPASS APPROXIMATELY 430 HERTZ. BIMODAL AMPLITUDES APPROXIMATELY 174 AND 179 JANSKYS. EVIDENCE AMPLITUDES ENCODE SEQUENCE OF PRIME NUMBERS. FULL LONGITUDE COVERAGE URGENTLY NEEDED. PLEASE CALL COLLECT FOR FURTHER INFORMATION IN COORDINATING OBSERVATIONS.
E. ARROWAY, DIRECTOR, PROJECT ARGUS, SOCORRO, NEW MEXICO, USA.

5

Decryption Algorithm

Oh, speak again, bright angel . . .

– WILLIAM SHAKESPEARE
Romeo and Juliet

The visiting scientists' quarters were now all occupied,
indeed overcrowded, by selected luminaries of the SETI
community. When the official delegations began arriving from Washington, they found no suitable accom-
modations at the Argus site and had to be billeted at
motels in nearby Socorro. Kenneth der Heer, the President's Science Adviser, was the only exception. He had
arrived the day after the discovery, in response to an
urgent call from Eleanor Arroway. Officials from the
National Science Foundation, the National Aeronautics
and Space Administration, the Department of Defense,
the President's Science Advisory Committee, the
National Security Council, and the National Security
Agency trickled in during the next few days. There were
a few government employees whose precise institutional
affiliations remained obscure.

The previous evening, some of them stood at the base
of Telescope 101 and had Vega pointed out to them for
the first time. Obligingly, its blue-white light flickered
prettily.

'I mean, I've seen it before, but I never knew what it
was called,' one of them remarked. Vega appeared brighter than the other stars in the sky, but in no other way
noteworthy. It was merely one of the few thousand
naked-eye stars.

The scientists were running a continuous research
seminar on the nature, origin, and possible significance

of the radio pulses. The project's public affairs office – larger than in most observatories because of widespread interest in the search for extraterrestrial intelligence – was assigned the task of filling in the lower-ranking officials. Every new arrival required an extensive personal briefing. Ellie, who was obliged to brief the senior officials, supervise the ongoing research, and respond to the entirely proper skeptical scrutiny being offered with some vigor by her colleagues, was exhausted. The luxury of a full night's sleep had eluded her since the discovery.

At first they had tried to keep the finding quiet. After all, they were not absolutely sure it was an extraterrestrial message. A premature or mistaken announcement would be a public relations disaster. But worse than that, it would interfere with the data analysis. If the press descended, the science would surely suffer. Washington as well as Argus was keen to keep the story quiet. But the scientists had told their families, the International Astronomical Union telegram had been sent all over the world, and still rudimentary astronomical data-basing systems in Europe, North America, and Japan were all carrying news of the discovery.

Although there had been a range of contingency plans for the public release of any findings, the actual circumstances had caught them largely unprepared. They drafted as innocuous a statement as they could and released it only when they had to. It caused, of course, a sensation.

They had asked the media's forbearance, but knew there would be only a brief period before the press would descend in force. They had tried to discourage reporters from visiting the site, explaining that there was no real information in the signals they were receiving, just tedious and repetitive prime numbers. The press was impatient with the absence of hard news. 'You can only do so many sidebars on "What is a prime number?"' one reporter explained to Ellie over the telephone.

Television camera crews in fixed-wing air taxis and chartered helicopters began making low passes over the facility, sometimes generating strong radio interference easily detected by the telescopes. Some reporters stalked the officials from Washington when they returned to their motels at night. A few of the more enterprising had attempted to enter the facility unobserved – by beach buggy, motorcycle, and in one case on horseback. She had been forced to inquire about bulk rates on cyclone fencing.

Immediately after der Heer arrived, he had received an early version of what was by now Ellie's standard briefing: the surprising intensity of the signal, its location in very much the same part of the sky as the star Vega, the nature of the pulses.

'I may be the President's Science Adviser,' he had said, 'but I'm only a biologist. So please explain it to me slowly. I understand that if the radio source is twenty-six light-years away, then the message had to be sent twenty-six years ago. In the 1960s, some funny-looking people with pointy ears thought we'd want to know that they like prime numbers. But prime numbers aren't difficult. It's not like they're boasting. It's more like they're sending us remedial arithmetic. Maybe we should be insulted.'

'No, look at it this way,' she said, smiling. 'This is a beacon. It's an announcement signal. It's designed to attract our attention. We get strange patterns of pulses from quasars and pulsars and radio galaxies and God-knows-what. But prime numbers are very specific, very artificial. No even number is prime, for example. It's hard to imagine some radiating plasma or exploding galaxy sending out a regular set of mathematical signals like this. The prime numbers are to attract our attention.'

'But what *for*?' he had asked, genuinely baffled.

'I don't know. But in this business you have to be very patient. Maybe in a while the prime numbers will turn

82

off and be replaced by something else, something very rich, the real message. We just have to keep on listening.'

This was the hardest part to explain to the press, that the signals had essentially no content, no meaning – just the first few hundred prime numbers in order, a cycling back to the beginning, and again the simple binary arithmetic representations: 1, 2, 3, 5, 7, 11, 13, 17, 19, 23, 29, 31 . . . Nine wasn't a prime number, she'd explain, because it was divisible by 3 (as well as 9 and 1, of course). Ten wasn't a prime number because 5 and 2 went into it (as well as 10 and 1). Eleven was a prime number because it was divisible only by 1 and itself. But why transmit prime numbers? It reminded her of an idiot savant, one of those people who might be grossly deficient in ordinary social or verbal skills but who could perform mind-boggling feats of mental arithmetic – such as figuring out, after a moment's thought, on what day of the week June first in the year 11,977 will fall. It wasn't *for* anything; they did it because they liked doing it, because they were *able* to do it.

She knew it was only a few days after receipt of the message, but she was at once exhilarated and deeply disappointed. After all these years, they had finally received a signal – sort of. But its content was shallow, hollow, empty. She had imagined receiving the *Encyclopaedia Galactica*.

We've only achieved the capacity for radio astronomy in the last few decades, she reminded herself, in a Galaxy where the average star is billions of years old. The chance of receiving a signal from a civilization exactly as advanced as we are should be minuscule. If they were even a little behind us, they would lack the technological capability to communicate with us at all. So the most likely signal would come from a civilization much more advanced. Maybe they would be able to write full and melodic mirror fugues: The counterpoint would be the theme written backwards. No, she decided. While this was a kind of genius without a doubt, and certainly beyond her ability, it was a tiny extrapolation from what human beings could do. Bach and Mozart had made at least respectable stabs at it.

She tried to make a bigger leap, into the mind of someone who was enormously, orders of magnitude, more intelligent than she was, smarter than Drumlin, say, or Eda, the young Nigerian physicist who had just won the Nobel Prize. But it was impossible. She could muse about demonstrating Fermat's Last Theorem or the Goldbach Conjecture in only a few lines of equations. She could imagine problems enormously beyond us that would be old hat to them. But she couldn't get into their minds; she couldn't imagine what thinking would be like if you were much more capable than a human being. Of course. No surprise. What did she expect? It was like trying to visualize a new primary color or a world in which you could recognize several hundred acquaintances individually only by their smells. . . . She could talk about this, but she couldn't experience it. By definition, it has to be mighty hard to understand the behavior of a being much smarter than you are. But even so, even so: Why only prime numbers?

The Argus radio astronomers had made progress in the last few days. Vega had a known motion – a known component of its velocity toward or away from the Earth, and a known component laterally, across the sky, against the background of more distant stars. The Argus telescopes, working together with radio observatories in West Virginia and Australia, had determined that the source was moving with Vega. Not only was the signal coming, as carefully as they could measure, from where Vega was in the sky; but the signal also shared the peculiar and characteristic motions of Vega. Unless this was a hoax of heroic proportions, the source of the prime number pulses was indeed in the Vega system. There was no additional Doppler effect due to the motion of the transmitter, perhaps tied to a planet, about Vega. The extraterrestrials had compensated for the orbital motion. Perhaps it was a kind of interstellar courtesy.

'It's the goddamnedest most wonderful thing I ever heard of. And it's got nothing to do with our shop,' said an official of the Defense Advanced Research Projects Agency, preparing to return to Washington.

As soon as the discovery had been made, Ellie had assigned a handful of the telescopes to examine Vega in a range of other frequencies. Sure enough, they had found the same signal, the same monotonous succession of prime numbers, beeping away in the 1420 megahertz hydrogen line, the 1667 megahertz hydroxyl line, and at many other frequencies. All over the radio spectrum, with an electromagnetic orchestra, Vega was bleating out prime numbers.

'It doesn't make sense,' said Drumlin, casually touching his belt buckle. 'We couldn't have missed it before. Everybody's looked at Vega. For years. Arroway observed it from Arecibo a decade ago. Suddenly last Tuesday Vega starts broadcasting prime numbers? Why now? What's so special about now? How come they start transmitting just a few years after Argus starts listening?'

'Maybe their transmitter was down for repairs for a couple of centuries,' Valerian suggested, 'and they just got it back on-line. Maybe their duty cycle is to broadcast to us just one year out of every million. There are all those other candidate planets that might have life on them, you know. We're probably not the only kid on the block.' But Drumlin, plainly dissatisfied, only shook his head.

Although his nature was the opposite of conspiratorial, Valerian thought he had caught an undercurrent in Drumlin's last question: Could all this be a reckless, desperate attempt by Argus scientists to prevent a premature closing down of the project? It wasn't possible. Valerian shook his head. As der Heer walked by, he found himself confronted by two senior experts on the

85

SETI problem silently shaking their heads at one another.

Between the scientists and the bureaucrats there was a kind of unease, a mutual discomfort, a clash of fundamental assumptions. One of the electrical engineers called it an impedance mismatch. The scientists were too speculative, too quantitative, and too casual about talking to anybody for the tastes of many of the bureaucrats. The bureaucrats were too unimaginative, too qualitative, too uncommunicative for many of the scientists. Ellie and especially der Heer tried hard to bridge the gap, but the pontoons kept being swept downstream.

This night, cigarette butts and coffee cups were everywhere. The casually dressed scientists, Washington officials in lightweight suits, and an occasional flag-rank military officer filled the control room, the seminar room, the small auditorium, and spilled out of doors, where, illuminated by cigarettes and starlight, some of the discussions continued. But tempers were frayed. The strain was showing.

'Dr Arroway, this is Michael Kitz, Assistant Secretary of Defense for C^3I.'

Introducing Kitz and positioning himself just a step behind him, der Heer was communicating . . . what? Some unlikely mix of emotions. Bemusement in the arms of prudence? He seemed to be appealing for restraint. Did he think her such a hothead? 'C^3I' – pronounced cee-cubed-eye – stood for Command, Control, Communications, and Intelligence, important responsibilities at a time when the United States and the Soviet Union were gamely making major phased reductions in their strategic nuclear arsenals. It was a job for a cautious man.

Kitz settled himself in one of the two chairs across the desk from Ellie, leaned forward, and read the Kafka quote. He was unimpressed.

'Dr Arroway, let me come right to the point. We're concerned about whether it's in the best interest of the

United States for this information to be generally known. We were not overjoyed about your sending that telegram all over the world.'

'You mean to China? To Russia? To India?' Her voice, despite her best effort, had a discernible edge to it. 'You wanted to keep the first 261 prime numbers secret? Do you suppose, Mr Kitz, the extraterrestrials intended to communicate only with Americans? Don't you think that a message from another civilization belongs to the whole world?'

'You might have asked our advice.'

'And risk losing the signal? Look, for all we know, something essential, something unique might have been broadcast after Vega had set here in New Mexico but when it was high in the sky over Beijing. These signals aren't exactly a person-to-person call to the US of A. They're not even a person-to-person call to the Earth. It's station-to-station to any planet in the solar system. We just happened to be lucky enough to pick up the phone.'

Der Heer was radiating something again. What was he trying to tell her? That he liked that elementary analogy, but ease up on Kitz?

'In any case,' she continued, 'it's too late. Everybody knows now that there's some kind of intelligent life in the Vega system.'

'I'm not sure it's too late, Dr Arroway. You seem to think there'll be some information-rich transmission, a message, still to come. Dr der Heer here' – he paused to listen to the unexpected assonance – 'Dr der Heer says you think these prime numbers are an announcement, something to make us pay attention. If there *is* a message and it's subtle – something those other countries wouldn't pick up right away – I want it kept quiet until we can talk about it.'

'Many of us have wants, Mr Kitz,' she found herself saying sweetly, ignoring der Heer's raised eyebrows. There was something irritating, almost provocative, about Kitz's manner. And probably hers as well. 'I, for

87

example, have a want to understand what the meaning of this signal is, and what's happening on Vega, and what it means for the Earth. It's possible that scientists in other nations are the key to that understanding. Maybe we'll need their data. Maybe we'll need their brains. I could imagine this might be a problem too big for one country to handle all by itself.'

Der Heer now appeared faintly alarmed. 'Uh, Dr Arroway. Secretary Kitz's suggestion isn't all that unreasonable. It's very possible we'd bring other nations in. All he's asking is to talk about it with us first. And that's only if there's a new message.'

His tone was calming but not unctuous. She looked at him closely again. Der Heer was not a patently handsome man, but he had a kind and intelligent face. He was wearing a blue suit and a crisp oxford shirt. His seriousness and air of self-possession were moderated by the warmth of his smile. Why, then, was he shilling for this jerk? Part of his job? Could it be that Kitz was talking sense?

'It's a remote contingency anyway.' Kitz sighed as he got to his feet. 'The Secretary of Defense would appreciate your cooperation.' He was trying to be winning. 'Agreed?'

'Let me think about it,' she replied, taking his proffered hand as if it were a dead fish.

'I'll be along in a few minutes, Mike,' der Heer said cheerfully.

His hand on the lintel of the door, Kitz had an apparent afterthought, removed a document from his inside breast pocket, returned, and placed it gingerly on the corner of her desk. 'Oh yes, I forgot. Here's a copy of the Hadden Decision. You probably know it. It's about the government's right to classify material vital to the security of the United States. Even if it didn't originate in a classified facility.'

'You want to classify the prime numbers?' she asked, her eyes wide in mock incredulity.

88

'See you outside, Ken.'

She began talking the moment Kitz left her office. 'What's he after? Vegan death rays? World blower-uppers? What's this really about?'

'He's just being prudent, Ellie. I can see you don't think that's the whole story. Okay. Suppose there's some message – you know, with real content – and in it there's something offensive to Muslims, say, or to Methodists. Shouldn't we release it carefully, so the United States doesn't get a black eye?'

'Ken, don't bullshit me. That man is an Assistant Secretary of *Defense*. If they're worried about Muslims and Methodists, they would have sent me an Assistant Secretary of State, or – I don't know – one of those religious fanatics who preside at presidential prayer breakfasts. You're the President's Science Adviser. What did you advise her?'

'I haven't advised her anything. Since I've been here, I've only talked to her once, briefly, on the phone. And I'll be frank with you, she didn't give me any instructions about classification. I thought what Kitz said was way off base. I think he's acting on his own.'

'Who *is* he?'

'As far as I know, he's a lawyer. He was a top executive in the electronics industry before joining the Administration. He really knows C^3I, but that doesn't make him knowledgeable about anything else.'

'Ken, I trust you. I believe you didn't set me up for this Hadden Decision threat.' She waved the document in front of her and paused, seeking his eyes. 'Do you know that Drumlin thinks there's another message in the polarization?'

'I don't understand.'

'Just a few hours ago, Dave finished a rough statistical study of the polarization. He's represented the Stokes parameters by Poincaré spheres; there's a nice movie of them varying in time.'

Der Heer looked at her blankly. Don't biologists use

polarized light in their microscopes? she asked herself.

'When a wave of light comes at you – visible light, radio light, any kind of light – it's vibrating at right angles to your line of sight. If that vibration rotates, the wave is said to be elliptically polarized. If it rotates clockwise, the polarization is called right-handed; counterclockwise, it's left-handed. I know it's a dumb designation. Anyway, by varying between the two kinds of polarization, you could transmit information. A little right polarization and that's a zero; a little left and it's a one. Follow? It's perfectly possible. We have amplitude modulation and frequency modulation, but our civilization, by convention, ordinarily just doesn't do polarization modulation.

'Well, the Vega signal looks as if it has polarization modulation. We're busy checking it out right now. But Dave found that there wasn't an equal amount of the two sorts of polarization. It wasn't left polarized as much as it was right polarized. It's just possible that there's another message in the polarization that we've missed so far. That's why I'm suspicious about your friend. Kitz isn't just giving me general gratuitous advice. He knows we may be onto something else.'

'Ellie, take it easy. You've hardly slept for four days. You've been juggling the science, the administration, and the press. You've already made one of the major discoveries of this century, and if I understand you right, you might be on the verge of something even more important. You've got every right to be a little on edge. And threatening to militarize the project was clumsy of Kitz. I don't have any trouble understanding why you're suspicious of him. But there's some sense to what he says.'

'Do you know the man?'

'I've been in a few meetings with him. I can hardly say I know him. Ellie, if there's a possibility of a real message coming in, wouldn't it be a good idea to thin out the crowd a little?'

'Sure. Give me a hand with some of the Washington deadwood.'

'Okay. And if you leave that document on your desk, someone'll be in here and draw the wrong conclusion. Why don't you put it away somewhere?'

'You're going to help?'

'If the situation stays anything like what it is now, I'll help. We're not going to make our best effort if this thing gets classified.'

Smiling, Ellie knelt before her small office safe, and punched in the six-digit combination, 314159. She took one last glance at the document that was titled in large black letters THE UNITED STATES VS. HADDEN CYBERNETICS, and locked it away.

It was a group of about thirty people – technicians and scientists associated with Project Argus, a few senior government officials, including the Deputy Director of the Defense Intelligence Agency in civilian clothes. Among them were Valerian, Drumlin, Kitz, and der Heer. Ellie was the only woman. They had set up a large television projection system, focused on a two-meter-by-two-meter screen set flush against the far wall. Ellie was simultaneously addressing the group and the de-cryption program, her fingers on the keyboard before her.

'Over the years we've prepared for the computer decryption of many kinds of possible messages. We've just learned from Dr Drumlin's analysis that there's information in the polarization modulation. All that frenetic switching between left and right means some-thing. It's not random noise. It's as if you're flipping a coin. Of course, you expect as many heads as tails, but instead you get twice as many heads as tails. So you conclude that the coin is loaded or, in our case, that the polarization modulation isn't random; it has content. . . . Oh, look at this. What the computer has just now told us is even more interesting. The precise sequence of heads and tails repeats. It's a long sequence, so it's a pretty complex message, and the transmitting civilization must want us to be sure to get it right.

'Here, you see? This is the repeating message. We're now into the first repetition. Every bit of information, every dot and dash – if you want to think of them that way – is identical to what it was in the last block of data. Now we analyze the total number of bits. It's a number in the tens of billions. Okay, bingo! It's the product of three prime numbers.'

Although Drumlin and Valerian were both beaming, it seemed to Ellie they were experiencing quite different emotions.

'So what? What do some more prime numbers mean?' a visitor from Washington asked.

'It means – maybe – that we're being sent a picture. You see, this message is made up of a large number of bits of information. Suppose that large number is the product of three smaller numbers; it's a number times a number times a number. So there's three dimensions to the message. I'd guess either it's a single static three-dimensional picture like a stationary hologram, or it's a two-dimensional picture that changes with time – a movie. Let's assume it's a movie. If it's a hologram, it'll take us longer to display anyway. We've got an ideal decryption algorithm for this one.'

On the screen, they made out an indistinct moving pattern composed of perfect whites and perfect blacks.

'Willie, put in some gray interpolation program, would you? Anything reasonable. And try rotating it about ninety degrees counterclockwise.'

'Dr Arroway, there seems to be an auxiliary sideband channel. Maybe it's the audio to go with the movie.'

'Punch it up.'

The only other practical application of prime numbers she could think of was public-key cryptography, now widely used in commercial and national security contexts. One application was to make a message clear to dummies; the other was to keep a message hidden from the tolerably intelligent.

Ellie scanned the faces before her. Kitz looked uncomfortable. Perhaps he was anticipating some alien invader or, worse, the design drawings of a weapon too secret for her staff to be trusted with. Willie looked very earnest and was swallowing over and over again. A picture is different from mere numbers. The possibility of a visual message was clearly rousing unexamined fears and fantasies in the hearts of many of the onlookers. Der Heer had a wonderful expression on his face; for the moment he seemed much less the official, the bureaucrat, the presidential adviser, and much more the scientist.

The picture, still unintelligible, was joined by a deep rumbling glissando of sounds, sliding first up and then down the audio spectrum until it gravitated to rest somewhere around the octave below middle C. Slowly the group became aware of faint but swelling music. The picture rotated, rectified, and focused.

Ellie found herself staring at a black-and-white grainy image of . . . a massive reviewing stand adorned with an immense art deco eagle. Clutched in the eagle's concrete talons . . .

'Hoax! It's a hoax!' There were cries of astonishment, incredulity, laughter, mild hysteria.

'Don't you see? You've been hoodwinked,' Drumlin was saying to her almost conversationally. He was smiling. 'It's an elaborate practical joke. You've been wasting the time of everybody here.'

Clutched in the eagle's concrete talons, she could now see clearly, was a swastika. The camera zoomed in above the eagle to find the smiling face of Adolf Hitler, waving to a rhythmically chanting crowd. His uniform, devoid of military decorations, conveyed a modest simplicity. The deep baritone voice of an announcer, scratchy but unmistakably speaking German, filled the room. Der Heer moved toward her.

'Do you know German?' she whispered. 'What's it saying?'

'The Fuehrer,' he translated slowly, 'welcomes the world to the German Fatherland for the opening of the 1936 Olympic Games.'

6

Palimpsest

And if the Guardians are not happy, who else can be?

> – ARISTOTLE
> *The Politics*
> Book 2, Chapter 5

As the plane reached cruising altitude, with Albuquerque already more than a hundred miles behind them, Ellie idly glanced at the small white cardboard rectangle imprinted with blue letters that had been stapled to her airline ticket envelope. It read, in language unchanged since her first commercial flight, 'This is not the luggage ticket (baggage check) described by Article 4 of the Warsaw Convention.' Why were the airlines so worried, she wondered, that passengers might mistake this piece of cardboard for the Warsaw Convention ticket? For that matter, what was a Warsaw Convention ticket? Why had she never seen one? Where were they storing them? In some forgotten key event in the history of aviation, an inattentive airline must have forgotten to print this caveat on cardboard rectangles and was sued into bankruptcy by irate passengers laboring under the misapprehension that this *was* the Warsaw luggage ticket. Doubtless there were sound financial reasons for this worldwide concern, never otherwise articulated, about which pieces of cardboard are not described by the Warsaw Convention. Imagine, she thought, all those cumulative lines of type devoted instead to something useful – the history of world exploration, say, or incidental facts of science, or even the average number of passenger miles until your airplane crashed.

If she had accepted der Heer's offer of a military

airplane, she would be having other casual associations. But that would have been far too cozy, perhaps some aperture leading to an eventual militarization of the project. They had preferred to travel by commercial carrier. Valerian's eyes were already closed as he finished settling into the seat beside her. There had been no particular hurry, even after taking care of those last-minute details on the data analysis, with the hint that the second layer of the onion was about to unpeel. They had been able to make a commercial flight that would arrive in Washington well before tomorrow's meeting; in fact, in plenty of time for a good night's sleep.

She glanced at the telefax system neatly zipped into a leather carrying case under the seat in front of her. It was several hundred kilobits per second faster than Peter's old model and displayed much better graphics. Well, maybe tomorrow she would have to use it to explain to the President of the United States what Adolf Hitler was doing on Vega. She was, she admitted to herself, a little nervous about the meeting. She had never met a President before, and by late-twentieth-century standards, this one wasn't half bad. She hadn't had time to get her hair done, much less a facial. Oh well, she wasn't going to the White House to be looked at.

What would her stepfather think? Did he still believe she was unsuited for science? Or her mother, now confined to a wheelchair in a nursing home? She had managed only one brief phone call to her mother since the discovery over a week ago, and promised herself to call again tomorrow.

As she had done a hundred times before, she peered out the airplane window and imagined what impression the Earth would make on an extraterrestrial observer, at this cruising altitude of twelve or fourteen kilometers, and assuming the alien had eyes something like ours. There were vast areas of the Midwest intricately geometrized with squares, rectangles, and circles by those with agricultural or urban predilections; and, as here, vast areas of the Southwest in which the only sign of intelligent life was an occasional straight line heading between mountains and across deserts. Are the worlds of more advanced civilizations totally geometrized, entirely rebuilt by their inhabitants? Or would the signature of a *really* advanced civilization be that they left no sign at all? Would they be able to tell in one swift glance precisely which stage we were in some great cosmic evolutionary sequence in the development of intellectual beings?

What else could they tell? From the blueness of the sky, they could make a rough estimate of Loschmidt's Number, how many molecules there were in a cubic centimeter at sea level. About three times ten to the nineteenth. They could easily tell the altitudes of the clouds from the length of their shadows on the ground. If they knew that the clouds were condensed water, they could roughly calculate the temperature lapse rate of the atmosphere, because the temperature had to fall to about minus forty degrees Centigrade at the altitude of the highest cloud she could see. The erosion of landforms, the dendritic patterns and oxbows of rivers, the presence of lakes and battered volcanic plugs all spoke of an ancient battle between land-forming and erosional processes. Really, you could see at a glance that this was an antique planet with a brand new civilization.

Most of the planets in the Galaxy would be venerable and pre-technical, maybe even lifeless. A few would harbor civilizations much older than ours. Worlds with technical civilizations just beginning to emerge must be spectacularly rare. It was perhaps the only quality fundamentally unique about the Earth.

Through lunch, the landscape slowly turned verdant as they approached the Mississippi Valley. There was hardly any sense of motion in modern air travel, Ellie thought. She looked at Peter's still sleeping form; he had rejected with some indignation the prospect of an airline lunch. Beyond him, across the aisle, was a very young human being, perhaps three months old, comfortably nestled in its father's arms. What was an infant's view of air travel? You go to a special place, walk into a large room with seats in it, and sit down. The room rumbles and shakes for four hours. Then you get up and walk off. Magically, you're somewhere else. The means of transportation seems obscure to you, but the basic idea is easy to grasp, and precocious mastery of the Navier-Stokes equations is not required.

It was late afternoon when they circled Washington, awaiting permission to land. She could make out, between the Washington Monument and the Lincoln Memorial, a vast crowd of people. It was, she had read only an hour earlier in the *Times* telefax, a massive rally of black Americans protesting economic disparities and educational inequities. Considering the justice of their grievances, she thought, they had been very patient. She wondered how the President would respond to the rally and to the Vega transmission, on both of which some official public comment would have to be made tomorrow.

'What do you mean, Ken, "They get out"?'

'I mean, Ms President, that our television signals leave this planet and go out into space.'

'Just exactly how far do they go?'

'With all due respect, Ms President, it doesn't work that way.'

'Well, how *does* it work?'

'The signals spread out from the Earth in spherical waves, a little like ripples in a pond. They travel at the speed of light – 186,000 miles a second – and essentially go on forever. The better some other civilization's receivers are, the farther away they could be and still pick up our TV signals. Even *we* could detect a strong TV transmission from a planet going around the nearest star.'

For a moment, the President stood ramrod straight, staring out the French doors into the Rose Garden. She turned toward der Heer. 'You mean . . . everything?'

'Yes. Everything.'

'You mean to say, all that crap on television? The car crashes? Wrestling? The porno channels? The evening news?'

'Everything, Ms President.' Der Heer shook his head in sympathetic consternation.

'Der Heer, do I understand you correctly? Does this mean that all my press conferences, my debates, my inaugural address, are out there?'

'That's the good news, Ms President. The bad news is, so are all the television appearances of your predecessor. And Dick Nixon. And the Soviet leadership. And so are a lot of nasty things your opponent said about you. It's a mixed blessing.'

'My God. Okay, go on.' The President had turned away from the French doors and was now apparently preoccupied in examining a marble bust of Tom Paine, newly restored from the basement of the Smithsonian Institution, where it had been consigned by the previous incumbent.

'Look at it this way: Those few minutes of television from Vega were originally broadcast in 1936, at the opening of the Olympic Games in Berlin. Even though it was only shown in Germany, it was the first television transmission on Earth with even moderate power. Unlike the ordinary radio transmission in the thirties, those TV signals got through our ionosphere and trickled out into space. We're trying to find out exactly what was transmitted back then, but it'll probably take some time. Maybe that welcome from Hitler is the only fragment of the transmission they were able to pick up on Vega.

'So from their point of view, Hitler is the first sign of intelligent life on Earth. I'm not trying to be ironic. They don't know what the transmission means, so they record it and transmit it back to us. It's a way of saying "Hello, we heard you." It seems to me a pretty friendly gesture.'

'Then you say there wasn't any television broadcasting until after the Second World War?'

'Nothing to speak of. There was a local broadcast in England on the coronation of George the Sixth, a few things like that. Big-time television transmission began in the late forties. All those programs are leaving the Earth at the speed of light. Imagine the Earth is here' – der Heer gestured in the air – 'and there's a little spherical wave running away from it at the speed of light, starting out in 1936. It keeps expanding and receding from the Earth. Sooner or later, it reaches the nearest civilization. They seem to be surprisingly close, only twenty-six light-years away, on some planet of the star Vega. They record it and play it back to us. But it takes another twenty-six years for the Berlin Olympics to return to Earth. So the Vegans didn't take decades to figure it out. They must have been pretty much tuned, all set up, ready to go, waiting for our first television signals. They detect them, record them, and after a while play them back to us. But unless they've already been here – you know, some survey mission a hundred years ago – they couldn't have known we were about to invent television. So Dr Arroway thinks this civilization is monitoring all the nearby planetary systems, to see if any of its neighbors develop high technology.'

'Ken, there's a lot of things here to think about. Are you sure those – what do you call them, Vegans? – you sure they don't understand what that television program was about?'

'Ms President, there's no doubt they're smart. That was a very weak signal in 1936. Their detectors have to be fantastically sensitive to pick it up. But I don't see how they could possibly understand what it means. They probably look very different from us. They must have different history, different customs. There's no way for them to know what a swastika is or who Adolf Hitler was.'

'Adolf Hitler! Ken, it makes me *furious*. Forty million

people die to defeat that megalomaniac, and he's the star of the first broadcast to another civilization? He's repre-*sent*ing us. And *them*. It's that madman's wildest dream come true.'

She paused and continued in a calmer voice. 'You know, I never thought Hitler could manage that Hitler salute. He never gave it straight on, it was always skewed at some wacko angle. And then there was that fruity bent elbow salute. If anyone else had done his Heil Hitlers so incompetently he would've been sent to the Russian front.'

'But isn't there a difference? He was only returning the salutes of others. He wasn't Heiling Hitler.'

'Oh yes he was,' returned the President and, with a gesture, ushered der Heer out of the Rose Room and down a corridor. Suddenly she stopped and regarded her Science Adviser.

'What if the Nazis didn't have television in 1936? Then what would have happened?'

'Well, then I suppose it would be the coronation of George the Sixth, or one of the transmissions about the New York World's Fair in 1939, if any of them were strong enough to be received on Vega. Or some pro-grams from the late forties, early fifties. You know, Howdy Doody, Milton Berle, the Army-McCarthy hearings – all those marvelous signs of intelligent life on Earth.'

'Those goddamn programs are our ambassadors into space . . . the Emissary from Earth.' She paused a mo-ment to savor the phrase. 'With an ambassador, you're supposed to put your best foot forward, and we've been sending mainly crap to space for forty years. I'd like to see the network executives come to grips with this one. And that madman Hitler, that's the first news they have about Earth? What are they going to think of us?'

As der Heer and the President entered the Cabinet Room, those who had been standing in small groups fell silent, and some who had been seated made efforts to stand. With a perfunctory gesture, the President conveyed a preference for informality and casually greeted the Secretary of State and an Assistant Secretary of Defense. With a slow and deliberate turn of the head, she scanned the group. Some returned her gaze expectantly. Others, detecting an expression of minor annoyance on the President's face, averted their eyes.

'Ken, isn't that astronomer of yours here? Arrowsmith? Arrowroot?'

'Arroway, Ms President. She and Dr Valerian arrived last night. Maybe they've been held up in traffic.'

'Dr Arroway called from her hotel, Ms President,' volunteered a meticulously groomed young man. 'She said there were some new data coming through on her telefax, and she wanted to bring it to this meeting. We're supposed to start without her.'

Michael Kitz leaned forward, his tone and expression incredulous. 'They're transmitting new data on this subject over an open telephone, insecure, in a Washington hotel room?'

Der Heer responded so softly that Kitz had to lean still further forward to hear. 'Mike, I think there's at least commercial encryption on her telefax. But remember there are no security guidelines established in this matter. I'm sure that Dr Arroway will be cooperative if guidelines are established.'

'All right, let's begin,' said the President. 'This is a joint informal meeting of the National Security Council and what for the time being we're calling the Special Contingency Task Group. I want to impress on all of you that nothing said in this room – I mean *nothing* – is to be discussed with anyone who isn't here, except for the Secretary of Defense and the Vice President, who are overseas. Yesterday, Dr der Heer gave most of you a briefing on this unbelievable TV program from the star Vega. It's the view of Dr der Heer and others' – she looked around the table – 'that it's just a fluke that the first

102

television program to get to Vega starred Adolf Hitler. But it's . . . an embarrassment. I've asked the Director of Central Intelligence to prepare an assessment of any national security implications in all of this. Is there any direct threat from whoever the hell is sending this? Are we going to be in trouble if there's some new message, and some other country decodes it first? But first let me ask, Marvin, does this have anything to do with flying saucers?'

The Director of Central Intelligence, an authoritative man in late middle age, wearing steel-rimmed glasses, summarized. Unidentified Flying Objects, called UFO's, have been of intermittent concern to the CIA and the Air Force, especially in the '50s and '60s, in part because rumors about them might be a means for a hostile power to spread confusion or to overload communications channels. A few of the more reliably reported incidents turned out to be penetrations of US air space or overflights of US overseas bases by high-performance aircraft from the Soviet Union or Cuba. Such overflights are a common means of testing a potential adversary's readiness, and the United States had more than its fair share of penetrations, and feints at penetration, of Soviet air space. A Cuban MiG penetrating 200 miles up the Mississippi Basin before being detected was considered undesirable publicity by NORAD. The routine procedure had been for the Air Force to deny that any of *its* aircraft were in the vicinity of the UFO sighting, and to volunteer nothing about unauthorized penetrations, thus solidifying public mystification. At these explanations, the Air Force Chief of Staff looked marginally uncomfortable but said nothing.

The great majority of UFO reports, the DCI continued, were natural objects misapprehended by the observer. Unconventional or experimental aircraft, automobile headlights reflected off overcast, balloons, birds, luminescent insects, even planets and stars seen under unusual atmospheric conditions, had all been reported as UFO's. A significant number of reports turned out to be hoaxes or real psychiatric delusions. There had been more than a million UFO sightings reported worldwide since the term 'flying saucer' had been invented in the late '40s, and not one of them seemed on good evidence to be connected with an extraterrestrial visitation. But the idea generated powerful emotions, and there were fringe groups and publications, and even some academic scientists, that kept alive the supposed connection between UFO's and life on other worlds. Recent millenarian doctrine included its share of saucer-borne extraterrestrial redeemers. The official Air Force investigation, called in one of its final incarnations Project Blue Book, had been closed down in the '60s for lack of progress, although a low-level continuing interest had been maintained jointly by the Air Force and the CIA. The scientific community had been so convinced there was nothing to it that when Jimmy Carter requested the National Aeronautics and Space Administration to make a comprehensive study of UFO's, NASA uncharacteristically refused a presidential request.

'In fact,' interjected one of the scientists at the table, unfamiliar with the protocol in meetings such as this, 'the UFO business has made it more difficult to do serious SETI work.'

'All right.' The President sighed. 'Is there anybody around this table who thinks UFO's and this signal from Vega have anything to do with each other?' Der Heer inspected his fingernails. No one spoke.

'Just the same, there's going to be an awful lot of I-told-you-so's from the UFO yo-yos. Marvin, why don't you continue?'

'In 1936, Ms President, a very faint television signal transmits the opening ceremonies of the Olympic Games to a handful of television receivers in the Berlin area. It's an attempt at a public relations coup. It shows the progress and superiority of German technology. There were a few earlier TV transmissions, but all at very low power levels. Actually, we did it before the Germans. Secretary of Commerce Herbert Hoover made a brief television appearance on . . . April twenty-seventh, 1927. Anyway, the German signal leaves the Earth at the speed of light, and twenty-six years later it arrives on Vega. They sit on the signal for a few years – whoever "they" are – and then send it back to us hugely amplified. Their ability to receive that very weak signal is impressive, and their ability to return it at such high power levels is impressive. There certainly are security implications here. The electronic intelligence community, for example, would like to know how such weak signals can be detected. Those people, or whatever they are, on Vega are certainly more advanced than we are – maybe only a few decades further along, but maybe much further along than that.

'They've given us no other information about themselves – except at some frequencies the transmitted signal doesn't show the Doppler effect from the motion of their planet around their star. They've simplified that data reduction step for us. They're . . . helpful. So far, nothing of military or any other interest has been received. All they've been saying is that they're good at radio astronomy, they like prime numbers, and they can return our first TV transmissions back to us. It couldn't hurt for any other nation to know that. And remember: All those other countries are receiving this same three-minute Hitler clip, over and over again. They just haven't figured out how to read it yet. The Russians or the Germans or someone is likely to tumble to this polarization modulation sooner or later. My personal impression, Ms President – I don't know if State agrees – is that it would be better if we released it to the world before we're accused of covering something up. If the situation remains static – with no big change from where we are right now – we could think about making a public announcement, or even releasing that three-minute film clip.

'Incidentally, we haven't been able to find any record from German archives of what was in that original broadcast. We can't be absolutely sure that the people on Vega haven't made some change in the content before sending it back to us. We can recognize Hitler, all right, and the part of the Olympic stadium we see corresponds accurately to Berlin in 1936. But if at that moment Hitler had really been scratching his mustache instead of smiling as in that transmission, we'd have no way to know.'

Ellie arrived slightly breathless, followed by Valerian. They attempted to take obscure chairs against the wall, but der Heer noticed and directed the President's attention to them.

'Dr Arrow-uh-way? I'm glad to see you've arrived safely. First, let me congratulate you on a splendid discovery. Splendid. Um, Marvin . . .'

'I've reached a stopping point, Ms President.'

'Good. Dr Arroway, we understand you have something new. Would you care to tell us about it?'

'Ms President, sorry to be late, but I think we've just hit the cosmic jackpot. We've . . . It's . . . Let me try and explain it this way: In classical times, thousands of years ago, when parchment was in short supply, people would write over an old parchment, making what's called a palimpsest. There was writing under writing under writing. This signal from Vega is, of course, very strong. As you know, there's the prime numbers, and "underneath" them, in what's called polarization modulation, this eerie Hitler business. But underneath the sequence of prime numbers and underneath the retransmitted Olympic broadcast, we've just uncovered an incredibly rich message – at least we're pretty sure it's a message. As far as we can tell, it's been there all along. We've just detected it. It's weaker than the announcement signal, but I'm embarrassed we didn't find it sooner.'

'What does it say?' the President asked. 'What's it about?'

'We haven't the foggiest idea, Ms President. Some of

106

the people at Project Argus tumbled to it early this morning Washington time. We've been working on it all night.'

'Over an open phone?' asked Kitz.

'With standard commercial encryption.' Ellie looked a little flushed. Opening her telefax case, she quickly generated a transparency printout and, with an overhead projector, cast its image against a screen.

'Here's all we know up to now: We'll get a block of information comprising about a thousand bits. There'll be a pause, and then the same block will be repeated, bit for bit. Then there'll be another pause, and we'll go on to the next block. *It's* repeated as well. The repetition of every block is probably to minimize transmission errors. They must think it's very important that we get whatever it is they're saying down accurately. Now, let's call each of these blocks of information a page. Argus is picking up a few dozen of these pages a day. But we don't know what they're about. They're not a simple picture code like the Olympic message. This is something much deeper and much richer. It appears to be, for the first time, information *they've* generated. The only clue we have so far is that the pages seem to be numbered. At the beginning of every page there's a number in binary arithmetic. See this one here? And every time another pair of identical pages shows up, it's labeled with the next higher number. Right now we're on page . . . 10,413. It's a big book. Calculating back, it seems that the message began about three months ago. We're lucky to have picked it up as early as we did.'

'I was right, wasn't I?' Kitz leaned across the table to der Heer. 'This isn't the kind of message you want to give to the Japanese or the Chinese or the Russians, is it?'

'Is it going to be easy to figure out?' the President asked over the whispering Kitz.

'We will, of course, make our best efforts. And it probably would be useful to have the National Security Agency work on it also. But without an explanation from Vega, without a primer, my guess is that we're not going to make much progress. It certainly doesn't seem to be written in English or German or any other Earthly language. Our hope is that the Message will come to an end, maybe on page 20,000 or page 30,000, and then start right over from the beginning, so we'll be able to fill in the missing parts. Maybe before the whole Message repeats, there'll be a primer, a kind of *McGuffey's Reader*, that will enable us to understand the Message.'

'If I may, Ms President –'

'Ms President, this is Dr Peter Valerian of the California Institute of Technology, one of the pioneers in this field.'

'Please go ahead, Dr Valerian.'

'This is an intentional transmission to us. They know we're here. They have some idea, from having intercepted our 1936 broadcast, of where our technology is, of how smart we are. They wouldn't be going to all this trouble if they didn't want us to understand the Message. Somewhere in there is the key to help us understand it. It's only a question of accumulating all the data and analyzing it very carefully.'

'Well, what do you suppose the Message is about?'

'I don't see any way to tell, Ms President. I can only repeat what Dr Arroway said. It's an intricate and complex Message. The transmitting civilization is eager for us to receive it. Maybe all this is one small volume of the *Encyclopaedia Galactica*. The star Vega is about three times more massive than the Sun and about fifty times brighter. Because it burns its nuclear fuel so fast, it has a much shorter lifetime than the Sun –'

'Yes. Maybe something's about to go wrong on Vega,' the Director of Central Intelligence interrupted. 'Maybe their planet will be destroyed. Maybe they want someone else to know about their civilization before they're wiped out.'

'Or,' offered Kitz, 'maybe they're looking for a new place to move to, and the Earth would suit them just fine.

Maybe it's no accident they chose to send us a picture of Adolf Hitler.'

'Hold on,' Ellie said, 'there are a lot of possibilities, but not *every*thing is possible. There's no way for the transmitting civilization to know whether we've received the Message, much less whether we're making any progress in decoding it. If we find the Message offensive we're not obliged to reply. And even if we did reply, it would be twenty-six years before they received the reply, and another twenty-six years before they can answer it. The speed of light is fast, but it's not infinitely fast. We're very nicely quarantined from Vega. And if there's anything that worries us about this new Message, we have decades to decide what to do about it. Let's not panic quite yet.' She enunciated these last words while offering a pleasant smile to Kitz.

'I appreciate those remarks, Dr Arroway,' returned the President. 'But things are happening fast. Too damn fast. And there are too many maybes. I haven't even made a public announcement about all of this. Not even the prime numbers, never mind the Hitler bullcrap. Now we have to think about this "book" you say they're sending. And because you scientists think nothing of talking to each other, the rumors are flying. Phyllis, where's that file? Here, look at these headlines.'

Brandished successively at arm's length, they all carried the same message, with minor variations in journalistic artistry: 'Space Doc Says Radio Show from Bug-Eyed Monsters,' 'Astronomical Telegram Hints at Extraterrestrial Intelligence,' 'Voice from Heaven?' and 'The Aliens Are Coming! The Aliens Are Coming!' She let the clippings flutter to the table.

'At least the Hitler story hasn't broken yet. I'm waiting for *those* headlines: "Hitler Alive and Well in Space, US Says." And worse. Much worse. I think we'd better curtail this meeting and reconvene later.'

'If I may, Ms President,' der Heer interrupted haltingly, with evident reluctance. 'I beg your pardon, but there are some international implications that I think have to be raised now.'

The President merely exhaled, acquiescing.

Der Heer continued. 'Tell me if I have this right, Dr Arroway. Every day the star Vega rises over the New Mexico desert, and then you get whatever page of this complex transmission – whatever it is – they happen to be sending to the Earth at the moment. Then, eight hours later or something, the star sets. Right so far? Okay. Then the next day the star rises again in the east, but you've lost some pages during the time you weren't able to look at it, after it had set the previous night. Right? So it's as if you were getting pages thirty through fifty and then pages eighty through a hundred, and so on. No matter how patiently we observe, we're going to have enormous amounts of information missing. Gaps. Even if the message eventually repeats itself, we're going to have gaps.'

'That's entirely right.' Ellie rose and approached an enormous globe of the world. Evidently the White House was opposed to the obliquity of the Earth; the axis of this globe was defiantly vertical. Tentatively, she gave it a spin. 'The Earth turns. You need radio telescopes distributed evenly over many longitudes if you don't want gaps. Any one nation observing only from its own territory is going to dip into the message and dip out – maybe even at the most interesting parts. Now this is the same kind of problem that an American interplanetary spacecraft faces. It broadcasts its findings back to Earth when it passes by some planet, but the United States might be facing the other way at the time. So NASA has arranged for three radio tracking stations to be distributed evenly in longitude around the Earth. Over the decades they've performed superbly. But . . .' Her voice trailed off diffidently, and she looked directly at P. L. Garrison, the NASA Administrator. A thin, sallow, friendly man, he blinked.

'Uh, thank you. Yes. It's called the Deep Space Network, and we're very proud of it. We have stations in the Mojave Desert, in Spain, and in Australia. Of course, we're underfunded, but with a little help, I'm sure we could get up to speed.'

'Spain and Australia?' the President asked.

'For purely scientific work,' the Secretary of State was saying, 'I'm sure there's no problem. However, if this research program had political overtones, it might be a little tricky.'

American relations with both countries had become cool of late.

'There's no question this has political overtones,' the President replied a little testily.

'But we don't have to be tied to the surface of the Earth,' interjected an Air Force general. 'We can beat the rotation period. All we need is a large radio telescope in Earth orbit.'

'All right.' The President again glanced around the table. 'Do we have a space radio telescope? How long would it take to get one up? Who knows about this? Dr Garrison?'

'Uh, no, Ms President. We at NASA have submitted a proposal for the Maxwell Observatory in each of the last three fiscal years, but OMB has removed it from the budget each time. We have a detailed design study, of course, but it would take years – well, three years anyway – before we could get it up. And I feel I should remind everybody that until last fall the Russians had a working millimeter and submillimeter wave telescope in Earth orbit. We don't know why it failed, but they'd be in a better position to send some cosmonauts up to fix it than we'd be to build and launch one from scratch.'

'That's it?' the President asked. 'NASA has an ordinary telescope in space but no big radio telescope. Isn't there anything suitable up there already? What about the intelligence community? National Security Agency? Nobody?'

'So, just to follow this line of reasoning,' der Heer said,

'it's a strong signal and it's on lots of frequencies. After Vega sets over the United States, there are radio telescopes in half a dozen countries that are detecting and recording the signal. They're not as sophisticated as Project Argus, and they probably haven't figured out the polarization modulation yet. If we wait to prepare a space radio telescope and launch it, the message might be finished by then, gone altogether. So doesn't it follow that the only solution is immediate cooperation with a number of other nations, Dr Arroway?'

'I don't think any nation can accomplish this project alone. It will require many nations, spread out in longitude, all the way around the Earth. It will involve every major radio astronomy facility now in place – the big radio telescopes in Australia, China, India, the Soviet Union, the Middle East, and Western Europe. It would be irresponsible if we wind up with gaps in the coverage because some critical part of the Message came when there's no telescope looking at Vega. We'll have to do something about the Eastern Pacific between Hawaii and Australia, and maybe something about the Mid-Atlantic also.'

'Well,' the Director of Central Intelligence responded grudgingly, 'the Soviets have several satellite tracking ships that are good in S-band through X-band, the *Akademik Keldysh*, for example. Or the *Marshal Nedelin*. If we make some arrangement with them, they might be able to station ships in the Atlantic or the Pacific and fill in the gaps.'

Ellie pursed her lips to respond, but the President was already talking.

'All right, Ken. You may be right. But I say again this is moving too damn fast. There are some other things I have to attend to right now. I'd appreciate it if the Director of Central Intelligence and the National Security staff would work overnight on whether we have any options besides cooperation with other countries – especially countries that aren't our allies. I'd like the Secretary

112

of State to prepare, in cooperation with the scientists, a contingency list of nations and individuals to be approached if we have to cooperate, and some assessment of the consequences. Is some nation going to be mad at us if we don't ask them to listen? Can we be blackmailed by somebody who promises the data and then holds back? Should we try to get more than one country at each longitude? Work through the implications. And for God's sake' – her eyes moved from face to face around the long polished table – 'keep quiet about this. You too, Arroway. We've got problems enough.'

7

The Ethanol in W-3

No credence whatever is to be given to the opinion . . . that the demons act as messengers and interpreters between the gods and men to carry all petitions from us to the gods, and to bring back to us the help of the gods. On the contrary, we must believe them to be spirits most eager to inflict harm, utterly alien from righteousness, swollen with pride, pale with envy, subtle in deceit . . .

> – AUGUSTINE
> *The City of God*, VIII, 22

That Heresies should arise, we have the prophesie of Christ; but that old ones should be abolished, we hold no prediction.

> – THOMAS BROWNE
> *Religio Medici*, I, 8 (1642)

She had planned to meet Vaygay's plane in Albuquerque and drive him back to the Argus facility in the Thunderbird. The rest of the Soviet delegation would have traveled in the observatory cars. She would have enjoyed speeding to the airport in the cool dawn air, perhaps again past an honor guard of rampant coneys. And she had been anticipating a long and substantial private talk with Vaygay on the return. But the new security people from the General Services Administration had vetoed the idea. Media attention and the President's sober announcement at the end of her press conference two weeks before had brought enormous crowds to the isolated desert site. There was a potential for violence, they had told Ellie. She must in future travel only in government cars, and then only with discreetly armed escorts. Their little convoy was wending its way toward Albuquerque at a pace so sober and responsible that she found her right foot of its own volition depressing an imaginary accelerator on the rubber mat before her.

It would be good to spend some time with Vaygay again. She had last seen him in Moscow three years before, during one of those periods in which he was forbidden to visit the West. Authorization for foreign travel had waxed and waned through the decades in response to changing policy fashions and Vaygay's own unpredictable behavior. Permission would be denied him after some mild political provocation about which he seemed unable to restrain himself, and then granted again when no one of comparable ability could be found to flesh out one or another scientific delegation. He received invitations from all over the world for lectures, seminars, colloquia, conferences, joint study groups, and international commissions. As a Nobel laureate in physics, and as a full member of the Soviet Academy of Sciences, he could afford to be a little more independent than most. He often seemed poised precariously at the outer limits of the patience and restraint of the governmental orthodoxy.

His full name was Vasily Gregorovich Lunacharsky, known throughout the global community of physicists as Vaygay after the initials of his first name and patronymic. His fluctuating and ambiguous relations with the Soviet regime puzzled her and others in the West. He was a distant relative of Anatoly Vasilyevich Lunacharsky, an old Bolshevik colleague of Gorky, Lenin, and Trotsky; the elder Lunacharsky had later served as People's Commissar for Education and as Soviet Ambassador to Spain until his death in 1933. Vaygay's mother had been Jewish. He had, it was said, worked on Soviet nuclear weapons, although surely he was too young to have played much of a role in fashioning the first Soviet thermonuclear explosion.

His institute was well staffed and well equipped, and his scientific productivity was prodigious, indicating at most infrequent distractions by the Committee for State Security. Despite the ebb and flow of permission for foreign travel, he had been a frequent attendee at major international conferences including the 'Rochester' symposia on high-energy physics, the 'Texas' meetings on relativistic astrophysics, and the informal but occasionally influential 'Pugwash' scientific gatherings on ways of reducing international tension.

In the 1960s, she had been told, Vaygay visited the University of California at Berkeley and was delighted with the proliferation of irreverent, scatological, and politically outrageous slogans imprinted on inexpensive buttons. You could, she recalled with faint nostalgia, size up someone's most pressing social concerns at a glance. Buttons were also popular and fiercely traded in the Soviet Union, but usually they celebrated the 'Dynamo' soccer team, or one of the successful spacecraft of the *Luna* series, which had been the first spacecraft to land on the Moon. The Berkeley buttons were different. Vaygay had brought dozens of them, but delighted in wearing one in particular. It was the size of his palm and read, 'Pray for Sex.' He even displayed it at scientific meetings. When asked about its appeal, he would say, 'In your country, it is offensive in only one way. In my country, it is offensive in two independent ways.' If pressed further, he would only comment that his famous Bolshevik relative had written a book on the place of religion in a socialist society. Since then, his English had improved enormously – much more than Ellie's Russian – but his propensity for wearing offensive lapel buttons had, sadly, diminished.

Once, during a vigorous discussion on the relative merits of the two political systems, Ellie had boasted that she had been free to march in front of the White House protesting American involvement in the Vietnam War. Vaygay replied that in the same period he had been

116

equally free to march in front of the Kremlin protesting American involvement in the Vietnam War.

He had never been inclined, say, to photograph the garbage scows burdened with malodorous refuse and squawking seagulls lumbering in front of the Statue of Liberty, as another Soviet scientist had when for fun she had escorted him on the Staten Island ferry during a break in a meeting in New York City. Nor had he, as had some of his colleagues, ardently photographed the tumble-down shanties and corrugated metal huts of the Puerto Rican poor during a bus excursion from a luxurious beachfront hotel to the Arecibo Observatory. To whom did they submit these pictures? Ellie wondered. She conjured up some vast KGB library dedicated to the infelicities, injustices, and contradictions of capitalist society. Did it warm them, when disconsolate with some of the failures of Soviet society, to browse through the fading snapshots of their imperfect American cousins?

There were many brilliant scientists in the Soviet Union who, for unknown offenses, had not been permitted out of Eastern Europe in decades. Konstantinov, for example, had never been to the West until the mid-1960s. When, at an international meeting in Warsaw – over a table encumbered with dozens of depleted Azerbaijani brandy snifters, their missions completed – Konstantinov was asked why, he replied, 'Because the bastards know, they let me out, I never come back.' Nevertheless, they had let him out, sure enough, during the thaw in scientific relations between the two countries in the late '60s and early '70s, and he had come back every time. But now they let him out no more, and he was reduced to sending his Western colleagues New Year's cards in which he portrayed himself forlornly cross-legged, head bowed, seated on a sphere below which was the Schwarzschild equation for the radius of a black hole. He was in a deep potential well, he would tell visitors to Moscow in the metaphors of physics. They would never let him out again.

117

In response to questions, Vaygay would say that the official Soviet position was that the Hungarian revolution of 1956 had been organized by cryptofascists, and that the Prague Spring of 1968 was brought about by an unrepresentative anti-socialist group in the leadership. But, he would add, if what he had been told was mistaken, if these were genuine popular uprisings, then his country had been wrong in suppressing them. On Afghanistan he did not even bother quoting the official justifications. Once in his office at the Institute he had insisted on showing Ellie his personal shortwave radio, on which were frequencies labeled London and Paris and Washington, neatly spelled out in Cyrillic letters. He was free, he told her, to listen to the propaganda of all nations.

There had been a time when many of his fellows had surrendered to national rhetoric about the yellow peril. 'Imagine the entire frontier between China and the Soviet Union occupied by Chinese soldiers, shoulder to shoulder, an invading army,' one of them requested, challenging Ellie's powers of imagination. They were standing around the samovar in the Director's office at the Institute. 'How long would it be, with the present Chinese birthrate, before they all passed over the border?' And the answer was pronounced, in an unlikely mix of dark foreboding and arithmetic delight, 'Never.' William Randolph Hearst would have felt at home. But not Lunacharsky. Stationing so many Chinese soldiers on the frontier would automatically reduce the birthrate, he argued; their calculations were therefore in error. He had phrased it as though the misuse of mathematical models was the subject of his disapproval, but few mistook his meaning. In the worst of the Sino-Soviet tensions, he had never, so far as Ellie knew, allowed himself to be swept up in the endemic paranoia and racism.

Ellie loved the samovars and could understand the Russian affection for them. Their *Lunakhod*, the successful unmanned lunar rover that looked like a bathtub on wire wheels, seemed to her to have a little samovar technology somewhere in its ancestry. Vaygay had once taken her to see a model of *Lunakhod* in a sprawling exhibition park outside of Moscow on a splendid June morning. There, next to a building displaying the wares and charms of the Tadzhik Autonomous Republic, was a great hall filled to the rafters with full-scale models of Soviet civilian space vehicles. *Sputnik 1*, the first orbital spacecraft; *Sputnik 2*, the first spacecraft to carry an animal, the dog Laika, who died in space; *Luna 2*, the first spacecraft to reach another celestial body; *Luna 3*, the first spacecraft to photograph the far side of the Moon; *Venera 7*, the first spacecraft to land safely on another planet; and *Vostok 1*, the first manned spacecraft, that carried Hero of the Soviet Union Cosmonaut Yuri A. Gagarin on a single orbit of the Earth. Outside, children were using the fins of the Vostok launch booster as slides, their pretty blond curls and red Komsomol neckerchiefs flaring as, to much hilarity, they descended to land. *Zemlya*, it was called in Russian. The large Soviet island in the Arctic Sea was called Novaya Zemlya, New Land. It was there in 1961 that they had detonated a fifty-eight-megaton thermonuclear weapon, the largest single explosion so far contrived by the human species. But on that spring day, with the vendors hawking the ice cream in which Moscovites take so much pride, with families on outings and a toothless old man smiling at Ellie and Lunacharsky as if they were lovers, the old land had seemed nice enough.

In her infrequent visits to Moscow or Leningrad, Vaygay would often arrange the evenings. A group of six or eight of them would go to the Bolshoi or the Kirov ballet. Lunacharsky somehow would arrange for the tickets. She would thank her hosts for the evening, and they – explaining that it was only in the company of foreign visitors that they themselves were able to attend such performances – would thank her. Vaygay would only smile. He never brought his wife, and Ellie had never met her. She was, he said, a physician who was devoted to her patients. Ellie had asked him what his greatest regret was, because his parents had not, as they had once contemplated, emigrated to America. 'I have only one regret,' he had said in his gravelly voice. 'My daughter married a Bulgarian.'

Once he arranged a dinner at a Caucasian restaurant in Moscow. A professional toastmaster, or *tamada*, named Khaladze had been engaged for the evening. The man was a master of this art form, but Ellie's Russian was bad enough that she was obliged to ask for most of the toasts to be translated. He turned to her and, foreshadowing the rest of the evening, remarked, 'We call the man who drinks without a toast an alcoholic.' An early and comparatively mediocre toast had ended 'To peace on all planets,' and Vaygay had explained to her that the word *mir* meant world, peace and a self-governing community of peasant households that went back to ancient times. They had talked about whether the world had been more peaceful when its largest political units had been no larger than villages. 'Every village is a planet,' Lunacharsky had said, his tumbler held high. 'And every planet a village,' she had returned.

Such gatherings would be a little raucous. Enormous quantities of brandy and vodka would be drunk, but no one ever seemed seriously inebriated. They would emerge noisily from the restaurant at one or two in the morning and try, often vainly, to find a taxicab. Several times he had escorted her on foot a distance of five or six kilometers from the restaurant back to her hotel. He was attentive, a little avuncular, tolerant in his political judgments, fierce in his scientific pronouncements. Although his sexual escapades were legendary among his colleagues, he never permitted himself so much as a goodnight kiss with Ellie. This had always distressed her a little, although his affection for her was plain.

There were many women in the Soviet scientific community, proportionately more so than in the United States. But they tended to occupy menial to middle-level positions, and male Soviet scientists, like their American counterparts, were puzzled about a pretty woman with evident scientific competence who forcefully expressed her views. Some would interrupt her or pretend not to hear her. Then, Lunacharsky would always lean over and ask in a louder voice than usual, 'What did you say, Dr Arroway? I didn't quite manage to hear.' The others would then fall silent and she would continue about doped gallium arsenide detectors, or the ethanol content of the galactic cloud W-3. The quantity of 200-proof alcohol in this single interstellar cloud was more than enough to maintain the present population of the Earth, if every adult were a dedicated alcoholic, for the age of the solar system. The *tamada* had appreciated the remark. In their subsequent toasts, they had speculated on whether other forms of life would be intoxicated by ethanol, whether public drunkenness was a Galaxy-wide problem, and whether a toastmaster on any other world could be a skilled as our Trofim Sergeivich Khaladze.

They arrived at the Albuquerque airport to discover that, miraculously, the commercial flight from New York with the Soviet delegation aboard had landed a half hour early. Ellie found Vaygay at an airport souvenir shop negotiating the price of some trinket. He must have seen her out of the corner of his eye. Without turning to face her, he lifted a finger: 'One second, Arroway. Nineteen ninety-five?' he continued, addressing the elaborately disinterested sales clerk. 'I saw the identical set in New York yesterday for seventeen fifty.' She edged closer and observed Vaygay spreading a set of holographic playing cards displaying nudes of both sexes in poses, now considered merely indecorous, that would have scandalized the previous generation. The clerk was making halfhearted attempts to gather the cards up as Lunacharsky made vigorous and successful efforts to cover the counter with the cards. Vaygay was winning. 'I'm sorry, sir, I don't set prices. I only work here,' complained the clerk.

'You see the deficiencies of a planned economy,' Vaygay said to Ellie while proffering a twenty-dollar bill to the clerk. 'In a true free-enterprise system, I probably could purchase this for fifteen dollars. Maybe twelve ninety-five. Don't look at me in that way, Ellie. This is not for me. With the jokers there are fifty-four cards here. Each of them will make a nice gift for some worker at my institute.'

She smiled and took his arm. 'It's good to see you again, Vaygay.'

'A rare pleasure, my dear.'

On the drive to Socorro, by mutual but unspoken agreement, they mainly talked pleasantries. Valerian and the driver, one of the new security people, were in the front seats. Peter, not a voluble man even in ordinary circumstances, was content to lean back and listen to their conversation, which touched only tangentially on the issue the Soviets had come to discuss: the third level of the palimpsest, the elaborate, complex, and still undecoded Message they were collectively receiving. the US government had, more or less reluctantly, concluded that Soviet participation was essential. This was true especially because the signal from Vega was so intense that even modest radio telescopes could detect it. Years before, the Soviets had prudently deployed a number of small telescopes across the entire Eurasian land mass, stretching 9,000 kilometers over the surface of the Earth, and recently had completed a major radio observatory near Samarkand. In addition, Soviet oceangoing satellite tracking vessels were patrolling both the Atlantic and the Pacific.

Some of the Soviet data were redundant, because observatories in Japan, China, India, and Iraq were recording those signals as well. Indeed, every substantial radio telescope in the world that had Vega in its sky was listening. Astronomers in Britain, France, the Netherlands, Sweden, Germany, and Czechoslovakia, in Canada and Venezuela and Australia, were recording small pieces of the Message, following Vega from starrise to starset. In some observatories the detection equipment was not sensitive enough even to make out the individual pulses. They listened anyway to an audio blur. Each of these nations had a piece of the jigsaw puzzle, because, as Ellie had reminded Kitz, the Earth turns. Every nation tried to make some sense out of the pulses. But it was difficult. No one could tell even if the Message was written in symbols or in pictures.

It was perfectly conceivable that they would not decrypt the Message until it cycled back to page one – if it ever did – and began again with the introduction, the primer, the decoding key. Maybe it was a very long message, Ellie thought as Vaygay idly compared taiga with scrub desert; maybe it wouldn't cycle back for a hundred years. Or maybe there was no primer. Maybe the Message (all over the planet, the word was beginning to be capitalized) was an intelligence test, so those worlds too stupid to decrypt it would be unable to misuse its contents. It suddenly struck her what a humiliation she would feel for the human species if in the end they failed to understand the Message. The moment the Americans and the Soviets decided to collaborate and the Memorandum of Agreement was solemnly signed, every other nation with a radio telescope had agreed to cooperate. There was a kind of World Message Consortium, and people were actually talking in those terms. They needed one another's data and brain power if the Message was to be decrypted.

The newspapers were full of little else. The pitiful few facts that were known – the prime numbers, the Olympic broadcast, the existence of a complex message – were endlessly reviewed. It was hard to find anyone on the planet who had not in one way or another heard about the Message from Vega.

Religious sects, established and marginal, and some newly invented for the purpose, were dissecting the theological implications of the Message. Some thought it was from God, and some from the Devil. Astonishingly, some were even unsure. There was a nasty resurgence of interest in Hitler and the Nazi regime, and Vaygay mentioned to her that he had found a total of eight swastikas in the advertisements in that Sunday's *New York Times Book Review*. Ellie replied that eight was about par, but she knew she was exaggerating; some weeks there were only two or three. A group that called themselves 'Spacaryans' offered definitive evidence that flying saucers had been invented in Hitler Germany. A new 'unmongrelized' race of Nazis had grown up on Vega and was now ready to put things right on Earth.

There were those who considered listening to the signal an abomination and who urged the observatories to stop; there were those who considered it a Token of Advent and urged the construction of still larger radio telescopes, some of them in space. Some cautioned against working with the Soviet data, on grounds that they might be falsified or fraudulent, although in the longitudes of overlap they agreed well with the Iraqi, Indian, Chinese, and Japanese data. And there were those who sensed a change in the world political climate and contended that the very existence of the Message, even if it was never decrypted, was exercising a steadying influence on the quarrelsome nation states. Since the transmitting civilization was clearly more advanced than ours, and because it clearly – at least as of twenty-six years ago – had not destroyed itself, it followed, some argued, that technological civilizations did not inevitably self-destruct. In a world gingerly experimenting with major divestitures of nuclear weapons and their delivery systems, the Message was taken by whole populations as a reason for hope. Many considered the Message the best news in a long time. For decades, young people had tried not to think too carefully about tomorrow. Now, there might be a benign future after all.

Those with predispositions favoring such cheerful prognoses sometimes found themselves edging uncomfortably toward ground that had been occupied for a decade by the chiliastic movement. Some chiliasts held that the imminent arrival of the Third Millennium would be accompanied by the return of Jesus or Buddha or Krishna or The Prophet, who would establish on Earth a benevolent theocracy, severe in its judgment of mortals. Perhaps this would presage the mass celestial Ascent of the Elect. But there were other chiliasts, and there were far more of these, who held that the physical destruction of the world was the indispensable prerequisite for the Advent, as had been unerringly foretold in various otherwise mutually contradictory ancient prophetic works. The Doomsday Chiliasts were uneasy with the whiff of world community in the air and troubled by the steady annual decline in the global stockpiles of strategic weapons. The most readily available means for fulfilling the central tenet of their faith was being disassembled day by day. Other candidate catastrophes – overpopulation, industrial pollution, earthquakes, volcanic explosions, greenhouse warming, ice ages, or cometary impact with the Earth – were too slow, too improbable, or insufficiently apocalyptic for the purpose.

Some chiliast leaders had assured mass rallies of devoted followers that, except for accidents, life insurance was a sign of wayward faith; that, except for the very elderly, to purchase a gravesite or make funeral arrangements in other than urgent necessity was a flagrant impiety. All who believed would be raised bodily to heaven and would stand before the throne of God in only a few years.

Ellie knew that Lunacharsky's famous relative had been that rarest of beings, a Bolshevik revolutionary with a scholarly interest in the world's religions. But the attention Vaygay directed to the growing worldwide theological ferment was apparently muted. 'The main religious question in my country,' he said, 'will be whether the Vegans have properly denounced Leon Trotsky.'

As they approached the Argus site, the roadside became dense with parked automobiles, recreation vehicles, campers, tents, and great crowds of people. At night the once tranquil Plains of San Augustin were illuminated by campfires. The people along the highway were by no means all well-to-do. She noticed two young couples. The men were in T-shirts and worn jeans, belted around their hips, swaggering a little as they had been taught by their seniors upon entering high school, talking animatedly. One of them pushed a ragged stroller in which sat a carefree boy about two years old. The women followed behind their husbands, one of them holding the hand of a toddler new to the human art of walking, and the other cantilevered forward with what in another month or two would be a further life born on this obscure planet.

There were mystics from sequestered communities outside Taos who used psilocybin as a sacrament, and nuns from a convent near Albuquerque who used ethanol for the same purpose. There were leather-skinned, crinkly-eyed men who had spent their whole lives under the open sky, and bookish, sallow-faced students from the University of Arizona in Tucson. There were silk cravats and burnished silver string ties sold by Navajo entrepreneurs at exorbitant prices, a small reversal of the historical commercial relations between whites and Native Americans. Chewing tobacco and bubble gum were being vigorously deployed by enlisted men on leave from Davis-Monthan Air Force Base. An elegantly attired white-haired man in a $900 suit with a color-coordinated Stetson was, just possibly, a rancher. There were people who lived in barracks and skyscrapers, adobe hovels, dormitories, trailer parks. Some came because they had nothing better to do, some because they wanted to tell their grandchildren that they had been there. Some arrived hoping for failure, others were confident of witnessing a miracle. Sounds of quiet devotion, raucous hilarity, mystic ecstasy, and subdued expectation rose from the crowd into the brilliant afternoon sunlight. A few heads glanced incuriously at the passing caravan of automobiles, each marked US GOVERNMENT INTERAGENCY MOTOR POOL.

Some people were lunching on the tailgates of hatchbacks; others were sampling the wares of vendors whose wheeled emporia were boldly lettered SNACKMOBILE or SPACE SOUVENIRS. There were long lines in front of small sturdy structures with maximum occupancy of one person that the project had thoughtfully provided. Children scampered among the vehicles, sleeping bags, blankets, and portable picnic tables almost never chided by the adults – except when they came too close to the highway or to the fence nearest Telescope 61, where a group of shaven-headed, kowtowed, saffron-robed young adults were solemnly intoning the sacred syllable 'Om.' There were posters with imagined representations of extraterrestrial beings, some made popular by comic books or motion pictures. One read, 'There Are Aliens Among Us.' A man with golden earrings was shaving, using the side-view mirror of someone's pickup truck, and a black-haired woman in a serape raised a cup of coffee in salute as the convoy sped by.

As they drove toward the new main gate, near Telescope 101, Ellie could see a young man on a jerrybuilt platform importuning a sizable crowd. He was wearing a T-shirt that depicted the Earth being struck by a bolt of celestial lightning. Several others in the crowd, she noticed, were wearing the same enigmatic adornment. At Ellie's urging, once through the gate, they pulled off the side of the road, rolled down the window, and listened. The speaker was turned away from them and they could see the faces in the crowd. These people are deeply moved, Ellie thought to herself.

127

He was in mid-oration: '. . . and others say there's been a pact with the Devil, that the scientists have sold their souls. There are precious stones in every one of these telescopes.' He waved his hand toward Telescope 101. 'Even the scientists admit that. Some people say it's the Devil's part of the bargain.'

'Religious hooliganism,' Lunacharsky muttered darkly, his eyes yearning for the open road before them.

'No, no. Let's stay,' she said. A half smile of wonderment was playing on her lips.

'There are some people – religious people, God-fearing people – who believe this Message comes from beings in space, entities, hostile creatures, aliens who want to harm us, enemies of Man.' He fairly shouted this last phrase, and then paused for effect. 'But all of you are wearied and disgusted by the corruption, the decay in this society, a decay brought on by unthinking, un-bridled, ungodly technology. I don't know which of you is right. I can't tell you what the Message means, or who it's from. I have my suspicions. We'll know soon enough. But I do know the scientists and the politicians and the bureaucrats are holding out on us. They haven't told us all they know. They're deceiving us, like they always do. For too long, O God, we have swallowed the lies they feed us, the corruption they bring.'

To Ellie's astonishment a deep rumbling chorus of assent rose from the crowd. He had tapped some well of resentment she had only vaguely apprehended.

'These scientists don't believe we're the children of God. They think we're the offspring of apes. There are known communists among them. Do you want people like that to decide the fate of the world?'

The crowd responded with a thunderous 'No!'

'Do you want a pack of unbelievers to do the talking to God?'

'No!' they roared again.

'Or the Devil? They are bargaining away our future

128

with monsters from an alien world. My brothers and sisters, there is an evil in this place.'

Ellie had thought the orator was unaware of their presence. But now he half turned and pointed through the cyclone fence directly at the idling convoy.

'They don't speak for us! They don't represent us! They have no right to parley in our name!'

Some of the crowd nearest the fence began jostling and rhythmically pushing. Both Valerian and the driver became alarmed. The engines had been left running, and in a moment they accelerated from the gate toward the Argus administration building, still many miles distant across the scrub desert. As they pulled away, over the sound of squealing tires and the murmur of the crowd, Ellie could hear the orator, his voice ringing clearly.

'The evil in this place will be stopped. I swear it.'

8

Random Access

The theologian may indulge the pleasing task of describing Religion as she descended from Heaven, arrayed in her native purity. A more melancholy duty is imposed on the historian. He must discover the inevitable mixture of error and corruption which she contracted in a long residence upon Earth, among a weak and degenerate race of beings.

> – EDWARD GIBBON
> *The Decline and Fall of the Roman Empire, XV*

Ellie ignored random access and advanced sequentially through the television stations. *Lifestyles of the Mass Murderers* and *You Bet Your Ass* were on adjacent channels. It was clear at a glance that the promise of the medium remained unfulfilled. There was a spirited basketball game between the Johnson City Wildcats and the Union-Endicott Tigers; the young men and women players were giving their all. On the next channel was an exhortation in Parsi on proper versus improper observances of Ramadan. Beyond was one of the locked channels, this one apparently devoted to universally abhorrent sexual practices. She next came upon one of the premier computer channels, dedicated to fantasy role-playing games and now fallen on hard times. Accessed to your home computer, it offered a single entry into a new adventure, today's apparently called *Galactic Gilgamesh*, in hopes that you would find it sufficiently attractive to order the corresponding floppy disk on one of the vending channels. Proper electronic precautions were taken so you could not record the program during your single play. Most of these video games, she thought, were desperately flawed attempts to prepare adolescents for an unknown future.

Her eye was caught by an earnest anchorman from one of the old networks discussing with unmistakable concern what was described as an unprovoked attack by North Vietnamese torpedo boats on two destroyers of the US Seventh Fleet in the Gulf of Tonkin, and the request by the President of the United States that he be authorized to 'take all necessary measures' in response. The program was one of her few favorites, *Yesterday's News*, reruns of network news shows of earlier years. The second half of the program consisted of a point-by-point dissection of the misinformation in the first half, and the obdurate credulity of the news organizations before any claims by any administration, no matter how unsupported and self-serving. It was one of several television series produced by an organization called REALITV – including *Promises, Promises*, devoted to follow-up analyses of unfulfilled campaign pledges at local, state, and national levels, and *Bamboozles and Baloney*, a weekly debunking of what were said to be widespread prejudices, propaganda, and myths. The date at the bottom of the screen was August 5, 1964, and a wave of recollection – nostalgia was not the appropriate word – about her days in high school washed over her. She pressed on.

Cycling through the channels, she rushed past an Oriental cooking series devoted this week to the hibachi, an extended advertisement for the first generation of general-purpose household robots by Hadden Cybernetics, the Soviet Embassy's Russian-language news and comment program, several children's and news frequencies, the mathematics station displaying the dazzling computer graphics of the new Cornell analytic geometry course, the local apartments and real estate channel, and a tight cluster of execrable daytime serials until she came upon the religious networks, where, with sustained and

131

general excitement, the Message was being discussed.

Attendance in churches had soared all over America. The Message, Ellie believed, was a kind of mirror in which each person sees his or her own beliefs challenged or confirmed. It was considered a blanket vindication of mutually exclusive apocalyptic and eschatological doctrines. In Peru, Algeria, Mexico, Zimbabwe, Ecuador, and among the Hopi, serious public debates took place on whether their progenitor civilizations had come from space; supporting opinions were attacked as colonialist. Catholics debated the extraterrestrial state of grace. Protestants discussed possible earlier missions of Jesus to nearby planets, and of course a return to Earth. Muslims were concerned that the Message might contravene the commandment against graven images. In Kuwait, a man announced himself as the Hidden Imam of the Shiites. Messianic fervor had arisen among the Sossafer Chasids. In other congregations of Orthodox Jews there was a sudden renewal of interest in Astruc, a zealot fearful that knowledge would undermine faith, who in 1305 had induced the Rabbi of Barcelona, the leading Jewish cleric of the time, to forbid the study of science or philosophy by those under twenty-five, on pain of excommunication. Similar currents were increasingly discernible in Islam. A Thessalonian philosopher, auspiciously named Nicholas Polydemos, was attracting attention with a set of passionate arguments for what he called the 'reunification' of the religions, governments, and peoples of the world. Critics began by questioning the 're.'

UFO groups had organized round-the-clock vigils at Brooks Air Force Base, near San Antonio, where the perfectly preserved bodies of four occupants of a flying saucer that had crash-landed in 1947 were said to be languishing in freezers; the extraterrestrials were reputed to be one meter tall and to have tiny flawless teeth. Apparitions of Vishnu had been reported in India, and of the Amida Buddha in Japan; miraculous cures by the hundreds were announced at Lourdes; a new Bodhisattva proclaimed herself in Tibet. A novel cargo cult was imported from New Guinea into Australia; it preached the construction of crude radio telescope replicas to attract extraterrestrial largesse. The World Union of Free Thinkers called the Message a disproof of the existence of God. The Mormon Church declared it a second revelation by the angel Moroni.

The Message was taken by different groups as evidence for many gods or one god or none. Chiliasm was rife. There were those who predicted the Millennium in 1999 – as a cabalistic inversion of 1666, the year that Sabbatai Zevi had adopted for his millennium; others chose 1996 or 2033, the presumed two thousandth anniversaries of the birth or death of Jesus. The Great Cycle of the ancient Maya was to be completed in the year 2011, when – according to this independent cultural tradition – the cosmos would end. The convolution of the Mayan prediction with Christian millenarianism was producing a kind of apocalyptic frenzy in Mexico and Central America. Some chiliasts who believed in the earlier dates had begun giving away their wealth to the poor, in part because it would soon be worthless anyway and in part as earnest money to God, a bribe for the Advent.

Zealotry, fanaticism, fear, hope, fervent debate, quiet prayer, agonizing reappraisal, exemplary selflessness, closed-minded bigotry, and a zest for dramatically new ideas were epidemic, rushing feverishly over the surface of the tiny planet Earth. Slowly emerging from this mighty ferment, Ellie thought she could see, was a dawning recognition of the world as one thread in a vast cosmic tapestry. Meanwhile, the Message itself continued to resist attempts at decryption.

On the vilification channels, protected by the First Amendment, she, Vaygay, der Heer, and to a lesser extent Peter Valerian were being castigated for a variety of offenses, including atheism, communism, and hoarding the Message for themselves. In her opinion, Vaygay wasn't much of a Communist, and Valerian had a deep, quiet, but sophisticated Christian faith. If they were lucky enough to come anywhere near cracking the Message, she was willing to deliver it personally to this sanctimonious twit of a television commentator. David Drumlin, however, was being made out as the hero, the man who had really decrypted the prime number and Olympic broadcasts; he was the kind of scientist we needed more of. She sighed and changed the channel once again.

She had come around to TABS, the Turner–American Broadcasting System, the only survivor of the large commercial networks that had dominated television broadcasting in the United States until the advent of widespread direct satellite broadcasting and 180-channel cable. On this station, Palmer Joss was making one of his rare television appearances. Like most Americans, Ellie instantly recognized his resonant voice, his slightly unkempt good looks, and the discoloration beneath his eyes that made you think he never slept for worrying about the rest of us.

'What has science really done for us?' he declaimed. 'Are we really happier? I don't mean just holographic receivers and seedless grapes. Are we fundamentally *happier*? Or do the scientists bribe us with toys, with technological trinkets, while they undermine our faith?'

Here was a man, she thought, who was hankering for a simpler age, a man who has spent his life attempting to reconcile the irreconcilable. He has condemned the most flagrant excesses of pop religion and thinks that justifies attacks on evolution and relativity. Why not attack the existence of the electron? Palmer Joss never saw one, and the Bible is innocent of electromagnetism. Why believe in electrons? Although she had never before listened to him speak, she was sure that sooner or later he would come around to the Message, and he did:

'The scientists keep their findings to themselves, give us little bits and pieces – enough to keep us quiet. They think we're too stupid to understand what they do. They give us conclusions without evidence, findings as if they were holy writ and not speculations, theories, hypotheses – what ordinary people would call guesses. They never ask if some new theory is as good for people as the belief that it tries to replace. They overestimate what they know and underestimate what we know. When we ask for explanations, they tell us it takes years to understand. I know about that, because in religion also there are things that take years to understand. You can spend a lifetime and never come close to understanding the nature of Almighty God. But you don't see the scientists coming to religious leaders to ask them about *their* years of study and insight and prayer. They never give us a second thought, except when they mislead us and deceive us.

'And now they say they have a Message from the star Vega. But a star can't send a message. *Some*one is sending it. Who? Is the purpose of the Message divine or satanic? When they decode the Message, will it end "Yours truly, God" . . . or "Sincerely, the Devil"? When the scientists get around to telling us what's in the Message, will they tell us the whole truth? Or will they hold something back because they think we can't understand it, or because it doesn't match what *they* believe? Aren't these the people who taught us how to annihilate ourselves?

'I tell you, my friends, science is too important to be left to the scientists. Representatives of the major faiths ought to be part of the process of decoding. We ought to be looking at the raw data. That's what the scientists call it, "raw." Otherwise . . . otherwise, where will we be? They'll tell us something about the Message. Maybe what they really believe. Maybe not. And we'll have to accept it, whatever they tell us. There are some things the scientists know about. There are other things – take my word for it – they know nothing about. Maybe they've received a message from another being in the heavens. Maybe not. Can they be sure the Message isn't a Golden

135

Calf? I don't think they'd know one if they saw one. These are the folks who brought us the hydrogen bomb. Forgive me, Lord, for not being more grateful to these kind souls.

'I have seen God face to face. I worship Him, trust Him, love Him, with my entire soul, with all of my being. I don't think anyone could believe more than I do. I can't see how the scientists could believe in science more than I do in God.

'They're ready to throw away their "truths" when a new idea comes round. They're proud of it. They don't see any end to knowing. They imagine we're locked in ignorance until the end of time, that there's no certainty anywhere in nature. Newton overthrew Aristotle. Einstein overthrew Newton. Tomorrow someone else'll overthrow Einstein. As soon as we get to understand one theory, there's another one in its place. I wouldn't mind so much if they had warned us that the old ideas were tentative. Newton's *law* of gravitation, they called it. They still call it that. But if it was a law of nature, how could it be wrong? How could it be overthrown? Only God can repeal the laws of nature, not the scientists. They just got it wrong. If Albert Einstein was right, Isaac Newton was an amateur, a bungler.

'Remember, the scientists don't always get it right. They want to take away our faith, our beliefs, and they offer us nothing of spiritual value in return. I do not intend to abandon God because the scientists write a book and say it is a message from Vega. I will not worship science. I will not defy the First Commandment. I will not bow down before a Golden Calf.'

When he was a very young man, before he became widely known and admired, Palmer Joss had been a carnival roustabout. It was mentioned in his profile in *Timesweek*; it was no secret. To help make his fortune he had arranged for a map of the Earth in cylindrical projection to be painstakingly tattooed on his torso. He would exhibit himself at county fairs and sideshows from Oklahoma to Mississippi, one of the stragglers and remnants of a more vigorous age of rural itinerant entertainment. In the expanse of blue ocean were the four gods of the winds, their cheeks puffing forth prevailing westerlies and nor'easters. By flexing his pectorals, he could make Boreas swell along with the Mid-Atlantic. Then, he would declaim to the astonished onlookers from Book 6 of Ovid's *Metamorphoses*:

> Monarch of Violence, rolling on clouds,
> I toss wide waters, and I fell huge trees . . .
> Possessed of daemon-rage, I penetrate,
> Sheer to the utmost caverns of old Earth;
> And straining, up from those unfathomed deeps,
> Scatter the terror-stricken shades of Hell;
> And hurl death-dealing earthquakes throughout the
>   world!

Fire and brimstone from old Rome. With some help from his hands, he would demonstrate continental drift, pressing West Africa against South America, so they joined, like the pieces of a jigsaw puzzle, almost perfectly at the longitude of his navel. They billed him as 'Geos, the Earth Man.'

Joss was a great reader and, being unencumbered by a formal education past grade school, had not been told that science and classics were unseemly fare for ordinary people. Aided by his casual, rumpled good looks, he would ingratiate himself with librarians in the towns along the carnival's trek and ask what serious books he should read. He wanted, he told them, to improve himself. Dutifully, he read about winning friends and investing in real estate and intimidating your acquaintances without their noticing, but felt these books somehow shallow. By contrast, in ancient literature and in modern science he thought he detected quality. When there were layovers, he would haunt the local town or county library. He taught himself some geography and history. They were job-related, he told Elvira the Elephant Girl, who questioned him closely on his absences. She suspected him of compulsive dalliances – a librarian in every port, she once said – but she had to admit his professional patter was improving. The contents were too highbrow, but the delivery was down home. Surprisingly, Joss's little stall began to make money for the carnival.

His back to the audience, he was one day demonstrating the collision of India with Asia and the resulting crinkling up of the Himalayas, when, out of a gray but rainless sky, a lightning bolt flashed and struck him dead. There had been twisters in south-eastern Oklahoma, and the weather was unusual throughout the South. He had a perfectly lucid sense of leaving his body – pitifully crumbled on the sawdust-covered planking, being regarded with caution and something akin to awe by the small crowd – and rising, rising as if through a long dark tunnel, slowly approaching a brilliant light. And in the radiance he gradually discerned a figure of heroic, indeed of Godlike, proportions.

When he awoke he found a part of himself disappointed to be alive. He was lying on a cot in a modestly furnished bedroom. Leaning over him was the Reverend Billy Jo Rankin, not the present incumbent of that name, but his father, a venerable surrogate preacher of the third quarter of the twentieth century. In the background, Joss thought he could see a dozen hooded figures singing the *Kyrie Eleison*. But he couldn't be sure.

'Am I gonna live or die?' the young man whispered.

'My boy, you're gonna do both,' the Reverend Mr Rankin replied.

Joss was soon overcome with a poignant sense of discovery at the existence of the world. But in a way that was difficult for him to articulate, this feeling was in conflict with the beatific image that he had beheld, and with the infinite joy that vision portended. He could sense the two feelings in conflict within his breast. In various circumstances, sometimes in mid-sentence, he would become aware of one or the other of these feelings

138

making some claim on speech or action. After a while, he was content to live with both.

He really *had* been dead, they told him afterwards. A doctor had pronounced him dead. But they had prayed over him, they had sung hymns, and they had even tried to revive him by body massage (mainly in the vicinity of Mauritania). They had returned him to life. He had been truly and literally reborn. Since this corresponded so well to his own perception of the experience, he accepted the account, and gladly. While he almost never talked about it, he became convinced of the significance of the event. He had not been struck dead for nothing. He had not been brought back for no reason.

Under his patron's tutelage, he began to study Scripture seriously. He was deeply moved by the idea of the Resurrection and the doctrine of Salvation. He assisted the Reverend Mr Rankin at first in small ways, eventually filling in for him in the more onerous or more distant preaching assignments – especially after the younger Billy Jo Rankin left for Odessa, Texas, in answer to a call from God. Soon Joss found a preaching style that was his own, not so much exhortatory as explanatory. In simple language and homely metaphors, he would explain baptism and the afterlife, the connection of Christian Revelation with the myths of classical Greece and Rome, the idea of God's plan for the world, and the conformity of science and religion when both were properly understood. This was not the conventional preaching, and it was too ecumenical for many tastes. But it proved unaccountably popular.

'You've been reborn, Joss,' the elder Rankin told him. 'So you ought to change your name. Except Palmer Joss is such a fine name for a preacher, you'd be a fool not to keep it.'

Like doctors and lawyers, the vendors of religion rarely criticize one another's wares, Joss observed. But one night he attended services at the new Church of God, Crusader, to hear the younger Billy Jo Rankin, triumphantly returned from Odessa, preach to the multitude. Billy Jo enunciated a stark doctrine of Reward, Retribution, and the Rapture. But tonight was a healing night. The curative instrument, the congregation was told, was the holiest of relics – holier than the splinter of the True Cross, holier even than the thigh bone of Saint Teresa of Avila that Generalissimo Francisco Franco had kept in his office to intimidate the pious. What Billy Jo Rankin brandished was the actual amniotic fluid that surrounded and protected our Lord. The liquid had been carefully preserved in an ancient earthenware vessel that once belonged, so it was said, to Saint Ann. The tiniest drop of it would cure what ails you, he promised, through a special act of Divine Grace. This holiest of holy waters was with us tonight.

Joss was appalled, not so much that Rankin would attempt so transparent a scam but that any of the parishioners were so credulous as to accept it. In his previous life he had witnessed many attempts to bamboozle the public. But that was entertainment. This was different. This was religion. Religion was too important to gloss the truth, much less to manufacture miracles. He took to denouncing this imposture from the pulpit.

As his fervor grew, he railed against other deviant forms of Christian fundamentalism, including those aspirant herpetologists who tested their faith by fondling snakes in accord with the biblical injunction that the pure of heart shall not fear the venom of serpents. In one widely quoted sermon he paraphrased Voltaire. He never thought, he said, that he would find men of the cloth so venal as to lend support to the blasphemers who taught that the first priest was the first rogue who met the first fool. These religions were damaging religion. He shook his finger gracefully in the air.

Joss argued that in every religion there was a doctrinal line beyond which it insulted the intelligence of its practitioners. Reasonable people might disagree as to where that line should be drawn, but religions trespassed well beyond it at their peril. People were not fools, he said. The day before his death, as he was putting his affairs in order, the elder Rankin sent word to Joss that he never wanted to lay eyes on him again.

At the same time, Joss began to preach that science didn't have all the answers either. He found inconsistencies in the theory of evolution. The embarrassing findings, the facts that don't fit, the scientists just sweep under the rug, he said. They don't really know that the Earth is 4.6 billion years old, any more than Archbishop Ussher knew that it was 6,000 years old. Nobody has seen evolution happen, nobody has been marking time since the Creation. ('Two-hundred-quadrillion-Mississippi . . .' he once imagined the patient timekeeper intoning, counting up the seconds from the origin of the world.)

And Einstein's theory of relativity was also unproved. You couldn't travel faster than light no matter what, Einstein had said. How could he know? How close to the speed of light had *he* gone? Relativity was only a way of understanding the world. Einstein couldn't restrict what mankind could do in the far future. And Einstein sure couldn't set limits on what God could do. Couldn't God travel faster than light if He wanted to? Couldn't God make *us* travel faster than light if He wanted to? There were excesses in science and there were excesses in religion. A reasonable man wouldn't be stampeded by either one. There were many interpretations of Scripture and many interpretations of the natural world. Both were created by God, so both must be mutually consistent. Wherever a discrepancy seems to exist, either a scientist or a theologian – maybe both – hasn't been doing his job.

Palmer Joss combined his evenhanded criticism of science and religion with a fervent plea for moral rectitude and a respect for the intelligence of his flock. In slow stages he acquired a national reputation. In debates on the teaching of 'scientific creationism' in the schools, on the ethical status of abortion and frozen embryos, on the admissibility of genetic engineering, he attempted in his way to steer a middle course, to reconcile caricatures of science and religion. Both contending camps were outraged at his interventions, and his popularity grew. He became a confidant of presidents. His sermons were excerpted on the Op Ed pages of major secular newspapers. But he resisted many invitations and some proffered blandishments to found an electronic church. He continued to live simply, and rarely – except for presidential invitations and ecumenical congresses – left the rural South. Beyond a conventional patriotism, he made it a rule not to meddle in politics. In a field filled with competing entries, many of dubious probity, Palmer Joss became, in erudition and moral authority, the preeminent Christian fundamentalist preacher of his day.

Der Heer had asked if they could have a quiet dinner somewhere. He was flying in for the summary session with Vaygay and the Soviet delegation on the latest progress in the interpretation of the Message. But south-central New Mexico was crawling with the world's press, and there was no restaurant for a hundred miles in which they could talk unobserved and unheard. So she made dinner herself in her modest apartment near the visiting scientists' quarters at the Argus facility. There was a great deal to talk about. Sometimes it seemed that the fate of the whole project was hanging by a presidential thread. But the little tremor of anticipation she felt just before Ken's arrival was occasioned, she was vaguely aware, by more than that. Joss was not exactly business, so they got around to him while loading the dishwasher.

'The man is scared stiff,' Ellie said. 'His perspective is narrow. He imagines the Message is going to be unacceptable biblical exegesis or something that shakes his faith. He has no idea about how a new scientific paradigm subsumes the previous one. He wants to know what science has done for him lately. And he's supposed to be the voice of reason.'

'Compared to the Doomsday Chiliasts and the Earth-

142

Firsters, Palmer Joss is the soul of moderation,' der Heer replied. 'Maybe we haven't explained the methods of science as well as we should have. I worry about that a lot these days. And Ellie, can you really be sure that it isn't a message from –'

'From God or the Devil? Ken, you can't be serious.'

'Well, how about advanced beings committed to what we might call good or evil, who somebody like Joss would consider indistinguishable from God or the Devil?'

'Ken, whoever those beings are in the Vega system, I guarantee they didn't create the universe. And they're nothing like the Old Testament God. Remember, Vega, the Sun, and all the other stars in the solar neighborhood are in some backwater of an absolutely humdrum galaxy. Why should I Am That I Am hang out around here? There must be more pressing things for him to do.'

'Ellie, we're in a bind. You know Joss is very influential. He's been close to three presidents, including the present incumbent. The President is inclined to make some concession to Joss, although I don't think she wants to put him and a bunch of other preachers on the Preliminary Decryption Committee with you, Valerian, and Drumlin – to say nothing of Vaygay and his colleagues. It's hard to imagine the Russians going along with fundamentalist clergy on the Committee. The whole thing could unravel over this. So why don't we go and talk to him? The President says that Joss is really fascinated by science. Suppose we won him over?'

'We're going to *convert* Palmer *Joss*?'

'I'm not imagining making him change his religion – let's just make him understand what Argus is about, how we don't have to answer the Message if we don't like what it says, how interstellar distances quarantine us from Vega.'

'Ken, he doesn't even believe that the velocity of light is a cosmic speed limit. We're going to be talking past each other. Also, I've got a long history of failure in accommodating to the conventional religions. I tend to blow my top at their inconsistencies and hypocrisies. I'm not sure a meeting between Joss and me is what you want. Or the President.'

'Ellie,' he said, 'I know who I'd put *my* money on. I don't see how getting together with Joss could make things much worse.'

She allowed herself to return his smile.

With the tracking ships now in place and a few small but adequate radio telescopes installed in such places as Reykjavik and Jakarta, there was now redundant coverage of the signal from Vega at every longitude swath. A major conference was scheduled to be held in Paris of the full World Message Consortium. In preparation, it was natural for the nations with the largest fraction of the data to hold a preparatory scientific discussion. They had been meeting for the better part of four days, and this summary session was intended mainly to bring those such as der Heer, who served as intermediaries between the scientists and the politicians, up to speed. The Soviet delegation, while nominally headed by Lunacharsky, included several scientists and technical people of equal distinction. Among them were Genrikh Arkhangelsky, recently named head of the Soviet-led international space consortium called Intercosmos, and Timofei Gotsridze, listed as Minister of Medium Heavy Industry, and a member of the Central Committee.

Vaygay clearly felt himself under unusual pressures: he had resumed chain smoking. He held the cigarette between his thumb and forefinger, palm up, as he talked.

'I agree that there is adequate overlap in longitude, but I'm still worried about redundancy. A failure in the helium liquifier on board the *Marshal Nedelin* or a power failure in Reykjavik, and the continuity of the Message is in jeopardy. Suppose the Message takes two years to cycle around to the beginning. If we miss a piece, we will have to wait two more years to fill in the gap. And remember, we don't know that the Message will be repeated. If there's no repeat, the gaps will never be repaired. I think we need to plan even for unlikely possibilities.'

'What are you thinking of?' der Heer asked. 'Something like emergency generators for every observatory in the Consortium?'

'Yes, and independent amplifiers, spectrometers, autocorrelators, disk drives, and so forth at each observatory. And some provision for fast airlift of liquid helium to remote observatories if necessary.'

'Ellie, do you agree?'

'Absolutely.'

'Anything else?'

'I think we should continue to observe Vega on a very broad range of frequencies,' Vaygay said. 'Perhaps tomorrow a different message will come through on only one of the message frequencies. We should also monitor other regions of the sky. Maybe the key to the Message won't come from Vega, but from somewhere else –'

'Let me say why I think Vaygay's point is important,' interjected Valerian. 'This is a unique moment, when we're receiving a message but have made no progress at all in decrypting it. We have no previous experience along these lines. We have to cover all the bases. We don't want to wind up a year or two from now kicking ourselves because there was some simple precaution we forgot to take, or some simple measurement that we overlooked. The idea that the Message will cycle back on itself is the merest guess. There's nothing in the Message itself, as far as we can see, that promises cycling back. Any opportunities lost now may be lost for all time. I also agree there's more instrumental development that needs doing. For all we know there's a fourth layer to the palimpsest.'

'There's also the question of personnel,' Vaygay continued. 'Suppose this message goes on not for a year or

145

two but for decades. Or suppose this is just the first in a long series of messages from all over the sky. There are at most a few hundred really capable radio astronomers in the world. That is a very small number when the stakes are so high. The industrialized countries must start producing many more radio astronomers and radio engineers with first-rate training.'

Ellie noted that Gotsridze, who had said little, was taking detailed notes. She was again struck by how much more literate the Soviets were in English than the Americans in Russian. Near the beginning of the century, scientists all over the world spoke – or at least read – German. Before that it had been French, and before that Latin. In another century there might be some other obligatory scientific language – Chinese, perhaps. For the moment it was English, and scientists all over the planet struggled to learn its ambiguities and irregularities.

Lighting a fresh cigarette from the glowing tip of its predecessor, Vaygay went on. 'There is something else to be said. This is just speculation. It's not even as plausible as the idea that the Message will cycle back on itself – which Professor Valerian quite properly stressed was only a guess. I would not ordinarily mention so speculative an idea at such an early stage. But if the speculation is sound, there are certain further actions we must begin thinking about immediately. I would not have the courage to raise this possibility if Academician Arkhangelsky had not come tentatively to the same conclusion. He and I have disagreed about the quantization of quasar red shifts, the explanation of superluminal light sources, the rest mass of the neutrino, quark physics in neutron stars . . . We have had many disagreements. I must admit that sometimes he has been right and sometimes I have been right. Almost never, it seems to me, in the early speculative stage of a subject, have we agreed. But on this, we agree.

'Genrikh Dmit'ch, would you explain?'

Arkhangelsky seemed tolerant, even amused. He and Lunacharsky had been for years engaged in personal rivalry, heated scientific disputes, and a celebrated controversy on the prudent level of support for Soviet fusion research.

'We guess,' he said, 'that the Message is the instructions for building a machine. Of course, we have no knowledge about how to decode the Message. The evidence is in internal references. I give you an example. Here on page 15441 is a clear reference to an earlier page, 13097, which, by luck, we also have. The later page was received here in New Mexico, the earlier one at our observatory near Tashkent. On page 13097 there is another reference, this to a time when we were not covering all longitudes. There are many cases of this back referencing. In general, and this is the important point, there are complicated instructions on a recent page, but simpler instructions on an earlier page. In one case there are eight citations to earlier material on a single page.'

'That's now an awfully compelling argument, guys,' replied Ellie. 'Maybe it's a set of mathematical exercises, the later ones building on the earlier ones. Maybe it's a long novel – they might have very long lifetimes compared to us – in which events are connected with childhood experiences or whatever they have on Vega when they're young. Maybe it's a tightly cross-referenced religious manual.'

'The Ten Billion Commandments.' Der Heer laughed.

'Maybe,' said Lunacharsky, staring through a cloud of cigarette smoke out the window at the telescopes. They seemed to be staring longingly at the sky. 'But when you look at the patterns of cross-references, I think you'll agree it looks more like the instruction manual for building a machine. God knows what the machine is supposed to do.'

9

The Numinous

Wonder is the basis of worship

– THOMAS CARLYLE
Sartor Resartus (1833–34)

I maintain that the cosmic religious feeling is the strongest and noblest motive for scientific research.

– ALBERT EINSTEIN
Ideas and Opinions (1954)

She could recall the exact moment when, on one of many trips to Washington, she discovered that she was falling in love with Ken der Heer.

Arrangements for the meeting with Palmer Joss seemed to be taking forever. Apparently Joss was reluctant to visit the Argus facility; it was the impiety of the scientists, not their interpretation of the Message, he now said, that interested him. And to probe their character, some more neutral ground was needed. Ellie was willing to go anywhere, and a special assistant to the President was negotiating. Other radio astronomers were not to go; the President wanted it to be Ellie alone.

Ellie was also waiting for the day, still some weeks off, when she would fly to Paris for the first full meeting of the World Message Consortium. She and Vaygay were coordinating the global data-collection program. The signal acquisition was now fairly routine, and in recent months there had been not one gap in the coverage. So she found to her surprise that she had a little time on her hands. She vowed to have a long talk with her mother, and to remain civil and friendly no matter what provocation was offered. There was an absurd amount of backed-up paper and electronic mail to go through, not just congratulations and criticisms from colleagues, but religious admonitions, pseudoscientific speculations proposed with great confidence, and fan mail from all over the world. She had not read *The Astrophysical Journal* in months, although she was the first author of a very recent paper that was surely the most extraordinary article that had ever appeared in that august publication. The signal from Vega was so strong that many amateurs – tired of 'ham' radio – had begun constructing their own small radio telescopes and signal analyzers. In the early stages of Message acquisition, they had turned up some useful data, and Ellie was still besieged by amateurs who thought they had acquired something unknown to the SETI professionals. She felt an obligation to write encouraging letters. There were other meritorious radio astronomy programs at the facility – the quasar survey, for example – that needed attending to. But instead of doing all these things, she found herself spending almost all her time with Ken.

Of course, it was her duty to involve the President's Science Adviser in Project Argus as deeply as he wished. It was important that the President be fully and competently informed. She hoped the leaders of other nations would be as thoroughly briefed on the findings from Vega as was the President of the United States. This President, while untrained in science, genuinely liked the subject and was willing to support science not only for its practical benefits but, at least a little for the joy of knowing. This had been true of few previous American leaders since James Madison and John Quincy Adams.

Still, it was remarkable how much time der Heer was able to spend at Argus. He did devote an hour or more each day in high-bandpass scrambled communications with his Office of Science and Technology Policy in the Old Executive Office Building in Washington. But the rest of the time, as far as she could see, he was simply . . .

149

around. He would poke into the innards of the computer system, or visit individual radio telescopes. Sometimes an assistant from Washington would be with him; more often he would be alone. She would see him through the open door of the spare office they had assigned him, his feet propped up on the desk, reading some report or talking on the phone. He would offer her a cheery wave and return to his work. She would find him talking casually with Drumlin or Valerian; but equally so with junior technicians and with the secretarial staff, who had on more than one occasion pronounced him, within Ellie's hearing, 'charming.'

Der Heer had many questions for her as well. At first they were purely technical and programmatic, but soon they extended to plans for a wide variety of conceivable future events, and then to untrammeled speculation. These days it almost seemed that discussion of the project was only a pretext to spend a little time together.

One fine autumn afternoon in Washington, the President was obliged to delay a meeting of the Special Contingency Task Group because of the Tyrone Free crisis. After an overnight flight from New Mexico, Ellie and der Heer found themselves with an unscheduled few hours, and decided to visit the Vietnam Memorial, designed by Maya Ying Lin when she was still an undergraduate architectural student at Yale. Amidst the somber and doleful reminders of a foolish war, der Heer seemed inappropriately cheerful, and Ellie began again to speculate about flaws in his character. A pair of General Service Administration plainclothes security people, their custom-molded, flesh-colored earpieces in place, followed discreetly.

He had coaxed an exquisite blue caterpillar to climb aboard a twig. It briskly padded along, its iridescent body rippling with the motion of fourteen pairs of feet. At the end of the twig, it held on with its last five segments and flailed the air in a plucky attempt to find a new perch. Unsuccessful, it turned itself around smartly

150

and retraced its many steps. Der Heer then changed his clutch on the twig so that when the caterpillar returned to its starting point, there was again nowhere to go. Like some caged mammalian carnivore, it paced back and forth many times, but in the last few passages, it seemed to her, with increasing resignation. She was beginning to feel pity for the poor creature, even if it proved to be, say, the larva responsible for the barley blight.

'What a wonderful program in this little guy's head!' he exclaimed. 'It works every time – optimum escape software. And he knows not to fall off. I mean the twig is effectively suspended in air. The caterpillar never experiences that in nature, because the twig is always connected to something. Ellie, did you ever wonder what that program would feel like if it was in your head? I mean, would it just seem obvious to you what you had to do when you came to the end of a twig? Would you have the impression you were thinking it through? Would you wonder how you knew to shake your front ten feet in the air but hold on tight with the other eighteen?'

She inclined her head slightly and examined him rather than the caterpillar. He seemed to have little difficulty imagining her as an insect. She tried to reply noncommittally, reminding herself that for him this would be a matter of professional interest.

'What'll you do with it now?'

'I'll put it back down in the grass, I guess. What else would you do with it?'

'Some people might kill it.'

'It's hard to kill a creature once it lets you see its consciousness.' He continued to carry both twig and larva.

They walked for a while in silence past almost 55,000 names engraved in reflecting black granite.

'Every government that prepares for war paints its adversaries as monsters,' she said. 'They don't want you thinking of the other side as human. If the enemy can think and feel, you might hesitate to kill them. And

151

killing is very important. Better to see them as monsters.'

'Here, look at this beauty,' he replied after a moment. 'Really. Look closely.'

She did. Fighting back a small tremor of revulsion, she tried to see it through his eyes.

'Watch what it does,' he continued. 'If it was as big as you or me, it would scare everybody to death. It would be a *genuine* monster, right? But it's little. It eats leaves, minds its own business, and adds a little beauty to the world.'

She took the hand not preoccupied with the caterpillar, and they walked wordlessly past the ranks of names, inscribed in chronological order of death. These were, of course, only the American casualties. Except in the hearts of their families and friends, there was no comparable memorial anywhere on the planet for the two million people of Southeast Asia who had also died in the conflict. In America, the most common public comment about this war was about political hamstringing of military power, psychologically akin, she thought, to the 'stab-in-the-back' explanation by German militarists of their World War I defeat. The Vietnam war was a pustule on the national conscience that no President so far had the courage to lance. (Subsequent policies of the Democratic Republic of Vietnam had not made this task easier.) She remembered how common it was for American soldiers to call their Vietnamese adversaries 'gooks,' 'slope-heads,' 'slant-eyes,' and worse. Could we possibly manage the next phase of human history without first dealing with this penchant for dehumanizing the adversary?

In everyday conversation, der Heer didn't talk like an academic. If you met him at the corner newsstand buying a paper, you'd never guess he was a scientist. He hadn't lost his New York street accent. At first the apparent incongruity between his language and the quality of his scientific work seemed amusing to his colleagues. As his research and the man himself became better known, his accent became merely idiosyncratic. But his pronunciation of, say, guanosine triphosphate, seemed to give this benign molecule explosive properties.

They had been slow in recognizing that they were falling in love. It must have been apparent to many others. A few weeks before, when Lunacharsky was still at Argus, he launched himself on one of his occasional tirades on the irrationality of language. This time it was the turn of American English.

'Ellie, why do people say "make the same mistake again"? What does "again" add to the sentence? And am I right that "burn up" and "burn down" mean the same thing? "Slow up" and "slow down" mean the same thing? So if "screw up" is acceptable, why not "screw down"?'

She nodded wearily. She had heard him more than once complain to his Soviet colleagues on the inconsistencies of the Russian language, and was sure she would hear a French edition of all this at the Paris conference. She was happy to admit that languages had infelicities, but they had so many sources and evolved in response to so many small pressures that it would be astonishing if they were perfectly coherent and internally consistent. Vaygay had such a good time complaining, though, that she ordinarily did not have the heart to remonstrate with him.

'And take this phrase "head over heels in love,"' he continued. 'This is a common expression, yes? But it's exactly backward. Or, rather, upside down. You are *ordinarily* head over heels. When you are in love you should be heels over *head*. Am I right? *You* would know about falling in love. But whoever invented this phrase did not know about love. He imagined you walk around in the usual way, instead of floating upside down in the air, like the work of that French painter – what's his name?'

'He was Russian,' she replied. Marc Chagall had provided a narrow pathway out of a somehow awkward

153

conversational thicket. Afterward she wondered if Vaygay had been teasing her or probing for a response. Perhaps he had only unconsciously recognized the growing bond between Ellie and der Heer.

At least part of der Heer's reluctance was clear. Here he was, the President's Science Adviser, devoting an enormous amount of time to an unprecedented, delicate, and volatile matter. To become emotionally involved with one of the principals was risky. The President certainly wanted his judgment unimpaired. He should be able to recommend courses of action that Ellie opposed, and to urge rejection of options that she supported. Falling in love with Ellie would on some level compromise der Heer's effectiveness.

For Ellie it was more complicated. Before she had acquired the somewhat staid respectability of the directorship of a major radio observatory, she had had many partners. While she had felt herself in love and declared herself so, marriage had never seriously tempted her. She dimly remembered the quatrain – was it William Butler Yeats? – with which she had tried to reassure her early swains, heartbroken because, as always, she had determined that the affair was over:

> You say there is no love, my love,
> Unless it lasts for aye.
> Ah, folly, there are episodes
> Far better than the play.

She recalled how charming John Staughton had been to her while courting her mother, and how easily he had cast off this pose after he became her stepfather. Some new and monstrous persona, hitherto barely glimpsed, could emerge in men shortly after you married them. Her romantic predispositions made her vulnerable, she thought. She was not going to repeat her mother's mistake. A little deeper was a fear of falling in love without reservation, of committing herself to someone who might then be snatched from her. Or simply leave

154

her. But if you never really fall in love, you can never really miss it. (She did not dwell on this sentiment, dimly aware that it did not ring quite true.) Also, if she never really fell in love with someone, she could never really betray him, as in her heart of hearts she felt that her mother had betrayed her long-dead father. She still missed him terribly.

With Ken it *seemed* to be different. Or had her expectations been gradually compromised over the years? Unlike many other men she could think of, when challenged or stressed Ken displayed a gentler, more compassionate side. His tendency to compromise and his skill in scientific politics were part of the accoutrements of his job; but underneath she felt she had glimpsed something solid. She respected him for the way he had integrated science into the whole of his life, and for the courageous support for science that he had tried to inculcate into two administrations.

They had, as discreetly as possible, been staying together, more or less, in her small apartment at Argus. Their conversations were a joy, with ideas flying back and forth like shuttlecocks. Sometimes they responded to each other's uncompleted thoughts with almost perfect foreknowledge. He was a considerate and inventive lover. And anyway, she liked his pheromones.

She was sometimes amazed at what she was able to do and say in his presence, because of their love. She came to admire him so much that his love for her affected her own self-esteem: She liked herself better because of him. And since he clearly felt the same, there was a kind of infinite regress of love and respect underlying their relationship. At least, that was how she described it to herself. In the presence of so many of her friends, she had felt an undercurrent of loneliness. With Ken, it was gone.

She was comfortable describing to him her reveries, snatches of memories, childhood embarrassments. And he was not merely interested but fascinated. He would question her for hours about her childhood. His questions were always direct, sometimes probing, but without exception gentle. She began to understand why lovers talk baby talk to one another. There was no other socially acceptable circumstance in which the children inside her were permitted to come out. If the one-year-old, the five-year-old, the twelve-year-old, and the twenty-year-old all find compatible personalities in the beloved, there is a real chance to keep all of these sub-personas happy. Love ends their long loneliness. Perhaps the depth of love can be calibrated by the number of different selves that are actively involved in a given relationship. With her previous partners, it seemed, at most one of these selves was able to find a compatible opposite number; the other personas were grumpy hangers-on.

The weekend before the scheduled meeting with Joss, they were lying in bed as the late-afternoon sunlight, admitted between the slats of the venetian blinds, played patterns on their intertwined forms.

'In ordinary conversation,' she was saying, 'I can talk about my father without feeling more than . . . a slight pang of loss. But if I allow myself to *really* remember him – his sense of humor, say, or that . . . passionate fairness – then the facade crumbles, and I want to weep because he's gone.'

'No question; language can free us of feeling, or almost,' der Heer replied, stroking her shoulder. 'Maybe that's one of its functions – so we can understand the world without becoming entirely overwhelmed by it.'

'If so, then the intention of language isn't only a blessing. You know, Ken, I'd give anything – I really mean anything I have – if I could just spend a few minutes with my dad.'

She imagined a heaven with all those nice moms and dads floating about or flapping over to a nearby cloud. It would have to be a commodious place to accommodate all the tens of billions of people who had lived and died since the emergence of the human species. It might be very crowded, she was thinking, unless the religious heaven was built on a scale something like the astronomical heaven. Then there'd be room to spare.

'There must be some number,' Ellie said, 'that measures the total population of intelligent beings in the Milky Way. How many do you suppose it is? If there's a million civilizations, each with about a billion individuals, that's um, ten to the fifteenth power intelligent beings. But if most of them are more advanced than we are, maybe the idea of individuals becomes inappropriate; maybe that's just another Earth chauvinism.'

'Sure. And then you can calculate the galactic production rate of Gauloises and Twinkies and Volga sedans and Sony pocket communicators. Then we could calculate the Gross Galactic Product. Once we have that in hand, we could work on the Gross Cosmic . . .'

'You're making fun of me,' she said with a soft smile, not at all displeased. 'But think about such numbers. I mean *really* think about them. All those planets with all those beings, more advanced than we are. Don't you get a kind of tingle thinking about it?'

She could tell what he was thinking, but rushed on. 'Here, look at this. I've been reading up for the meeting with Joss.'

She reached toward the bedside table for Volume 16 of an old *Encyclopaedia Britannica Macropaedia*, titled 'Rubens to Somalia,' and opened to a page where a scrap of computer printout had been inserted as a bookmark. She pointed to an article called 'Sacred or Holy.'

'The theologians seem to have recognized a special, nonrational – I wouldn't call it irrational – aspect of the feeling of sacred or holy. They call it "numinous." The term was first used by . . . let's see . . . somebody named Rudolph Otto in a 1923 book, *The Idea of the Holy*. He believed that humans were predisposed to detect and revere the numinous. He called it the *misterium tremendum*. Even *my* Latin is good enough for that.

'In the presence of the *misterium tremendum*, people feel

157

utterly insignificant but, if I read this right, not personally alienated. He thought of the numinous as a thing
"wholly other," and the human response to it as "absolute astonishment." Now, if that's what religious people
talk about when they use words like sacred or holy, I'm
with them. I felt something like that just in *listening* for a
signal, never mind in actually receiving it. I think all of
science elicits that sense of awe.'

'Now listen to this.' She read from the text:

Throughout the past hundred years a number of philosophers
and social scientists have asserted the disappearance of the
sacred, and predicted the demise of religion. A study of the
history of religions shows that religious forms change and that
there has never been unanimity on the nature and expression of
religion. Whether or not man . . .

'Sexists write and edit religious articles, too, of
course.' She returned to the text.

Whether or not man is now in a new situation for developing
structures of ultimate values radically different from those
provided in the traditionally affirmed awareness of the sacred is
a vital question.

'So?'

'So, I think the bureaucratic religions try to insti-
tutionalize your perception of the numinous instead of
providing the means so you can perceive the numinous
directly – like looking through a six-inch telescope. If
sensing the numinous is at the heart of religion, who's
more religious would you say – the people who follow
the bureaucratic religions or the people who teach themselves science?'

'Let's see if I've got this straight,' he returned. It was a
phrase of hers that he had adopted. 'It's a lazy Saturday
afternoon, and there's this couple lying naked in bed
reading the *Encyclopaedia Britannica* to each other, and
arguing about whether the Andromeda Galaxy is more
"numinous" than the Resurrection. Do they know how
to have a good time, or don't they?'

Part II

THE MACHINE

The Almighty Lecturer, by displaying the principles of science in the structure of the universe, has invited man to study and to imitation. It is as if He had said to the inhabitants of this globe that we call ours, 'I have made an earth for man to dwell upon, and I have rendered the starry heavens visible, to teach him science and the arts. He can now provide for his own comfort, and learn from my munificence to all to be kind to each other.'

– THOMAS PAINE
The Age of Reason (1794)

10
Precession of the Equinoxes

*Do we, holding that the gods exist, deceive ourselves
with insubstantial dreams and lies, while random careless
chance and change alone control the world?*

– EURIPIDES
Hecuba

It was odd the way it had worked out. She had imagined
that Palmer Joss would come to the Argus facility, watch
the signal being gathered in by the radio telescopes, and
take note of the huge room full of magnetic tapes and
disks on which the previous many months of data were
stored. He would ask a few scientific questions and then
examine, in its multiplicity of zeros and ones, some of the
reams of computer printout displaying the still incomprehensible Message. She hadn't imagined spending
hours arguing philosophy or theology. But Joss had
refused to come to Argus. It wasn't magnetic tape he
wanted to scrutinize, he said, it was human character.
Peter Valerian would have been ideal for this discussion:
unpretentious, able to communicate clearly, and bul-
warked by a genuine Christian faith that engaged him
daily. But the President had apparently vetoed the idea;
she had wanted a small meeting and had explicitly asked
that Ellie attend.

Joss had insisted that the discussion be held here, at the
Bible Science Research Institute and Museum in Modesto, California. She glanced past der Heer and out the
glass partition that separated the library from the exhibit
area. Just outside was a plaster impression from a Red
River sandstone of dinosaur footprints interspersed with
those of a pedestrian in sandals, proving, so the caption

said, that Man and Dinosaur were contemporaries, at least in Texas. Mesozoic shoemakers seemed also to be implied. The conclusion drawn in the caption was that evolution was a fraud. The opinion of many paleontologists – that the sandstone was the fraud – remained, Ellie had noted two hours earlier, unmentioned. The intermingled footprints were part of a vast exhibit called 'Darwin's Default.' To its left was a Foucault pendulum demonstrating the scientific assertion, this one apparently uncontested, that the Earth turns. To its right, Ellie could see part of a lavish Matsushita holography unit on the podium of a small theater, from which three-dimensional images of the most eminent divines could communicate directly to the faithful.

Communicating still more directly to her at this moment was the Reverend Billy Jo Rankin. She had not known until the last moment that Joss had invited Rankin, and she was surprised at the news. There had been continuing theological disputation between them, on whether an Advent was at hand, whether Doomsday is a necessary accompaniment of the Advent, and on the role of miracles in the ministry, among other matters. But they had recently effected a widely publicized reconciliation, done, it was said, for the common good of the fundamentalist community in America. The signs of rapprochement between the United States and the Soviet Union were having worldwide ramifications in the arbitration of disputes. Holding the meeting here was perhaps part of the price Palmer Joss had to pay for the reconciliation. Conceivably, Rankin felt the exhibits would provide factual support for his position, were there any scientific points in dispute. Now, two hours into their discussion, Rankin was alternately castigating and imploring. His suit was immaculately tailored, his nails freshly manicured, and his beaming smile stood in some contrast to Joss's rumpled, distracted, and more weatherbeaten appearance. Joss, the faintest of smiles on his face, had his eyes half closed and his head

162

bowed in what seemed very close to an attitude of prayer. He had not had to say much. Rankin's remarks so far – except for the Rapture rap, she guessed – were doctrinally indistinguishable from Joss's television address.

'You scientists are so shy,' Rankin was saying. 'You love to hide your light under a bushel basket. You'd never guess what's in those articles from the titles. Einstein's first work on the Theory of Relativity was called "The Electrodynamics of Moving Bodies." No $E = mc^2$ up front. No sir. "The Electrodynamics of Moving Bodies." I suppose if God appeared to a whole gaggle of scientists, maybe at one of those big Association meetings, they'd write something all about it and call it, maybe, "On Spontaneous Dendritoform Combustion in Air." They'd have lots of equations; they'd talk about "economy of hypothesis"; but they'd never say a word about God.

'Y'see, you scientists are too skeptical.' From the sidewise motion of his head, Ellie deduced that der Heer was also included in this assessment. 'You question everything, or try to. You never heard about "Leave well enough alone," or "If it ain't broke, don't fix it." You always want to check out if a thing is what you call "true." And "true" means only empirical, sense data, things you can see and touch. There's no room for inspiration or revelation in your world. Right from the beginning you rule out of court almost everything religion is about. I mistrust the scientists because the scientists mistrust everything.'

Despite herself, she thought Rankin had put his case well. And he was supposed to be the dumb one among the modern video evangelists. No, not dumb, she corrected herself; he was the one who considered his parishioners dumb. He could, for all she knew, be very smart indeed. Should she respond at all? Both der Heer and the local museum people were recording the discussion, and although both groups had agreed that the recordings were not for public use, she worried about

163

embarrassing the project or the President if she spoke her mind. But Rankin's remarks had become increasingly outrageous, and no interventions were being made either by der Heer or by Joss.

'I suppose you want a reply,' she found herself saying. 'There isn't an "official" scientific position on any of these questions, and I can't pretend to talk for all scientists or even for the Argus Project. But I can make some comments, if you'd like.'

Rankin nodded his head vigorously, smiling encouragement. Languidly, Joss merely waited.

'I want you to understand that I'm not attacking anybody's belief system. As far as I'm concerned, you're entitled to any doctrine you like, even if it's demonstrably wrong. And many of the things you're saying, and that the Reverend Joss has said – I saw your talk on television a few weeks ago – can't be dismissed instantly. It takes a little work. But let me try to explain why I think they're improbable.'

So far, she thought, I've been the soul of restraint.

'You're uncomfortable with scientific skepticism. But the reason it developed is that the world is complicated. It's subtle. Everybody's first idea isn't necessarily right. Also, people are capable of self-deception. Scientists, too. All sorts of socially abhorrent doctrines have at one time or another been supported by scientists, well-known scientists, famous brand-name scientists. And, of course, politicians. And respected religious leaders. Slavery, for instance, or the Nazi brand of racism. Scientists make mistakes, theologians make mistakes, everybody makes mistakes. It's part of being human. You say it yourselves: "To err is."

'So the way you avoid the mistakes, or at least reduce the chance that you'll make one, is to be skeptical. You test the ideas. You check them out by rigorous standards of evidence. I don't think there is such a thing as a received truth. But when you let the different opinions debate, when any skeptic can perform his or her own

164

experiment to check some contention out, then the truth tends to emerge. That's the experience of the whole history of science. It isn't a perfect approach, but it's the only one that seems to work.

'Now, when I look at religion, I see lots of contending opinions. For example, the Christians think the universe is a finite number of years old. From the exhibits out there, it's clear that some Christians (and Jews, and Muslims) think that the universe is only six thousand years old. The Hindus, on the other hand – and there are lots of Hindus in the world – think that the universe is infinitely old, with an infinite number of subsidiary creations and destructions along the way. Now they can't both be right. Either the universe is a certain number of years old or its infinitely old. Your friends out there' – she gestured out the glass door toward several museum workers ambling past 'Darwin's Default' – 'ought to debate Hindus. God seems to have told them something different from what he told you. But you tend to talk only to yourselves.'

Maybe a little too strong? she asked herself.

'The major religions on the Earth contradict each other left and right. You can't all be correct. And what if all of you are wrong? It's a possibility, you know. You must care about the truth, right? Well, the way to winnow through all the differing contentions is to be skeptical. I'm not any more skeptical about your religious beliefs than I am about every new scientific idea I hear about. But in my line of work, they're called hypotheses, not inspiration and not revelation.'

Joss now stirred a little, but it was Rankin who replied.

'The revelations, the confirmed predictions by God in the Old Testament and the New are legion. The coming of the Saviour is foretold in Isaiah fifty-three, in Zechariah fourteen, in First Chronicles seventeen. That He would be born in Bethlehem was prophesied in Micah five. That He would come from the line of David was foretold in Matthew one and –'

165

'In Luke. But that ought to be an embarrassment for you, not a fulfilled prophecy. Matthew and Luke give Jesus totally different genealogies. Worse than that, they trace the lineage from David to Joseph, not from David to Mary. Or don't you believe in God the Father?'

Rankin continued smoothly on. Perhaps he hadn't understood her. '. . . the Ministry and Suffering of Jesus are foretold in Isaiah fifty-two and fifty-three, and the Twenty-second Psalm. That He would be betrayed for thirty pieces of silver is explicit in Zechariah eleven. If you're honest, you can't ignore the evidence of fulfilled prophecy.

'And the Bible speaks to our own time. Israel and the Arabs, Gog and Magog, America and Russia, nuclear war – it's all there in the Bible. Anybody with an ounce of sense can see it. You don't have to be some fancy college professor.'

'Your trouble,' she replied, 'is a failure of the imagination. These prophecies are – almost every one of them – vague, ambiguous, imprecise, open to fraud. They admit lots of possible interpretations. Even the straightforward prophecies direct from the top you try to weasel out of – like Jesus' promise that the Kingdom of God would come in the lifetime of some people in his audience. And don't tell me the Kingdom of God is within me. His audience understood him quite literally. You only quote the passages that seem to you fulfilled, and ignore the rest. And don't forget there was a hunger to see prophecy fulfilled.

'But imagine that your kind of god – omnipotent, omniscient, compassionate – really wanted to leave a record for future generations, to make his existence unmistakable to, say, the remote descendants of Moses. It's easy, trivial. Just a few enigmatic phrases, and some fierce commandment that they be passed on unchanged . . .'

Joss leaned forward almost imperceptibly. 'Such as . . . ?'

166

'Such as "The Sun is a star." Or "Mars is a rusty place with deserts and volcanos, like Sinai." Or "A body in motion tends to remain in motion." Or – let's see now' – she quickly scribbled some numbers on a pad – ' "The Earth weighs a million million million million times as much as a child." Or – I recognize that both of you seem to have some trouble with special relativity, but it's confirmed every day routinely in particle accelerators and cosmic rays – how about "There are no privileged frames of reference"? Or even "Thou shalt not travel faster than light." Anything they couldn't possibly have known three thousand years ago.'

'Any others?' Joss asked.

'Well, there's an indefinite number of them – or at least one for every principle of physics. Let's see . . . "Heat and light hide in the smallest pebble." Or even "The way of the Earth is as two, but the way of the lodestone is as three." I'm trying to suggest that the gravitational force follows an inverse square law, while the magnetic dipole force follows an inverse cube law. Or in biology' – she nodded toward der Heer, who seemed to have taken a vow of silence – 'how about "Two strands entwined is the secret of life"?'

'Now that's an interesting one,' said Joss. 'You're talking, of course, about DNA. But you know the physician's staff, the symbol of medicine? Army doctors wear it on their lapels. It's called the caduceus. Shows two serpents intertwined. It's a perfect double helix. From ancient times that's been the symbol of preserving life. Isn't this exactly the kind of connection you're suggesting?'

'Well, I thought it's a spiral, not a helix. But if there are enough symbols and enough prophecies and enough myth and folklore, eventually a few of them are going to fit some current scientific understanding purely by accident. But I can't be sure. Maybe you're right. Maybe the caduceus *is* a message from God. Of course, it's not a Christian symbol, or a symbol of any of the major religions

167

today. I don't suppose you'd want to argue that the gods talked only to the ancient Greeks. What I'm saying is, if God wanted to send us a message, and ancient writings were the only way he could think of doing it, he could have done a better job. And he hardly had to confine himself to writings. Why isn't there a monster crucifix orbiting the Earth? Why isn't the surface of the Moon covered with the Ten Commandments? Why should God be so clear in the Bible and so obscure in the world?'

Joss had apparently been ready to reply a few sentences back, a look of genuine pleasure unexpectedly on his face, but Ellie's rush of words was gathering momentum, and perhaps he felt it impolite to interrupt.

'Also, why would you think that God has abandoned us? He used to chat with patriarchs and prophets every second Tuesday, you believe. He's omnipotent, you say, and omniscient. So it's no particular effort for him to remind us directly, unambiguously, of his wishes at least a few times in every generation. So how come, fellas? Why don't we see him with crystal clarity?'

'We *do*.' Rankin put enormous feeling in this phrase. 'He is all around us. Our prayers are answered. Tens of millions of people in this country have been born again and have witnessed God's glorious grace. The Bible speaks to us as clearly in this day as it did in the time of Moses and Jesus.'

'Oh, come off it. You know what I mean. Where are the burning bushes, the pillars of fire, the great voice that says "I am that I am" booming down at us out of the sky? Why should God manifest himself in such subtle and debatable ways when he can make his presence completely unambiguous?'

'But a voice from the sky is just what you say you found.' Joss made this comment casually while Ellie paused for breath. He held her eyes with his own.

Rankin quickly picked up the thought. 'Absolutely. Just what I was going to say. Abraham and Moses, they didn't have radios or telescopes. They couldn't have heard the Almighty talking on FM. Maybe today God talks to us in new ways and permits us to have a new understanding. Or maybe it's not God –'

'Yes, Satan. I've heard some talk about that. It sounds crazy. Let's leave that one alone for a moment, if it's okay with you. You think maybe the Message is the Voice of God, your God. Where in your religion does God answer a prayer by repeating the prayer back?'

'I wouldn't call a Nazi newsreel a prayer, myself,' Joss said. 'You say it's to attract our attention.'

'Then why do you think God has chosen to talk to scientists? Why not preachers like yourself?'

'God talks to *me* all the time.' Rankin's index finger audibly thumped his sternum. 'And the Reverend Joss here. God has told me that a revelation is at hand. When the end of the world is nigh, the Rapture will be upon us, the judgment of sinners, the ascension to heaven of the elect –'

'Did he tell you he was going to make that announcement in the radio spectrum? Is your conversation with God recorded somewhere, so we can verify that it really happened? Or do we have only your say-so? Why would God choose to announce it to radio astronomers and not to men and women of the cloth? Don't you think it's a little strange that the first message from God in two thousand years or more is prime numbers . . . and Adolf Hitler at the 1936 Olympics? Your God must have quite a sense of humor.'

'My God can have any sense He wants to have.'

Der Heer was clearly alarmed at the first appearance of real rancor. 'Uh, maybe I could remind us all about what we hope to accomplish at this meeting,' he began.

Here's Ken in his mollifying mode, Ellie thought. On some issues he's courageous, but chiefly when he has no responsibility for action. He's a brave talker . . . in private. But on scientific politics, and especially when representing the President, he becomes very accommodating, ready to compromise with the Devil himself. She

169

caught herself. The theological language was getting to her.

'That's another thing.' She interrupted her own train of thought as well as der Heer's. 'If that signal is from God, why does it come from just one place in the sky – in the vicinity of a particularly bright nearby star? Why doesn't it come from all over the sky at once, like the cosmic black-body background radiation? Coming from one star, it looks like a signal from another civilization. Coming from everywhere, it would look much more like a signal from your God.'

'God can make a signal come from the bunghole of the Little Bear if He wants.' Rankin's face was becoming bright red. 'Excuse me, but you've gotten me riled up. God can do *anything*.'

'Anything you don't understand, Mr Rankin, you attribute to God. God for you is where you sweep away all the mysteries of the world, all the challenges to our intelligence. You simply turn your mind off and say God did it.'

'Ma'am, I didn't come here to be insulted . . .'

' "Come here"? I thought this was where you *lived*.'

'Ma'am –' Rankin was about to say something, but then thought better of it. He took a deep breath and continued. 'This is a Christian country and Christians have true knowledge on this issue, a sacred responsibility to make sure that God's sacred word is understood . . .'

'I'm a Christian and you don't speak for me. You've trapped yourself in some sort of fifth-century religious mania. Since then the Renaissance has happened, the Enlightenment has happened. Where've you been?'

Both Joss and der Heer were half out of their chairs. 'Please,' Ken implored, looking directly at Ellie. 'If we don't keep more to the agenda, I don't see how we can accomplish what the President asked us to.'

'Well, you wanted "a frank exchange of views." '

'It's nearly noon,' Joss observed. 'Why don't we take a little break for lunch?'

Outside the library conference room, leaning on the railing surrounding the Foucault pendulum, Ellie began a brief whispered exchange with der Heer.

'I'd like to punch out that cocksure, know-it-all, holier-than-thou . . .'

'Why, exactly, Ellie? Aren't ignorance and error painful enough?'

'Yes, if he'd shut up. But he's corrupting millions.'

'Sweetheart, he thinks the same about you.'

When she and der Heer came back from lunch, Ellie noticed immediately that Rankin appeared subdued, while Joss, who was first to speak, seemed cheerful, certainly beyond the requirements of mere cordiality.

'Dr Arroway,' he began, 'I can understand that you're impatient to show us your findings, and that you didn't come here for theological disputation. But please bear with us just a bit longer. You have a sharp tongue. I can't recall the last time Brother Rankin here got so stirred up on matters of the faith. It must be years.'

He glanced momentarily at his colleague, who was doodling, apparently idly, on a yellow legal pad, his collar unbuttoned and his necktie loosened.

'I was struck by one or two things you said this morning. You called yourself a Christian. May I ask? In what sense are you a Christian?'

'You know, this wasn't in the job description when I accepted the directorship of the Argus Project.' She said this lightly. 'I'm a Christian in the sense that I find Jesus Christ to be an admirable historical figure. I think the Sermon on the Mount is one of the greatest ethical statements and one of the best speeches in history. I think that "Love your enemy" might even be the long-shot solution to the problem of nuclear war. I wish he was alive today. It would benefit everybody on the planet. But I think Jesus was only a man. A great man, a brave man, a man with insight into unpopular truths. But I

171

don't think he was God or the son of God or the grandnephew of God.'

'You don't *want* to believe in God.' Joss said it as a simple statement. 'You figure you can be a Christian and not believe in God. Let me ask you straight out: *Do* you believe in God?'

'The question has a peculiar structure. If I say no, do I mean I'm convinced God *doesn't* exist, or do I mean I'm not convinced he *does* exist? Those are two very different statements.'

'Let's see if they are so different, Dr Arroway. May I call you "Doctor"? You believe in Occam's Razor, isn't that right? If you have two different, equally good explanations of the same experience, you pick the simplest. The whole history of science supports it, you say. Now, if you have serious doubts about whether there *is* a God – enough doubts so you're unwilling to commit yourself to the Faith – then you must be able to imagine a world *without* God: a world that comes into being without God, a world that goes about its everyday life without God, a world where people die without God. No punishment. No reward. All the saints and prophets, all the faithful who have ever lived – why, you'd have to believe they were foolish. Deceived themselves, you'd probably say. That would be a world in which we weren't here on Earth for any good reason – I mean for any purpose. It would all be just complicated collisions of atoms – is that right? Including the atoms that are inside human beings.

'To me, that would be a hateful and inhuman world. I wouldn't want to live in it. But if *you* can imagine that world, why straddle? Why occupy some middle ground? If you believe all that already, isn't it much simpler to say there's no God? You're not being true to Occam's Razor. I think you're waffling. How can a thoroughgoing conscientious scientist be an agnostic if you can even *imagine* a world without God? Wouldn't you just *have* to be an atheist?'

172

'I thought you were going to argue that God is the simpler hypothesis,' Ellie said, 'but this is a much better point. If it were only a matter of scientific discussion, I'd agree with you, Reverend Joss. Science is essentially concerned with examining and correcting hypotheses. If the laws of nature explain all the available facts without supernatural intervention, or even do only as well as the God hypothesis, then for the time being I'd call myself an atheist. Then, if a single piece of evidence was discovered that doesn't fit, I'd back off from atheism. We're fully able to detect some breakdown in the laws of nature. The reason I don't call myself an atheist is because this isn't mainly a scientific issue. It's a religious issue and a political issue. The tentative nature of scientific hypothesis doesn't extend into these fields. *You* don't talk about God as a hypothesis. You think you've cornered the truth, so I point out that you may have missed a thing or two. But if you ask, I'm happy to tell you: I can't be *sure* I'm right.'

'I've always thought an agnostic is an atheist without the courage of his convictions.'

'You could just as well say that an agnostic is a deeply religious person with at least a rudimentary knowledge of human fallibility. When I say I'm an agnostic, I only mean that the evidence isn't in. There isn't compelling evidence that God exists – at least your kind of god – and there isn't compelling evidence that he doesn't. Since more than half the people on the Earth aren't Jews or Christians or Muslims, I'd say that there aren't any compelling arguments for your kind of god. Otherwise, everybody on Earth would have been converted. I say again, if your God wanted to convince us, he could have done a much better job.

'Look at how clearly authentic the Message is. It's being picked up all over the world. Radio telescopes are humming away in countries with different histories, different languages, different politics, different religions. Everybody's getting the same kind of data from the same

173

place in the sky, at the same frequencies with the same polarization modulation. The Muslims, the Hindus, the Christians, and the atheists are all getting the same message. Any skeptic can hook up a radio telescope – it doesn't have to be very big – and get the identical data.'

'You're not suggesting that your radio message *is* from God,' Rankin offered.

'Not at all. Just that the civilization on Vega – with powers infinitely less than what you attribute to your God – was able to make things very clear. If your God wanted to talk to us through the unlikely means of word-of-mouth transmission and ancient writings over thousands of years, he could have done it so there was no room left for debate about his existence.'

She paused, but neither Joss nor Rankin spoke, so she tried again to steer the conversation to the data.

'Why don't we just withhold judgment for a while until we make some more progress on decrypting the Message? Would you like to see some of the data?'

This time they assented, readily enough it seemed. But she could produce only reams of zeros and ones, neither edifying nor inspirational. She carefully explained about the presumed pagination of the Message and the hoped-for primer. By unspoken agreement, she and der Heer said nothing about the Soviet view that the Message was the blueprint for a machine. It was at best a guess, and had not yet been publicly discussed by the Soviets. As an afterthought, she described something about Vega itself – its mass, surface temperature, color, distance from the Earth, lifetime, and the ring of orbiting debris around it that had been discovered by the Infrared Astronomy Satellite in 1983.

'But beyond its being one of the brightest stars in the sky, is there anything special about it?' Joss wanted to know. 'Or anything that connects it up with the Earth?'

'Well, in terms of stellar properties, anything like that, I can't think of a thing. But there is one incidental fact: Vega was the Pole Star about twelve thousand years ago, and it

174

'will be again about fourteen thousands years from now.'

'I thought the polestar was the Pole Star.' Rankin, still doodling, said this to the pad of paper.

'It is, for a few thousand years. But not forever. The Earth is like a spinning top. Its axis is slowly precessing in a circle.' She demonstrated, using her pencil as the Earth's axis. 'It's called the precession of the equinoxes.'

'Discovered by Hipparchus of Rhodes,' added Joss. 'Second century BC.' This seemed a surprising piece of information for him to have at his fingertips.

'Exactly. So right now,' she continued, 'an arrow from the center of the Earth to the North Pole points to the star we call Polaris, in the constellation of the Little Dipper, or the Little Bear. I believe you were referring to this constellation just before lunch, Mr Rankin. As the Earth's axis slowly precesses, it points in some different direction in the sky, not toward Polaris, and over 26,000 years the place in the sky to which the North Pole points makes a complete circle. The North Pole points right now very near Polaris, close enough to be useful in navigation. Twelve thousand years ago, by accident, it pointed to Vega. But there's no physical connection. How the stars are distributed in the Milky Way has nothing to do with the Earth's axis of rotation being tipped twenty-three and a half degrees.'

'Now, twelve thousand years ago is 10,000 BC, the time when civilization was just starting up. Isn't that right?' Joss asked.

'Unless you believe that the Earth was created in 4004 BC.'

'No, we don't believe that, do we, Brother Rankin? We just don't think the age of the Earth is known with the same precision that you scientists do. On the question of the age of the Earth, we're what you might call agnostics.' He had a most attractive smile.

'So if folks were navigating ten thousand years ago, sailing the Mediterranean, say, or the Persian Gulf, Vega would have been their guide?'

175

'That's still in the last Ice Age, Probably a little early for navigation. But the hunters who crossed the Bering land bridge to North America were around then. It must have seemed an amazing gift – providential, if you like – that such a bright star was exactly to the north. I'll bet a lot of people owed their lives to that coincidence.'

'Well now, that's mighty interesting.'

'I don't want you to think I used the word "providential" as anything but a metaphor.'

'I'd never think that, my dear.'

Joss was by now giving signs that the afternoon was drawing to a close, and he did not seem displeased. But there were still a few items, it seemed, on Rankin's agenda.

'It amazes me that you don't think it was Divine Providence, Vega being the Pole Star. My faith is so strong I don't need proofs, but every time a new fact comes along it simply confirms my faith.'

'Well then, I guess you weren't listening very closely to what I was saying this morning. I resent the idea that we're in some kind of faith contest, and you're the hands-down winner. So far as I know you've never tested your faith. Are you willing to put your life on the line for your faith? I'm willing to do it for mine. Here, take a look out that window. There's a big Foucault pendulum out there. The bob must weigh five hundred pounds. My faith says that the amplitude of a free pendulum – how far it'll swing away from the vertical position – can never increase. It can only decrease. I'm willing to go out there, put the bob in front of my nose, let go, have it swing away and then back toward me. If my beliefs are in error, I'll get a five-hundred-pound pendulum smack in the face. Come on. You want to test my faith?'

'Truly, it's not necessary. I believe you,' replied Joss. Rankin, though, seemed interested. He was imagining, she guessed, what she would look like afterward.

'But would *you* be willing,' she went on, 'to stand a

176

foot closer to this same pendulum and pray to God to shorten the swing? What if it turns out that you've gotten it all wrong, that what you're teaching isn't God's will at all? Maybe it's the work of the Devil. Maybe it's pure human invention. How can you be *really* sure?'

'Faith, inspiration, revelation, awe,' Rankin answered. 'Don't judge everyone else by your own limited experience. Just the fact that you've rejected the Lord doesn't prevent other folks from acknowledging His glory.'

'Look, we all have a thirst for wonder. It's a deeply human quality. Science and religion are both bound up with it. What I'm saying is, you don't have to make stories up, you don't have to exaggerate. There's wonder and awe enough in the real world. Nature's a lot better at inventing wonders than we are.'

'Perhaps we are all wayfarers on the road to truth,' Joss replied.

On this hopeful note, der Heer stepped in deftly, and amidst strained civilities they prepared to leave. She wondered whether anything useful had been accomplished. Valerian would have been much more effective and much less provocative, Ellie thought. She wished she had kept herself in better check.

'It's been a most interesting day, Dr Arroway, and I thank you for it.' Joss seemed a little remote again, courtly but distracted. He shook her hand warmly, though. On the way out to the waiting government car, past a lavishly rendered three-dimensional exhibit on 'The Fallacy of the Expanding Universe,' a sign read, 'Our God Is Alive and Well. Sorry About Yours.'

She whispered to der Heer, 'I'm sorry if I made your job more difficult.'

'Oh no, Ellie. You were fine.'

'That Palmer Joss is a very attractive man. I don't think I did much to convert him. But I'll tell you, he almost converted me.' She was joking, of course.

11
The World Message Consortium

The world is nearly all parceled out, and what there is left of it is being divided up, conquered, and colonized. To think of these stars that you see overhead at night, these vast worlds which we can never reach. I would annex the planets if I could; I often think of that. It makes me sad to see them so clear and yet so far.

– CECIL RHODES
Last Will and Testament (1902)

From their table by the window she could see the downpour spattering the street outside. A soaked pedestrian, his collar up, gamely hurried by. The proprietor had cranked the striped awning over the tubs of oysters, segregated according to size and quality and providing a kind of street advertisement for the specialty of the house. She felt warm and snug inside the restaurant, the famous theatrical gathering place, Chez Dieux. Since fair weather had been predicted, she was without raincoat or umbrella.

Likewise unencumbered, Vaygay introduced a new subject: 'My friend, Meera,' he announced, 'is an ecdysiast – that is the right word, yes? When she works in your country she performs for groups of professionals, at meetings and conventions. Meera says that when she takes off her clothes for working-class men – at trade union conventions, that sort of thing – they become wild, shout out improper suggestions, and try to join her on the stage. But when she gives exactly the same performance for doctors or lawyers, they sit there motionless. Actually, she says, some of them lick their lips. My question is: Are the lawyers healthier than the steelworkers?'

That Vaygay had diverse female acquaintances had always been apparent. His approaches to women were so direct and extravagant – herself, for some reason that both pleased and annoyed her, excluded – that they could always say no without embarrassment. Many said yes. But the news about Meera was a little unexpected.

They had spent the morning in a last-minute comparison of notes and interpretations of the new data. The continuing Message transmission had reached an important new stage. Diagrams were being transmitted from Vega the way newspaper wirephotos are transmitted. Each picture was an array raster. The number of tiny black and white dots that made up the picture was the product of two prime numbers. Again prime numbers were part of the transmission. There was a large set of such diagrams, one following the other, and not at all interleaved with the text. It was like a section of glossy illustrations inserted in the back of a book. Following transmission of the long sequence of diagrams, the unintelligible text continued. From at least some of the diagrams it seemed obvious that Vaygay and Arkhangelsky had been right, that the Message was in part at least the instructions, the blueprints, for building a machine. Its purpose was unknown. At the plenary session of the World Message Consortium, to be held tomorrow at the Elysée Palace, she and Vaygay would present for the first time some of the details to representatives of the other Consortium nations. But word had quietly been passed about the machine hypothesis.

Over lunch, she had summarized her encounter with Rankin and Joss. Vaygay had been attentive, but asked no questions. It was as if she had been confessing some unseemly personal predilection, and perhaps that had triggered his train of association.

179

'You have a friend named Meera who's a striptease artist? With international venue?'

'Since Wolfgang Pauli discovered the Exclusion Principle while watching the Folies-Bergère, I have felt it my professional duty as a physicist to visit Paris as much as possible. I think of it as my homage to Pauli. But somehow I can never persuade the officials in my country to approve trips solely for this purpose. Usually I must do some pedestrian physics as well. But in such establishments – that's where I met Meera – I am a student of nature, waiting for insight to strike.'

Abruptly his tone of voice shifted from expansive to matter-of-fact. 'Meera says American professional men are sexually repressed and have gnawing doubts and guilt.'

'Really. And what does Meera say about Russian professional men?'

'Ah, in that category she knows only me. So, of course, she has a good opinion. I think I'd rather be with Meera tomorrow.'

'But all your friends will be at the Consortium meeting,' she said lightly.

'Yes, I'm glad you'll be there,' he replied morosely.

'What's worrying you, Vaygay?'

He took a long time before answering, and began with a slight but uncharacteristic hesitation. 'Perhaps not worries. Maybe only concerns. . . . What if the Message really *is* the design drawings of a machine? Do we build the machine? *Who* builds it? Everybody together? The Consortium? The United Nations? A few nations in competition? What if it's enormously expensive to build? Who pays? Why should they want to? What if it doesn't work? Could building the machine injure some nations economically? Could it injure them in some other way?'

Without interrupting this torrent of questions, Lunacharsky emptied the last of the wine into their glasses. 'Even if the Message cycles back and even if we

180

completely decrypt it, how good could the translation be? You know the opinion of Cervantes? He said that reading a translation is like examining the *back* of a piece of tapestry. Maybe it's not possible to translate the Message perfectly. Then we wouldn't build the machine perfectly. Also, are we really confident we have all the data? Maybe there's essential information at some other frequency that we haven't discovered yet.

'You know, Ellie, I thought people would be very cautious about building this machine. But there may be some coming tomorrow who will urge immediate construction – I mean, immediately after we receive the primer and decrypt the Message, assuming that we do. What is the American delegation going to propose?'

'I don't know,' she said slowly. But she remembered that soon after the diagrammatic material had been received der Heer began asking whether it was likely that the machine was within reach of the Earth's economy and technology. She could offer him little reassurance on either score. She recalled again how preoccupied Ken had seemed in the last few weeks, sometimes even jittery. His responsibilities in this matter were, of course –

'Are Dr der Heer and Mr Kitz staying at the same hotel as you?'

'No, they're staying at the Embassy.'

It was always the case. Because of the nature of the Soviet economy and the perceived necessity of buying military technology instead of consumer goods with their limited hard currency, Russians had little walking-around money when visiting the West. They were obliged to stay in second- or third-rate hotels, even rooming houses, while their Western colleagues lived in comparative luxury. It was a continuing source of embarrassment for scientists of both countries. Picking up the bill for this relatively simple meal would be effortless for Ellie but a burden for Vaygay, despite his comparatively exalted status in the Soviet scientific hierarchy. Now, what was Vaygay . . .

'Vaygay, be straight with me. What are you saying? You think Ken and Mike Kitz are jumping the gun?'

' "Straight." An interesting word; not right, not left, but progressively forward. I'm concerned that in the next few days we will see premature discussion about building something that we have no right to build. The politicians think we know everything. In fact, we know almost nothing. Such a situation could be dangerous.'

It finally dawned on her that Vaygay was taking a personal responsibility for figuring out the nature of the Message. If it led to some catastrophe, he was worried it might be his fault. He had less personal motives as well, of course.

'You want me to talk to Ken?'

'If you think it's appropriate. You have frequent opportunities to talk to him?' He said this casually.

'Vaygay, you're not jealous, are you? I think you picked up on my feelings for Ken before I did. When you were back at Argus. Ken and I've been more or less together for the last two months. Do you have some reservations?'

'Oh no, Ellie. I am not your father or a jealous lover. I wish only great happiness for you. It's just that I see so many unpleasant possibilities.'

But he did not further elaborate.

They returned to their preliminary interpretations of some of the diagrams, with which the table was eventually covered. For counterpoint, they also discussed a little politics – the debate in America over the Mandala Principles for resolving the crisis in South Africa, and the growing war of words between the Soviet Union and the German Democratic Republic. As always, Arroway and Lunacharsky enjoyed denouncing their own countries' foreign policies to one another. This was far more interesting than denouncing the foreign policies of each other's nation, which would have been equally easy to do. Over their ritual dispute about whether the check should be shared, she noticed that the downpour had diminished to a discreet drizzle.

By now, the news of the Message from Vega had reached every nook and cranny of the planet Earth. People who knew nothing of radio telescopes and had never heard of a prime number had been told a peculiar story about a voice from the stars, about strange beings – not exactly men, but not exactly gods either – who had been discovered living in the night sky. They did not come from Earth. Their home star could easily be seen, even with a full moon. Amidst the continuing frenzy of sectarian commentary, there was also – all over the world, it was now apparent – a sense of wonder, even of awe. Something transforming, something almost miraculous was happening. The air was full of possibility, a sense of new beginning.

'Mankind has been promoted to high school,' an American newspaper editorialist had written.

There were other intelligent beings in the universe. We could communicate with them. They were probably older than we, possibly wiser. They were sending us libraries of complex information. There was a widespread anticipation of imminent secular revelation. So the specialists in every subject began to worry. Mathematicians worried about what elementary discoveries they might have missed. Religious leaders worried that Vegan values, however alien, would find ready adherents, especially among the uninstructed young. Astronomers worried that there might be fundamentals about the nearby stars that they had gotten wrong. Politicians and government leaders worried that some other systems of government, some quite different from those currently fashionable, might be admired by a superior civilization. Whatever Vegans knew had not been influenced by peculiarly human institutions, history, or biology. What if much that we think true is a misunderstanding, a special case, or a logical blunder?

Experts uneasily began to reassess the foundations of their subjects.

Beyond this narrow vocational disquiet was a great and soaring perception of a new adventure for the human species, of turning a corner, of bursting into a new age – a symbolism powerfully amplified by the approach of the Third Millennium. There were still political conflicts, some of them – like the continuing South African crisis – serious. But there was also a notable decline in many quarters of the world of jingoist rhetoric and puerile self-congratulatory nationalism. There was a sense of the human species, billions of tiny beings spread over the world, collectively presented with an unprecedented opportunity, or even a grave common danger. To many, it seemed absurd for the contending nation states to continue their deadly quarrels when faced with a non-human civilization of vastly greater capabilities. There was a whiff of hope in the air. Some people were unaccustomed to it and mistook it for something else – confusion, perhaps, or cowardice.

For decades after 1945, the world stockpile of strategic nuclear weapons had steadily grown. Leaders changed, weapons systems changed, strategy changed, but the number of strategic weapons only increased. The time came when there were more than 25,000 of them on the planet, ten for every city. The technology was pushing toward short flight time, incentives for hard-target first strike, and at least de facto launch-on-warning. Only so monumental a danger could undo so monumental a foolishness, endorsed by so many leaders in so many nations for so long a time. But finally the world came to its senses, at least to this extent, and an accord was signed by the United States, the Soviet Union, Britain, France, and China. It was not intended to rid the world of nuclear weapons. Few expected it to carry some Utopia in its wake. But the Americans and the Russians undertook to diminish their strategic arsenals down to a thousand nuclear weapons each. The details were carefully designed so that neither superpower was at any significant disadvantage at any stage of the dismantling process. Britain, France, and China agreed to begin reducing their arsenals once the superpowers had gone below the 3,200 mark. The Hiroshima Accords were signed, to world-wide rejoicing, next to the famous commemorative plaque for the victims in the first city ever obliterated by a nuclear weapon: 'Rest in peace, for it shall never happen again.'

Every day the fission triggers from an equal number of US and Soviet warheads were delivered to a special facility run by American and Russian technicians. The plutonium was extracted, logged, sealed, and transported by bilateral teams to nuclear power plants where it was consumed and converted into electricity. This scheme, known as the Gayler Plan after an American admiral, was widely hailed as the ultimate in beating swords into plowshares. Since each nation still retained a devastating retaliatory capability, even the military establishments eventually welcomed it. Generals no more wish for their children to die than anyone else, and nuclear war is the negation of the conventional military virtues; it is hard to find much valor in pressing a button. The first divestment ceremony – televised live, and rebroadcast many times – featured white-clad American and Soviet technicians wheeling in two of the dull gray metallic objects, each about as big as an ottoman and festooned variously with stars and stripes, hammers and sickles. It was witnessed by a huge fraction of the world population. The evening television news programs regularly counted how many strategic weapons on both sides had been disassembled, how many more to go. In a little over two decades, this news, too, would reach Vega.

In the following years, the divestitures continued, almost without a hitch. At first the fat in the arsenals was surrendered, with little change in strategic doctrine; but now the cuts were being felt, and the most destabilizing weapons systems were being dismantled. It was something the experts had called impossible and declared 'contrary to human nature.' But a sentence of death, as Samuel Johnson had noted, concentrates the mind wonderfully. In the past half year, the dismantling of nuclear weapons by the United States and the Soviet Union had made major new strides, with fairly intrusive inspection teams of each nation soon to be installed on the territory of the other – despite the disapproval and concern publicly voiced by the military staffs of both nations. The United Nations found itself unexpectedly effective in mediating international disputes, with the West Irian and the Chile-Argentina border wars both apparently resolved. There was even talk, not all of it fatuous, of a nonaggression treaty between NATO and the Warsaw Pact.

The delegates arriving at the first plenary session of the World Message Consortium were predisposed toward cordiality to an extent unparalleled in recent decades.

Every nation with even a handful of Message bits was represented, sending both scientific and political delegates; a surprising number sent military representatives as well. In a few cases, national delegations were led by foreign ministers or even heads of state. The United Kingdom delegation included Viscount Boxforth, the Lord Privy Seal – an honorific Ellie privately found hilarious. The USSR delegation was headed by B. Ya. Abukhimov, President of the Soviet Academy of Sciences, with Gotsridze, the Minister of Medium Heavy Industry, and Arkhangelsky playing significant roles. The President of the United States had insisted that der Heer head the American delegation, although it included Undersecretary of State Elmo Honicutt and Michael Kitz, among others, for the Department of Defense.

A vast and elaborate map in equal-area projection showed the disposition of radio telescopes over the planet, including the Soviet oceangoing tracking vessels.

Ellie glanced around the newly completed conference hall, adjacent to the offices and residence of the President of France. In only the second year of his seven-year term, he was making every effort to guarantee the meeting's success. A multitude of faces, flags, and national dress was reflected off the long arcing mahogany tables and the mirrored walls. She recognized few of the political and military people, but in every delegation there seemed to be at least one familiar scientist or engineer: Annunziata and Ian Broderick from Australia; Fedirka from Czechoslovakia; Braude, Crebillon, and Boileau from France; Kumar Chandrapurana and Devi Sukhavati from India; Hironaga and Matsui from Japan . . . Ellie reflected on the strong technological rather than radio-astronomical background of many of the delegates, especially the Japanese. The idea that the construction of some vast machine might be on the agenda of this meeting had motivated last-minute changes in the composition of delegations.

She also recognized Malatesta of Italy; Bedenbaugh, a physicist fallen into politics, Clegg, and the venerable Sir Arthur Chatos chatting behind the sort of Union Jack one can find on restaurant tables in European resorts; Jaime Ortiz of Spain; Prebula from Switzerland, which was puzzling, since Switzerland did not, so far as she knew, even *have* a radio telescope; Bao, who had done brilliantly in putting together the Chinese radio telescope array; Wintergaden from Sweden. There were surprisingly large Saudi, Pakistani and Iraqi delegations; and, of course, the Soviets, among whom Nadya Rozhdestvenskaya and Genrikh Arkhangelsky were sharing a moment of genuine hilarity.

Ellie looked for Lunacharsky, and finally spotted him with the Chinese delegation. He was shaking hands with Yu Renqiong, the director of the Beijing Radio Observatory. She recalled that the two men had been friends and colleagues during the period of Sino-Soviet cooperation. But the hostilities between their two nations had ended all contact between them, and Chinese restrictions on foreign travel by their senior scientists were still almost as severe as Soviet constraints. She was witnessing, she realized, their first meeting in perhaps a quarter century.

'Who's the old Chinaperson Vaygay's shaking hands with?' This was, for Kitz, an attempt at cordiality. He had been making small offerings of this sort for the last few days – a development she regarded as unpromising.

'Yu, Director of the Beijing Observatory.'

'I thought those guys hated each other's guts.'

'Michael,' she said, 'the world is both better and worse than you imagine.'

'You can probably beat me on "better,"' he replied, 'but you can't hold a candle to me on "worse."'

After the welcome by the President of France (who, to mild astonishment, stayed to hear the opening presentations) and a discussion of procedure and agenda by der Heer and Abukhimov as conference co-chairmen, Ellie and Vaygay together summarized the data. They made what were by now standard presentations – not too technical, because of the political and military people – of how radio telescopes work, the distribution of nearby stars in space, and the history of the palimpsest Message. Their tandem presentation concluded with a survey, displayed on the monitors before each delegation, of the diagrammatic material recently received. She was careful to show how the polarization modulation was converted into a sequence of zeros and ones, how the zeros and ones fit together to make a picture, and how in most cases they had not the vaguest notion of what the picture conveyed.

The data points reassembled themselves on the computer screens. She could see faces illuminated in white, amber, and green by the monitors in the now partly darkened hall. The diagrams showed intricate branching networks; lumpy, almost indecently biological forms; a perfectly formed regular dodecahedron. A long series of pages had been reassembled into an elaborately detailed three-dimensional construction which slowly rotated. Each enigmatic object was joined by an unintelligible caption.

Vaygay stressed the uncertainties still more strongly than she did. Nevertheless, it was, in his opinion, now beyond doubt that the Message was a handbook for the construction of a machine. He neglected to mention that the idea of the Message as a blueprint had originally been his and Arkhangelsky's, and Ellie seized the opportunity to rectify the oversight.

She had talked about the subject enough over the past few months to know that both scientific and general audiences were often fascinated by the details of the unraveling of the Message, and tantalized by the still unproved concept of a primer. But she was unprepared for the response from this – one would expect – staid audience. Vaygay and she had interdigitated their presentations. As they finished, there was a sustained thunder of applause. The Soviets and Eastern European delegations applauded in unison, with a frequency of about two or three handclaps per heartbeat. The Americans and many others applauded separately, their unsynchronized clapping a sea of white noise rising from the crowd. Enveloped by an unfamiliar kind of joy, she could not resist thinking about the differences in national character – the Americans as individualists, and the Russians engaged in a collective endeavor. Also, she recalled that Americans in crowds tried to maximize their distance from their fellows, while Soviets tended to lean on each other as much as possible. Both styles of applause, the American clearly dominant, delighted her. For just a moment she permitted herself to think about her stepfather. And her father.

After lunch there was a succession of other presentations on the data collection and interpretation. David Drumlin gave an extraordinarily capable discussion of a statistical analysis he had recently performed of all previous pages of the Message that referred to the new numbered diagrams. He argued that the Message contained not just a blueprint for building a machine but also descriptions of the designs and means of fabrication of components and subcomponents. In a few cases, he thought, there were descriptions of whole new industries not yet known on Earth. Ellie, mouth agape, shook her finger toward Drumlin, silently asking Valerian whether he had known about this. His lips pursed, Valerian hunched his shoulders and rotated his hands palms up. She scanned the other delegates for some expression of emotion, but could detect mainly signs of fatigue; the depth of technical material and the necessity, sooner or later, of making political decisions were already producing strain. After the session, she complimented Drumlin on the interpretation but asked why she had not heard of it until now. He replied before walking away, 'Oh, I didn't think it was important enough to bother you with. It was just a little something I did while you were out consulting religious fanatics.'

If Drumlin had been her thesis adviser, she would *still* be pursuing her PhD, she thought. He had never fully accepted her. They would never share an easygoing collegial relationship. Sighing, she wondered whether Ken had known about Drumlin's new work. But as conference co-chairman, der Heer was sitting with his Soviet opposite number on a raised dais facing the horseshoe of delegate tiers. He was, as he had been for weeks, nearly inaccessible. Drumlin was not obliged to discuss his findings with her, of course; she knew they both had been preoccupied recently. But in conversation with him why was she always accommodating – and argumentative only in extremis? A part of her evidently felt that the granting of her doctorate and the opportunity to pursue her science were still future possibilities firmly in Drumlin's hands.

On the morning of the second day, a Soviet delegate was given the floor. He was unknown to her. 'Stefan

Alexeivich Baruda,' the vitagraphics on her computer screen read out, 'Director, Institute for Peace Studies, Soviet Academy of Sciences, Moscow; Member, Central Committee, Communist Party of the USSR.'

'Now we start to play hardball,' she heard Michael Kitz say to Elmo Honicutt of the State Department.

Baruda was a dapper man, wearing an elegantly tailored and impeccably fashionable Western business suit, perhaps of Italian cut. His English was fluent and almost unaccented. He had been born in one of the Baltic republics, was young to be head of such an important organization – formed to study the long-term implications for strategic policy of the deaccessioning of nuclear weapons – and was a leading example of the 'new wave' in the Soviet leadership.

'Let us be frank,' Baruda was saying. 'A Message is being sent to us from the far reaches of space. Most of the information has been gathered by the Soviet Union and the United States. Essential pieces have also been obtained by other countries. All of those countries are represented at this conference. Any one nation – the Soviet Union, for example – could have waited until the Message repeated itself several times, as we all hope it will, and fill in the many missing pieces in such a way. But it would take years, perhaps decades, and we are a little impatient. So we have all shared the data.

'Any one nation – the Soviet Union, for example – could place into orbit around the Earth large radio telescopes with sensitive receivers that work at the frequencies of the Message. The Americans could do this as well. Perhaps Japan or France or the European Space Agency could. Then any one nation by itself could acquire all the data, because in space a radio telescope can point at Vega all the time. But that might be thought a hostile act. It is no secret that the United States or the Soviet Union might be able to shoot down such satellites. So, perhaps for this reason, too, we have all shared the data.

'It is better to cooperate. Our scientists wish to

exchange not only the data they have gathered, but also their speculations, their guesses, their . . . dreams. All you scientists are alike in that respect. I am not a scientist. My specialty is government. So I know that the nations are also alike. Every nation is cautious. Every nation is suspicious. None of us would give an advantage to a potential adversary if we could prevent it. And so there have been two opinions – perhaps more, but at least two – one that counsels exchange all of the data, and another that counsels each nation to seek advantage over the others. "You can be sure the other side is seeking some advantage," they say. It is the same in most countries.

'The scientists have won this debate. So, for example, most of the data – although, I wish to point out, not all – acquired by the United States and the Soviet Union have been exchanged. Most of the data from all other countries have been exchanged worldwide. We are happy we have made this decision.'

Ellie whispered to Kitz, 'This doesn't sound like "hardball" to me.'

'Stay tuned,' he whispered back.

'But there are other kinds of dangers. We would like now to raise one of them for the Consortium to consider.' Baruda's tone reminded her of Vaygay's at lunch the other day. What was the bee in the Soviet bonnet?

'We have heard Academician Lunacharsky, Dr Arroway, and other scientists agree that we are receiving the instructions for building a complex machine. Suppose that, as everyone seems to expect, the end of the Message comes; the Message recycles to the beginning; and we receive the introduction or – the English word is "primer"? – primer which lets us read the Message. Suppose also that we continue to cooperate fully, all of us. We exchange all the data, all the fantasies, all the dreams.

'Now the beings on Vega, they are not sending us these instructions for their amusement. They want us to build a machine. Perhaps they will tell us what the machine is supposed to do. Perhaps not. But even if they do, why should we believe them? So I raise my own fantasy, my own dream. It is not a happy one. What if this machine is a Trojan Horse? We build the machine at great expense, turn it on, and suddenly an invading army pours out of it. Or what if it is a Doomsday Machine? We build it, turn it on, and the Earth blows up. Perhaps this is their way to suppress civilizations just emerging into the cosmos. It would not cost much; they pay only for a telegram, and the upstart civilization obediently destroys itself.

'What I am about to ask is only a suggestion, a talking point. I raise it for your consideration. I mean it to be constructive. On this issue, we all share the same planet, we all have the same interests. No doubt I will put it too bluntly. Here is my question: Would it be better to burn the data and destroy the radio telescopes?'

A commotion ensued. Many delegations asked simultaneously to be recognized. Instead, the conference co-chairmen seemed mainly motivated to remind the delegates that sessions were not to be recorded or video-taped. No interviews were to be granted to the press. There would be daily press releases, agreed upon by the conference co-chairmen and the leaders of delegations. Even the integuments of the present discussion were to remain in this conference chamber.

Several delegates asked for clarification from the Chair. 'If Baruda is right about a Trojan Horse or a Doomsday Machine,' shouted out a Dutch delegate, 'isn't it our duty to inform the public?' But he had not been recognized and his microphone had not been activated. They went on to other, more urgent, matters.

Ellie had quickly punched into the institutional computer terminal before her for an early position in the queue. She discovered that she was scheduled second, after Sukhavati and before one of the Chinese delegates.

Ellie knew Devi Sukhavati slightly. A stately woman in her mid-forties, she was wearing a Western coiffure, high-heeled sling-back pumps, and an exquisite silk sari. Originally trained as a physician, she had become one of the leading Indian experts in molecular biology and now shared her time between King's College, Cambridge, and the Tata Institute in Bombay. She was one of a handful of Indian Fellows of the Royal Society of London, and was said to be well-placed politically. They had last met a few years before, at an international symposium in Tokyo, before receipt of the Message had eliminated the obligatory question marks in the titles of some of their scientific papers. Ellie had sensed a mutual affinity, due only in part to the fact that they were among the few women participating in scientific meetings on extraterrestrial life.

'I recognize that Academician Baruda has raised an important and sensitive issue,' Sukhavati began, 'and it would be foolish to dismiss the Trojan Horse possibility carelessly. Given most of recent history, this is a natural idea, and I'm surprised it took so long to be raised. However, I would like to caution against such fears. It is unlikely in the extreme that the beings on a planet of the star Vega are exactly at our level of technological advance. Even on our planet, cultures do not evolve in lockstep. Some start earlier, others later. I recognize that some cultures can catch up at least technologically. When there were high civilizations in India, China, Iraq, and Egypt, there were, at best, iron-age nomads in Europe and Russia, and stone-age cultures in America.

'But the differences in the technologies will be much greater in the present circumstances. The extraterrestrials are likely to be far ahead of us, certainly more than a few hundred years farther along – perhaps thousands of years ahead of us, or even millions. Now, I ask you to compare that with the pace of human technological advancement in the last century.

'I grew up in a tiny village in South India. In my grandmother's time the treadle sewing machine was a technological wonder. What would beings who are thousands of years ahead of us be capable of? Or millions? As a philosopher in our part of the world once said: "The artifacts of a sufficiently advanced extraterrestrial civilization would be indistinguishable from magic."

'We can pose no threat to them whatever. They have nothing to fear from us, and that will be true for a very long time. This is no confrontation between Greeks and Trojans, who were evenly matched. This is no science-fiction movie where beings from different planets fight with similar weapons. If they wish to destroy us, they can certainly do so with or without our coopera –'

'But at what cost?' someone interrupted from the floor. 'Don't you see? That's the point. Baruda is saying our television broadcasts to space are their notice that it's time to destroy us, and the Message is the means. Punitive expeditions are dear. The Message is cheap.'

Ellie could not make out who had shouted out this intervention. It seemed to be someone in the British delegation. His remarks had not been amplified by the audio system, because again the speaker had not been recognized by the Chair. But the acoustics in the conference hall were sufficiently good that he could be heard perfectly well. Der Heer, in the Chair, tried to keep order. Abukhimov leaned over and whispered something to an aide.

'You think there is a danger in building the machine,' Sukhavati replied. 'I think there is a danger in *not* building the machine. I would be ashamed of our planet if we turned our back on the future. Your ancestors' – she shook a finger at her interlocutor – 'were not so timid when they first set sail for India or America.'

This meeting was getting to be full of surprises, Ellie thought, although she doubted whether Clive or Raleigh were the best role models for present decision making. Perhaps Sukhavati was only tweaking the British for past colonial offenses. She waited for the green speaker's light on her console to illuminate, indicating that her microphone was activated.

195

'Mr Chairman.' She found herself in this formal and public posture addressing der Heer, whom she had hardly seen in the last few days. They had arranged to spend tomorrow afternoon together during a break in the meeting, and she felt some anxiety about what they would say. Oops, wrong thought, she thought.

'Mr Chairman, I believe we can shed some light on these two questions – the Trojan Horse and the Dooms-day Machine. I had intended to discuss this tomorrow morning, but it certainly seems relevant now.' On her console, she punched in the code numbers for a few of her slides. The great mirrored hall darkened.

'Dr Lunacharsky and I are convinced that these are different projections of the same three-dimensional configuration. We showed the entire configuration in computer-simulated rotation yesterday. We think, though we can't be sure, that this is what the interior of the machine will look like. There is as yet no clear indication of scale. Maybe it's a kilometer across, maybe it's submicroscopic. But notice these five objects evenly spaced around the periphery of the main interior chamber, inside the dodecahedron. Here's a closeup of one of them. They're the only things in the chamber that look at all recognizable.

'This appears to be an ordinary overstuffed armchair, perfectly configured for a human being. It's very unlikely that extraterrestrial beings, evolved on another quite different world, would resemble us sufficiently to share our preferences in living-room furniture. Here, look at this close-up. It looks like something from my mother's spare room when I was growing up.'

Indeed, it almost seemed to have flowered slipcovers. A small flutter of guilt entered her mind. She had neglected to call her mother before leaving for Europe, and, if truth be told, had called her only once or twice since the Message was received. Ellie, how *could* you? she remonstrated with herself.

She looked again at the computer graphics. The

fivefold symmetry of the dodecahedron was reflected in the five interior chairs, each facing a pentagonal surface. 'So it's our contention – Dr Lunacharsky and I – that the five chairs are meant for us. For people. That would mean that the interior chamber of the machine is only a few meters across, the exterior, perhaps ten or twenty meters across. The technology is undoubtedly formidable, but we don't think we're talking about building something the size of a city. Or as complex as an aircraft carrier. We might very well be able to build this, whatever it is, if we all work together.

'What I'm trying to say is that you don't put chairs inside a bomb. I don't think this is a Doomsday Machine, or a Trojan Horse. I agree with what Dr Sukhavati said, or maybe only implied; the idea that this is a Trojan Horse is itself an indication of how far we have to go.'

Again there was an outburst. But this time der Heer made no effort to stop it; indeed, he actually turned the complainant's microphone on. It was the same delegate who had interrupted Sukhavati a few minutes earlier, Philip Bedenbaugh of the United Kingdom, a Labour Party minister in the shaky coalition government.

'. . . simply doesn't understand what our concern is. If it was literally a wooden horse, we would not be tempted to bring the alien device within the city gates. We have read our Homer. But flounce it up with some upholstery and our suspicions are allayed. Why? Because we are being flattered. Or bribed. There's an historic adventure implied. There's the promise of new technologies. There's a hint of acceptance by – how to put it? – greater beings. But I say no matter what lofty fantasies the radio astronomers may entertain, if there is even a tiny chance the machine is a means of destruction, it should not be built. Better, as the Soviet delegate has proposed, to burn the data tapes and make the construction of radio telescopes a capital crime.'

The meeting was becoming unruly. Scores of delegates were electronically queuing for authorization to speak. The hubbub rose to a subdued roar that reminded Ellie of her years of listening to radio-astronomical static. A consensus did not seem readily within reach, and the co-chairmen were clearly unable to restrain the delegates.

As the Chinese delegate rose to speak, the vitagraphics were slow to appear on Ellie's screen and she looked around for help. She had no idea who this man was either. Nguyen 'Bobby' Bui, a National Security Council staffer now assigned to der Heer, leaned over and said: 'Xi Qiaomu's his name. Spelled "ex," "eye." Pronounced "she." Heavy dude. Born on the Long March. Volunteer as a teenager in Korea. Government official, mainly political. Knocked down for a nine count in the Cultural Revolution. Central Committee member now. Very influential. Been in the news lately. Also directs Chinese archeological digging.'

Xi Qiaomu was a tall, broad-shouldered man around sixty. The wrinkles on his face made him seem older, but his posture and physique gave him an almost youthful appearance. He wore his tunic buttoned at the collar in the fashion that was as obligatory for Chinese political leaders as three-piece suits were for American governmental leaders, the President, of course, excepted. The vitagraphics now came through on her console, and she could remember having read a long article about Xi Qiaomu in one of the video newsmagazines.

'If we are frightened,' he was saying, 'we will do nothing. That will delay them a little. But remember, they know we are here. Our television arrives at their planet. Every day they are reminded of us. Have you looked at our television programs? They will not forget us. If we do nothing and if they are worried about us, they will come to us, machine or no machine. We cannot hide from them. If we had kept quiet, we would not face this problem. If we had cable television only and no big military radar, then maybe they would not know about us. But now it is too late. We cannot go back. Our course is set.

198

'If you are seriously frightened about this machine destroying the Earth, do not build it on the Earth. Build it somewhere else. Then if it *is* a Doomsday Machine and blows up a world . . . it will not be our world. But this will be very expensive. Probably too expensive. Or if we are not *so* frightened, build it in some isolated desert. You could have a very big explosion in the Takopi Wasteland in Xinjing Province and still kill nobody. And if we are not frightened at all, we can build it in Washington. Or Moscow. Or Beijing. Or in this beautiful city.

'In Ancient China, Vega and two nearby stars were called Chih Neu. It means the young woman with the spinning wheel. It is an auspicious symbol, a machine to make new clothes for the people of the Earth.

'We have received an invitation. A very unusual invitation. Maybe it is to go to a banquet. The Earth has never been invited to a banquet before. It would be impolite to refuse.'

12

The One-Delta Isomer

> Looking at the stars always makes me dream, as simply
> as I dream over the black dots representing towns and
> villages on a map. Why, I ask myself, shouldn't the
> shining dots of the sky be as accessible as the black dots
> on the map of France?
>
> — VINCENT VAN GOGH

It was a splendid autumn afternoon, so unseasonably
warm that Devi Sukhavati had left her coat behind. She
and Ellie walked along the crowded Champs-Elysées
toward the Place de la Concorde. The ethnic diversity
was rivaled by London, Manhattan, and only a few other
cities on the planet. Two women walking together, one
in a skirt and sweater, the other in a sari, were in no way
unusual.

Outside a tobacconist's there was a long, orderly, and
polyglot line of people attracted by the first week of
legalized sale of cured cannabis cigarettes from the
United States. By French law they could not be sold to or
consumed by those under eighteen years of age. Many in
line were middle-aged and older. Some might have been
naturalized Algerians or Moroccans. Especially potent
varieties of cannabis were grown, mainly in California
and Oregon, for the export trade. Featured here was a
new and admired strain, which had in addition been
grown in ultraviolet light, converting some of the inert
cannabinoids into the $^1\Delta$ isomer. It was called 'Sun-
Kissed.' The package, illustrated in a window display a
meter and a half high, bore in French the slogan 'This will
be deducted from your share in Paradise.'

The shop windows along the boulevard were a riot of

color. The two women bought chestnuts from a street vendor and reveled in the taste and texture. For some reason, every time Ellie saw a sign advertising BNP, the Banque Nationale de Paris, she read it as the Russian word for beer, with the middle letter inverted left to right. BEER, the signs – lately corrupted from their usual and respectable fiduciary vocations – seemed to be exhorting her, RUSSIAN BEER. The incongruity amused her, and only with difficulty could she convince the part of her brain in charge of reading that this was the Latin, not the Cyrillic alphabet. Further on, they marveled at L'Obélisque – an ancient military commemorative stolen at great expense to become a modern military commemorative. They decided to walk on.

Der Heer had broken the date, or at least that's what it amounted to. He had called her up this morning, apologetic but not desperately so. There were too many political issues being raised at the plenary session. The Secretary of State was flying in tomorrow, interrupting a visit to Cuba. Der Heer's hands were full, and he hoped Ellie would understand. She understood. She hated herself for sleeping with him. To avoid an afternoon alone she had dialed Devi Sukhavati.

'One of the Sanskrit words for "victorious" is *abhijit*. That's what Vega was called in ancient India. Abhijit. It was under the influence of Vega that the Hindu divinities, our culture heroes, conquered the asuras, the gods of evil. Ellie, are you listening? . . . Now, it's a curious thing. In Persia there are asuras also, but in Persia the asuras were the gods of good. Eventually religions sprang up in which the chief god, the god of light, the Sun god, was called Ahura-Mazda. The Zoroastrians, for example, and the Mithraists. Ahura, Asura, it's the same name. There are still Zoroastrians today, and the Mithraists gave the early Christians a good fright. But in this same story, those Hindu divinities – they were mainly female, by the way – were called Devis. It's the origin of my own name. In India, the Devis are gods of

201

good. In Persia, the Devis become gods of evil. Some scholars think this is where the English word "devil" ultimately comes from. The symmetry is complete. All this is probably some vaguely remembered account of the Aryan invasion that pushed the Dravidians, my ancestors, to the south. So, depending on which side of the Kirthar Range one lives on, Vega supports either God or the Devil.'

This cheerful story had been proffered as a gift by Devi, who clearly had heard something of Ellie's California religious adventures two weeks before. Ellie was grateful. But it reminded her that she had not even mentioned to Joss the possibility that the Message was the blueprint for a machine of unknown purpose. Now he would soon enough be hearing all this through the media. She should really, she told herself sternly, make an overseas call to explain to him the new developments. But Joss was said to be in seclusion. He had offered no public statement following their meeting in Modesto. Rankin, in a press conference, announced that while there might be some dangers, he was not opposed to letting the scientists receive the full Message. But translation was another matter. Periodic review by all segments of society was required, he said, especially by those entrusted to safeguard spiritual and moral values.

They were now approaching the Tuileries Gardens, where the garish hues of autumn were on display. Frail and elderly men – Ellie judged them to be from Southeast Asia – were in vigorous dispute. Ornamenting the black cast-iron gates were multicolored balloons on sale. At the center of a pool of water was a marble Amphitrite. Around her, toy sailboats were racing, urged on by an exuberant crowd of small children with Magellanic aspirations. A catfish suddenly broke water, swamping the lead boat, and the boys and girls became subdued, chastened by this wholly unexpected apparition. The Sun was low in the west, and Ellie felt a momentary chill.

They approached L'Orangerie, in the annex of which was a special exhibition, so the poster proclaimed, 'Images Martiennes.' The joint American-French-Soviet robot roving vehicles on Mars had produced a spectacular windfall of color photographs, some – like the *Voyager* images of the outer solar system around 1980 – soaring beyond their mere scientific purpose and becoming art. The poster featured a landscape photographed on the vast Elysium Plateau. In the foreground was a three-sided pyramid, smooth, highly eroded, with an impact crater near the base. It had been produced by millions of years of high-speed sandblasting by the fierce Martian winds, the planetary geologists had said. A second rover – assigned to Cydonia, on the other side of Mars – had become mired in a drifting dune, and its controllers in Pasadena had been so far unable to respond to its forlorn cries for help.

Ellie found herself riveted on Sukhavati's appearance: her huge black eyes, erect bearing, and yet another magnificent sari. She thought to herself, I'm not graceful. Usually she found herself able to continue her part of a conversation while mentally addressing other matters as well. But today she had trouble following one line of thought, never mind two. While they were discussing the merits of the several opinions on whether to build the Machine, in her mind's eye she returned to Devi's image from the Aryan invasion of India 3,500 years ago: a war between two peoples, each of whom claimed victory, each of whom patriotically exaggerated the historical accounts. Ultimately, the story is transformed into a war of the gods. 'Our' side, of course, is good. The other side, of course, is evil. She imagined the goateed, spade-tailed, cloven-hoofed Devil of the West evolving by slow evolutionary steps over thousands of years from some Hindu antecedent who, for all Ellie knew, had the head of an elephant and was painted blue.

'Baruda's Trojan Horse – maybe it's not a completely foolish idea,' she found herself saying. 'But I don't see that we have any choice, as Xi said. They can *be* here in twenty-some-odd years if they want to.'

They arrived at a monumental arch in the Roman style surmounted by a heroic, indeed apotheotic, statue of Napoleon as chariot driver. From the long view, from an extraterrestrial perspective, how pathetic this posturing was. They rested on a nearby bench, their long shadows cast over a bed of flowers planted in the colors of the French Republic.

Ellie longed to discuss her own emotional predicament, but that might have political overtones. It would, at the very least, be indiscreet. She did not know Sukhavati very well. Instead she encouraged her companion to speak about *her* personal life. Sukhavati acquiesced readily enough.

She had been born to a Brahman but unprosperous family with matriarchal proclivities in the southern state of Tamil Nadu. Matriarchal households were still common all over South India. She matriculated at Banares Hindu University. At medical school in England she had met and fallen deeply in love with Surindar Ghosh, a fellow medical student. But Surindar was a harijan, an untouchable, of a caste so loathed that the mere sight of them was held by orthodox Brahmans to be polluting. Surindar's ancestors had been forced to live a nocturnal existence, like bats and owls. Her family threatened to disown her if they married. Her father declared that he had no daughter who would consider such a union. If she married Ghosh, he would mourn her as though she were dead. She married him anyway. 'We were too much in love,' she said. 'I really had no choice.' Within the year, he died from septicemia acquired while performing an autopsy under inadequate supervision.

Instead of reconciling her to her family, however, Surindar's death accomplished the opposite, and after receiving her medical degree, Devi decided to remain in England. She discovered a natural affinity for molecular biology and considered it an effortless continuation of her medical studies. She soon found she had real talent in this meticulous discipline. Knowledge of nucleic acid replication led her to work on the origin of life, and that in turn led her to consider life on other planets.

'You could say that my scientific career has been a sequence of free associations. One thing just led to another.'

She had recently been working on the characterization of Martian organic matter, measured in a few locales on Mars by the same roving vehicles whose stunning photographic products they had just seen advertised. Devi had never remarried, although she had made it plain there were some who pursued her. Lately she had been seeing a scientist in Bombay whom she described as a 'computer wallah.'

Walking a little farther on, they found themselves in the Cour Napoleon, the interior courtyard of the Louvre Museum. In its center was the newly completed and wildly controversial pyramidal entrance, and in high niches around the courtyard were sculptural representations of the heroes of French civilization. Captioned under each statue of a revered man – they could see little evidence of revered women – was his surname. Occasionally, letters were eroded – by natural weathering, or in a few cases perhaps effaced by some offended passerby. For one or two statues, it was difficult to piece together who the savant had been. On the statue that had evidently evoked the greatest public resentment, only the letters LTA remained.

Although the Sun was setting and the Louvre was open until mid-evening, they did not enter, but instead ambled along the Seine embankment, following the river back along the Quai d'Orsay. The proprietors of bookstalls were fastening shutters and closing up shop for the day. For a while they strolled on, arm in arm in the European manner.

A French couple was walking a few paces ahead of them, each parent holding one hand of their daughter, a girl of about four who would periodically launch herself off the pavement. In her momentary suspension in zero g, she experienced, it was apparent, something akin to ecstasy. The parents were discussing the World Message Consortium, which was hardly a coincidence since the newspapers had been full of little else. The man was for building the Machine; it might create new technologies and increase employment in France. The woman was more cautious, but for reasons she had difficulty articulating. The daughter, braids flying, was wholly unconcerned about what to do with a blueprint from the stars.

Der Heer, Kitz, and Honicutt had called a meeting at the American Embassy early the following morning to prepare for the arrival of the Secretary of State later in the day. The meeting was to be classified and held in the Embassy's Black Room, a chamber electromagnetically decoupled from the outside world, making even sophisticated electronic surveillance impossible. Or so it was claimed. Ellie thought there might be instrumentation developed that could make an end run around these precautions.

After spending the afternoon with Devi Sukhavati, she had received the message at her hotel and had tried to call der Heer, but was able only to reach Michael Kitz. She opposed a classified meeting on this subject, she said; it was a matter of principle. The Message was clearly intended for the entire planet. Kitz replied that there were no data being withheld from the rest of the world, at least by Americans; and that the meeting was merely advisory – to assist the United States in the difficult procedural negotiations ahead. He appealed to her patriotism, to her self-interest, and at last invoked again the Hadden Decision. 'For all I know, that thing is still sitting in your safe unread. Read it,' he urged.

She tried, again unsuccessfully, to reach der Heer. First the man turns up everywhere in the Argus facility, like a bad penny. He moves in with you in your apartment.

You're sure, for the first time in years, you're in love. The next minute you can't even get him to answer the phone. She decided to attend the meeting, if only to see Ken face to face.

Kitz was enthusiastically for building the Machine, Drumlin cautiously in favor, der Heer and Honicutt at least outwardly uncommitted, and Peter Valerian in an agony of indecision. Kitz and Drumlin were even talking about where to build the thing. Freightage costs alone made manufacture or even assembly on the far side of the Moon prohibitively expensive, as Xi had guessed.

'If we use aerodynamic braking, it's cheaper to send a kilogram to Phobos or Deimos than to the far side of the Moon,' Bobby Bui volunteered.

'Where the hell is Fobuserdeemus?' Kitz wanted to know.

'The moons of Mars. I was talking about aerodynamic braking in the Martian atmosphere.'

'And how long does it take to get to Phobos or Deimos?' Drumlin was stirring his cup of coffee.

'Maybe a year, but once we have a fleet of interplanetary transfer vehicles and the pipeline is full –'

'Compared with three days to the Moon?' sputtered Drumlin. 'Bui, stop wasting our time.'

'It's only a suggestion,' he protested. 'You know, just something to think about.'

Der Heer seemed impatient, distracted. He was clearly under great pressure – alternately avoiding her eyes and, she thought, making some unspoken appeal. She took it as a hopeful sign.

'If you want to worry about Doomsday Machines,' Drumlin was saying, 'you have to worry about energy supplies. If it doesn't have access to an enormous amount of energy, it can't be a Doomsday Machine. So as long as the instructions don't ask for a gigawatt nuclear reactor, I don't think we have to worry about Doomsday Machines.'

'Why are you guys in such a hurry to commit to

construction?' she asked Kitz and Drumlin collectively. They were sitting next to each other with a plate of croissants between them.

Kitz looked from Honicutt to der Heer before answering: 'This is a classified meeting,' he began. 'We all know you won't pass anything said here on to your Russian friends. It's like this: We don't know what the Machine will do, but it's clear from Dave Drumlin's analysis that there's new technology in it, probably new industries. Constructing the Machine is bound to have economic value – I mean, think of what we'd learn. And it might have military value. At least that's what the Russians are thinking. See, the Russians are in a box. Here's a whole new area of technology they're going to have to keep up with the US on. Maybe there's instructions for some decisive weapon in the Message, or some economic advantage. They can't be sure. They'll have to bust their economy trying. Did you notice how Baruda kept referring to what was cost–effective? If all this Message stuff went away – burn the data, destroy the telescopes – then the Russians could maintain military parity. That's why they're so cautious. So, of course, that's why we're gung ho for it.' He smiled.

Temperamentally, Kitz was bloodless, she thought; but he was far from stupid. When he was cold and withdrawn, people tended not to like him. So he had developed an occasional veneer of urbane amiability. In Ellie's view, it was a molecular monolayer thick.

'Now let me ask *you* a question,' he continued. 'Did you catch Baruda's remark about withholding some of the data? *Is* there any missing data?'

'Only from very early on,' she replied. 'Only from the first few weeks, I'd guess. There were a few holes in the Chinese coverage a little after that. There's still a small amount of data that hasn't been exchanged, on all sides. But I don't see any signs of serious holding back. Anyway, we'll pick up any missing data swatches after the Message recycles.'

208

'*If* the Message recycles,' Drumlin growled.

Der Heer moderated a discussion on contingency planning: what to do when the primer was received; which American, German, and Japanese industries to notify early about possible major development projects; how to identify key scientists and engineers for constructing the Machine, if the decision was made to go ahead; and, briefly, the need to build enthusiasm for the project in Congress and with the American public. Der Heer hastened to add that these would be contingency plans only, that no final decision was being made, and that no doubt Soviet concerns about a Trojan Horse were at least partly genuine.

Kitz asked about the composition of 'the crew.' 'They're asking us to put people in five upholstered chairs. Which people? How do we decide? It'll probably have to be an international crew. How many Americans? How many Russians? Anybody else? We don't know what happens to those five people when they sit down in those chairs, but we want to have the best men for the job.'

Ellie did not rise to the bait, and he continued. 'Now a major question is going to be who pays for what, who builds what, who's in charge of overall systems integration. I think we can do some real horse trading on this, in exchange for significant American representation in the crew.'

'But we still want to send the best possible people,' der Heer noted, a little obviously.

'Sure,' returned Kitz, 'but what do we mean by "best"? Scientists? People with military intelligence backgrounds? Physical strength and endurance? Patriotism? (That's not a dirty word, you know.) And then' – he looked up from buttering another croissant to glance directly at Ellie – 'there's the question of sex. Sexes, I mean. Do we send only men? If it's men and women, there has to be more of one sex than the other. There's five places, an odd number. Are all the crew members going to work together okay? If we go ahead with this project, there's gonna be a lot of tough negotiation.'

'This doesn't sound right to me,' said Ellie. 'This isn't some ambassadorship you buy with a campaign contribution. This is serious business. Also, do you want some muscle-bound moron up there, some kid in his twenties who knows nothing about how the world works – just how to run a respectable hundred-yard dash and how to obey orders? Or some political hack? That *can't* be what this trip is about.'

'No, you're right.' Kitz smiled. 'I think we'll find people who satisfy all our criteria.'

Der Heer, the bags under his eyes making him look almost haggard, adjourned the meeting. He managed to give Ellie a small private smile, but it was all lips, no teeth. The Embassy limousines were waiting to take them back to the Elysée Palace.

'I'll tell you why it would be better to send Russians,' Vaygay was saying. 'When you Americans were opening up your country – pioneers, trappers, Indian scouts, all that – you were unopposed, at least by anyone at your level of technology. You raced across your continent from the Atlantic to the Pacific. After a while, you *expected* everything would be easy. Our situation was different. We were conquered by the Mongols. Their horse technology was much superior to ours. When we expanded eastward we were careful. We never crossed the wilderness and expected it would be easy. We're more adjusted to adversity than you are. Also, Americans are used to being ahead technologically. We're used to catching up technologically. Now, everybody on Earth is a Russian – you understand, I mean in our historical position. This mission needs Soviets more than it needs Americans.'

Merely meeting with her alone entailed certain risks for Vaygay – and for her as well, as Kitz had gone out of his way to remind her. Sometimes, during a scientific meeting in America or Europe, Vaygay would be permitted to spend an afternoon with her. More often he was accompanied by colleagues or a KGB baby-sitter – who would be described as a translator, even when his English was clearly inferior to Vaygay's; or as a scientist from the secretariat of this or that Academy commission, except that his knowledge of the scientific matters often proved superficial. Vaygay would shake his head when asked about them. But by and large, he considered the baby-sitters a part of the game, the price you must pay when they let you visit the West, and more than once she thought she detected a note of affection in Vaygay's voice when he talked to the baby-sitter: To go to a foreign country and pretend to be expert in a subject you know poorly must be filled with anxiety. Perhaps, in their heart of hearts, the baby-sitters detested their assignment as much as Vaygay did.

They were seated at the same window table at Chez Dieux. A distinct chill was in the air, a premonition of winter, and a young man wearing a long blue scarf as his only concession to the cold strode briskly past the tubs of chilled oysters outside the window. From Lunacharsky's continuing (and uncharacteristically) guarded remarks, she deduced disarray in the Soviet delegation. The Soviets were concerned that the Machine might somehow redound to the strategic advantage of the United States in the five-decade-old global competition. Vaygay had in fact been shocked by Baruda's question about burning the data and destroying the radio telescopes. He had had no advance knowledge of Baruda's position. The Soviets had played a vital role in gathering the Message, with the largest longitude coverage of any nation, Vaygay stressed, and they had the only serious ocean-going radio telescopes. They would expect a major role in whatever came next. Ellie assured him that, as far as she was concerned, they should have such a role.

'Look, Vaygay, they know from our television transmissions that the Earth rotates, and that there are many different nations. The Olympic broadcast alone might have told them that. Subsequent transmissions from other nations would have nailed it down. So if they're as good as we think, they could have phased the transmission with the Earth's rotation, so only one nation got the Message. They chose not to do that. They want the Message to be received by everybody on the planet. They're expecting the Machine to be built by the whole planet. This *can't* be an all-American or an all-Russian project. It's not what our . . . client wants.'

But she was not sure, she told him, that she would be playing any role in decisions on Machine construction or crew selection. She was returning to the United States the next day, mainly to get on top of the new radio data from the past few weeks. The Consortium plenary sessions seemed interminable, and no closing date had been set. Vaygay had been asked by his people to stay on at least a little longer. The Foreign Minister had just arrived and was now leading the Soviet delegation.

'I'm worried all this will end badly,' he said. 'There are so many things that can go wrong. Technological failures. Political failures. Human failures. And even if we get through all that, if we don't have a war because of the Machine, if we build it correctly and without blowing ourselves up, I'm still worried.'

'About what? How do you mean?'

'The best that can happen is we will be made fools of.'

'Who will?'

'Arroway, don't you understand?' A vein in Lunacharsky's neck throbbed. 'I'm amazed you don't see it. The Earth is a . . . ghetto. Yes, a ghetto. All human beings are trapped here. We have heard vaguely that there are big cities out there beyond the ghetto, with broad boulevards filled with droshkys and beautiful perfumed women in furs. But the cities are too far away, and we are too poor ever to go there, even the richest of us. Anyway, we know they don't want us. That's why

212

they've left us in this pathetic little village in the first place.

'And now along comes an invitation. As Xi said. Fancy, elegant. They have sent us an engraved card and an empty droshky. We are to send five villagers and the droshky will carry them to – who knows? – Warsaw. Or Moscow. Maybe even Paris. Of course, some are tempted to go. There will always be people who are flattered by the invitation, or who think it is a way to escape our shabby village.

'And what do you think will happen when we get there? Do you think the Grand Duke will have us to dinner? Will the President of the Academy ask us interesting questions about daily life in our filthy shtetl? Do you imagine the Russian Orthodox Metropolitan will enage us in learned discourse on comparative religion?

'No, Arroway. We will gawk at the big city, and they will laugh at us behind their hands. They will exhibit us to the curious. The more backward we are the better they'll feel, the more reassured they'll be.

'It's a quota system. Every few centuries, five of us get to spend a weekend on Vega. Have pity on the provincials, and make sure they know who their betters are.'

13

Babylon

With the basest of companions, I walked the streets of
Babylon . . .

— AUGUSTINE
Confessions, II, 3

The Cray 21 mainframe computer at Argus had been
instructed to compare each day's harvest of data from
Vega with the earliest records of Level 3 of the palimpsest. In effect, one long and incomprehensible sequence
of zeros and ones was being compared automatically
with another, earlier, such sequence. This was part of a
massive statistical intercomparison of various segments
of the still undecrypted text. There were some short
sequences of zeros and ones – 'words' the analysts called
them, hopefully – which were repeated again and again.
Many sequences would appear only once in thousands of
pages of text. This statistical approach to message decryption was familiar to Ellie since high school. But the
subroutines applied by the experts from the National
Security Agency – made available only as a result of a
presidential directive, and even then armed with instructions to self-destruct if examined closely – were brilliant.

What prodigies of human inventivenes, Ellie reflected,
were being directed to reading each other's mail. The
global confrontation between the United States and the
Soviet Union – now, to be sure, easing somewhat – was
still eating up the world. It was not just the financial
resources dedicated to the military establishments of all
nations. That was approaching two trillion dollars a year,
and by itself was ruinously expensive when there were so
many other urgent human needs. But still worse, she

knew, was the intellectual effort dedicated to the arms race.

Almost half the scientists on the planet, it had been estimated, were employed by one or another of the almost two hundred military establishments worldwide. And they were not the dregs of the doctoral programs in physics and mathematics. Some of her colleagues would console themselves with this thought when the awkward problem arose of what to tell a recent doctoral candidate being courted by, say, one of the weapons laboratories. 'If he was any good, he'd be offered an assistant professorship at Stanford, at least,' she could recall Drumlin once saying. No, a certain kind of mind and character was drawn to the military applications of science and mathematics – people who liked big explosions, for example; or those with no taste for personal combat who, to avenge some schoolyard injustice, aspired to military command; or inveterate puzzle solvers who longed to decrypt the most complex messages known. Occasionally the spur was political, tracing back to international disputes, immigration policies, wartime horrors, police brutality, or national propaganda by this nation or that decades earlier. Many of these scientists had real ability, Ellie knew, whatever reservations she might have about their motivations. She tried to imagine that massed talent really dedicated to the well-being of the species and the planet.

She pored over the studies that had accumulated during her absence. They were making almost no progress in decrypting the Message, although the statistical analyses now stacked into a pile of paper a meter tall. It was all very discouraging.

She wished there were someone, especially a close woman friend, at Argus to whom she could pour out her hurt and anger at Ken's behavior. But there was not, and she was disinclined even to use the telephone for this purpose. She did manage to spend a weekend with her college friend Becky Ellenbogen in Austin, but Becky, whose appraisals of men tended to be somewhere between wry and scathing, in this case was surprisingly mild in her criticism.

'He *is* the President's Science Adviser, and this is only the most amazing discovery in the history of the world. Don't be so hard on him,' Becky urged. 'He'll come around.'

But Becky was another of those who found Ken 'charming' (she had met him once at the dedication of the National Neutrino Observatory), and was perhaps too inclined to accommodate to power. Had der Heer treated Ellie in this shabby way while he was a mere professor of molecular biology somewhere, Becky would have marinated and skewered the man.

After returning from Paris, der Heer had mustered a regular campaign of apology and devotion. He had been overstressed, he told her, overwhelmed with a range of responsibilities including difficult and unfamiliar political issues. His position as leader of the American delegation and co-chairman of the plenary might have been rendered less effective if there had been public knowledge of his and Ellie's relationship. Kitz had been insufferable. Ken had had too many consecutive nights with only a few hours' sleep. Altogether, Ellie judged, there were too many explanations. But she permitted the relationship to continue.

When it happened, it was Willie once again, this time on the graveyard shift, who first noticed. Afterward, Willie would attribute the speed of the discovery less to the superconducting computer and the NSA programs than to the new Hadden context-recognition chips. At any rate, Vega had been low in the sky an hour or so before dawn when the computer triggered an understated alarm. With some annoyance, Willie put down what he was reading – it was a new textbook on Fast Fourier Transform Spectroscopy – and noticed these words being printed out on the screen:

As he watched, 41619 became 41620 and then 41621.
The digits after the slash were increasing in a continuous
blur. Both the number of pages and the correlation
coefficient, a measure of the improbability that the correlation was by chance, increased as he watched. He gave
it another two pages before picking up the direct line to
Ellie's apartment.

She had been in a deep sleep and was momentarily
disoriented. But she quickly turned on the bedside light
and after a moment gave instructions for senior Argus
staff to be assembled. She would, she told him, locate der
Heer, who was somewhere on the facility. This proved
not very difficult. She shook his shoulder.

'Ken, get up. There's word that we've repeated.'

'What?'

'The Message has cycled back. Or at least that's what
Willie says. I'm on my way there. Why don't you wait
another ten minutes so we can pretend you were in your
room in BSQ?'

She was almost at the door before he shouted after her,
'How can we recycle? We haven't gotten the primer yet.'

Racing across the screens was a paired sequence of
zeros and ones, a real-time comparison of the data just
being received and the data from an early page of text
received at Argus a year before. The program would
have culled out any differences. So far, there were none.
It reassured them that they had not mistranscribed, that
there were no apparent transmission errors, and that if
some small dense interstellar cloud between Vega and the
Earth was able to eat the occasional zero or one, this was
an infrequent occurrence. Argus was by now in real-time
communication with dozens of other telescopes that
were part of the World Message Consortium, and the
news of recycling was passed on to the next observing
stations westward, to California, Hawaii, the *Marshal*

Nedelin now in the South Pacific, and to Sydney. Had the discovery been made when Vega was over one of the other telescopes in the network, Argus would have been informed instantly.

The absence of the primer was an agonizing disappointment, but it was not the only surprise. The Message page numbers had jumped discontinuously from the 40,000s to the 10,000s, where recycling had been uncovered. Evidently Argus had discovered the transmission from Vega almost at the moment it first arrived at Earth. It was a remarkably strong signal, and would have been picked up even by small omnidirectional telescopes. But it was a surprising coincidence that the broadcast should arrive at Earth at the very moment Argus was looking at Vega. Also, what did it mean for the text to begin on a page in the 10,000s? Were there 10,000 pages of text missing? Was it a backward practice of the provincial Earth to start numbering books on page 1? Were these sequential numbers perhaps not page numbers but something else? Or – and this worried Ellie the most – was there some fundamental and unexpected difference between how humans thought of things and how the aliens thought? If so, it would have worrisome implications about the ability of the Consortium to understand the Message, primer or no primer.

The Message repeated exactly, the gaps were all filled in and nobody could read a word of it. It seemed unlikely that the transmitting civilization, meticulous in all else, had simply overlooked the need for a primer. At least the Olympic broadcast and the interior design of the Machine seemed to be tailored specifically for humans. They would hardly go to all this trouble to devise and transmit the Message without making some provision for humans to read it. So humans must have overlooked something. It soon became generally agreed that somewhere was a fourth layer to the palimpsest. But where?

The diagrams were published in an eight-volume 'coffee table' book set that was soon reprinted worldwide.

All over the planet people tried to figure out the pictures. The dodecahedron and the quasi-biological forms were especially evocative. Many clever suggestions were made by the public and carefully sifted by the Argus team. Many harebrained interpretations were also widely available, especially in weekly newspapers. Whole new industries developed – doubtless unforeseen by those who devised the Message – dedicated to using the diagrams to bilk the public. The Ancient and Mystical Order of the Dodecahedron was announced. The Machine was a UFO. The Machine was Ezekiel's Wheel. An angel revealed the meaning of the Message and the diagrams to a Brazilian businessman, who distributed – at first, at his own expense – his interpretation worldwide. With so many enigmatic diagrams to interpret, it was inevitable that many religions would recognize some of their iconography in the Message from the stars. A principal cross section of the Machine looked something like a chrysanthemum, a fact that stirred great enthusiasm in Japan. If there had been an image of a human face among all the diagrams, messianic fervor might have reached a flash point.

As it was, a surprisingly large number of people were winding up their affairs in preparation for the Advent. Industrial productivity was off worldwide. Many had given away all their possessions to the poor and then, as the end of the world was delayed, were obliged to seek help from a charity or the State. Because gifts of this sort constituted a major fraction of the resources of such charities, some of the philanthropists ended up being supported by their own gifts. Delegations approached government leaders to urge that schistosomiasis, say, or world hunger be ended by the Advent; otherwise there was no telling what would happen to us. Others counseled, more quietly, that if there was a decade of real world madness in the offing, there must be a considerable monetary or national advantage in it somewhere.

Some said that there *was* no primer, that the whole

exercise was to teach humans humility, or to drive us mad. There were newspaper editorials on how we're not as smart as we think we are, and some resentment directed at the scientists who, after all the support given to them by the governments, have failed us in our time of need. Or maybe humans are much dumber than the Vegans gave us credit for. Maybe there was some point that had been entirely obvious to all previous emerging civilizations so contacted, something no one in the history of the Galaxy had ever missed before. A few commentators embraced this prospect of cosmic humiliation with real enthusiasm. It demonstrated what they'd been saying about people all along. After a while, Ellie decided that she needed help.

They entered surreptitiously through the Enlil Gate, with an escort dispatched by the Proprietor. The General Services Administration security detail was edgy despite, or perhaps because of, the additional protection.

Although there was a little sunlight still left, the dirt streets were lit by braziers, oil lamps, and an occasional guttering torch. Two amphoras, each large enough to contain an adult human being, flanked the entrance to a retail olive oil establishment. The advertising was in cuneiform. On an adjacent public building was a magnificent bas-relief of a lion hunt from the reign of Assurbanipal. As they approached the Temple of Assur, there was a scuffle in the crowd, and her escort made a wide berth. She now had an unobstructed view of the Ziggurat down a wide torchlit avenue. It was more breathtaking than in the pictures. There was a martial flourish on an unfamiliar brass instrument; three men and a horse clattered by, the charioteer in Phrygian headdress. As in some medieval rendition of a cautionary tale from the book of Genesis, the top of the Ziggurat was enveloped in low twilit clouds. They left the Ishtarian Way and entered the Ziggurat through a side street. In the private elevator, her escort pressed the button for the topmost floor: 'Forty,' it read. No numerals. Just the word. And then, to leave no room for doubt, a glass panel flashed, 'The Gods.'

Mr Hadden would be with her shortly. Would she like something to drink while she waited? Considering the reputation of the place, Ellie demurred. Babylon lay spread out before her – magnificent, as everyone said, in its re-creation of a long-gone time and place. During daylight hours busloads from museums, a very few schools, and the tourist agencies would arrive at the Ishtar Gate, don appropriate clothes, and travel back in time. Hadden wisely donated all profits from his daytime clientele to New York City and Long Island charities. The daytime tours were immensely popular, in part because it was a respectable opportunity to look the place over for those who would not dream of visiting Babylon at night.

After dark, Babylon was called an adult amusement park. It was of an opulence, scale, and imaginativeness that dwarfed, say, the Reeperbahn in Hamburg. It was by far the largest tourist attraction in the New York metropolitan area, with by far the largest gross revenues. How Hadden had been able to convince the city fathers of Babylon, New York, and how he had lobbied for an 'easement' of local and state prostitution laws was well known. It was now a half-hour train ride from midtown Manhattan to the Ishtar Gate. Ellie had insisted on taking this train, despite the entreaties of the security people, and had found almost a third of the visitors to be women. There were no graffiti, little danger of mugging, but a much inferior brand of white noise compared with the conveyances of the New York City subway system.

Although Hadden was a member of the National Academy of Engineering, he had never, so far as Ellie knew, attended a meeting, and she had never set eyes on him. His face became well known to millions of Americans, however, years before as a result of the Advertising Council's campaign against him: 'The Unamerican' had been the caption under an unflattering portrait of Hadden. Even so, she was taken aback when in the midst of her reverie by the slanted glass wall she was interrupted by a small, fat beckoning person.

'Oh. Sorry. I never understand how anyone can be afraid of me.'

His voice was surprisingly musical. In fact, he seemed to talk in fifths. He hadn't thought it necessary to introduce himself and once again inclined his head to the door he had left ajar. It was hard to believe that some crime of passion was about to be visited upon her under these circumstances, and wordlessly she entered the next room.

He ushered her to a meticulously crafted tabletop model of an ancient city of less pretentious aspect than Babylon.

'Pompeii,' he said by way of explanation. 'The stadium here is the key. With the restrictions on boxing there aren't any healthy blood sports left in America. Very important. Sucks out some of the poisons from the national bloodstream. The whole thing is designed, permits issued, and now this.'

'What's "this"?'

'No gladiatorial games. I just got word from Sacramento. There's a bill before the legislature to outlaw gladiatorial games in California. Too violent, they say. They authorize a new skyscraper, they know they'll lose two or three construction workers. The unions know, the builders know, and that's just to build offices for oil companies or Beverly Hills lawyers. Sure, we'd lose a few. But we're geared more to trident and net than the short sword. Those legislators don't have their priorities straight.'

He beamed at her owlishly and offered a drink, which again she refused. 'So you want to talk to me about the Machine, and I want to talk to you about the Machine. You first. You want to know where the primer is?'

'We're asking for help from a few key people who

might have some insight. We thought with your record of invention – and since your context-recognition chip was involved in the recycling discovery – that you might put yourself in the place of the Vegans and think of where you'd put the primer. We recognize you're very busy, and I'm sorry to –'

'Oh, no. It's all right. It's true I'm busy. I'm trying to regularize my affairs, because I'm gonna make a big change in my life . . .'

'For the Millennium?' She tried to imagine him giving away S. R. Hadden and Company, the Wall Street brokerage house; Genetic Engineering, Inc.; Hadden Cybernetics; and Babylon to the poor.

'Not exactly. No. It was fun to think about. It made me feel good to be asked. I looked at the diagrams.' He waved at the commercial set of eight volumes spread in disarray on a worktable. 'There are wonderful things in there, but I don't think that's where the primer is hiding. Not in the diagrams. I don't know why you think the primer has to be *in* the Message. Maybe they left it on Mars or Pluto or in the Oort Comet Cloud, and we'll discover it in a few centuries. Right now, we know there's this wonderful Machine, with design drawings and thirty thousand pages of explanatory text. But we don't know whether we'd be able to build the thing if we could read it. So we wait a few centuries, improving our technology, knowing that sooner or later we'll have to be ready to build it. *Not* having the primer binds us up with future generations. Human beings are sent a problem that takes generations to solve. I don't think that's such a bad thing. Might be very healthy. Maybe you're making a mistake looking for a primer. Maybe it's better not to find it.'

'No, I want to find the primer right away. We don't know it'll be waiting for us forever. If they hang up because there was no answer, it would be much worse than if they'd never called at all.'

'Well, maybe you have a point. Anyway, I thought of

223

as many possibilities as I could. I'll give you a couple of trivial possibilities, and then a nontrivial possibility. Trivial first: The primer's in the Message but at a very different data rate. Suppose there was another message in there at a bit an hour – could you detect that?'

'Absolutely. We routinely check for long-term receiver drift in any case. But also a bit an hour only buys you – let me see – ten, twenty thousand bits tops before the Message recycles.'

'So that makes sense only if the primer is *much* easier than the Message. *You* think it isn't. *I* think it isn't. Now, what about much faster bit rates? How do you know that under every bit of your Machine Message there aren't a million bits of primer message?'

'Because it would produce monster bandwidths. We'd know in an instant.'

'Okay, so there's a fast data dump every now and then. Think of it as microfilm. There's a tiny dot of microfilm that's sitting in repetitious – I mean in repetitive – parts of the Message. I'm imagining a little box that says in your regular language, "I am the primer." Then right after that there's a dot. And in that dot is a hundred million bits, very fast. You might see if you've got any boxes.'

'Believe me, we would have seen it.'

'Okay, how about phase modulation? We use it in radar and spacecraft telemetry, and it hardly messes up the spectrum at all. Have you hooked up a phase correlator?'

'No. That's a useful idea. I'll look into it.'

'Now, the nontrivial idea is this: If the Machine ever gets made, if our people are gonna sit in it, somebody's gonna press a button and then those five are gonna go somewhere. Never mind where. Now, there's an interesting question whether those five are gonna come back. Maybe not. I like the idea that all this Machine design was invented by Vegan body snatchers. You know, their medical students, or anthropologists or something. They need a few human bodies. It's a big hassle to come to Earth – you need permission, passes from the transit authority – hell, it's more trouble than it's worth. But with a little effort you can send the Earth a Message and then the *earthlings*'ll go to all the trouble to ship you five bodies.

'It's like stamp collecting. I used to collect stamps when I was a kid. You could send a letter to somebody in a foreign country and most of the time they'd write back. It didn't matter what they said. All you wanted was the stamp. So that's my picture: There's a few stamp collectors on Vega. They send letters out when they're in the mood, and bodies come flying back to them from all over space. Wouldn't you like to see the collection?'

He smiled up at her and continued. 'Okay, so what does this have to do with finding the primer? Nothing. It's relevant only if I'm wrong. If my picture is wrong, if the five people are coming back to Earth, then it would be a big help if we've invented space-flight. No matter *how* smart they are, it's gonna be tough to land the Machine. Too many things are moving. God knows what the propulsion system is. If you pop out of space a few meters below ground, you've had it. And what's a few meters in twenty-six light-years? It's too risky. When the Machine comes back it'll pop out – or whatever it does – in space, somewhere near the Earth, but not on it or in it. So they have to be sure we have spaceflight, so the five people can be rescued in space. They're in a hurry and can't sit tight until the 1957 evening news arrives on Vega. So what do they do? They arrange so part of the Message can only be detected from space. What part is that? The primer. If you can detect the primer, you've got spaceflight and you can come back safe. So I imagine the primer is being sent at the frequency of the oxygen absorptions in the microwave spectrum, or in the near-infrared – some part of the spectrum you can't detect until you're well out of the Earth's atmosphere . . .'

'We've had the Hubble telescope looking at Vega all through the ultraviolet, visible, and near-infrared. Not a

hint of anything. The Russians have repaired their millimeter wave instrument. They've hardly been looking at
anything *besides* Vega and they haven't found anything.
But we'll keep looking. Other possibilities?'

'Sure you wouldn't like a drink? I don't drink myself,
but so many people do.' Ellie again declined. 'No, no
other possibilities. Now it's my turn?

'See, I want to ask you for something. But I'm not
good at asking for things. I never have been. My public
image is rich, funny-looking, unscrupulous – somebody
who looks for weaknesses in the system so he can make a
fast buck. And don't tell me you don't believe any of that.
Everybody believes at least some of it. You've probably
heard some of what I'm gonna say before, but give me
ten minutes and I'll tell you how all this began. I want
you to know something about me.'

She settled back, wondering what he could possibly
want of her, and brushed away idle fantasies involving
the Temple of Ishtar, Hadden, and perhaps a charioteer
or two thrown in for good measure.

Years before, he had invented a module that, when a
television commercial appeared, automatically muted
the sound. It wasn't at first a context-recognition device.
Instead, it simply monitored the amplitude of the carrier
wave. TV advertisers had taken to running their ads
louder and with less audio clutter than the programs that
were their nominal vehicles. News of Hadden's module
spread by word of mouth. People reported a sense of
relief, the lifting of a great burden, even a feeling of joy at
being freed from the advertising barrage for the six to
eight hours out of every day that the average American
spent in front of the television set. Before there could be
any coordinated response from the television advertising
industry, Adnix had become wildly popular. It forced
advertisers and networks into new choices of carrier-
wave strategy, each of which Hadden countered with a
new invention. Sometimes he invented circuits to defeat
strategies that the agencies and the networks had not yet

226

hit upon. He would say that he was saving them the trouble of making inventions, at great cost to their shareholders, which were at any rate doomed to failure. As his sales volume increased, he kept cutting prices. It was a kind of electronic warfare. And he was winning.

They tried to sue him – something about a conspiracy in restraint of trade. They had sufficient political muscle that his motion for summary dismissal was denied, but insufficient influence to actually win the case. The trial had forced Hadden to investigate the relevant legal codes. Soon after, he applied, through a well-known Madison Avenue agency in which he was now a major silent partner, to advertise his own product on commercial television. After a few weeks of controversy his commercials were refused. He sued all three networks and in *this* trial was able to prove conspiracy in restraint of trade. He received a huge settlement that was, at the time, a record for cases of this sort, and which contributed in its modest way to the demise of the original networks.

There had always been people who enjoyed the commercials, of course, and they had no need for Adnix. But they were a dwindling minority. Hadden made a great fortune by eviscerating broadcast advertising. He also made many enemies.

By the time context-recognition chips were commercially available, he was ready with Preachnix, a submodule which could be plugged into Adnix. It would simply switch channels if by chance a doctrinaire religious program should be tuned in. You could preselect key words, such as 'Advent' or 'Rapture,' and cut great swaths through the available programming. Preachnix was a godsend for a long-suffering but significant minority of television viewers. There was talk, some of it half-serious, that Hadden's next submodule would be called Jivenix, and would work only on public addresses by presidents and premiers.

As he further developed context-recognition chips, it became obvious to him that they had much wider applications – from education, science, and medicine, to military intelligence and industrial espionage. It was on this issue that the lines were drawn for the famous suit *United States* v. *Hadden Cybernetics*. One of Hadden's chips was considered too good for civilian life, and on recommendation of the National Security Agency, the facilities and key personnel for the most advanced context-recognition chip production were taken over by the government. It was simply too important to read the Russian mail. God knows, they told him, what would happen if the Russians could read our mail.

Hadden refused to cooperate in the takeover and vowed to diversify into areas that could not possibly be connected with national security. The government was nationalizing industry, he said. They claimed to be capitalists, but when push came to shove they showed their socialist face. He had found an unsatisfied public need and employed an existing and legal new technology to deliver what they wanted. It was classic capitalism. But there were many sober capitalists who would tell you that he had already gone too far with Adnix, that he had posed a real threat to the American way of life. In a dour column signed V. Petrov, *Pravda* called it a concrete example of the contradictions of capitalism. *The Wall Street Journal* countered, perhaps a little tangentially, by calling *Pravda*, which in Russian means 'truth,' a concrete example of the contradictions of communism.

He suspected that the takeover was only a pretext, that his real offense had been to attack advertising and video evangelism. Adnix and Preachnix were the essence of capitalist entrepreneurship, he argued repeatedly. The point of capitalism was supposed to be providing people with alternatives.

'Well, the *absence* of advertising is an alternative, I told them. There are huge advertising budgets only when there's no difference between the products. If the products really were different, people would buy the one that's better. Advertising teaches people not to trust their

228

judgment. Advertising teaches people to be stupid. A strong country needs smart people. So Adnix is patriotic. The manufacturers can use some of their advertising budgets to improve their products. The consumer will benefit. Magazines and newspapers and direct mail business will boom, and that'll ease the pain in the ad agencies. I don't see what the problem is.'

Adnix, much more than the innumerable libel suits against the original commercial networks, led directly to their demise. For a while there was a small army of unemployed advertising executives, down-and-out former network officials, and penniless divines who had sworn blood oaths to revenge themselves on Hadden. And there was an ever-growing number of still more formidable adversaries. Without a doubt, she thought, Hadden was an interesting man.

'So I figure it's time to go. I've got more money than I know what to do with, my wife can't stand me, and I've got enemies everywhere. I want to do something important, something worthy. I want to do something so that hundreds of years from now people will look back and be glad I was around.'

'You want –'

'I want to build the Machine. Look, I'm perfectly suited for it. I've got the best cybernetics expertise, practical cybernetics, in the business – better than Carnegie-Mellon, better than MIT, better than Stanford, better than Santa Barbara. And if there's anything clear from those plans, it's that this isn't a job for an old-time tool-and-die maker. And you're going to need something like genetic engineering. You won't find anybody more dedicated to this job. And I'll do it at cost.'

'Really, Mr Hadden, who builds the Machine, if we ever get to that point, isn't up to me. It's an international decision. All sorts of politics is involved. They're still debating in Paris about *whether* to build the thing, if and when we decrypt the Message.'

'Don't you think I know that? I'm also applying

through the usual channels of influence and corruption. I just want to have a good word put in for me for the right reasons, by the side of the angels. You understand? And speaking of angels, you really shook up Palmer Joss and Billy Jo Rankin. I haven't seen them so agitated since that trouble they had about Mary's waters. Rankin saying he was deliberately misquoted about supporting the Machine. My, my.'

He shook his head in mock consternation. That some longstanding personal enmity existed between these active proselytizers and the inventor of Preachnix seemed probable enough, and for some reason she was moved to their defense.

'They're both a lot smarter than you might think. And Palmer Joss is . . . well, there's something genuine about him. He's not a phony.'

'You're sure it's not just another pretty face? Excuse me, but it's important that people understand their feelings on this. It's too important not to. I know these clowns. Underneath, when push comes to shove, they're jackals. A lot of people find religion attractive – you know, personally, sexually. You ought to see what happens in the Temple of Ishtar.'

She repressed a small shiver of revulsion. 'I think I *will* have that drink,' she said.

Looking down from the penthouse, she could see the gradated tiers of the Ziggurat, each draped with flowers, some artificial, some real, depending on the season. It was a reconstruction of the Hanging Gardens of Babylon, one of the Seven Wonders of the Ancient World. Miraculously, it was so arranged that it did not closely resemble a Hyatt Hotel. Far below, she could make out a torchlit procession headed back from the Ziggurat to the Enlil Gate. It was led by a kind of sedan chair held by four burly men stripped to the waist. Who or what was in it she could not make out.

'It's a ceremony in honor of Gilgamesh, one of the ancient Sumerian culture heroes.'

230

'Yes, I've heard of him.'

'Immortality was his business.'

He said this matter-of-factly, by way of explanation, and looked at his watch.

'It's at the very top of the Ziggurat, you know, that the kings would go to receive instruction from the gods. Especially from Anu, the sky god. By the way, I looked up what they called Vega. It was Tiranna, the Life of Heaven. It's a funny thing to call it.'

'And have you gotten any instructions?'

'No, they went to your place, not mine. But there'll be another Gilgamesh procession at nine o'clock.'

'I'm afraid I won't be able to stay that long. But let me ask you something. Why Babylon?' she asked. 'And Pompeii. Here you are, one of the most inventive people around. You've created several major industries; you defeated the advertising industry on its own ground. Okay, so you got whipped on that security issue on the context-recognition chip. There's lots of other things you could have done. Why . . . this?'

Far away, the procession had reached the Temple of Assur.

'Why not something more . . . worthy?' he asked. 'I'm just trying to satisfy societal needs that the government overlooks or ignores. It's capitalism. It's legal. It makes a lot of people happy. And I think it's a safety valve for some of the crazies that this society keeps generating.

'But I didn't think all that through at the time. It's very simple. I can remember exactly the moment when the idea for Babylon hit me. I was in Walt Disney World, riding the Mississippi sternwheeler riverboat with my grandson, Jason. Jason was around four, maybe five. I was thinking about how smart the Disney people were to discontinue individual tickets for each ride and instead offer a one-day pass which admitted you to everything. They saved some salaries – some of the ticket takers', for instance. But much more important, people tended to

231

overestimate their appetites for rides. They'd pay a premium to be admitted to everything, and then they'd be happy with a lot less.

'Now, next to me and Jason was an eight-year-old boy with a faraway look in his eye. I'm guessing his age. Maybe he was ten. His father was asking him stuff and he was answering in monosyllables. The boy was fondling the barrel of a toy rifle he'd propped up on his deck chair. The stock was between his legs. All he wanted was to be left alone and stroke the rifle. Behind him were the towers and spires of the Magic Kingdom, and suddenly everything fell into place. You know what I'm saying?'

He filled a tumbler with diet cola and clicked it against her glass.

'Confusion to your enemies,' he toasted genially. 'I'll have them take you out by the Ishtar Gate. The procession's gonna make things too crowded toward the Enlil Gate.'

Both escorts magically appeared, and it was evident she was being dismissed. She had little desire to linger.

'Don't forget about the phase modulation, and looking in the oxygen lines. But even if I'm wrong about where the primer is, don't forget: I'm the only one to build the machine.'

Floodlights brilliantly illuminated the Ishtar Gate. It was covered with representations in glazed tile of some blue animal. The archeologists had called them dragons.

14

Harmonic Oscillator

Scepticism is the chastity of the intellect, and it is shameful to surrender it too soon or to the first comer: there is nobility in preserving it coolly and proudly through long youth, until at last, in the ripeness of instinct and discretion, it can be safely exchanged for fidelity and happiness.

– GEORGE SANTAYANA
Scepticism and Animal Faith, IX

It was on a mission of insurgency and subversion. The enemy was vastly larger and more powerful. But it knew the enemy's weakness. It could take over the alien government, turning the resources of the adversary to its own purpose. Now, with millions of dedicated agents in place . . .

She sneezed and tried to find a clean paper tissue in the bulging pocket of the terry-cloth presidential bathrobe. She had no makeup on, although her chapped lips revealed patches of mentholated balm.

'My doctor tells me I have to stay in bed or I'll get viral pneumonia. I ask him for an antibiotic, and he tells me there's no antibiotic for viruses. So how does he know I have a virus?'

Der Heer opened his mouth to answer, a gesture in the making, when the President cut him short.

'No, never mind. You'll start telling me about DNA and host recognition and I'll need what resources I've got left to listen to your story. If you're not afraid of my virus, pull up a chair.'

'Thank you, Ms President. This is about the primer. I have the report here. There's a long technical section that's included as an appendix. I thought you might be interested in it also. Briefly, we're reading and actually understanding the thing with almost no difficulty. It's a fiendishly clever learning program. I don't mean "fiendishly" in any literal sense, of course. We must have a vocabulary of three thousand words by now.'

'I don't understand how it's possible. I could see how they could teach you the names of their numbers. You make one dot and write the letters O N E underneath, and so on. I could see how you could have a picture of a star and then write S T A R under it. But I don't see how you could do verbs or the past tense or conditionals.'

'They do some of it with movies. Movies are perfect for verbs. And a lot of it they do with numbers. Even abstractions; they can communicate abstractions with numbers. It goes something like this: First they count out the numbers for us, and then they introduce some new words – words we don't understand. Here, I'll indicate their words by letters. We read something like this (the letters stand for symbols the Vegans introduce).' He wrote:

$$1A1B2Z$$
$$1A2B3Z$$
$$1A7B8Z$$

'What do you think it is?'

'My high school report card? You mean there's a combination of dots and dashes that A stands for, and a different combination of dots and dashes that B stands for, and so on?'

'Exactly. You know what one and two mean, but you don't know what A and B mean. What does a sequence like this tell you?'

'A means "plus" and B means "equals." Is that what you're getting at?'

'Good. But we don't yet understand what Z means, right? Now along comes something like this':

234

'You see?'
'Maybe. Give me another that ends in Y.'

2000A4000B0Y

'Okay, I think I got it. As long as I don't read the last three symbols as a word. Z means it's true, and Y means it's false.'

'Right. Exactly. Pretty good for a President with a virus and a South African crisis. So with a few lines of text they've taught us four words: plus, equals, true, false. Four pretty useful words. Then they teach division, divide one by zero, and tell us the word for infinity. Or maybe it's just the word for indeterminate. Or they say, "The sum of the interior angles of a triangle is two right angles." Then they comment that the statement is true if space is flat, but false if space is curved. So you've learned how to say "if" and −'

'I didn't know space *was* curved. Ken, what the hell are you talking about? How can space be curved? No, never mind, never mind. That can't have anything to do with the business in front of us.'

'Actually . . .'

'Sol Hadden tells me it was his idea where to find the primer. Don't look at me funny, der Heer. I talk to all types.'

'I didn't mean . . . ah . . . As I understand it, Mr Hadden volunteered a few suggestions, which had all been made by other scientists as well. Dr Arroway checked them out and hit paydirt with one of them. It's called phase modulation, or phase coding.'

'Yes. Now, is this correct, Ken? The primer is scattered throughout the Message, right? Lots of repetitions. And there was some primer shortly after Arroway first picked up the signal.'

'Shortly after she picked up the third layer of the palimpsest, the Machine design.'

'And many countries have the technology to read the primer, right?'

'Well, they need a device called a phase correlator. But, yes. The countries that count, anyway.'

'Then the Russians could have read the primer a year ago, right? Or the Chinese or the Japanese. How do you know they're not halfway to building the Machine right now?'

'I thought of that, but Marvin Yang says it's impossible. Satellite photography, electronic intelligence, people on the scene, all confirm that there's no sign of the kind of major construction project you'd need to build the Machine. No, we've *all* been asleep at the switch. We were seduced by the idea that the primer had to come at the beginning and not interspersed through the Message. It's only when the Message recycled and we discovered it wasn't there that we started thinking of other possibilities. All this work has been done in close cooperation with the Russians and everybody else. We don't think anybody has the jump on us, but on the other hand everybody has the primer now. I don't think there's any unilateral course of action for us.'

'I don't *want* a unilateral course of action for us. I just want to make sure that nobody *else* has a unilateral course of action. Okay, so back to your primer. You know how to say true–false, if–then, and space is curved. How do you build a Machine with that?'

'You know, I don't think this cold or whatever you've got has slowed you down a bit. Well, it just takes off from there. For example, they draw us a periodic table of the elements, so they get to name all the chemical elements, the idea of an atom, the idea of a nucleus, protons, neutrons, electrons. They they run through some quantum mechanics just to make sure we're paying attention – there are already some new insights for us in the remedial stuff. Then it starts concentrating on the particular materials needed for the construction. For example, for some reason we need two tons of erbium, so they run through a nifty technique to extract it from ordinary rocks.'

Der Heer raised his hand palm outward in a placatory gesture. 'Don't ask why we need two tons of erbium. Nobody has the faintest idea.'

'I wasn't going to ask that. I want to know how they told you how much a ton is.'

'They counted it out for us in Planck masses. A Planck mass is –'

'Never mind, never mind. It's something that physicists all over the universe know about, right? And I've never heard of it. Now, the bottom line. Do we understand the primer well enough to start reading the Message? Will we be able to build the thing or not?'

'The answer seems to be yes. We've only had the primer for a few weeks now, but whole chapters of the Message are falling into our lap in clear. Its painstaking design, redundant explanations, and as far as we can tell, tremendous redundancy in the Machine design. We should have a three-dimensional model of the Machine for you in time for that crew-selection meeting on Thursday, if you feel up to it. So far, we haven't a clue as to what the Machine does, or how it works. And there are some funny organic chemical components that don't make any sense as part of a machine. But almost everybody seems to think we can build the thing.'

'Who doesn't?'

'Well, Lunacharsky and the Russians. And Billy Jo Rankin, of course. There are still people who worry that the Machine will blow up the world or tip the Earth's axis, or something. But what's impressed most of the scientists is how careful the instructions are, and how many different ways they go about trying to explain the same thing.'

'And what does Eleanor Arroway say?'

'She says if they want to do us in, they'll be here in

twenty-five years or so and there's nothing we could do in twenty-five years to protect ourselves. They're too far ahead of us. So she says, Build it, and if you're worried about environmental hazards, build it in a remote place. Professor Drumlin says you can build it in downtown Pasadena for all he cares. In fact, he says he'll be there every minute it takes to construct the Machine, so he'll be the first to go if it blows up.'

'Drumlin, he's the fellow who figured out that this was the design for a Machine, right?'

'Not exactly, he –'

'I'll read all the briefing material in time for that Thursday meeting. You got anything else for me?'

'Are you seriously considering letting Hadden build the Machine?'

'Well, it's not only up to me, as you know. That treaty they're hammering out in Paris gives us about a one-quarter say. The Russians have a quarter, the Chinese and the Japanese together have a quarter, and the rest of the world has a quarter, roughly speaking. A lot of nations want to build the Machine, or at least parts of it. They're thinking about prestige, and new industries, new knowledge. As long as no one gets a jump on us, that all sounds fine to me. It's possible Hadden might have a piece of it. What's the problem? Don't you think he's technically competent?'

'He certainly is. It's just –' ·

'If there's nothing more, Ken, I'll see you Thursday, virus willing.'

As der Heer was shutting the door and entering the adjacent sitting room, there was an explosive presidential sneeze. The Warrant Officer of the Day, sitting stiffly on a couch, was visibly startled. The briefcase at his feet was crammed with authorization codes for nuclear war. Der Heer calmed him with a repetitive gesture of his hand, fingers spread, palm down. The officer gave an apologetic smile.

*

'That's Vega? That's what all the fuss is about?' the President asked with some disappointment. The photo opportunity for the press was now over, and her eyes had become almost dark-adapted after the onslaught of flashbulbs and television lighting. The pictures of the President gazing steely-eyed through the Naval Observatory telescope that appeared in all the papers the next day were, of course, a minor sham. She had been unable to see anything at all through the telescope until the photographers had left and darkness returned.

'Why does it wiggle?'

'It's turbulence in the air, Ms President,' der Heer explained. 'Warm bubbles of air go by and distort the image.'

'Like looking at Si across the breakfast table when there's a toaster between us. I can remember seeing one whole side of his face fall off,' she said affectionately, raising her voice so the presidential consort, standing nearby talking to the uniformed Commandant of the Observatory, could overhear.

'Yeah, no toaster on the breakfast table these days,' he replied amiably.

Seymour Lasker was before his retirement a high official of the International Ladies Garment Workers Union. He had met his wife decades before when she was representing the New York Girl Coat Company, and they had fallen in love over a protracted labor settlement. Considering the present novelty of both their positions, the apparent health of their relationship was noteworthy.

'I can do without the toaster, but I'm not getting enough breakfasts with Si.' She inflected her eyebrows in his general direction, and then returned to the monocular eyepiece. 'It looks like a blue amoeba, all . . . squishy.'

After the difficult crew-selection meeting, the President was in a lighthearted frame of mind. Her cold was almost gone.

'What if there was no turbulence, Ken? What would I see then?'

239

'Then it would be just like Space Telescope above the Earth's atmosphere. You'd see a steady, unflickering point of light.'

'Just the star? Just Vega? No planets, no rings, no laser battle stations?'

'No, Ms President. All that would be much too small and faint to see even with a very big telescope.'

'Well, I hope your scientists know what they're doing,' she said in a near whisper. 'We're making an awful lot of commitments on something we've never seen.'

Der Heer was a little taken aback. 'But we've seen thirty-one thousand pages of text – pictures, words, plus a huge primer.'

'In my book, that's not the same as *seeing* it. It's a little too . . . inferential. Don't tell me about scientists all over the world getting the same data. I know all that. And don't tell me about how clear and unambiguous the blueprints for the Machine are. I know that too. And if we back out, someone else is sure to build the Machine. I know all those things. But I'm still nervous.'

The party ambled back through the Naval Observatory compound to the Vice President's residence. Tentative agreements on crew selection had been painstakingly worked out in Paris in the last weeks. The United States and the Soviet Union had argued for two crew positions each; on such matters they were reliable allies. But it was hard to sustain this argument with the other nations in the World Message Consortium. These days it was much more difficult for the United States and the Soviet Union – even on issues on which they agreed – to work their way with the other nations of the world than had once been the case.

The enterprise was now widely touted as an activity of the human species. The name 'World Message Consortium' was about to be changed to 'World Machine Consortium.' Nations with pieces of the Message tried to use this fact as an entree for one of their nationals as a member of the crew. The Chinese had quietly argued that by the middle of the next century there would be one and a half billion of them in the world, but with many born as only children because of the Chinese experiment on state-supported birth control. Those children, once grown, would be brighter, they predicted, and more emotionally secure than children of other nations with less stringent rules on family size. Since the Chinese would thus be playing a more prominent role in world affairs in another fifty years, they argued, they deserved at least one of the five seats on the Machine. It was an argument now being discussed in many nations by officials with no responsibility for the Message or the Machine.

Europe and Japan surrendered crew representation in exchange for major responsibility for the construction of Machine components, which they believed would be of major economic benefit. In the end, a seat was reserved for the United States, the Soviet Union, China, and India, with the fifth seat undecided. This represented a long and difficult multilateral negotiation, with population size, economic, industrial, and military power, present political alignments, and even a little of the history of the human species as considerations.

For the fifth seat, Brazil and Indonesia made representations based on population size and geographical balance; Sweden proposed a moderating role in case of political disputes; Egypt, Iraq, Pakistan and Saudi Arabia argued on grounds of religious equity. Others suggested that at least this fifth seat should be decided on grounds of individual merit rather than national affiliation. For the moment, the decision was left in limbo, a wild card for later.

In the four selected nations, scientists, national leaders, and others were going through the exercise of choosing their candidates. A kind of national debate ensued in the United States. In surveys and opinion polls, religious leaders, sports heroes, astronauts, Congressional Medal of Honor winners, scientists, movie actors, a former presidential spouse, television talk show hosts and news anchors, members of Congress, millionaires with political ambitions, foundation executives, singers of country-and-western and rock-and-roll music, university presidents, and the current Miss America were all endorsed with varying degrees of enthusiasm.

By long tradition, ever since the Vice President's residence was moved to the grounds of the Naval Observatory, the house servants had been Filipino petty officers on active duty in the US Navy. Wearing smart blue blazers with a patch embroidered 'Vice-President of the United States,' they were now serving coffee. Most of the participants in the all-day crew-selection meeting had not been invited to this informal evening session.

It had been Seymour Lasker's singular fate to be America's first First Gentleman. He bore his burden – the editorial cartoons, the smarmy jokes, the witticism that he had gone where no man had gone before – with such directness and good nature that at last America was able to forgive him for marrying a woman with the nerve to imagine that she could lead half the world. Lasker had the Vice President's wife and teenaged son laughing uproariously as the President guided der Heer into an adjacent library annex.

'All right,' she began. 'There's no official decision to be made today and no public announcement of our deliberations. But let's see if we can sum up. We don't know what the goddamn Machine will do, but it's a reasonable guess that it goes to Vega. Nobody has the slightest idea of how it would work or even how long it would take. Tell me again, how far away is Vega?'

'Twenty-six light-years, Ms President.'

'And so if this Machine were a kind of spaceship and could travel as fast as light – I know it can't travel as fast as light, only close to it, don't interrupt – then it would take twenty-six years for it to get there, but only as we measure time here on Earth. Is that right, der Heer?'

'Yes. Exactly. Plus maybe a year to get up to light speed and a year to decelerate into the Vega system. But from the standpoint of the crew members, it would take a lot less. Maybe only a couple of years, depending on how close to light speed they travel.'

'For a biologist, der Heer, you've been learning a lot of astronomy.'

'Thank you, Ms President. I've tried to immerse myself in the subject.'

She stared at him for just a moment and then went on. 'So as long as the Machine goes very close to the speed of light, it might not matter much how old the crew members are. But if it takes ten or twenty years or more – and you say that's possible – then we ought to have somebody young. Now, the Russians aren't buying this argument. We understand it's between Arkhangelsky and Lunacharsky, both in their sixties.'

She had read the names somewhat haltingly off a file card in front of her.

'The Chinese are almost certainly sending Xi. He's also in his sixties. So if I thought they knew what they're doing, I'd be tempted to say, "What the hell, let's send a sixty-year-old man."'

Drumlin, der Heer knew, was exactly sixty years old.

'On the other hand . . .' he counterposed.

'I know, I know. The Indian doctor; she's in her forties. . . . In a way, this is the stupidest thing I ever heard of. We're picking somebody to enter the Olympics, and we don't know what the events are. I don't know why we're talking about sending scientists. Mahatma Gandhi, that's who we should send. Or, while we're at it, Jesus Christ. Don't tell me they're not available, der Heer. I know that.'

'When you don't know what the events are, you send a decathlon champion.'

'And then you discover the event is chess, or oratory, or sculpture, and your athlete finishes last. Okay, you say that it ought to be someone who's thought about

243

extraterrestial life and who's been intimately involved with the receipt and decrypting of the Message.'

'At least a person like that will be intimately involved with how the Vegans think. Or at least how they expect us to think.'

'And for really top-rate people, you say that reduces the field to three.'

Again she consulted her notes. 'Arroway, Drumlin, and . . . the one who thinks he's a Roman general.'

'Dr Valerian, Ms President. I don't know that he *thinks* he's a Roman general; it's just his name.'

'Valerian wouldn't even answer the Selection Committee's questionnaire. He wouldn't consider it because he won't leave his wife? Is that right? I'm not criticizing him. He's no dope. He knows how to make a relationship work. It's not that his wife is sick or anything?'

'No, as far as I know, she's in excellent health.'

'Good. Good for them. Send her a personal note from me – something about how she must be some woman for an astronomer to give up the universe for her. But fancy up the language, der Heer. You know what I want. And throw in some quotation. Poetry, maybe. But not too gushy.' She waved her index finger at him. 'Those Valerians can teach us all something. Why don't we invite them to a state dinner? The King of Nepal's here in two weeks. That'll be about right.'

Der Heer was scribbling furiously. He would have to call the White House Appointments Secretary at home as soon as this meeting was over, and he had a still more urgent call. He had not been able to get to the telephone for hours.

'So that leaves Arroway and Drumlin. She's something like twenty years younger, but he's in terrific physical shape. He hang-glides, skydives, scuba dives . . . he's a brilliant scientist, he helped in a big way to crack the Message, and he'll have a fine time arguing with all the other old men. He didn't work on nuclear weapons, did he? I don't want to send anybody who worked on nuclear weapons.

'Now, Arroway's also a brilliant scientist. She's led this whole Argus Project, she knows all the ins and outs of the Message, and she has an inquiring mind. Everybody says that her interests are very broad. And she'd convey a younger American image.' She paused.

'And you like her, Ken. Nothing wrong with that. I like her too. But sometimes she's a loose cannon. Did you listen carefully to her questionnaire?'

'I think I know the passage you're talking about, Ms President. But the Selection Committee had been asking her questions for almost eight hours and sometimes she gets annoyed at what she considers dumb questions. Drumlin's the same way. Maybe she learned it from him. She was his student for a while, you know.'

'Yeah, he said some dumb things, too. Here, it's supposed to be all cued up for us on this VCR. First Arroway's questionnaire, then Drumlin's. Just press the "play" button, Ken.'

On the television screen, Ellie was being interviewed in her office at the Argus Project. He could even make out the yellowing piece of paper with the quote from Kafka. Perhaps, all things considered, Ellie would have been happier had she received only silence from the stars. There were lines around her mouth and bags under her eyes. There were also two unfamiliar vertical creases on her forehead just above her nose. Ellie on videotape looked terribly tired, and der Heer felt a pang of guilt.

'What do I think of "the world population crisis"?' Ellie was saying. 'You mean am I for it or against it? You think this is a key question I'm going to be asked on Vega, and you want to make sure I give the right answer? Okay. Overpopulation is why I'm in favor of homosexuality and a celibate clergy. A celibate clergy is an especially good idea, because it tends to suppress any hereditary propensity toward fanaticism.'

Ellie waited, deadpan, indeed frozen, for the next

question. The President had pushed the 'pause' button.

'Now, I admit that some of the questions may not have been the best,' the President continued. 'But we didn't want anybody in such a prominent position, on a project with really positive international implications, who turns out to be some racist bozo. We want the developing world on our side in this one. We had a good reason to ask a question like that. Don't you find her answer shows some . . . lack of tact? She's a bit of a wiseass, your Dr Arroway. Now take a look at Drumlin.'

Wearing a blue polka-dot bow tie, Drumlin was looking tanned and very fit. 'Yes, I know we all have emotions,' he was saying. 'but let's bear in mind exactly what emotions are. They're motivations for adaptive behavior from a time when we were too stupid to figure things out. But I can figure out that if a pack of hyenas are headed toward me with their fangs bared there's trouble ahead. I don't need a few cc's of adrenaline to help me understand the situation. I can even figure out that it might be important for me to make some genetic contribution to the next generation. I don't really need testosterone in my bloodstream to help me along. Are you sure that an extraterrestrial being far in advance of us is going to be saddled with emotions? I know there are people who think I'm too cold, too reserved. But if you really want to understand the extraterrestrials, you'll send *me*. I'm more like them than anyone else you'll find.'

'Some choice!' the President said. 'The one's an atheist, and the other thinks he's from Vega already. Why do we have to send scientists? Why can't we send somebody . . . normal? Just a rhetorical question,' she quickly added. 'I know why we have to send scientists. The Message is about science and it's written in scientific language. Science is what we know we share with the beings on Vega. No, those are good reasons, Ken. I remember them.'

'She's not an atheist. She's an agnostic. Her mind is

246

open. She's not trapped by dogma. She's intelligent, she's tough, and she's very professional. The range of her knowledge is broad. She's just the person we need in this situation.'

'Ken, I'm pleased by your commitment to uphold the integrity of this project. But there's a great deal of fear out there. Don't think I don't know how much the men out there have had to swallow already. More than half the people I talk to believe we've got no business building this thing. If there's no turning back, they want to send somebody absolutely safe. Arroway may be all the things you say she is, but safe she isn't. I'm catching a lot of heat from the Hill, from the Earth-Firsters, from my own National Committee, from the churches. I guess she impressed Palmer Joss in that California meeting, but she managed to infuriate Billy Jo Rankin. He called me up yesterday and said "Ms President" – he can't disguise his distaste at saying "Ms" – "Ms President," he says, "that Machine's gonna fly straight to God or the Devil. Whichever one it is, you better send an honest-to-God Christian." He tried to use his relationship with Palmer Joss to muscle me, for God's sake. I don't think there's any doubt he was angling to go himself. Drumlin's going to be much more acceptable to somebody like Rankin than Arroway is.

'I recognize Drumlin's something of a cold fish. But he's reliable, patriotic, sound. He has impeccable scientific credentials. And he wants to go. No, it has to be Drumlin. The best I can offer is to have her as a backup.'

'Can I tell her that?'

'We can't have Arroway knowing before Drumlin, can we? I'll let you know the moment a final decision is made and we've informed Drumlin. . . Oh, cheer up, Ken. Don't you *want* her to stay here on Earth?'

It was after six when Ellie finished her briefing of the State Department's 'Tiger Team' that was backstopping the American negotiators in Paris. Der Heer had promised to call her as soon as the crew-selection meeting was done. He wanted her to hear from him whether she had been selected, not from anybody else. She had been insufficiently deferential to the examiners, she knew, and might lose out for that reason among a dozen others. Nevertheless, she guessed, there might still be a chance.

There was a message waiting for her at the hotel – not a pink 'while you were out' form filled in by the hotel operator, but a sealed unstamped hand-delivered letter. It read: 'Meet me at the National Science and Technology Museum, 8:00 pm tonight. Palmer Joss.'

No hello, no explanations, no agenda, and no yours truly, she thought. This really *is* a man of faith. The stationery was her hotel's, and there was no return address. He must have sauntered in this afternoon, knowing from the Secretary of State himself, for all she knew, that Ellie was in town, and expecting her to be in. It had been a tiresome day, and she was annoyed at having to spend any time away from piecing together the Message. Although a part of her was reluctant to go, she showered, changed, bought a bag of cashews, and was in a taxi in forty-five minutes.

It was about an hour before closing, and the museum was almost empty. Huge dark machinery was stuffed into every corner of a vast entrance hall. Here was the pride of the nineteenth-century shoemaking, textile, and coal industries. A steam calliope from the 1876 Exposition was playing a jaunty piece, originally written for brass she judged, for a tourist group from West Africa. Joss was nowhere to be seen. She suppressed the impulse to turn on her heel and leave.

If you had to meet Palmer Joss in this museum, she thought, and the only thing you had ever talked to him about was religion and the Message, where would you meet him? It was a little like the frequency selection problem in SETI: You haven't yet received a message from an advanced civilization and you have to decide on which frequencies these beings – about whom you know

248

virtually nothing, not even their existence – have decided to transmit. It must involve some knowledge that both you and they share. You and they certainly both know what the most abundant kind of atom in the universe is, and the single radio frequency at which it characteristically absorbs and emits. That was the logic by which the 1420 megahertz line of neutral atomic hydrogen had been included in all the early SETI searches. What would the equivalent be here? Alexander Graham Bell's telephone? The telegraph? Marconi's – Of course.

'Does this museum have a Foucault pendulum?' she asked the guard.

The sound of her heels echoed on the marble floors as she approached the rotunda. Joss was leaning over the railing, peering at a mosaic tile representation of the cardinal directions. There were small vertical hour marks, some upright, others evidently knocked down by the bob earlier in the day. Around 7 P.M. someone had stopped its swing, and it now hung motionless. They were entirely alone. He had heard her approach for a minute at least and had said nothing.

'You've decided that prayer *can* stop a pendulum?' She smiled.

'That would be an abuse of faith,' he replied.

'I don't see why. You'd make an awful lot of converts. It's easy enough for God to do, and if I remember correctly, you talk to Him regularly. . . . That's not it, huh? You really want to test my faith in the physics of harmonic oscillators? Okay.'

A part of her was amazed that Joss would put her through this test, but she was determined to pass muster. She let her handbag slide off her shoulder and removed her shoes. He gracefully hurdled the brass guardrail and helped her over. They half walked and half slid down the tiled slope until they were standing alongside the bob. It had a dull black finish, and she wondered whether it was made of steel or lead.

'You'll have to give me a hand,' she said. She could

249

easily put her arms around the bob, and together they wrestled it until it was inclined at a good angle from the vertical and flush against her face. Joss was watching her closely. He didn't ask her whether she was sure, he neglected to warn her about falling forward, he offered no cautions about giving the bob a horizontal component of velocity as she let go. Behind her was a good meter or meter and a half of level floor, before it started sloping upward to become a circumferential wall. If she kept her wits about her, she said to herself, this was a lead-pipe cinch.

She let go. The bob fell away from her.

The period of a simple pendulum, she thought a little giddily, is 2π, square root L over g, where L is the length of the pendulum and g is the acceleration due to gravity. Because of friction in the bearing, the pendulum can never swing back farther than its original position. All I have to do is not sway forward, she reminded herself.

Near the opposite railing, the bob slowed and came to a dead stop. Reversing its trajectory, it was suddenly moving much faster than she had expected. As it careened toward her, it seemed to grow alarmingly in size. It was enormous and almost upon her. She gasped.

'I flinched,' Ellie said in disappointment as the bob fell away from her.

'Only the littlest bit.'

'No, I flinched.'

'You believe. You believe in science. There's only a tiny smidgen of doubt.'

'No, that's not it. That was a million years of brains fighting a billion years of instinct. That's why your job is so much easier than mine.'

'In this matter, our jobs are the same. My turn,' he said, and jarringly grabbed the bob at the highest point on its trajectory.

'But we're not testing *your* belief in the conservation of energy.'

He smiled and tried to dig in his feet.

'What you doin' down there?' a voice asked. 'Are you folks crazy?' A museum guard, dutifully checking that all visitors would leave by closing time, had come upon this unlikely prospect of a man, a woman, a pit and a pendulum in an otherwise deserted recess of the cavernous building.

'Oh, it's all right, officer,' Joss said cheerfully. 'We're just testing our faith.'

'You can't do that in the Smithsonian Institution,' the guard replied. 'This is a museum.'

Laughing, Joss and Ellie wrestled the bob to a nearly stationary position and clambered up the sloping tile walls.

'It must be permitted by the First Amendment,' she said.

'Or the First Commandment,' he replied.

She slipped on her shoes, shouldered her bag, and, head held high, accompanied Joss and the guard out of the rotunda. Without identifying themselves and without being recognized, they managed to talk him out of arresting them. But they were escorted out of the museum by a tight phalanx of uniformed personnel, who were concerned perhaps that Ellie and Joss might next sidle aboard the steam calliope in pursuit of an elusive God.

The street was deserted. They walked wordlessly along the Mall. The night was clear, and Ellie made out Lyra against the horizon.

'The bright one over there. That's Vega,' she said.

He stared at it for a long time. 'That decoding was a brilliant achievement,' he said at last.

'Oh, nonsense. It was trivial. It was the easiest message an advanced civilization could think of. It would have been a genuine disgrace if we hadn't been able to figure it out.'

'You don't take compliments well, I've noticed. No, this is one of those discoveries that change the future.

251

Our expectations of the future, anyway. It's like fire, or writing, or agriculture. Or the Annunciation.'

He stared again at Vega. 'If you could have a seat in that Machine, if you could ride it back to its Sender, what do you think you would see?'

'Evolution is a stochastic process. There are just too many possibilities to make reasonable predictions about what life elsewhere might be like. If you had seen the Earth before the origin of life, would you have predicted a katydid or a giraffe?'

'I know the answer to that question. I guess you imagine that we just make this stuff up. That we read it in some book, or pick it up in some prayer tent. But that's not how it is. I have certain, positive knowledge from my own direct experience. I can't put it any plainer than that. I have seen God face to face.'

About the depth of his commitment there seemed no doubt.

'Tell me about it.'

So he did.

'Okay,' she said finally, 'you were clinically dead, then you revived, and you remember rising through the darkness into a bright light. You saw a radiance with a human form that you took to be God. But there was nothing in the experience that told you the radiance made the universe or laid down moral law. The experience is an experience. You were deeply moved by it, no question. But there are other possible explanations.'

'Such as?'

'Well, like birth. Birth is rising through a long, dark tunnel into a brilliant light. Don't forget how brilliant it is – the baby has spent nine months in the dark. Birth is its first encounter with light. Think of how amazed and awed you'd be in your first contact with color, or light and shade, or the human face – which you're probably preprogrammed to recognize. Maybe, if you almost die, the odometer gets set back to zero for a moment. Understand, I don't insist on this explanation. It's just one of many possibilities. I'm suggesting you may have misinterpreted the experience.'

'You haven't seen what I've seen.'

He looked up once more at the cold flickering blue-white light from Vega, and then turned to her.

'Don't you ever feel . . . lost in your universe? How do you know what to do, how to behave, if there's no God? Just obey the law or get arrested?'

'You're not worried about being lost, Palmer. You're worried about not being central, not the reason the universe was created. There's plenty of order in my universe. Gravitation, electromagnetism, quantum mechanics, superunification, they all involve laws. And as for behavior, why can't we *figure out* what's in our best interest – as a species?'

'That's a warmhearted and noble view of the world, I'm sure, and I'd be the last to deny that there's goodness in the human heart. But how much cruelty has been done when there was no love of God?'

'And how much cruelty when there was? Savonarola and Torquemada loved God, or so they said. Your religion assumes that people are children and need a boogeyman so they'll behave. You want people to believe in God so they'll obey the law. That's the only means that occurs to you: a strict secular police force, and the threat of punishment by an all-seeing God for whatever the police overlook. You sell human beings short.

'Palmer, you think if I haven't had your religious experience I can't appreciate the magnificence of your god. But it's just the opposite. I listen to you, and I think, His god is too small! One paltry planet, a few thousand years – hardly worth the attention of a minor deity, much less the Creator of the universe.'

'You're confusing me with some other preacher. That museum was Brother Rankin's territory. I'm prepared for a universe billions of years old. I just say the scientists haven't proved it.'

'And I say you haven't understood the evidence. How can it benefit the people if the conventional wisdom, the religious "truths," are a lie? When you really believe that people can be adults, you'll preach a different sermon.'

There was a brief silence, punctuated only by the echoes of their footfalls.

'I'm sorry if I've been a little too strident,' she said. 'It happens to me from time to time.'

'I give you my word, Dr Arroway, I'll carefully ponder what you've said this evening. You've raised some questions I should have answers for. But in the same spirit, let me ask you a few questions. Okay?'

She nodded, and he continued. 'Think of what consciousness feels like, what it feels like this minute. Does that *feel* like billions of tiny atoms wiggling in place? And beyond the biological machinery, where in science can a child learn what love is? Here's –'

Her beeper buzzed. It was probably Ken with the news she had been waiting for. If so, it had been a very long meeting for him. Maybe it was good news nevertheless. She glanced at the letters and numbers forming in the liquid crystal: Ken's office number. There were no public telephones in sight, but after a few minutes they were able to flag down a taxicab.

'I'm sorry I have to leave so suddenly,' she apologized. 'I enjoyed our conversation, and I'll think seriously about your questions. . . . You wanted to pose one more?'

'Yes. What is there in the precepts of science that keeps a scientist from doing evil?'

15

Erbium Dowel

The earth, that is sufficient,
I do not want the constellations any nearer,
I know they are very well where they are,
I know they suffice for those who belong
to them.

— WALT WHITMAN
Leaves of Grass
'Song of the Open Road' (1855)

It took years, it was a technological dream and a diplomatic nightmare, but finally they got around to building the Machine. Various neologisms were proposed, and project names evocative of ancient myths. But from the beginning everyone had called it simply the Machine, and that became its official designation. The continuing complex and delicate international negotiations were described by Western editorial writers as 'Machine Politics.' When the first reliable estimate of the total cost was generated, even the titans of the aerospace industry gasped. Eventually, it came to half a trillion dollars a years for some years, roughly a third of the total military budget – nuclear and conventional – of the planet. There were fears that building the Machine would ruin the world economy. 'Economic Warfare from Vega?' asked the London *Economist*. The daily headlines in *The New York Times* were, by any dispassionate measure, more bizarre than any in the now defunct *National Enquirer* a decade earlier.

The record will show that no psychic, seer, prophet, or soothsayer, no person with claimed precognitive abilities, no astrologer, no numerologist, and no late-

December copywriter on 'The Year Ahead' had predicted the Message or the Machine – much less Vega, prime numbers, Adolf Hitler, the Olympics, and the rest. There were many claims, however, by those who had clearly foreseen the events but had carelessly neglected to write the precognition down. Predictions of surprising events always prove more accurate if not set down on paper beforehand. It is one of those odd regularities of everyday life. Many religions were in a slightly different category: A careful and imaginative perusal of their sacred writings will reveal, it was argued, a clear foretelling of these wondrous happenings.

For others, the Machine represented a potential bonanza for the world aerospace industry, which had been in worrisome decline since the Hiroshima Accords took full force. Very few new strategic weapons systems were under development. Habitats in space were a growing business, but they hardly compensated for the loss of orbiting laser battle stations and other accoutrements of the strategic defense envisioned by an earlier administration. Thus, some of those who worried about the safety of the planet if the Machine were to be built swallowed their scruples when contemplating the implications for jobs, profits, and career advancement.

A well-placed few argued that there was no richer prospect for the high-technology industries than a threat from space. There would have to be defenses, immensely powerful surveillance radars, eventual outposts on Pluto or in the Oort Comet Cloud. No amount of discourse about military disparities between terrestrials and extra-terrestrials could daunt these visionaries. 'Even if we can't defend ourselves against them,' they asked, 'don't you want us to see them coming?' There was profit here and they could smell it. They were building the Machine, of course, trillions of dollars' worth of Machine; but the Machine was only the beginning, if they played their cards right.

An unlikely political alliance coalesced behind the

re-election of President Lasker, which became in effect a national referendum on whether to build the Machine. Her opponent warned of Trojan Horses and Doomsday Machines and the prospect of demoralization of American ingenuity in the face of aliens who had already 'invented everything.' The President pronounced herself confident that American technology would rise to the challenge and implied, although she did not actually say, that American ingenuity would eventually equal anything they had on Vega. She was re-elected by a respectable but by no means overwhelming margin.

The instructions themselves were a decisive factor. Both in the primer on language and basic technology and in the Message on the construction of the Machine nothing was left unclear. Sometimes intermediate steps that seemed entirely obvious were spelled out in tedious detail – as when, in the foundations of arithmetic, it is proved that if two times three equals six, then three times two also equals six. At every stage of construction there were checkpoints: The erbium produced by this process should be 96 percent pure, with no more than a fraction of a percent impurity from the other rare earths. When Component 31 is completed and placed in a 6 molar solution of hydrofluoric acid, the remaining structural elements should look like the diagram in the accompanying figure. When Component 408 is assembled, application of a two megagauss transverse magnetic field should spin the rotor up to so many revolutions per second before it returns itself to a motionless state. If any of the tests failed, you went back and redid the whole business.

After a while you got used to the tests, and you expected to be able to pass them. It was akin to rote memorization. Many of the underlying components, constructed by special factories designed from scratch by following the primer instructions, defied human understanding. It was hard to see why they should work. But they did. Even in such cases, practical applications of the new technologies could be contemplated. Occasionally promising insights seemed to be available for the skimming – in metallurgy, for example, or in organic semiconductors. In some cases several alternative technologies were supplied to produce an equivalent component; the extraterrestrials could not be sure, apparently, which approach would be easiest for the technology of the Earth.

As the first factories were built and the first prototypes produced, pessimism diminished about human ability to reconstruct an alien technology from a Message written in no known language. There was the heady feeling of arriving unprepared for a school test and finding that you can figure out the answers from your general education and your common sense. As in all competently designed examinations, taking it was a learning experience. All the first tests were passed: The erbium was of adequate purity; the pictured superstructure was left after the inorganic material was etched away by hydrofluoric acid; the rotor spun up as advertised. The Message flattered the scientists and engineers, critics said; they were becoming caught up in the technology and losing sight of the dangers.

For the construction of one component, a particularly intricate set of organic chemical reactions was specified and the resulting product was introduced into a swimming pool-sized mixture of formaldehyde and aqueous ammonia. The mass grew, differentiated, specialized, and then just sat there – exquisitely more complex than anything like it humans knew how to build. It had an intricately branched network of fine hollow tubes, through which perhaps some fluid was to circulate. It was colloidal, pulpy, dark red. It did not make copies of itself, but it was sufficiently biological to scare a great many people. They repeated the procedure and produced something apparently identical. How the end product could be significantly more complicated than the instructions that went into building it was a mystery. The organic mass squatted on its platform and did, so far as anyone could tell, nothing. It was to go inside the dodecahedron, just above and below the crew area.

Identical machines were under construction in the United States and the Soviet Union. Both nations had chosen to build in fairly remote places, not so much to protect population centers in case it was a Doomsday Machine as to control access by curiosity seekers, protesters, and the media. In the United States the Machine was built in Wyoming; in the Soviet Union, just beyond the Caucasus, in the Uzbek SSR. New factories were established near the assembly sites. Where components could be manufactured with something like existing industry, manufacturing was widely dispersed. An optical subcontractor in Jena, for example; would make and test components to go to the American and Soviet Machines; and to Japan, where every component was systematically examined to understand how it worked, so far as was possible. Progress out of Hokkaido had been slow.

There was concern that a component subjected to a test unauthorized in the Message might destroy some subtle symbiosis of the various components in a functioning Machine. A major sub-structure of the Machine was three exterior concentric spherical shells, arranged with axes perpendicular to each other, and designed to spin at high velocities. The spherical shells were to have precise and intricate patterns cut into them. Would a shell that had been whirled a few times in an unauthorized test function improperly when assembled into the Machine? Would an inexperienced shell, by contrast, work perfectly?

Hadden Industries was the American prime contractor for Machine construction. Sol Hadden had insisted on no unauthorized testing or even mounting of components intended for eventual assembly into the Machine. The instructions, he ordered, were to be followed to the bit, there being no letters per se in the Message. He urged his employees to think of themselves as medieval necromancers, fastidiously following the words of a magic spell.

259

Do not dare to mispronounce a syllable, he told them.

This was, depending on which calendrical or eschatological doctrine you fancied, two years before the Millennium. So many people were 'retiring,' in happy anticipation of Doomsday or the Advent or both, that in some industries skilled laborers were in short supply. Hadden's willingness to restructure his work force to optimize Machine construction, and to provide incentives for subcontractors, was seen to be a major factor in the American success so far.

But Hadden had also 'retired' – a surprise, considering the well-known views of the inventor of Preachnix. 'The chiliasts made an atheist out of me,' he was quoted as saying. Key decisions were still in his hands, his subordinates said. But communication with Hadden was via fast asynchronous telenetting: His subordinates would leave progress reports, authorization requests, and questions for him in a locked box of a popular scientific telenetting service. His answers would come back in another locked box. It was a peculiar arrangement, but it seemed to be working. As the early, most difficult steps were cleared and the Machine actually was beginning to take shape, less and less was heard from S. R. Hadden. The executives of the World Machine Consortium were concerned, but after what was described as a lengthy visit with Mr Hadden in an unrevealed location, they came away reassured. His whereabouts were unknown to everyone else.

The world strategic inventories fell below 3,200 nuclear weapons for the first time since the middle 1950s. Multilateral talks on the more difficult stages of disarmament, down to a minimum nuclear deterrent, were making progress. The fewer the weapons on one side, the more dangerous would be the sequestering of a small number of weapons by the other. And with the number of delivery systems – which were much easier to verify – also diminishing steeply, with new means of automatic monitoring of treaty compliance being deployed, and with new agreements on on-site inspection, the prospects for further reductions seemed good. The process had generated a kind of momentum of its own in the minds of both the experts and the public. As occurs in the usual kind of arms race, the two powers were vying to keep up with one another but this time in arms reductions. In practical military terms they had not yet given up very much; they still retained the capability of destroying the planetary civilization. However, in the optimism generated for the future, in the hope engendered in the emerging generation, this beginning had already accomplished much. Aided perhaps by the imminent worldwide Millennial celebrations, both secular and canonical, the number of armed hostilities between nations per year had diminished still further. 'The Peace of God,' the Cardinal Archbishop of Mexico City had called it.

In Wyoming and Uzbekistan new industries had been created and whole cities were rising from the ground. The cost was borne disproportionately by the industrialized nations, of course, but the pro rata cost for everyone on Earth was something like one hundred dollars per year. For a quarter of the Earth's population, one hundred dollars was a significant fraction of annual income. The money spent on the Machine produced no goods or services directly. But in stimulating new technology, it was deemed a great bargain, even if the Machine itself never worked.

There were many who felt that the pace had been too swift, that every step should be understood before moving on to the next. If the construction of the Machine took generations, it was argued, so what? Spreading the development costs over decades would lessen the economic burden to the world economy of building the Machine. By many standards this was prudent advice, but it was difficult to implement. How could you develop only one component of the Machine? All over the world, scientists and engineers of varying disciplinary persuasions were straining to be let loose on those aspects of the Machine that overlapped their areas of expertise.

There were some who worried that were the Machine not built quickly, it would never be built. The American President and the Soviet Premier had committed their nations to the construction of the Machine. This was not guaranteed for all possible successors. Also, for perfectly understandable personal reasons, those controlling the project wished to see it completed while they were still in positions of responsibility. Some argued that there was an intrinsic urgency to a Message broadcast on so many frequencies so loudly and for so long. They were not asking us to build the Machine when we were ready. They were asking us to build it now. The pace quickened.

All the early subsystems were based on elementary technologies described in the first part of the primer. The prescribed tests had been passed readily enough. As the later, more complex subsystems were tested, occasional failures were noted. This was apparent in both nations, but was more frequent in the Soviet Union. Since no one knew how the components worked, it was usually impossible to trace backwards from failure mode to identification of the flawed step in the manufacturing process. In some cases the components were made in parallel by two different manufacturers, with competition for speed and accuracy. If there were two components, both of which had passed tests, there was a tendency for each nation to select the domestic product. Thus, the machines that were being assembled in the two countries were not absolutely identical.

Finally, in Wyoming, the day came to begin systems integration, the assembling of the separate components into a complete Machine. It was likely to be the easiest part of the construction process. Completion within a year or two seemed likely. Some thought that activating the Machine would end the world right on schedule.

*

The rabbits were much more astute in Wyoming. Or less. It was hard to figure out. The headlights on the Thunderbird had picked up an occasional rabbit near the road more than once. But hundreds of them organized in ranks – that custom, apparently, had not yet spread from New Mexico to Wyoming. The situation here was not much different from Argus, Ellie found. There was a major scientific facility surrounded by tens of thousands of square kilometers of lovely, almost uninhabited land-scape. She wasn't running the show, and she wasn't one of the crew. But she was *here*, working on one of the grandest enterprises ever contemplated. Surely, no matter what happened after the Machine was activated, the Argus discovery would be judged a turning point in human history.

Just at the moment when some additional unifying force is needed, this bolt comes from the blue. From the black, she corrected herself. From twenty-six light-years away, 230 trillion kilometers. It's hard to think of your primary allegiance as Scottish or Slovenian or Szechuanese when you're all being hailed indiscrimi-nately by a civilization millennia ahead of you. The gap between the most technologically backward nation on the Earth and the industrialized nations was, certainly, much smaller than the gap between the industrialized nations and the beings on Vega. Suddenly, distinctions that had earlier seemed transfixing – racial, religious, national, ethnic, linguistic, economic, and cultural – began to seem a little less pressing.

'We are all humans.' This was a phrase you heard often these days. It was remarkable, in previous decades, how infrequently sentiments of this sort had been expressed, especially in the media. We share the same small planet, it was said, and – very nearly – the same global civilization. It was hard to imagine the extraterrestrials taking seriously a plea for preferential parley from representa-tives of one or another ideological faction. The existence of the Message – even apart from its enigmatic function –

was binding up the world. You could see it happening before your eyes.

Her mother's first question when she heard that Ellie had not been selected was 'Did you cry?' Yes, she had cried. It was only natural. There was, of course, a part of her that longed to be aboard. But Drumlin was a first-rate choice, she had told her mother.

No decision had been made by the Soviets between Lunacharsky and Arkhangelsky; both would 'train' for the mission. It was hard to see what training might be appropriate beyond understanding the Machine as best they, or anyone else, could. Some Americans charged that this was merely an attempt by the Soviets to acquire two principal Machine spokesmen, but Ellie thought this was mean-spirited. Both Lunacharsky and Arkhangelsky were extremely capable. She wondered how the Soviets would decide which to send. Lunacharsky was in the United States, but not here in Wyoming. He was in Washington with a high-level Soviet delegation meeting with the Secretary of State and Michael Kitz, newly promoted to be Deputy Secretary of Defense. Arkhangelsky was back in Uzbekistan.

The new metropolis growing up in the Wyoming wilderness was called Machine; Machine, Wyoming. Its Soviet counterpart was given the Russian equivalent, Makhina. Each was a complex of residences, utilities, residential and business districts, and – most of all – factories. Some of them were unpretentious, at least on the outside. But in others you could see in a single glance their bizarre aspects – domes and minarets, miles of intricate exterior piping. Only the factories that were adjudged potentially dangerous – those manufacturing the organic components, for example – were here in the Wyoming wilderness. Technologies better understood were distributed worldwide. The core of the cluster of new industries was the Systems Integration Facility, built near what had once been Wagonwheel, Wyoming, to which completed components were consigned. Sometimes Ellie would see a component arrive and realize that she had been the first human being ever to see it as a design drawing. As each new part was uncrated, she would rush to inspect it. As components were mounted one upon another, and as subsystems passed their prescribed tests, she felt a kind of glow that she guessed was akin to maternal pride.

Ellie, Drumlin, and Valerian arrived for a routine and long-scheduled meeting on the now wholly redundant worldwide monitoring of the signal from Vega. When they arrived, they found everyone talking about the burning of Babylon. It had happened in the early hours of the morning, perhaps at a time when the place was prowled only by its most iniquitous and unregenerate habitués. A raiding party, equipped with mortars and incendiaries, had struck simultaneously through the Enlil and Ishtar gates. The Ziggurat had been put to the torch. There was a photograph of improbably and scantily clad people rushing from the Temple of Assur. Remarkably, no one was killed, although there were many injuries.

Just before the attack, the *New York Sun*, a paper controlled by the Earth-Firsters and sporting a globe shattered by a lightning bolt on its masthead, received a call announcing that the attack was under way. It was divinely inspired retribution, the caller volunteered, carried out on behalf of decency and American morality, by those sick and tired of filth and corruption. There were statements by the president of Babylon, Inc., decrying the attack and condemning an alleged criminal conspiracy, but – at least so far – not a word from S. R. Hadden, wherever he might be.

Because Ellie was known to have visited Hadden in Babylon, a few of the project personnel sought out her reaction. Even Drumlin was interested in her opinion on this matter, although from his evident knowledge of the geography of the place, it seemed possible that he had visited it more than once himself. She had no trouble imagining him as a charioteer. But perhaps he had only read about Babylon. Photomaps had been published in the weekly newsmagazines.

Eventually, they got back to business. Fundamentally, the Message was continuing on the same frequencies, bandpasses, time constants, and polarization and phase modulation; the Machine design and the primer were still sitting underneath the prime numbers and the Olympic broadcast. The civilization in the Vega system seemed very dedicated. Or maybe they had just forgotten to turn off the transmitter. Valerian had a faraway look in his eyes.

'Peter, why do you have to look at the ceiling when you think?'

Drumlin was reputed to have mellowed over the last few years, but, as with this comment, his reform was not always apparent. Being chosen by the President of the United States to represent the nation to the extraterrestrials was, he would say, a great honor. The trip, he told his intimates, would be the crowning point of his life. His wife, temporarily transplanted to Wyoming and still doggedly faithful, had to endure the same slide shows presented to new audiences of scientists and technicians building the Machine. Since the site was near his native Montana, Drumlin visited there briefly from time to time. Once Ellie had driven him to Missoula. For the first time in their relationship, he had been cordial to her for a few consecutive hours.

'Shhhh! I'm thinking,' replied Valerian. 'It's a noise-suppression technique. I'm trying to minimize the distractions in my visual field, and then you present a distraction in the audio spectrum. You might ask me why I don't just as well stare at a piece of blank paper. But the trouble is that the paper's too small. I can see things in my peripheral vision. Anyway, what I was thinking is this: Why are we still getting the Hitler message, the Olympic broadcast? Years have passed. They must have received the British Coronation broadcast by now. Why

266

haven't we seen some close-ups of Orb and Scepter and ermine, and a voice intoning '. . . now crowned as George the Sixth, by the Grace of God, King of England and Northern Ireland, and Emperor of India"?'

'Are you sure Vega was over England at the time of the Coronation transmission?' Ellie asked.

'Yes, we checked that out within a few weeks of receipt of the Olympic broadcast. And the intensity was stronger than the Hitler thing. I'm sure Vega could have picked up the Coronation transmission.'

'You're worried that they don't want us to know everything they know about us?' she asked.

'They're in a hurry,' said Valerian. He was given occasionally to delphic utterances.

'More likely,' offered Ellie, 'they want to keep reminding us that they know about Hitler.'

'That's not entirely different from what I'm saying,' Valerian replied.

'All right. Let's not waste too much time in Fantasyland,' Drumlin groaned. He was always impatient with speculation on extraterrestrial motivation. It was a total waste of time to guess, he would say; we'll know soon enough. Meanwhile, he urged all and sundry to concentrate on the Message; it was hard data – redundant, unambiguous, brilliantly composed.

'Here, a little reality might fix you two up. Why don't we go into the assembly area? I think they're doing systems integration with the erbium dowels.'

The geometric design of the Machine was simple. The details were extremely complex. The five chairs in which the crew would sit were amidships in the dodecahedron where it bulged out most prominently. There were no facilities for eating or sleeping or other bodily functions, clear evidence that the trip aboard the Machine – if there was one – would be short. Some thought this meant that the Machine, when activated, would quickly rendezvous with an interstellar space vehicle in the vicinity of the Earth. The only difficulty was that meticulous radar and optical searches could find no trace of such a ship. It seemed scarcely likely that the extraterrestrials had overlooked elementary human physiological needs. Maybe the machine didn't *go* anywhere. Maybe it *did* something to the crew. There were no instruments in the crew area, nothing to steer with, not even an ignition key – just the five chairs, pointed inward, so each crew member could watch the others. And there was a carefully prescribed upper limit on the weight of the crew and their belongings. In practice, the constraint worked to the advantage of people of small stature.

Above and below the crew area, in the tapering part of the dodecahedron, were the organics, with their intricate and puzzling architecture. Placed throughout the interior of this part of the dodecahedron, apparently at random, were the dowels of erbium. And surrounding the dodecahedron were the three concentric spherical shells, each in a way representing one of the three physical dimensions. The shells were apparently magnetically suspended – at least the instructions included a powerful magnetic field generator, and the space between the spherical shells and the dodecahedron was to be a high vacuum.

The Message did not name any Machine component. Erbium was identified as the atom with sixty-eight protons and ninety-nine neutrons. The various parts of the Machine were also described numerically – Component 31, for example. So the rotating concentric spherical shells were named benzels by a Czech technician who knew something of the history of technology; Gustav Benzel had, in 1870, invented the merry-go-round.

The design and function of the Machine were unfathomed, it required whole new technologies to construct, but it was made of matter, the structure could be diagrammed – indeed cutaway engineering drawings had appeared in mass media all over the world – and its finished form was readily visualized. There was a continuing mood of technological optimism.

Drumlin, Valerian, and Arroway went through the usual identification sequence, involving credentials, thumbprint and voice-print, and were then admitted to the vast assembly bay. Three-story overhead cranes were positioning erbium dowels in the organic matrix. Several pentagonal panels for the exterior of the dodecahedron were hanging from an elevated railroad track. While the Soviets had had some problems, the US subsystems had finally passed all their tests, and the overall architecture of the Machine was gradually emerging. It's all coming together, Ellie thought. She looked to where the benzels would be assembled. When completed, the Machine would look from the outside like one of those armillary spheres of the Renaissance astronomers. What would Johannes Kepler have made of all this?

The floor and the circumferential tracks at various altitudes in the assembly building were crowded with technicians, government officials, and representatives of the World Machine Consortium. As they watched, Valerian mentioned that the President had established an occasional correspondence with his wife, who would not tell Peter even what it was about. She had pleaded the right of privacy.

The positioning of the dowels was almost completed, and a major systems integration test was about to be attempted for the first time. Some thought the prescribed monitoring device was a gravity wave telescope. Just as the test was to begin, they walked around a stanchion to get a better view.

Suddenly Drumlin was in the air, flying. Everything else seemed to be flying, too. It reminded her of the tornado that had carried Dorothy to Oz. As in a slow motion film, Drumlin careened toward her, arms outstretched, and knocked her roughly to the ground. After all these years, she thought, was this his notion of a sexual overture? He had a lot to learn.

*

269

It was never determined who did it. Organizations publicly claiming responsibility included the Earth-Firsters, the Red Army Faction, the Islamic Jihad, the now underground Fusion Energy Foundation, the Sikh Separatists, Shining Path, the Khmer Vert, the Afghan Renaissance, the radical wing of Mothers Against the Machine, the Reunified Reunification Church, Omega Seven, the Doomsday Chiliasts (although Billy Jo Rankin denied any connection and claimed that the confessions were called in by the impious, in a doomed attempt to discredit God), the Broederbond, El Catorce de Febrero, the Secret Army of the Kuomintang, the Zionist League, the Party of God, and the newly resuscitated Symbionese Liberation Front. Most of these organizations did not have the wherewithal to execute the sabotage; the length of the list was merely an index of how widespread opposition to the Machine had become.

The Ku Klux Klan, the American Nazi Party, the Democratic National Socialist Party, and a few like-minded organizations restrained themselves and did not claim responsibility. An influential minority of their membership believed that the Message had been dispatched by Hitler himself. According to one version, he had been spirited off the Earth by German rocket technology in May 1945, and quite some progress had been made by the Nazis in the intervening years.

'I don't know where the Machine was going,' the President said some months later, 'but if it was half as whacked-out as this planet is, it probably wasn't worth the trip anyway.'

As reconstructed by the Commission of Inquiry, one of the erbium dowels was sundered by an explosion; the two pillbox-shaped fragments careened downward from a height of twenty meters, and were also propelled laterally with considerable velocity. A weight-bearing interior wall was struck and collapsed under the impact. Eleven people were killed and forty-eight injured. A number of major Machine components were destroyed;

and, since an explosion was not among the testing protocols prescribed by the Message, the explosion might have ruined apparently unaffected components. When you had no idea at all about how the thing worked, you had to be very careful about building it.

Despite the profusion of organizations that craved credit, suspicion in the United States focused immediatley on two of the few groups that had not claimed responsibility: the extraterrestrials and the Russians. Talk about Doomsday Machines filled the air once again. The extraterrestrials had designed the Machine to explode catastrophically when assembled, but fortunately, some said, we were careless in assembling it and only a small charge – perhaps the trigger for the Doomsday Machine – blew up. They urged halting construction before it was too late and burying the surviving components in widely dispersed salt mines.

But the Commission of Inquiry found evidence that the Machine Disaster, as it came to be known, was of more Earthly origin. The dowels had a central ellipsoidal cavity of unknown purpose, and its interior wall was lined with an intricate network of fine gadolinium wires. This cavity had been packed with plastic explosive and a timer, materials not on the Message's Inventory of Parts. The dowel had been machined, the cavity lined, and the finished product tested and sealed in a Hadden Cybernetics facility in Terre Haute, Indiana. The gadolinium wiring had been too intricate to do by hand; robot servomechanisms were required, and they in turn had required a major factory to be constructed. The cost of building the factory was defrayed entirely by Hadden Cybernetics, but there would be other, more profitable, applications for its wares.

The other three erbium dowels in the same lot were inspected and revealed no plastic explosive. (Soviet and Japanese crews had performed a range of remote sensing experiments before daring to split their dowels open.) Somebody had carefully packed a tamped charge and timer into the cavity near the end of the construction process in Terre Haute. Once out of the factory this dowel – and those from other batches – had been transported by special train and under armed guard to Wyoming. The timing of the explosion and the nature of the sabotage suggested someone with knowledge of the Machine construction; it was an inside job.

But the investigation made little progress. There were several dozen people – technicians, quality control analysts, inspectors who sealed the component for transshipment – who had the opportunity to commit the sabotage, if not the means and the motivation. Those who failed polygraph tests had ironclad alibis. None of the suspects let drop a confession in an unguarded moment at the neighborhood bar. None began to spend more than their means allowed. No one 'broke' under interrogation. Despite what were said to be vigorous efforts by law-enforcement agencies, the mystery remained unsolved.

Those who believed the Soviets responsible argued that their motive was to prevent the United States from activating its Machine first. The Russians had the technical capability for the sabotage, and, of course, detailed knowledge of Machine construction protocols and practice on both sides of the Atlantic. As soon as the disaster occurred, Anatoly Goldmann, a former student of Lunacharsky's, who was working as Soviet liaison in Wyoming, urgently called Moscow and told them to take down all their dowels. At face value, this conversation – which had been routinely monitored by the NSA – seemed to show no Russian involvement, but some argued that the phone call was a sham to deflect suspicion, or that Goldmann had not been told of the sabotage beforehand. The argument was picked up by those in the United States made uneasy by the late reduction of tensions between the two nuclear superpowers. Understandably, Moscow was outraged at the suggestion.

In fact, the Soviets were having more difficulties in

constructing their Machine than was generally known. Using the decrypted Message, the Ministry of Medium Heavy Industry made considerable progress in ore extraction, metallurgy, machine tools, and the like. The new microelectronics and cybernetics were more difficult, and most of those components for the Soviet Machine were produced under contract elsewhere in Europe and in Japan. Even more difficult for Soviet domestic industry was the organic chemistry, much of which required techniques developed in molecular biology.

A nearly fatal blow had been dealt Soviet genetics when in the 1930s Stalin decided that modern Mendelian genetics was ideologically unsuitable, and decreed as scientifically orthodox the crackpot genetics of a politically sophisticated agriculturalist named Trofim Lysenko. Two generations of bright Soviet students were taught essentially nothing of the fundamentals of heredity. Now, sixty years later, Soviet molecular biology and genetic engineering were comparatively backward, and few major discoveries in the subject had been made by Soviet scientists. Something similar had happened, but abortively, in the United States, where for theological reasons attempts had been made to prevent public school students from learning about evolution, the central idea of modern biology. The issue was clearcut, because a fundamentalist interpretation of the Bible was widely held to be inconsistent with the evolutionary process. Fortunately for American molecular biology, the fundamentalists were not as influential in the United States as Stalin had been in the Soviet Union.

The National Intelligence Estimate prepared for the President on the matter concluded that there was no evidence of Soviet involvement in the sabotage. Rather, since the Soviets had parity with the Americans in crew membership, they had strong incentives to support the completion of the American Machine. 'If your technology is at Level Three,' explained the Director of

Central Intelligence, 'and your adversary is ahead of you at Level Four, you're happy when, out of the blue, Level Fifteen technology apears. Provided you have equal access to it and adequate resources.' Few officials of the American government believed the Soviets were responsible for the explosion, and the President said as much publicly on more than one occasion. But old habits die hard.

'No crackpot group, however well organized, will deflect humanity from this historic goal,' the President declared. In practice, though, it was now much more difficult to achieve a national consensus. The sabotage had given new life to every objection, reasonable and unreasonable, that had earlier been raised. Only the prospect of the Soviets' completing their Machine kept the American project going.

His wife had wanted to keep Drumlin's funeral a family affair, but in this, as in much else, her well-meaning intentions were thwarted. Physicists, parasailors, hang-gliding aficionados, government officials, scuba enthusiasts, radio astronomers, sky divers, aquaplaners, and the world SETI community all wanted to attend. For a while, they had contemplated holding the services at the Cathedral of St John the Divine in New York City, as the only church in the country of adequate size. But Drumlin's wife won a small victory, and the ceremony was held outdoors in his hometown of Missoula, Montana. The authorities had agreed because Missoula simplified the security problems.

Although Valerian was not badly injured, his physicians advised him against attending the funeral; nevertheless, he gave one of the eulogies from a wheelchair. Drumlin's special genius was in knowing what questions to ask, Valerian said. He had approached the SETI problem skeptically, because skepticism was at the heart of science. Once it was clear that a Message was being received, no one was more dedicated or resourceful in figuring it out. The Deputy Secretary of Defense, Michael Kitz, representing the President, stressed Drumlin's personal qualities – his warmth, his concern for the feelings of others, his brilliance, his remarkable athletic ability. If not for this tragic and dastardly event, Drumlin would have gone down in history as the first American to visit another star.

No peroration from her, Ellie had told der Heer. No press interviews. Maybe a few photographs – she understood the importance of a few photographs. She didn't trust herself to say the right thing. For years she had served as a kind of public spokesperson for SETI, for Argus, and then for the Message and the Machine. But this was different. She needed some time to work this one through.

As nearly as she could tell, Drumlin had died saving her life. He had seen the explosion before others heard it, had spied the several-hundred-kilogram mass of erbium arcing toward them. With his quick reflexes, he had leaped to push her back behind the stanchion.

She had mentioned this as a possibility to der Heer, who replied, 'Drumlin was probably leaping to save himself, and you were just in the way.' The remark was ungracious; was it also intended to be ingratiating? Or perhaps, der Heer had gone on, sensing her displeasure, Drumlin had been thrown into the air by the concussion of the erbium hitting the staging surface.

But she was absolutely sure. She had seen the whole thing. Drumlin's concern was to save her life. And he had. Except for a few scratches, Ellie was physically unhurt. Valerian, who had been entirely protected by the stanchion, had both legs broken by a collapsing wall. She had been fortunate in more ways than one. She had not even been knocked unconscious.

Her first thought – as soon as she had understood what had happened – was not for her old teacher David Drumlin crushed horribly before her eyes; not amaze-

275

ment at the prospect of Drumlin giving up his life for hers; not the setback to the entire Machine Project. No, clear as a bell, her thought had been *I can go, they'll have to send me, there's nobody else, I get to go.*

She had caught herself in an instant. But it was too late. She was aghast at her self-involvement, at the contemptible egotism she had revealed to herself in this moment of crisis. It didn't matter that Drumlin might have had similar failings. She was appalled to find them, even momentarily, within her – so . . . vigorous, busy, planning future courses of action, oblivious of everything except herself. What she detested most was the absolute unselfconsciousness of her ego. It made no apologies, gave no quarter, and plunged on. It was unwholesome. She knew it would be impossible to tear it out, root and branch. She would have to work on it patiently, reason with it, distract it, maybe even threaten it.

When the investigators arrived on the scene, she was uncommunicative. 'I'm afraid I can't tell you much. The three of us were walking together in the staging area and suddenly there was an explosion and everything was flying up into the air. I'm sorry I can't help. I wish I could.'

She made it clear to her colleagues that she did not want to talk about it, and disappeared into her apartment for so long that they sent a scouting party to inquire after her. She tried recalling every nuance of the incident. She tried to reconstruct their conversation before they had entered the staging area, what she and Drumlin had talked about on their drive to Missoula, what Drumlin had seemed like when she first met him at the beginning of her graduate school career. Gradually she discovered that there was a part of her that had wished Drumlin dead – even before they became competitors for the American seat on the Machine. She hated him for having diminished her before the other students in class, for opposing Argus, for what he had said to her the moment after the Hitler film had been reconstructed. She had wanted him dead. And now he *was* dead. By a certain reasoning – she recognized it immediately as convoluted and spurious – she believed herself responsible.

Would he even have *been* here if not for her? Certainly, she told herself; someone else would have discovered the Message, and Drumlin would have leaped in. So to say. But had she not – through her own scientific carelessness, perhaps – provoked him into deeper involvement in the Machine Project? Step by step, she worked through the possibilities. If they were distasteful, she worked especially hard on them; there was something hiding there. She thought about men, men who for one reason or another she had admired. Drumlin. Valerian. Der Heer. Hadden. . . . Joss. Jesse. . . . Staughton? . . . Her father.

'Dr Arroway?'

Ellie was roused somewhat gratefully from this meditation by a stout blond woman of middle age in a blue print dress. Her face was somehow familiar. The cloth identification badge on her ample bosom read 'H. Bork, Gøteborg.'

'Dr Arroway, I'm so sorry for your . . . for our loss. David told me all about you.'

Of course! The legendary Helga Bork, Drumlin's scuba-diving companion in so many tedious graduate-student slide shows. Who, she wondered for the first time, had taken those pictures? Did they invite a photographer to accompany them on their underwater trysts?

'He told me how close you both were.'

What is this woman trying to tell me? Did Drumlin insinuate to her . . . Her eyes welled with tears.

'I'm sorry, Dr Bork, I don't feel very well right now.' Head lowered, she hurried away.

There were many at the funeral she wanted to see: Vaygay, Arkhangelsky, Gotsridze, Baruda, Yu, Xi, Devi. And Abonneba Eda, who was increasingly being talked about as the fifth crew member – if the nations had any sense, she thought, and if there was to be such a thing as a completed Machine. But her social stamina was in tatters and she could not now abide long meetings. For one thing, she didn't trust herself to speak. How much that she'd be saying would be for the good of the project, and how much to satisfy her own needs? The others were sympathetic and understanding. She had, after all, been the person closest to Drumlin when the erbium dowel struck and pulped him.

16

The Elders of Ozone

The God whom science recognizes must be a God of universal laws exclusively, a God who does a wholesale, not a retail business. He cannot accommodate his processes to the convenience of individuals.

— WILLIAM JAMES
The Varieties of Religious Experience (1902)

At a few hundred kilometers altitude, the Earth fills half your sky, and the band of blue that stretches from Mindanao to Bombay, which your eye encompasses in a single glance, can break your heart with its beauty. Home, you think. Home. This is my world. This is where I come from. Everyone I know, everyone I ever heard of, grew up down there, under that relentless and exquisite blue.

You race eastward from horizon to horizon, from dawn to dawn, circling the planet in an hour and a half. After a while, you get to know it, you study its idiosyncrasies and anomalies. You can see so much with the naked eye. Florida will soon be in view again. Has that tropical storm system you saw last orbit, swirling and racing over the Caribbean, reached Fort Lauderdale? Are any of the mountains in the Hindu Kush snow-free this summer? You tend to admire the aquamarine reefs in the Coral Sea. You look at the West Antarctic Ice Pack and wonder whether its collapse could really inundate all the coastal cities on the planet.

In the daylight, though, it's hard to see any sign of human habitation. But at night, except for the polar aurora, everything you see is due to humans, humming and blinking all over the planet. That swath of light is eastern North America, continuous from Boston to Washington, a megalopolis in fact if not in name. Over there is the burnoff of natural gas in Libya. The dazzling lights of the Japanese shrimp fishing fleet have moved toward the South China Sea. On every orbit, the Earth tells you new stories. You can see a volcanic eruption in Kamchatka, a Saharan sandstorm approaching Brazil, unseasonably frigid weather in New Zealand. You get to thinking of the Earth as an organism, a living thing. You get to worry about it, care for it, wish it well. National boundaries are as invisible as meridians of longitude, or the Tropics of Cancer and Capricorn. The boundaries are arbitrary. The planet is real.

Spaceflight, therefore, is subversive. If they are fortunate enough to find themselves in Earth orbit, most people, after a little meditation, have similar thoughts. The nations that had instituted spaceflight had done so largely for nationalistic reasons; it was a small irony that almost everyone who entered space received a startling glimpse of a transnational perspective, of the Earth as one world.

It wasn't hard to imagine a time when the predominant loyalty would be to this blue world, or even to the cluster of worlds huddling around the nearby yellow dwarf star on which humans, once unaware that every star is a sun, had bestowed the definite article: *the* Sun. It was only now, when many people were entering space for long periods and had been afforded a little time for reflection, that the power of the planetary perspective began to be felt. A significant number of these occupants of low Earth orbit, it turned out, were influential down there on Earth.

They had – from the beginning, from before humans ever entered space – sent animals up there. Amoebas, fruit flies, rats, dogs, and apes had become hardy space veterans. As spaceflights of longer and longer duration became possible, something unexpected was found. It had no effect on microorganisms and little effect on fruit flies. But for mammals, it seemed, zero gravity extended the lifespan. By 10 or 20 percent. If you lived in zero g, your body would spend less energy fighting the force of gravity, your cells would oxidize more slowly, and you would live longer. There were some physicians who claimed that the effects would be much more pronounced on humans than on rats. There was the faintest aroma of immortality in the air.

The rate of new cancers was down 80 percent for the orbital animals compared with a control group on the Earth. Leukemia and lymphatic carcinomas were down 90 percent. There was even some evidence, perhaps not yet statistically significant, that the spontaneous remission rate for neoplastic diseases was much greater in zero gravity. The German chemist Otto Warburg had, half a century before, proposed that oxidation was the cause of many cancers. The lower cellular oxygen consumption in the weightless condition suddenly seemed very attractive. People who in earlier decades would have made a pilgrimage to Mexico for laetrile now clamored for a ticket into space. But the price was exorbitant. Whether preventive or clinical medicine, spaceflight was for the few.

Suddenly, hitherto unheard-of sums of money became available for investment in civilian orbital stations. By the very end of the Second Millennium there were rudimentary retirement hotels a few hundred kilometers up. Aside from the expense, there was a serious disadvantage, of course: Progressive osteological and vascular damage would make it impossible for you ever to come back to the gravitational field at the surface of the Earth. But for some of the wealthy elderly, this was no major impediment. In exchange for another decade of life, they were happy to retire to the sky and, eventually, to die there.

There were those who worried that this was an imprudent investment of the limited wealth of the planet; there

281

were too many urgent needs and just grievances of the poor and powerless to spend it on pampering the rich and powerful. It was foolhardy, they said, to permit an elite class to emigrate to space, with the masses left back on Earth – a planet in effect given over to absentee landlords. Others professed it to be a godsend: The owners of the planet were picking up in droves and leaving; they couldn't do nearly as much damage up there, it was argued, as down here.

Hardly anyone anticipated the principal outcome, the transfer of a vivid planetary perspective to those who could do the most good. After some years, there were few nationalists left in Earth orbit. Global nuclear confrontation poses real problems for those with a penchant for immortality.

There were Japanese industrialists, Greek shipping tycoons, Saudi crown princes, one ex-President, a former Party General Secretary, a Chinese robber baron, and a retired heroin kingpin. In the West, aside from a few promotional invitations, there was only one criterion for residence in Earth orbit: You had to be able to pay. The Soviet hostel was different; it was called a space station, and the former Party Secretary was said to be there for 'gerontological research.' By and large, the multitudes were not resentful. One day, they imagined, they would go, too.

Those in Earth orbit tended to be circumspect, careful, quiet. Their families and staffs had similar personal qualities. They were the focus of discreet attention by other rich and powerful people still on Earth. They made no public pronouncements, but their views gradually permeated the thinking of leaders worldwide. The continuing divestment of nuclear weapons by the five nuclear powers was something the venerables in orbit supported. Quietly, they had endorsed the building of the Machine, because of its potential to unify the world. Occasionally nationalist organizations would write about a vast conspiracy in Earth orbit, doddering do-gooders selling out their Motherlands. There were pamphlets that purported to be stenographic transcripts of a meeting aboard *Methuselah* attended by representatives of the other private space stations who had been ferried over for the purpose. A list of 'action items' was produced, calculated to strike terror in the heart of the most lukewarm patriot. The pamphlets were spurious, *Timesweek* announced; it called them 'The Protocols of the Elders of Ozone.'

On the days immediately before launch, she tried to spend some time – often just after dawn – on Cocoa Beach. Ellie had borrowed an apartment that overlooked the beach and the Atlantic Ocean. She would bring pieces of bread along and practice throwing them to the seagulls. They were good at catching morsels on the fly, with a fielding average, she calculated, about that of a major league outfielder. There were moments when twenty or thirty seagulls would hover in the air just a meter or two above her head. They flapped vigorously to stay in place, their beaks wide, straining in anticipation of the miraculous appearance of food. They grazed past each other in apparent random motion, but the overall effect was a stationary pattern. On her way back, she noticed a small and, in its humble way, perfect palm frond lying at the edge of the beach. She picked it up and carried it back to her apartment, carefully wiping off the sand with her fingers.

Hadden had invited her up for a visit to his home away from home, his chateau in space. *Methuselah*, he called it. She could tell no one outside the government about the invitation, because of Hadden's passion to stay out of the public eye. Indeed, it was still not generally known that he had taken up residence in orbit, retired to the sky. All those inside the government she asked were for it. Der Heer's advice was 'The change of scene will do you good.' The President clearly was in favor of her visit, because a place had suddenly been made available on the next shuttle launch, the aging STS *Intrepid*. Passage to an orbiting rest home was usually by commercial carrier. A much larger nonreusable launch vehicle was undergoing final flight qualification. But the aging shuttle fleet was still the workhorse of US government space activities, both military and civilian.

'We jus' flake off tiles by the handful when we re-enter, and then we jus' stick 'em back on again before liftoff,' one of the astronaut-pilots explained to her.

Beyond general good health, there were no special physical requirements for the flight. Commercial launches tended to go up full and come back empty. By contrast, the shuttle flights were crowded both on the way up and on the way down. Before *Intrepid's* latest landing the previous week, it had rendezvoused and docked with *Methuselah* to return two passengers to Earth. She recognized their names; one was a designer of propulsion systems, the other a cryobiologist. Ellie wondered what they had been doing on *Methuselah*.

'You'll see,' the pilot continued, 'it'll be like fallin' off a log. Hardly anybody hates it, and most folks jus' love it.'

She did. Crowded in with the pilot, two mission specialists, a tight-lipped military officer, and an employee of the Internal Revenue Service, she experienced a flawless liftoff and the exhilaration of her first experience in zero gravity longer than the ride in the high-deceleration elevator at the World Trade Center in New York. One and a half orbits later, they rendezvoused with *Methuselah*. In two days the commercial transport *Narnia* would bring Ellie down.

The Chateau – Hadden insisted on calling it that – was slowly spinning, one revolution about every ninety minutes, so that the same side of it was always facing the Earth. Hadden's study featured a magnificent panorama on the Earthward bulkhead – not a television screen but a real transparent window. The photons she was seeing had been reflected off the snowy Andes just a fraction of a second ago. Except toward the periphery of the window,

284

where the slant path through the thick polymer was longer, hardly any distortion was evident.

There were many people she knew, even people who considered themselves religious, for whom the feeling of awe was an embarrassment. But you would have to be made of wood, she thought, to stand before this window and not feel it. They should be sending up young poets and composers, artists, filmmakers, and deeply religious people not wholly in thrall to the sectarian bureaucracies. This experience could easily be conveyed, she thought, to the average person on Earth. What a pity it had not yet been attempted seriously. The feeling was . . . numinous.

'You get used to it,' Hadden told her, 'but you don't get tired of it. From time to time it's still inspiring.'

Abstemiously he was nursing a diet cola. She had refused the offer of something stronger. The premium on ethanol in orbit must be high, she thought.

'Of course, you miss things – long walks, swimming in the ocean, old friends dropping in unannounced. But I was never much into those things anyway. And as you see, friends can come by for a visit.'

'At huge expense,' she replied.

'A woman comes up to visit Yamagishi, my neighbor in the next wing. Second Tuesday of every month, rain or shine. I'll introduce you to him later. He's quite a guy. Class A war criminal – but only indicted, you understand, never convicted.'

'What's the attraction?' she asked. 'You don't think the world is about to end. What are you doing up here?'

'I like the view. And there are certain legal niceties.'

She looked at him querulously.

'You know, someone in my position – new inventions, new industries – is always on the thin edge of breaking some law or other. Usually it's because the old laws haven't caught up with the new technology. You can spend a lot of your time in litigation. It cuts down your effectiveness. While all this' – he gestured expansively, taking in both the Chateau and the Earth – 'doesn't belong to any nation. This Chateau belongs to me, my friend Yamagishi, and a few others. There could never be anything illegal about supplying me with food and material needs. Just to be on the safe side, though we're working on closed ecological systems. There's no extradition treaty between this Chateau and any of the nations down there. It's more . . . efficient for me to be up here.

'I don't want you to think that I've done anything really illegal. But we're doing so many new things, it's smart to be on the safe side. For instance, there are people who actually believe I sabotaged the Machine, when I spent a ridiculous amount of my own money trying to build it. And you know what they did to Babylon. My insurance investigators think it might have been the same people in Babylon and Terre Haute. I seem to have a lot of enemies. I don't understand why. I think I've done a lot of good for people. Anyway, all in all, it's better for me to be up here . . .

'Now, it's the Machine I wanted to talk to you about. That was awful – that erbium-dowel catastrophe in Wyoming. I'm really sorry about Drumlin. He was a tough old pisser. And it must have been a big shock for you. Sure you don't want a drink?'

But she was content to look out at the Earth and listen.

'If *I'm* not disheartened about the Machine,' he went on, 'I don't see why you should be. You're probably worried that there never will be an American Machine, that there are too many people who want it to fail. The President's worried about the same thing. And those factories we built, those aren't assembly lines. We've been making custom-made products. It's gonna be expensive to replace all the broken parts. But mainly you're thinking, maybe it was a bad idea in the first place. Maybe we've been foolish to go so fast. So let's take a long, careful look at the whole thing. Even if you're not thinking like that, the President is.

'But if we don't do it soon, I'm worried we'll never do it. And there's another thing: I don't think this invitation is open forever.'

'Funny you should say that. That's just what Valerian, Drumlin, and I were talking about before the accident. The sabotage,' she corrected herself. 'Please go on.'

'You see, the religious people – most of them – really think this planet is an experiment. That's what their beliefs come down to. Some god or other is always fixing and poking, messing around with tradesmen's wives, giving tablets on mountains, commanding you to mutilate your children, telling people what words they can say and what words they can't say, making people feel guilty about enjoying themselves, and like that. Why can't the gods leave well enough alone? All this intervention speaks of incompetence. If God didn't want Lot's wife to look back, why didn't he make her obedient, so she'd do what her husband told her? Or if he hadn't made Lot such a shithead, maybe she would've listened to him more. If God is omnipotent and omniscient, why didn't he start the universe out in the first place so it would come out the way he wants? Why's he constantly repairing and complaining? No, there's one thing the Bible makes clear: The biblical God is a sloppy manufacturer. He's not good at design, he's not good at execution. He'd be out of business if there was any competition.

'That's why I don't believe we're an experiment. There might be lots of experimental planets in the universe, places where apprentice gods get to test out their skills. What a shame Rankin and Joss weren't born on one of those planets. But on *this* planet' – again he waved at the window – 'there isn't any microintervention. The gods don't drop in on us to fix things up when we've botched it. You look at human history and it's clear we've been on our own.'

'Until now,' she said. 'Deus ex machina? That's what

287

you think? You think the gods finally took pity on us and sent the Machine?'

'More like *Machina ex deo*, or whatever the right Latin is. No, I don't think we're the experiment. I think we're the control, the planet that nobody was interested in, the place where nobody intervened at all. A calibration world gone to seed. This is what happens if they don't intervene. The Earth is an object lesson for the apprentice gods. 'If you really screw up,' they get told, "you'll make something like Earth." But of course it'd be a waste to destroy a perfectly good world. So.they look in on us from time to time, just in case. Maybe each time they bring by the gods who screwed up. Last time they looked we're frolicking in the savannas, trying to outrace the antelopes. "Okay, that's fine," they say. "These guys aren't gonna give us any trouble. Look in on 'em in another ten million years. But just to be on the safe side, monitor 'em at radio frequencies."

'Then one day there's an alarm. A message from Earth. "What? They have television already? Let's see what they're into." Olympic stadium. National flags. Bird of prey. Adolf Hitler. Thousands of cheering people. "Uh-oh," they say. They know the warning signs. Quick as a flash they tell us, "Cut it out, you guys. That's a perfectly good planet you have there. Disorganized, but service-able. Here, build this Machine instead." They're worried about us. They see we're on a downward slope. They think we should be in a hurry to get repaired. So I think so, too. We *have* to build the Machine.'

She knew what Drumlin would have thought of arguments like this. Although much that Hadden had just said resonated with her own thinking, she was tired of these beguiling and confident speculations on what the Vegans had in mind. She wanted the project to continue, the Machine completed and activated, the new stage in human history begun. She still mistrusted her own motives, was still wary even when she was mentioned as a possible member of the crew on a completed Machine.

288

So the delays in resuming construction served a purpose for her. They bought time for her to work her problems through.

'We'll have dinner with Yamagishi. You'll like him. But we're a little worried about him. He keeps his oxygen partial pressure so low at night.'

'What do you mean?'

'Well, the lower the oxygen content in the air, the longer you live. At least that's what the doctors tell us. So we all get to pick the amount of oxygen in our rooms. In daytime you can't bring it much below twenty percent, because you get groggy. It impairs mental functioning. But at night, when you're sleeping anyway, you can lower the oxygen partial pressure. There's a danger, though. You can lower it too much. Yamagishi's down to fourteen percent these days, because he wants to live forever. As a result, he's not lucid until lunchtime.'

'I've been that way all my life, at twenty percent oxygen.' She laughed.

'Now he's experimenting with noötropic drugs to remove the grogginess. You know, like piracetam. They definitely improve memory. I don't know that it actually makes you smarter, but that's what they say. So Yamagishi is taking an awful lot of noötropics, and he's not breathing enough oxygen at night.'

'So does he behave cuckoo?'

'Cuckoo? It's hard to tell. I don't know very many ninety-two-year-old Class A war criminals.'

'That's why every experiment needs a control,' she said.

He smiled.

Even at his advanced age, Yamagishi displayed the erect bearing he had acquired during his long service in the Imperial Army. He was a small man, entirely bald, with an inconspicuous white mustache and a fixed, benign expression on his face.

'I am here because of hips,' he explained. 'I know about

cancer, and lifetimes. But I am here because of hips. At my age bones break easily. Baron Tsukuma died from falling from his futon onto his tatami. One-half meter, he fell. One-half meter. And his bones broke. In zero g, hips do not break.'

This seemed very sensible.

A few gastronomic compromises had been made, but the dinner was of surprising elegance. A specialized small technology had been developed for weightless dining. Serving utensils had lids, wine glasses had tops and straws. Foods such as nuts or dried corn flakes were prohibited.

Yamagishi urged the caviar on her. It was one of the few Western foods, he explained, that cost more per kilogram to buy on Earth than to ship to space. The cohesion of the individual caviar eggs was a lucky break, Ellie mused. She tried to imagine thousands of separate eggs in individual free-fall, clouding the passageways of this orbiting retirement home. Suddenly she remembered that her mother was also in a retirement home, several orders of magnitude more modest than this one. In fact, orienting herself by the Great Lakes, visible out the window at this moment, she could pinpoint her mother's location. She could spend two days chatting it up in Earth orbit with bad-boy billionaires, but couldn't spare fifteen minutes for a phone call with her mother? She promised herself to call as soon as she landed in Cocoa Beach. A communiqué from Earth orbit, she told herself, might be too much novelty for the senior citizens' rest home in Janesville, Wisconsin.

Yamagishi interrupted her train of thought to inform her that he was the oldest man in space. Ever. Even the former Chinese Vice Premier was younger. He removed his coat, rolled up his right sleeve, flexed his biceps, and asked her to feel his muscle. He was soon full of vivid and quantitative detail about the worthy charities to which he had been a major contributor.

She tried to make polite conversation. 'It's very placid

and quiet up here. You must be enjoying your retirement.'

She had addressed this bland remark to Yamagishi, but Hadden replied.

'It's not entirely uneventful. Occasionally there's a crisis and we have to move fast.'

'Solar flare, extremely bad. Make you sterile,' Yamagishi volunteered.

'Yeah, if there's a major solar flare monitored by telescope, you have about three days before the charged particles hit the Chateau. So the permanent residents, like Yamagishi-san and me, we go to the storm shelter. Very spartan, very confined. But it has enough radiation shielding to make a difference. There's some secondary radiation, of course. The thing is, all the nonpermanent staff and visitors have to leave in the three-day period. That kind of an emergency can tax the commercial fleet. Sometimes we have to call in NASA or the Soviets to rescue people. You wouldn't believe who you flush out in solar-flare events – Mafiosi, heads of intelligence services, beautiful men and women . . .'

'Why do I get the feeling that sex is high on the list of imports from Earth?' she asked a little reluctantly.

'Oh, it is, it is. There's lots of reasons. The clientele, the location. But the main reason is zero g. In zero g you can do things at eighty you never thought possible at twenty. You ought to take a vacation up here – with your boyfriend. Consider it a definite invitation.'

'Ninety,' said Yamagishi.

'I beg your pardon?'

'You can do things at ninety you didn't dream of at twenty. That's what Yamagishi-san is saying. That's why everyone wants to come up here.'

Over coffee, Hadden returned to the topic of the Machine.

'Yamagishi-san and me are partners with some other people. He's the Honorary Chairman of the Board of Yamagishi Industries. As you know, they're the prime

291

contractor for the Machine component testing going on in Hokkaido. Now imagine our problem. I'll give you a for-instance. There are three big spherical shells, one inside the other. They're made of a niobium alloy, they have peculiar patterns cut into them, and they're obviously designed to rotate in three orthogonal directions very fast in a vacuum. Benzels, they're called. You know all this, of course. What happens if you make a scale model of the three benzels and spin them very fast? What happens? All knowledgeable physicists think nothing will happen. But, of course, nobody's done the experiment. This precise experiment. So nobody really knows. Suppose something does happen when the full Machine is activated. Does it depend on the speed of rotation? Does it depend on the composition of the benzels? On the pattern of the cutouts? Is it a question of scale? So we've been building these things, and running them – scale models and full-scale copies, both. We want to spin our version of the big benzels, the ones that'll be mated to the other components in the two Machines. Suppose nothing happens then. Then we'd want to add additional components, one by one. We'd keep plugging them in, a small systems integration job at every step, and then maybe there'd be a time when we plug in a component, not the last one, and the machine does something that knocks our socks off. We're only trying to figure out how the Machine works. You see what I'm driving at?'

'You mean you've been secretly assembling an identical copy of the Machine in Japan?'

'Well, it's not exactly a secret. We're testing out the individual components. Nobody said we can only test them one at a time. So here's what Yamagishi-san and I propose: We change the schedule on the experiments in Hokkaido. We do full-up systems integration now, and if nothing works we'll do the component-by component testing later. The money's all been allocated anyway.

292

'We think it'll be months – maybe years – before the American effort gets back on track. And we don't think the Russians can do it even in that time. Japan's the only possibility. We don't have to announce it right away. We don't have to make a decision about activating the Machine right away. We're just testing components.'

'Can you two make this kind of decision on your own?'

'Oh, it's well within what they call our designated responsibilities. We figure we can catch up to where the Wyoming Machine was in about six months. We'll have to be much more careful about sabotage, of course. But if the components are okay, I think the Machine will be okay: Hokkaido's kind of hard to get to. Then, when everything is checked and ready, we can ask the World Machine Consortium if they'd like to give it a try. If the crew is willing, I bet you the Consortium will go along. What do you think, Yamagishi-san?'

Yamagishi had not heard the question. He was softly singing 'Free-Fall' to himself; it was a current hit song full of vivid detail about succumbing to temptation in Earth orbit. He did not know all the words, he explained when the question was repeated.

Unperturbed, Hadden continued. 'Now some of the components will have been spun or dropped or something. But in any case they'll have to pass the prescribed tests. I didn't think that would be enough to scare you off. Personally, I mean.'

'Personally? What makes you think I'm going? Nobody's asked me, for one thing, and there are a number of new factors.'

'The probability is very high that the Selection Committee will ask you, and the President will be for it. Enthusiastically. C'mon,' he said, grinning, 'you wanna spend your whole life in the sticks?'

It was cloudy over Scandinavia and the North Sea, and the English Channel was covered with a lacy, almost transparent, cobweb of fog.

'Yes, you go.' Yamagishi was on his feet, his hands stiffly at his sides. He gave her a deep bow.

'Speaking for the twenty-two million employees of the corporations I control, very nice to meet you.'

She dozed fitfully in the sleeping cubicle they had assigned her. It was tethered loosely to two walls so she would not, in the course of turning over in zero g, propel herself against some obstacle. She awoke while everyone else seemed to be still asleep and pulled herself along a series of handholds until she found herself before the grand window. They were over the night side. The Earth was in darkness except for a patchwork and sprinkle of light, the plucky attempt of humans to compensate for the opacity of the Earth when their hemisphere was averted from the Sun. Twenty minutes later, at sunrise, she decided that, if they asked her, she would say yes.

Hadden came up behind her, and she started just a little.

'It looks great, I admit. I've been up here for years and it still looks great. But doesn't it bother you that there's a spaceship around you? See, there's an experience no one's ever had yet. You're in a space suit, there's no tether, no spacecraft. Maybe the Sun is behind you, and you're surrounded on all sides by stars. Maybe the Earth is below you. Or maybe some other planet. I kind of fancy Saturn myself. There you are, floating in space, like you really are one with the cosmos. Space suits nowadays have enough consumables to last you for hours. The spacecraft that dropped you off could be long gone. Maybe they'll rendezvous with you in an hour. Maybe not.

'The best would be if the ship wasn't coming back. Your last hours, surrounded by space and stars and worlds. If you had an incurable disease, or if you just wanted to give yourself a really nifty last indulgence, how could you top that?'

'You're serious? You want to market this . . . scheme?'

'Well, too soon to market. Maybe it's not exactly the right way to go about it. Let's just say I'm thinking of feasability testing.'

She decided that she would not tell Hadden of her decision, and he did not ask. Later, as the *Narnia* was beginning its rendezvous and docking with *Methuselah*, Hadden took her aside.

'We were saying that Yamagishi is the oldest person up here. Well, if you talk about *permanently* up here – I don't mean staff and astronauts and dancing girls – I'm the *youngest* person up here. I've got a vested interest in the answer, I know, but it's a definite medical possibility that zero g'll keep me alive for centuries. See, I'm engaged in an experiment on immortality.

'Now, I'm not bringing this up so I can boast. I'm bringing it up for a practical reason. If we're figuring out ways to extend our lifespans, think of what those creatures on Vega must have done. They probably *are* immortal, or close enough. I'm a practical person, and I've thought a lot now about immortality. I've probably thought longer and more seriously about it than anybody else. And I can tell you one thing for sure about immortals: They're very careful. They don't leave things to chance. They've invested too much effort in becoming immortal. I don't know what they look like, I don't know what they want from you, but if you ever get to see them, this is the only piece of practical advice I have for you: Something you think is dead cinch safe, they'll consider an unacceptable risk. If there's any negotiating you get to do up there, don't forget what I'm telling you.'

17

The Dream of the Ants

Human speech is like a cracked kettle on which we tap
crude rhythms for bears to dance to, while we long to
make music that will melt the stars.

— GUSTAVE FLAUBERT
Madame Bovary (1857)

Popular theology. . . . is a massive inconsistency derived
from ignorance. . . . The goods exist because nature
herself has imprinted a conception of them on the minds
of men.

— CICERO
De Natura Deorum, I, 16

Ellie was in the midst of packing notes, magnetic tapes,
and a palm frond for shipment to Japan when she received word that her mother had suffered a stroke.
Immediately afterward, she was brought a letter by
project courier. It was from John Staughton, and there
were no polite preliminaries:

Your mother and I would often discuss your deficiencies and
shortcomings. It was always a difficult conversation. When I
defended you (and, although you may not believe it, this
happened often), she told me that I was putty in your hands.
When I criticized you, she told me to mind my own business.
  But I want you to know that your unwillingness to visit her
in the last few years, since this Vega business, was a source of
continuing pain to her. She would tell her cronies at the
dreadful nursing home she insisted on going to that you'd be
visiting her soon. For years she told them that. 'Soon.' She
planned how she would show her famous daughter around, in
what order she'd introduce you to that decrepit bunch.

You probably won't want to hear this, and I tell it to you with sorrow. But it's for your own good. Your behavior was more painful to her than anything that ever happened to her, even your father's death. You may be a big shot now, your hologram available all over the world, hobnobbing with politicians and so on, but as a human being, you haven't learned anything since high school . . .

Her eyes welling with tears, she began to crumple the letter and its envelope, but discovered some stiff piece of paper inside, a partial hologram made from an old two-dimensional photograph by a computer extrapolation technique. You had a faint but satisfactory sense of being able to see around edges and corners. It was a photo she had never seen before. Her mother as a young woman, quite lovely, smiled out of the picture, her arm casually draped over the shoulder of Ellie's father, who sported what seemed to be a day's growth of beard. They both seemed radiantly happy. With a surge of anguish, guilt, fury at Staughton, and a little self-pity, Ellie weighed the evident reality that she would never see either of the people in that picture again.

Her mother lay immobile in the bed. Her expression was oddly neutral, registering neither joy nor regret, merely . . . a kind of waiting. Her only motion was an occasional blink of her eyes. Whether she could hear or understand what Ellie was saying was unclear. Ellie thought about communications schemes. She couldn't help it; the thought arose unbidden: one blink for yes, two blinks for no. Or hook up an encephalograph with a cathode ray tube that her mother could see, and teach her to modulate her beta waves. But this was her *mother*, not Alpha Lyrae, and what was called for here was not decryption algorithms but feeling.

She held her mother's hand and talked for hours. She rambled on about her mother and her father, her childhood. She recalled being a toddler among the newly washed sheets, being swept up to the sky. She talked about John Staughton. She apologized for many things. She cried a little.

Her mother's hair was awry and, finding a brush, she prettified her. She examined the lined face and recognized her own. Her mother's eyes, deep and moist, stared fixedly, with only an occasional blink into, it seemed, a great distance.

'I know where I come from,' Ellie told her softly.

Almost imperceptibly, her mother shook her head from side to side, as though she were regretting all those years in which she and her daughter had been estranged. Ellie gave her mother's hand a little squeeze and thought she felt one in return.

Her mother's life was not in danger, she was told. If there was any change in her condition, they would call at once to her office in Wyoming. In a few days, they would be able to move her from the hospital back to the nursing home, where the facilities, she was assured, were adequate.

Staughton seemed subdued, but with a depth of feeling for her mother she had not guessed at. She would call often, she told him.

The austere marble lobby displayed, perhaps incongruously, a real statue – not a holograph – of a nude woman in the style of Praxiteles. They ascended in an Otis-Hitachi elevator, in which the second language was English rather than braille, and she found herself ushered through a large barn of a room in which people were huddled over word processors. A word would be typed in Hiragana, the fifty-one-letter Japanese phonetic alphabet, and on the screen would appear the corresponding Chinese ideogram in Kanji. There were hundreds of thousands of such ideograms, or characters, stored in the computer memories, although only three or four thousand were generally needed to read a newspaper. Because many characters of entirely different

298

meanings were expressed by the same spoken word, all possible translations into Kanji were printed out, in order of probability. The word processor had a contextual subroutine in which the candidate characters were also queued according to the computer's estimate of the intended meaning. It was rarely wrong. In a language which had until recently never had a typewriter, the word processor was working a communications revolution not fully admired by traditionalists.

In the conference room they seated themselves on low chairs – an evident concession to Western tastes – around a low lacquered table, and tea was poured. In Ellie's field of view, beyond the window was the city of Tokyo. She was spending much time before windows, she thought. The newspaper was the *Asahi Shimbun* – the Rising Sun News – and she was interested to see that one of the political reporters was a woman, a rarity by the standards of the American and Soviet media. Japan was engaged in a national reassessment of the role of women. Traditional male privileges were being surrendered slowly in what seemed to be an unreported street-by-street battle. Just yesterday the president of a firm called Nanoelectronics had bemoaned to her that there wasn't a 'girl' in Tokyo who still knew how to tie an obi. As with clip-on bow ties, an easily donned simulacrum had captured the market. Japanese women had better things to do than spend half an hour every day wrapping and tucking. The reporter was dressed in an austere business suit, the hem falling to her calves.

To maintain security, no press visitors were permitted at the Hokkaido Machine site. Instead, when crew members or project officials came to the main island of Honshu, they routinely scheduled a round of interviews with the Japanese and foreign news media. As always, the questions were familiar. Reporters all over the world had nearly the same approach to the Machine, if you made a few allowances for local idiosyncrasies. Was she pleased that, after the American and Soviet 'disappointments,' a Machine was being built in Japan? Did she feel isolated in the northern island of Hokkaido? Was she concerned because the Machine components being used in Hokkaido had been tested beyond the strictures of the Message?

Before 1945, this district of the city had been owned by the Imperial Navy, and indeed, immediately adjacent she could see the roof of the Naval Observatory, its two silver domes housing telescopes still used for time-keeping and calendrical functions. They were gleaming in the noonday Sun.

Why did the Machine include a dodecahedron and the three spherical shells called benzels? Yes, the reporters understood that she didn't know. But what did she *think*? She explained that on an issue of this sort it was foolish to have an opinion in the absence of evidence. They persisted, and she pleaded the virtues of a tolerance for ambiguity. If there was a real danger, should they send robots instead of people, as a Japanese artificial intelligence expert had recommended? Are there any personal effects she would be taking with her? Any family pictures? Microcomputers? A Swiss Army knife?

Ellie noticed two figures emerge through a trapdoor onto the roof of the nearby observatory. Their faces were obscured by visors. They were garbed in the blue-gray quilted armor of medieval Japan. Brandishing wood staffs taller than they were, they bowed one to another, paused for a heartbeat, and then pummeled and parried for the next half hour. Her answers to the reporters became a little stilted; she was mesmerized by the spectacle before her. No one else seemed to notice. The staffs must have been heavy, because the ceremonial combat was slow, as if they were warriors from the ocean bottom.

Had she known Dr Lunacharsky and Dr Sukhavati for many years before the receipt of the Message? What about Dr Eda? Mr Xi? What did she think of them, their accomplishments? How well were the five of them getting on? Indeed, she marveled to herself that she was a member of such a select group.

What were her impressions of the quality of the Japanese components? What could she say about the meeting the Five had had with Emperor Akihito? Were their discussions with Shinto and Buddhist leaders part of a general effort by the Machine Project to gain the insights of world religious figures before the Machine was activated, or just a courtesy to Japan as the host country? Did she think the device could be a Trojan Horse or a Doomsday Machine? In her answers she tried to be courteous, succinct, and noncontroversial. The Machine Project public relations officer who had accompanied her was visibly pleased.

Abruptly the interview was over. They wished her and her colleagues all success, the Managing Editor said. They had every expectation of interviewing her when she returned. They hoped she would visit Japan often afterward.

Her hosts were smiling and bowing. The quilted warriors had retreated down the trapdoor. She could see her security people, eyes darting, outside the now open door of the conference room. On the way out she asked the woman reporter about the apparitions from medieval Japan.

'Oh yes,' she replied. 'They are astronomers for the Coast Guard. They practice Kendo at their lunch hour every day. You can set your watch by them.'

Xi had been born on the Long March, and had fought the Kuomintang as a youngster during the Revolution. He served as an intelligence officer in Korea, rising eventually to a position of authority over Chinese strategic technology. But in the Cultural Revolution he was publicly humiliated and condemned to domestic exile, although later he was rehabilitated with some fanfare.

One of Xi's crimes in the eyes of the Cultural Revolution had been to admire some of the ancient Confucian virtues, and especially one passage from the *Great Learning*, which for centuries before every Chinese with even a rudimentary education knew by heart. It was upon this passage, Sun Yat-sen had said, that his own revolutionary nationalist movement at the beginning of the twentieth century was based:

The ancients who wished to illustrate illustrious virtue throughout the Kingdom first ordered well their own states. Wishing to order well their states, they first regulated their families. Wishing to regulate their families, they first cultivated their persons. Wishing to cultivate their persons, they first rectified their hearts. Wishing to rectify their hearts, they first sought to be sincere in their thoughts. Wishing to be sincere in their thoughts, they first extended to the utmost their knowledge. Such extension of knowledge lay in the investigation of things.

Thus, Xi believed, the pursuit of knowledge was central for the well-being of China. But the Red Guards had thought otherwise.

During the Cultural Revolution, Xi had been consigned as a worker on an impoverished collective farm in Ningxia Province, near the Great Wall, a region with a rich Muslim tradition – where, while plowing an unpromising field, he uncovered an intricately ornamented bronze helmet from the Han Dynasty. When reestablished in the leadership, he turned his attention from strategic weapons to archeology. The Cultural Revolution had attempted to sever a 5,000-year-old continuous Chinese cultural tradition. Xi's response was to help build bridges to the nation's past. Increasingly he devoted his attention to the excavation of the underground funerary city of Xian.

It was there that the great discovery had been made of the terra-cotta army of the Emperor after whom China itself was named. His official name was Qin Shi Huangdi, but through the vagaries of transliteration had come to be widely known in the West as Ch'in. In the third century B.C., Qin unified the country, built the Great Wall, and compassionately decreed that upon his death lifelike terra-cotta models be substituted for the members of his entourage – soldiers, servants, and nobles – who, according to earlier tradition, would have been buried alive with his body. The terra-cotta army was composed of 7,500 soldiers, roughly a division. Every one of them had distinct facial features. You could see that people from all over China were represented. The Emperor had welded many separate and warring provinces into one nation. A nearby grave contained the almost perfectly preserved body of the Marchioness of Tai, a minor functionary in the Emperor's court. The technology for preserving bodies – you could clearly see the severe expression on the face of the Marchioness, refined perhaps from decades of dressing down the servants – was vastly superior to that of ancient Egypt.

Qin had simplified the writing, codified the law, built roads, completed the Great Wall, and unified the country. He also confiscated weapons. While he was accused of massacring scholars who criticized his policies, and burning books because some knowledge was unsettling, he maintained that he had eliminated endemic corruption and instituted peace and order. Xi was reminded of the Cultural Revolution. He imagined reconciling these conflicting tendencies in the heart of a single person. Qin's arrogance had reached staggering proportions – to punish a mountain that had offended him, he ordered it denuded of vegetation and painted red, the color worn by condemned criminals. Qin was great, but he was also mad. Could you unify a collection of diverse and contentious nations without being a little mad? You'd have to be crazy even to attempt it, Xi laughingly told Ellie.

With increasing fascination, Xi had arranged for massive excavations at Xian. Gradually, he became convinced that the Emperor Qin himself was also lying in wait, perfectly preserved, in some great tomb near the disinterred terra-cotta army. Nearby, according to ancient records, was also buried under a great mound a detailed model of the nation of China in 210 B.C., with every temple and pagoda meticulously represented. The rivers, it was said, were made of mercury, with the Emperor's barge in miniature perpetually navigating his underground domain. When the ground at Xian was found to be contaminated with mercury, Xi's excitement grew.

Xi had unearthed a contemporary account that described a great dome the Emperor had commissioned to overarch this miniature realm, called, like the real one, the Celestial Kingdom. As written Chinese had hardly changed in 2,200 years, he was able to read the account directly, without benefit of an expert linguist. A chronicler from the time of Qin was speaking to Xi directly. Many nights Xi would put himself to sleep trying to envision the great Milky Way that sundered the vault of the sky in the domed tomb of the great Emperor, and the night ablaze with comets which had appeared at his passing to honor his memory.

The search for Qin's tomb and for his model of the universe had occupied Xi over the last decade. He had not found it yet; but his quest had captured the imagination of China. It was said of him, 'There are a billion people in China, but there is only one Xi.' In a nation slowly easing restraints on individuality, he was seen as exerting a constructive influence.

Qin, it was clear, had been obsessed by immortality. The man who gave his name to the most populous nation on Earth, the man who built what was then the largest structure on the planet, was, predictably enough, afraid he would be forgotten. So he caused more monumental structures to be erected; preserved, or reproduced for the ages, the bodies and faces of his courtiers; built his own still-elusive tomb and world model; and sent repeated expeditions into the Eastern Sea to seek the elixir of life. He complained bitterly of the expense as he launched each new voyage. One of these missions involved scores of oceangoing junks and a crew of 3,000 young men and women. They never returned, and their fate is unknown. The water of immortality was unavailable.

Just fifty years later, wet rice agriculture and iron metallurgy suddenly appeared in Japan – developments that profoundly altered the Japanese economy and created a class of warrior aristocrats. Xi argued that the Japanese name for Japan clearly reflected the Chinese origin of Japanese culture: The Land of the Rising Sun. Where would you have to be standing, Xi asked, for the Sun to be rising over Japan? So the very name of the daily newspaper that Ellie had just visited was, Xi proposed, a reminder of the life and times of the Emperor Qin. Ellie thought that Qin made Alexander the Great a schoolyard bully by comparison. Well, almost.

If Qin had been obsessed with immortality. Xi was obsessed with Qin. Ellie told him about her visit to Sol Hadden in Earth orbit, and they agreed that were the Emperor Qin alive in the waning years of the twentieth century, Earth orbit is where he would be. She introduced Xi to Hadden by videophone and then left them to talk alone. Xi's excellent English had been honed during his recent involvement in the transfer of the Crown Colony of Hong Kong to the Chinese People's Republic. They were still talking when the *Methuselah* set, and had to continue through the network of communications satellites in geosynchronous orbit. They must have hit it off. Soon after, Hadden requested that the activation of the Machine be synchronized so that he would be overhead at that moment. He wanted Hokkaido in the focus of his telescope, he said, when the time came.

'Do Buddhists believe in God, or not?' Ellie asked on their way to have dinner with the Abbot.

'Their position seems to be,' Vaygay replied dryly, 'that their God is so great he doesn't even have to exist.'

As they sped through the countryside, they talked about Utsumi, the Abbot of the most famous Zen

Buddhist monastery in Japan. A few years before, at ceremonies marking the fiftieth anniversary of the destruction of Hiroshima, Utsumi had delivered a speech that commanded worldwide attention. He was well connected in Japanese political life, and served as a kind of spiritual adviser to the ruling political party, but he spent most of his time in monastic and devotional activities.

'His father was also the Abbot of a Buddhist monastery,' Sukhavati mentioned.

Ellie raised her eyebrows.

'Don't look so surprised. Marriage was permitted to them, like the Russian Orthodox clergy. Isn't that right, Vaygay?'

'That was before my time,' he said, a little distractedly.

The restaurant was set in a grove of bamboo and was called Ungetsu – the Clouded Moon; and indeed there was a clouded moon in the early evening sky. Their Japanese hosts had arranged that there be no other guests. Ellie and her companions removed their shoes and, padding in their stocking feet, entered a small dining room which looked out on stalks of bamboo.

The Abbot's head was shaved, his garment a robe of black and silver. He greeted them in perfect colloquial English, and his Chinese, Xi later told her, turned out to be passable as well. The surroundings were restful, the conversation lighthearted. Each course was a small work of art, edible jewels. She understood how nouvelle cuisine had its origins in the Japanese culinary tradition. If the custom were to eat the food blindfolded, she would have been content. If, instead, the delicacies were brought out only to be admired and never to be eaten, she would also have been content. To look and eat both was an intimation of heaven.

Ellie was seated across from the Abbot and next to Lunacharsky. Others inquired about the species – or at least the kingdom – of this or that morsel. Between the sushi and the ginkgo nuts, the conversation turned, after a fashion, to the mission.

'But *why* do we communicate?' the Abbot asked.

'To exchange information,' replied Lunacharsky, seemingly devoting full attention to his recalcitrant chopsticks.

'But why do we *wish* to exchange information?'

'Because we feed on information. Information is necessary for our survival. Without information we die.'

Lunacharsky was intent on a ginkgo nut that slipped off his chopsticks each time he attempted to raise it to his mouth. He lowered his head to meet the chopsticks halfway.

'I believe,' continued the Abbot, 'that we communicate out of love or compassion.' He reached with his fingers for one of his own ginkgo nuts and placed it squarely in his mouth.

'Then you think,' she asked, 'that the Machine is an instrument of compassion? You think there is no risk?'

'I can communicate with a flower,' he went on as if in response. 'I can talk to a stone. You would have no difficulty understanding the beings – that is the proper word? – of some other world.'

'I am perfectly prepared to believe that the stone communicates to you,' Lunacharsky said, chewing on the ginkgo nut. He had followed the Abbot's example. 'But I wonder about you communicating to the stone. How would you convince us that you can communicate with a stone? The world is full of error. How do you know you are not deceiving yourself?'

'Ah, scientific skepticism.' The Abbot flashed a smile that Ellie found absolutely winning; it was innocent, almost childlike.

'To communicate with a stone, you must become much less . . . preoccupied. You must not do so much thinking, so much talking. When I say I commuunicate with a stone, I am not talking about words. The Christians say, "In the beginning was the Word." But I am talking about a communication much earlier, much more fundamental than that.'

307

'It's only the Gospel of Saint John that talks about the Word,' Ellie commented – a little pedantically, she thought as soon as the words were out of her mouth. 'The earlier Synoptic Gospels say nothing about it. It's really an accretion from Greek philosophy. What kind of preverbal communication do you mean?'

'Your question is made of words. You ask me to use words to describe what has nothing to do with words. Let me see. There is a Japanese story called "The Dream of the Ants." It is set in the Kingdom of the Ants. It is a long story, and I will not tell it to you now. But the point of the story is this: To understand the language of the ants, you must become an ant.'

'The language of the ants is in fact a chemical language,' said Lunacharsky, eyeing the Abbot keenly. 'They lay down specific molecular traces to indicate the path they have taken to find food. To understand the language of the ants, I need a gas chromatograph, or a mass spectrometer. I do not need to become an ant.'

'Probably, that is the only way you know to become an ant,' returned the Abbot, looking at no one in particular. 'Tell me, why do people study the signs left by the ants?'

'Well,' Ellie offered, 'I guess an entomologist would say it's to understand the ants and ant society. Scientists take pleasure in understanding.'

'That is only another way of saying that they love the ants.'

She suppressed a small shudder.

'Yes, but those who fund the entomologists say something else. They say it's to control the behavior of ants, to make them leave a house they've infested, say, or to understand the biology of soil for agriculture. It might provide an alternative to pesticides. I guess you could say there's some love of the ants in that,' Ellie mused.

'But it's also in our self-interest,' said Lunacharsky. 'The pesticides are poisonous to us as well.'

'Why are you talking about pesticides in the midst of

308

such a dinner?' shot Sukhavati from across the table.

'We will dream the dream of the ants another time,' the Abbot said softly to Ellie, flashing again that perfect, untroubled smile.

Reshod with the aid of meter-long shoehorns, they approached their small fleet of automobiles, while the serving women and proprietress smiled and bowed ceremoniously. Ellie and Xi watched the Abbot enter a limousine with some of their Japanese hosts.

'I asked him, If he could talk with a stone, could he communicate with the dead?' Xi told her.

'And what did he say?'

'He said the dead were easy. His difficulties were with the living.'

18

Superunification

A rough sea!
Stretched out over Sado
The Milky Way.

— MATSUO BASHO (1644–94)
Poem

Perhaps they had chosen Hokkaido because of its maverick reputation. The climate required construction techniques that were highly unconventional by Japanese standards, and this island was also the home of the Ainu, the hairy aboriginal people still despised by many Japanese. Winters were as severe as the ones in Minnesota or Wyoming. Hokkaido posed certain logistical difficulties, but it was out of the way in case of a catastrophe, being physically separated from the other Japanese islands. It was by no means isolated, however, now that the fifty-one-kilometer-long tunnel connecting it with Honshu had been completed; it was the longest submarine tunnel in the world.

Hokkaido had seemed safe enough for the testing of individual Machine components. But concern had been expressed about actually assembling the Machine in Hokkaido. This was, as the mountains that surrounded the facility bore eloquent testimony, a region surging with recent volcanism. One mountain was growing at a rate of a meter a day. Even the Soviets – Sakhalin Island was only forty-three kilometers away, across the Soya, or La Pérouse Strait – had voiced some misgivings on this score. But in for a kopek, in for a ruble. For all they knew, even a Machine built on the far side of the Moon could blow up the Earth when activated. The decision to build the Machine was the key fact in assessing dangers; *where* the thing was built was an entirely secondary consideration.

By early July, the Machine was once again taking shape. In America, it was still embroiled in political and sectarian controversy; and there were apparently serious technical problems with the Soviet Machine. But here – in a facility much more modest than that in Wyoming – the dowels had been mounted and the dodecahedron completed, although no public announcement had been made. The ancient Pythagoreans, who first discovered the dodecahedron, had declared its very existence a secret, and the penalties for disclosure were severe. So perhaps it was only fitting that this house-sized dode-cahedron, halfway around the world and 2,600 years later, was known only to a few.

The Japanese Project Director had decreed a few days' rest for everyone. The nearest city of any size was Obihiro, a pretty place at the confluence of the Yubetsu and Tokachi rivers. Some went to ski on strips of un-melted snow on Mount Asahi; others to dam thermal streams with a makeshift rock wall, warming themselves with the decay of radioactive elements cooked in some supernova explosion billions of years before. A few of the project personnel went to the Bamba races, in which massive draft horses pulled heavy ballasted sledges over parallel strips of farmland. But for a serious cele-bration, the Five flew by helicopter to Sapporo, the largest city on Hokkaido, situated less than 200 kilo-meters away.

Propitiously enough, they arrived in time for the Tanabata Festival. The security risk was considered small, because it was the Machine itself much more than these five people that was essential for the success of the project. They had undergone no special training, beyond thorough study of the Message, the Machine, and the miniaturized instruments they would take with them. In a rational world, they would be easy to replace, Ellie

311

thought, although the political impediments in selecting five humans acceptable to all members of the World Machine Consortium had been considerable.

Xi and Vaygay had 'unfinished business,' they said, which could not be completed except over sake. So she, Devi Sukhavati, and Abonneba Eda found themselves guided by their Japanese hosts along one of the side streets of the Odori Promenade, past elaborate displays of paper streamers and lanterns, pictures of leaves, turtles, and ogres, and appealing cartoon representations of a young man and woman in medieval costume. Between two buildings was stretched a large piece of sailcloth on which had been painted a peacock rampant.

She glanced at Eda in his flowing, embroidered linen robe and high stiff cap, and at Sukhavati in another stunning silk sari, and delighted in the company. The Japanese Machine had so far passed all the prescribed tests, and a crew had been agreed upon that was not merely representative – if imperfectly – of the population of the planet, but which included genuine individuals not stamped out by the official cookie cutters of five nations. Every one of them was in some sense a rebel.

Eda, for instance. Here he was, the great physicist, the discoverer of what was called superunification – one elegant theory, which included as special cases physics that ran the gamut from gravitation to quarks. It was an achievement comparable to Isaac Newton's or Albert Einstein's, and Eda was being compared to both. He had been born a Muslim in Nigeria, not unusual in itself, but he was an adherent of an unorthodox Islamic faction called the Ahmadiyah, which encompassed the Sufis. The Sufis, he explained after the evening with Abbot Utsumi, were to Islam what Zen was to Buddhism. Ahmadiyah proclaimed 'a *jihad* of the pen, not the sword.'

Despite his quiet, indeed humble demeanor, Eda was a fierce opponent of the more conventional Muslim concept of *jihad*, holy war, and argued instead for the most

312

vigorous free exchange of ideas. In this he was an embarrassment for much of conservative Islam, and opposition to his participation in the Machine crew had been made by some Islamic nations. Nor were they alone. A black Nobel laureate – said occasionally to be the smartest person on Earth – proved too much for some who had masked their racism as a concession to the new social amenities. When Eda visited Tyrone Free in prison four years earlier, there was a marked upsurge in pride among black Americans, and a new role model for the young. Eda brought out the worst in the racists and the best in everyone else.

'The time necessary to do physics is a luxury,' he told Ellie. 'There are many people who could do the same if they had the same opportunity. But if you must search the streets for food, you will not have enough time for physics. It is my obligation to improve conditions for young scientists in my country.'

As he had slowly become a national hero in Nigeria, he spoke out increasingly about corruption, about an unfair sense of entitlement, about the importance of honesty in science and everywhere else, about how great a nation Nigeria could be. It had as many people as the United States in the 1920s, he said. It was rich in resources, and its many cultures were a strength. If Nigeria could overcome its problems, he argued, it would be a beacon for the rest of the world. Seeking quiet and isolation in all other things, on these issues he spoke out. Many Nigerian men and women – Muslims, Christians, and Animists, the young but not only the young – took his vision seriously.

Of Eda's many remarkable traits, perhaps the most striking was his modesty. He rarely offered opinions. His answers to most direct questions were laconic. Only in his writings – or in spoken language after you knew him well – did you glimpse his depth. Amidst all the speculation about the Message and the Machine and what would happen after its activation, Eda had volunteered

313

only one comment: In Mozambique, the story goes, monkeys do not talk, because they know if they utter even a single word some man will come and put them to work.

With such a voluble crew it was strange to have someone as taciturn as Eda. Like many others, Ellie paid especial attention to even his most casual utterances. He would describe as 'foolish errors' his earlier, only partly successful version of superunification. The man was in his thirties and, Ellie and Devi had privately agreed, devastatingly attractive. He was also, she knew, happily married to one wife; she and their children were in Lagos at the moment.

A stand of bamboo cuttings that had been planted for such occasions was adorned, festooned, indeed weighed down with thousands of strips of colored paper. Young men and women especially could be seen augmenting the strange foliage. The Tanabata Festival is unique in Japan for its celebration of love. Representations of the central story were displayed on multipaneled signs and in a performance on a makeshift outdoor stage: Two stars were in love, but separated by the Milky Way. Only once a year, on the seventh day of the seventh month of the lunar calendar, could the lovers contrive to meet – provided it did not rain. Ellie looked up at the crystalline blue of this alpine sky and wished the lovers well. The young man star, the legend went, was a Japanese sort of cowboy, and was represented by the A7 dwarf star Altair. The young woman was a weaver, and represented by Vega. It seemed odd to Ellie that Vega should be central to a Japanese festival a few months before Machine activation. But if you survey enough cultures, you will probably find interesting legends about every bright star in the sky. The legend was of Chinese origin, and had been alluded to by Xi when she had heard him years ago at the first meeting of the World Message Consortium in Paris.

In most of the big cities, the Tanabata Festival was

314

dying. Arranged marriages had ceased to be the norm, and the anguish of the separated lovers no longer struck so responsive a chord as it once had. But in a few places – Sapporo, Sendai, a few others – the Festival grew more popular each year. In Sapporo it had a special poignancy because of the still widespread outrage at Japanese-Ainu marriages. There was an entire cottage industry of detectives on the island who would, for a fee, investigate the relatives and antecedents of possible spouses for your children. Ainu ancestry was still held to be a ground for summary rejection. Devi, remembering her young husband of many years before, was especially scathing. Eda doubtless had heard a story or two along the same line, but he was silent.

The Tanabata Festival in the Honshu city of Sendai was now a staple on Japanese television for people who now could rarely see the real Altair or Vega. She wondered if the Vegans would continue broadcasting the same Message to the Earth forever. Partly because the Machine was being completed in Japan, it received considerable attention in the television commentary accompanying this year's Tanabata Festival. But the Five, as they were now sometimes called, had not been required to appear on Japanese television, and their presence here in Sapporo for the Festival was not generally known. Nevertheless, Eda, Sukhavati, and she were readily recognized, and they made their way back to the Obori Promenade to the accompaniment of polite scattered applause by passersby. Many also bowed. A loudspeaker outside a music shop blared a rock-and-roll piece that Ellie recognized. It was 'I Wanna Ricochet Off You,' by the black musical group White Noise. In the afternoon sun was a rheumy-eyed, elderly dog, which, as she approached, wagged its tail feebly.

Japanese commentators talked of Machindo, the Way of the Machine – the increasingly common perspective of the Earth as a planet and of all humans sharing an equal stake in its future. Something like it had been proclaimed

315

in some, but by no means all, religions. Practitioners of those religions understandably resented the insight being attributed to an alien Machine. If the acceptance of a new insight on our place in the universe represents a religious conversion, she mused, then a theological revolution was sweeping the Earth. Even the American and European chiliasts had been influenced by Machindo. But if the Machine didn't work and the Message went away, how long, she wondered, would the insight last? Even if we had made some mistake in interpretation or construction, she thought, even if we never understood anything more about the Vegans, the Message demonstrated beyond a shadow of a doubt that there were other beings in the universe, and that they were more advanced than we. That should help keep the planet unified for a while, she thought.

She asked Eda if he had ever had a transforming religious experience.

'Yes,' he said.

'When?' Sometimes you had to encourage him to talk.

'When I first picked up Euclid. Also when I first understood Newtonian gravitation. And Maxwell's equations, and general relativity. And during my work on superunification. I have been fortunate enough to have had many religious experiences.'

'No,' she returned. 'You know what I mean. Apart from science.'

'Never,' he replied instantly. 'Never apart from science.'

He told her a little of the religion he had been born into. He did not consider himself bound by all its tenets, he said, but he was comfortable with it. He thought it could do much good. It was a comparatively new sect – contemporaneous with Christian Science or the Jehovah's Witnesses – founded by Mirza Ghulam Ahmad in the Punjab. Devi apparently knew something about the Ahmadiyah as a proselytizing sect. It had been especially successful in West Africa. The origins of the religion

316

were wrapped in eschatology. Ahmad had claimed to be the Mahdi, the figure Muslims expect to appear at the end of the world. He also claimed to be Christ come again, an incarnation of Krishna, and a *buruz*, or reappearance of Mohammed. Christian chiliasm had now infected the Ahmadiyah, and his reappearance was imminent according to some of the faithful. The year 2008, the centenary of Ahmad's death, was now a favored date for his Final Return as Mahdi. The global messianic fervor, while sputtering, seemed on average to be swelling still further, and Ellie confessed concern about the irrational predilections of the human species.

'At a Festival of Love,' said Devi, 'you should not be such a pessimist.'

In Sapporo there had been an abundant snowfall, and the local custom of making snow and ice sculptures of animals and mythological figures was updated. An immense dodecahedron had been meticulously carved and was shown regularly, as a kind of icon, on the evening news. After unseasonably warm days, the ice sculptors could be seen packing, chipping, and grinding, repairing the damage.

That the activation of the Machine might, one way or another, trigger a global apocalypse was a fear now often being voiced. The Machine Project responded with confident guarantees to the public, quiet assurances to the governments, and decrees to keep the activation time secret. Some scientists proposed activation on November 17, an evening on which was predicted the most spectacular meteor shower of the century. An agreeable symbolism, they said. But Valerian argued that if the machine was to leave the Earth at that moment, having to fly through a cloud of cometary debris would provide an additional and unnecessary hazard. So activation was postponed for a few weeks, until the end of the last month of nineteen hundred and anything. While this date was not literally the Turn of the Millennium, but a year

317

before, celebrations on a lavish scale were planned by those who could not be bothered to understand the calendrical conventions, or who wished to celebrate the coming of the Third Millennium in two consecutive Decembers.

Although the extraterrestrials could not have known how much each crew member weighed, they specified in painstaking detail the mass of each machine component and the total permissible mass. Very little was left over for equipment of terrestrial design. This fact had some years before been used as an argument for an all-woman crew, so that the equipment allowance could be increased; but the suggestion had been rejected as frivolous.

There was no room for space suits. They would have to hope the Vegans would remember that humans had a propensity for breathing oxygen. With virtually no equipment of their own, with their cultural differences and their unknown destination, it was clear that the mission might entail great risk. The world press discussed it often; the Five themselves, never.

A variety of miniature cameras, spectrometers, superconducting supercomputers, and microfilm libraries were being urged on the crew. It made sense and it didn't make sense. There were no sleeping or cooking or toilet facilities on board the Machine. They were taking only a minimum of provisions, some of them stuffed in the pockets of their coveralls. Devi was to carry a rudimentary medical kit. As far as she was concerned, Ellie thought, she was barely planning to bring a toothbrush and a change of underwear. If they can get me to Vega in a chair, she thought, they'll probably be able to provide the amenities as well. If she needed a camera, she told project officials, she'd just ask the Vegans for one.

There was a body of opinion, apparently serious, that the Five should go naked; since clothing had not been specified it should not be included, because it might somehow disturb the functioning of the Machine. Ellie and Devi, among many others, were amused, and noted that there was no proscription *against* wearing clothing, a popular human custom evident in the Olympic broadcast. The Vegans knew we wore clothes, Xi and Vaygay protested. The only restrictions were on total mass. Should we also extract dental work, they asked, and leave eyeglasses behind? Their view carried the day, in part because of the reluctance of many nations to be associated with a project culminating so indecorously. But the debate generated a little raw humor among the press, the technicians, and the Five.

'For that matter,' Lunacharsky said, 'it doesn't actually specify that human beings are to go. Maybe they would find five chimpanzees equally acceptable.'

Even a single two-dimensional photograph of an alien machine could be invaluable, she was told. And imagine a picture of the aliens themselves. Would she please reconsider and bring a camera? Der Heer, who was now on Hokkaido with a large American delegation, told her to be serious. The stakes were too high, he said, for – but she cut him short with a look so withering that he could not complete the sentence. In her mind, she knew what he was going to say – for childish behavior. Amazingly, der Heer was acting as if he had been the injured party in their relationship. She described it all to Devi, who was not fully sympathetic. Der Heer, she said, was 'very sweet.' Eventually, Ellie agreed to take an ultraminiaturized video camera.

In the manifest that the project required, under 'Personal Effects,' she listed 'Frond, palm, 0.811 kilograms.'

Der Heer was sent to reason with her. 'You know there's a splendid infrared imaging system you can carry along for two-thirds of a kilogram. Why would you want to take the branch of a tree?'

'A frond. It's a palm frond. I know you grew up in New York, but you must know what a palm tree is. It's all in *Ivanhoe*. Didn't you read it in high school? At the time of the Crusades, pilgrims who made the long

319

journey to the Holy Land took back a palm frond to show they'd really been there. It's to keep my spirits up. I don't care *how* advanced they are. The Earth is *my* Holy Land. I'll bring a frond to them to show them where I came from.'

Der Heer only shook his head. But when she described her reasons to Vaygay, he said, 'This I understand very well.'

Ellie remembered Vaygay's concerns and the story he had told her in Paris about the droshky sent to the impoverished village. But this was not her worry at all. The palm frond served another purpose, she realized. She needed something to remind her of Earth. She was afraid she might be tempted not to come back.

The day before the Machine was to be activated she received a small package that had been delivered by hand to her apartment on the site in Wyoming and trans-shipped by courier. There was no return address and, inside, no note and no signature. The package held a gold medallion on a chain. Conceivably, it could be used as a pendulum. An inscription had been engraved on both sides, small but readable. One side read

> Hera, superb Queen
> With the golden robes,
> Commanded Argus,
> Whose glances bristle
> Out through the world.

On the obverse, she read:

This is the response of the defenders of Sparta to the Commander of the Roman Army: 'If you are a god, you will not hurt those who have never injured you. If you are a man, advance – and you will find men equal to yourself.' And women.

She knew who had sent it.

★

Next day, Activation Day, they took an opinion poll of the senior staff on what would happen. Most thought nothing would happen, that the Machine would not work. A smaller number believed that the Five would somehow find themselves very quickly in the Vega system, relativity to the contrary notwithstanding. Others suggested, variously, that the Machine was a vehicle for exploring the solar system, the most expensive practical joke in history, a classroom, a time machine, or a galactic telephone booth. One scientist wrote: 'Five very ugly replacements with green scales and sharp teeth will slowly materialize in the chairs.' This was the closest to the Trojan Horse scenario in any of the responses. Another, but only one, read 'Doomsday Machine.'

There was a ceremony of sorts. Speeches were made, food and drink were served. People hugged one another. Some cried quietly. Only a few were openly skeptical. You could sense that if anything at all happened on Activation the response would be thunderous. There was an intimation of joy in many faces.

Ellie managed to call the nursing home and wish her mother goodbye. She spoke the word into the mouthpiece on Hokkaido, and in Wisconsin the identical sound was generated. But there was no response. Her mother was recovering some motor functions on her stricken side, the nurse told her. Soon she might be able to speak a few words. By the time the call had been completed, Ellie was feeling almost lighthearted.

The Japanese technicians were wearing *hachimaki*, cloth bands around their heads, that were traditionally donned in preparation for mental, physical, or spiritual effort, especially combat. Printed on the headband was a conventional projection of the map of the Earth. No single nation held a dominant position.

There had not been much in the way of national briefings. As far as she could tell, no one had been urged to rally round the flag. National leaders sent short state-

321

ments on videotape. The President's was especially fine, Ellie thought:

'This is not a briefing, and not a farewell. It's just a so long. Each of you makes this journey on behalf of a billion souls. You represent all the peoples of the planet Earth. If you are to be transported to somewhere else, then see for all of us – not just the science, but everything you can learn. You represent the entire human species, past, present, and future. Whatever happens, your place in history is secure. You are heroes of our planet. Speak for all of us. Be wise. And . . . come back.'

A few hours later, for the first time, they entered the Machine – one by one, through a small airlock. Recessed interior lights, very low-key, came on. Even after the Machine had been completed and had passed every prescribed test, they were afraid to have the Five take their places prematurely. Some project personnel worried that merely sitting down might induce the Machine to operate, even if the benzels were stationary. But here they were, and nothing extraordinary was happening so far. This was the first moment she was able to lean back, a little gingerly to be sure, into the molded and cushioned plastic. She had wanted chintz; chintz slipcovers would have been perfect for these chairs. But even this, she discovered, was a matter of national pride. The plastic seemed more modern, more scientific, more serious.

Knowing of Vaygay's careless smoking habits, they had decreed that no cigarettes could be carried on board the Machine. Lunacharsky had uttered fluent maledictions in ten languages. Now he entered after the others, having finished his last Lucky Strike. He wheezed just a little as he sat down beside her. There were no seat belts in the design extracted from the Message, so there were none in the Machine. Some project personnel had argued, nevertheless, that it was foolhardy to omit them.

The Machine *goes* somewhere, she thought. It was a means of conveyance, an aperture to elsewhere . . . or elsewhen. It was a freight train barreling and wailing into the night. If you had climbed aboard, it could carry you out of the stifling provincial towns of your childhood, to the great crystal cities. It was discovery and escape and an end to loneliness. Every logistical delay in manufacture and every dispute over the proper interpretation of some subcodicil of the instructions had plunged her into despair. It was not glory she was seeking . . . not mainly, not much . . . but instead a kind of liberation.

She was a wonder junkie. In her mind, she was a hill tribesman standing slack-jawed before the real Ishtar Gate of ancient Babylon; Dorothy catching her first glimpse of the vaulted spires of the Emerald City of Oz; a small boy from darkest Brooklyn plunked down in the Corridor of Nations of the 1939 World's Fair, the Trylon and Perisphere beckoning in the distance; she was Pocahontas sailing up the Thames estuary with London spread out before her from horizon to horizon.

Her heart sang in anticipation. She would discover, she was sure, what else is possible, what could be accomplished by other beings, great beings – beings who had, it seemed likely, been voyaging between the stars when the ancestors of humans were still brachiating from branch to branch in the dappled sunlight of the forest canopy.

Drumlin, like many others she had known over the years, had called her an incurable romantic; and she found herself wondering again why so many people thought it some embarrassing disability. Her romanticism had been a driving force in her life and a fount of delights. Advocate and practitioner of romance, she was off to see the Wizard.

A status report came through by radio. There were no apparent malfunctions, so far as could be detected with the battery of instrumentation that had been set up exterior to the machine. Their main wait was for the evacuation of the space between and around the benzels. A system of extraordinary efficiency was pumping out the air to attain the highest vacuum ever reached on Earth. She double-checked the stowage of her video microcamera system and gave the palm frond a pat. Powerful lights on the exterior of the dodecahedron had turned on. Two of the spherical shells had now spun up to what the Message had defined as critical speed. It was already a blur to those watching outside. The third benzel would be there in a minute. A strong electrical charge was building up. When all three spherical shells with their mutually perpendicular axes were up to speed, the Machine would be activated. Or so the Message had said.

Xi's face showed fierce determination, she thought; Lunacharsky's a deliberate calm; Sukhavati's eyes were open wide; Eda revealed only an attitude of quiet attentiveness. Devi caught her glance and smiled.

She wished she had had a child. It was her last thought before the walls flickered and became transparent and, it seemed, the Earth opened up and swallowed her.

Part III

THE GALAXY

So I walk on uplands unbounded,
and know that there is hope
for that which Thou didst mold out of dust
to have consort with things eternal.

— The Dead Sea Scrolls

19

Naked Singularity

. . . . mount to paradise
By the stairway of surprise.

— RALPH WALDO EMERSON
'Merlin,' *Poems* (1847)

It is not impossible that to some infinitely superior being
the whole universe may be as one plain, the distance
between planet and planet being only as the pores in a
grain of sand, and the spaces between system and system
no greater than the intervals between one grain and the
grain adjacent.

— SAMUEL TAYLOR COLERIDGE
Omniania

They were falling. The pentagonal panels of the dodecahedron had become transparent. So had the roof and
the floor. Above and below she could make out the
organosilicate lacework and the implanted erbium
dowels, which seemed to be stirring. All three benzels
had disappeared. The dodecahedron plunged, racing
down a long dark tunnel just broad enough to permit its
passage. The acceleration seemed somewhere around
one g. As a result, Ellie, facing forward, was pressed
backward in her chair, while Devi, opposite her, was
bending slightly at the waist. Perhaps they should have
added seat belts.

It was hard not to entertain the thought that they had
plunged into the mantle of the Earth, bound for its core
of molten iron. Or maybe they were on their way
straight to . . . She tried to imagine this improbable
conveyance as a ferryboat upon the River Styx.

There was a texture to the tunnel walls, from which she could sense their speed. The patterns were irregular soft-edged mottlings, nothing with a well-defined form. The walls were not memorable for their appearance, only for their function. Even a few hundred kilometers beneath the Earth's surface the rocks would be glowing with red heat. There was no hint of that. No minor demons were managing the traffic, and no cupboards with jars of marmalade were in evidence.

Every now and then a forward vertex of the dodecahedron would brush the wall, and flakes of an unknown material would be scraped off. The dodec itself seemed unaffected. Soon, quite a cloud of fine particles was following them. Every time the dodecahedron touched the wall, she could sense an undulation, as if something soft had retreated to lessen the impact. The faint yellow lighting was diffuse, uniform. Occasionally the tunnel would swerve gently, and the dodec would obligingly follow the curvature. Nothing, so far as she could see, was headed toward them. At these speeds, even a collision with a sparrow would produce a devastating explosion. Or what if this was an endless fall into a bottomless well? She could feel a continuous physical anxiety in the pit of her stomach. Even so, she entertained no second thoughts.

Black hole, she thought. *Black hole*. I'm falling through the event horizon of a black hole toward the dread singularity. Or maybe this isn't a black hole and I'm headed toward a naked singularity. That's what the physicists called it, a naked singularity. Near a singularity, causality could be violated, effects could precede causes, time could flow backward, and you were unlikely to survive, much less remember the experience. For a rotating black hole, she dredged up from her studies years before, there was not a point but a ring singularity or something still more complex to be avoided. Black holes were nasty. The gravitational tidal forces were so great that you would be stretched into a long thin thread

328

if you were so careless as to fall in. You would also be crushed laterally. Happily, there was no sign of any of this. Through the gray transparent surfaces that were now the ceiling and floor, she could see a great flurry of activity. The organosilicate matrix was collapsing on itself in some places and unfolding in others; the embedded erbium dowels were spinning and tumbling. Everything inside the dodec – including herself and her companions – looked quite ordinary. Well, maybe a bit excited. But they were not yet long thin threads.

These were idle ruminations, she knew. The physics of black holes was not her field. Anyway, she could not understand how this could have anything to *do* with black holes, which were either primordial – made during the origin of the universe – or produced in a later epoch by the collapse of a star more massive than the Sun. Then, the gravity would be so strong that – except for quantum effects – even light could not escape, although the gravitational field certainly would remain. Hence 'black,' hence 'hole.' But they hadn't collapsed a star, and she couldn't see any way in which they had captured a primordial black hole. Anyway, no one knew where the nearest primordial black hole might be hiding. They had only built the Machine and spun up the benzels.

She glanced over to Eda, who was figuring something on a small computer. By bone conduction, she could feel as well as hear a low-pitched roaring every time the dodec scraped the wall, and she raised her voice to be heard.

'Do you understand what's going on?'

'Not at all,' he shouted back. 'I can almost prove this can't be happening. Do you know the Boyer-Lindquist coordinates?'

'No, sorry.'

'I'll explain it to you later.'

She was glad he thought there would be a 'later.'

Ellie felt the deceleration before she could see it, as if they had been on the downslope of a roller coaster, had leveled out, and now were slowly climbing. Just before the deceleration set in, the tunnel had made a complex sequence of bobs and weaves. There was no perceptible change either in the color or in the brightness of the surrounding light. She picked up her camera, switched to the long-focal-length lens, and looked as far ahead of her as she could. She could see only to the next jag in the tortuous path. Magnified, the texture of the wall seemed intricate, irregular, and, just for a moment, faintly self-luminous.

The dodecahedron had slowed to a comparative crawl. No end to the tunnel was in sight. She wondered if they would make it to wherever they were going. Perhaps the designers had miscalculated. Maybe the Machine had been built imperfectly, just a little bit off; perhaps what had seemed on Hokkaido an acceptable technological imperfection would doom their mission to failure here in . . . in wherever this was. Or, glancing at the cloud of fine particles following and occasionally overtaking them, she thought maybe they had bumped into the walls one time too often and lost more momentum than had been allowed for in the design. The space between the dodec and the walls seemed very narrow now. Perhaps they would find themselves stuck fast in this never-never land and languish until the oxygen ran out. Could the Vegans have gone to all this trouble and forgotten that we need to breathe? Hadn't they noticed all those shouting Nazis?

Vaygay and Eda were deep in the arcana of gravitational physics – twistors, renormalization of ghost propagators, time-like Killing vectors, non-Abelian gauge invariance, geodesic refocusing, eleven-dimensional Kaluza-Klein treatments of supergravity, and, of course, Eda's own and quite different superunification. You could tell at a glance that an explanation was not readily within their grasp. She guessed that in another few hours the two physicists would make some progress on the problem. Superunification embraced virtually all scales and aspects of physics known on Earth. It was hard to believe that this . . . tunnel was not itself some hitherto unrealized solution of the Eda Field Equations.

Vaygay asked, 'Did anyone see a naked singularity?'

'I don't know what one looks like,' Devi replied.

'I beg your pardon. It probably wouldn't be naked. Did you sense any causality inversion, anything bizarre – really crazy – maybe about how you were thinking, anything like scrambled eggs reassembling themselves into whites and yolks . . . ?'

Devi looked at Vaygay through narrowed lids.

'It's okay,' Ellie quickly interjected. Vaygay's a little excited, she added to herself. 'These are genuine questions about black holes. They only sound crazy.'

'No,' replied Devi slowly, 'except for the question itself.' But then she brightened. 'In fact it was a marvelous ride.'

They all agreed. Vaygay was elated.

'This is a very strong version of cosmic censorship,' he was saying. 'Singularities are invisible even *inside* black holes.'

'Vaygay is only joking,' Eda added. 'Once you're inside the event horizon, there is no way to escape the black hole singularity.'

Despite Ellie's reassurance, Devi was glancing dubiously at both Vaygay and Eda. Physicists had to invent words and phrases for concepts far removed from everyday experience. It was their fashion to avoid pure neologisms and instead to evoke, even if feebly, some analogous commonplace. The alternative was to name discoveries and equations after one another. This they did also. But if you didn't know it was physics they were talking, you might very well worry about them.

She stood up to cross over to Devi, but at the same moment Xi roused them with a shout. The walls of the tunnel were undulating, closing in on the dodecahedron, squeezing it forward. A nice rhythm was being established. Every time the dodec would slow almost to a halt, it was given another squeeze by the walls. She felt a slight motion sickness rising in her. In some places it was tough going, the walls working hard, waves of contraction and expansion rippling down the tunnel. Elsewhere, especially on the straightaways, they would fairly skip along.

A great distance away, Ellie made out a dim point of light, slowly growing in intensity. A blue-white radiance began flooding the inside of the dodecahedron. She could see it glint off the black erbium cylinders, now almost stationary. Although the journey seemed to have taken only ten or fifteen minutes, the contrast between the subdued, restrained ambient light for most of the trip and the swelling brillance ahead was striking. They were rushing toward it, shooting up the tunnel, and then erupting into what seemed to be ordinary space. Before them was a huge blue-white sun, disconcertingly close. Ellie knew in an instant it was Vega.

She was reluctant to look at it directly through the long-focal-length lens; this was foolhardy even for the Sun, a cooler and dimmer star. But she produced a piece of white paper, moved it so it was in the focal plane of the long lens and projected a bright image of the star. She could see two great sunspot groups and a hint, she thought, a shadow, of some of the material in the ring plane. Putting down the camera, she held her hand at arm's length, palm outward, to just cover the disk of Vega, and was rewarded by seeing a brilliant extended corona around the star; it had been invisible before, washed out in Vega's glare.

Palm still outstretched, she examined the ring of debris that surrounded the star. The nature of the Vega system had been the subject of worldwide debate ever since receipt of the prime number Message. Acting on behalf of the astronomical community of the planet Earth, she hoped she was not making any serious mistakes. She videotaped at a variety of f/stops and frame speeds. They had emerged almost in the ring plane, in a debris-free circumstellar gap. The ring was extremely thin compared with its vast lateral dimensions. She could make out faint color gradations within the rings, but none of the individual ring particles. If they were at all like the rings of Saturn, a particle a few meters across would be a giant. Perhaps the Vegan rings were composed entirely of specks of dust, clods of rock, shards of ice.

She turned around to look back at where they had emerged and saw a field of black – a circular blackness, blacker than velvet, blacker than the night sky. It eclipsed that leeward portion of the Vega ring system which was otherwise – where not obscured by this somber apparition – clearly visible. As she peered through the lens more closely, she thought she could see faint erratic flashes of light from its very center. Hawking radiation? No, its wavelength would be much too long. Or light from the planet Earth still rushing down the tube? On the other side of that blackness was Hokkaido.

Planets. Where were the planets? She scanned the ring plane with the long-focal-length lens, searching for embedded planets – or at least for the home of the beings who had broadcast the Message. In each break in the rings she looked for a shepherding world whose gravitational influence had cleared the lanes of dust. But she could find nothing.

'You can't find any planets?' Xi asked.

'Nothing. There's a few big comets in close. I can see the tails. But nothing that looks like a planet. There must be thousands of separate rings. As far as I can tell, they're all made of debris. The black hole seems to have cleared out a big gap in the rings. That's where we are right now, slowly orbiting Vega. The system is very young – only a few hundred million years old – and some astronomers thought it was too soon for there to be planets. But then where did the transmission come from?'

'Maybe this isn't Vega,' Vaygay offered. 'Maybe our radio signal comes from Vega, but the tunnel goes to another star system.'

'Maybe, but it's a funny coincidence that your other star should have roughly the same color temperature as Vega – look, you can see it's bluish – and the same kind of debris system. It's true, I can't check this out from the constellations because of the glare. I'd still give you ten-to-one odds this is Vega.'

'But then where are they?' Devi asked.

Xi, whose eyesight was acute, was staring up – through the organosilicate matrix, out the transparent pentagonal panels, into the sky far above the ring plane. He said nothing, and Ellie followed his gaze. There was something there, all right, gleaming in the sunlight and with a perceptible angular size. She looked through the long lens. It was some vast irregular polyhedron, each of its faces covered with . . . a kind of circle? Disk? Dish? Bowl?

'Here, Qiaomu, look through here. Tell us what you see.'

'Yes, I see. Your counterparts . . . radio telescopes. Thousands of them, I suppose, pointing in many directions. It is not a world. It is only a device.'

They took turns using the long lens. She concealed her impatience to look again. The fundamental nature of a radio telescope was more or less specified by the physics of radio waves, but she found herself disappointed that a civilization able to make, or even just use, black holes for some kind of hyperrelativistic transport would still be using radio telescopes of recognizable design, no matter how massive the scale. It seemed backward of the Vegans . . . unimaginative. She understood the advantage of putting the telescopes in polar orbit around the star, safe except for twice each revolution from collisions with ring plane debris. But radio telescopes pointing all over the sky – thousands of them – suggested some comprehensive sky survey, an Argus in earnest. Innumerable candidate worlds were being watched for television transmission, military radar, and perhaps other varieties of early radio transmission unknown on Earth. Did they

334

find such signals often, she wondered, or was the Earth their first success in a million years of looking? There was no sign of a welcoming committee. Was a delegation from the provinces so unremarkable that no one had been assigned even to note their arrival?

When the lens was returned to her she took great care with focus, f/stop, and exposure time. She wanted a permanent record, to show the National Science Foundation what really serious radio astronomy was like. She wished there was a way to determine the size of the polyhedral world. The telescopes covered it like barnacles on a whale. A radio telescope in zero g could be essentially any size. After the pictures were developed, she would be able to determine the angular size (maybe a few minutes of arc), but the linear size, the real dimensions, that was impossible to figure out unless you knew how far away the thing was. Nevertheless she sensed it was vast.

'If there are no worlds here,' Xi was saying, 'then there are no Vegans. No one lives here. Vega is only a guardhouse, a place for the border patrol to warm their hands.'

'Those radio telescopes' – he glanced upward – 'are the watchtowers of the Great Wall. If you are limited by the speed of light, it is difficult to hold a galactic empire together. You order the garrison to put down a rebellion. Ten thousand years later you find out what happened. Not good. Too slow. So you give autonomy to the garrison commanders. Then, no more empire. But *those*' – and now he gestured at the receding blot covering the sky behind them – '*those* are imperial roads. Persia had them. Rome had them. China had them. Then you are not restricted to the speed of light. With roads you can hold an empire together.'

But Eda, lost in thought, was shaking his head. Something about the physics was bothering him.

The black hole, if that was what it really was, could now be seen orbiting Vega in a broad lane entirely clear of debris; both inner and outer rings gave it wide berth. It was hard to believe how black it was.

As she took short video pans of the debris ring before her, she wondered whether it would someday form its own planetary system, the particles colliding, sticking, growing ever larger, gravitational condensations taking place until at last only a few large worlds orbited the star. It was very like the picture astronomers had of the origin of the planets around the Sun four and a half billion years ago. She could now make out inhomogeneities in the rings, places with a discernible bulge where some debris had apparently accreted together.

The motion of the black hole around Vega was creating a visible ripple in the bands of debris immediately adjacent. The dodecahedron was doubtless producing some more modest wake. She wondered if these gravitational perturbations, these spreading rarefactions and condensations, would have any long-term consequence, changing the pattern of subsequent planetary formation. If so, then the very existence of some planet billions of years in the future might be due to the black hole and the Machine . . . and therefore to the Message, and therefore to Project Argus. She knew she was overpersonalizing; had she never lived, some other radio astronomer would surely have received the Message, but earlier, or later. The Machine would have been activated at a different moment and the dodec would have found its way here in some other time. So some future planet in this system might still owe its existence to her. Then, by symmetry, she had snatched out of existence some other world that was destined to form had she never lived. It was vaguely burdensome, being responsible by your innocent actions for the fates of unknown worlds.

She attempted a panning shot, beginning inside the dodecahedron, then out to the struts joining the transparent pentagonal panels, and beyond to the gap in the debris rings in which they, along with the black hole, were orbiting. She followed the gap, flanked by two

336

bluish rings, further and further from her. There was something a little odd up ahead, a kind of bowing in the adjacent inner ring.

'Qiaomu,' she said, handing him the long lens, 'look over there. Tell me what you see.'

'Where?'

She pointed again. After a moment he had found it. She could tell because of his slight but quite unmistakable intake of breath.

'Another black hole,' he said. 'Much bigger.'

They were falling again. This time the tunnel was more commodious, and they were making better time.

'That's *it*?' Ellie found herself shouting at Devi. 'They take us to Vega to show off their black holes. They give us a look at their radio telescopes from a thousand kilometers away. We spend ten minutes there, and they pop us into another black hole and ship us back to Earth. That's why we spent two trillion dollars?'

'Maybe we're beside the point,' Lunacharsky was saying. 'Maybe the only real point was to plug themselves into the Earth.'

She imagined nocturnal excavations beneath the gates of Troy.

Eda, fingers of both hands outspread, was making a calming gesture. 'Wait and see,' he said. 'This is a different tunnel. Why should you think it goes back to Earth?'

'Vega's not where we're intended to go?' Devi asked.

'The experimental method. Let's see where we pop out next.'

In this tunnel there was less scraping of the walls and fewer undulations. Eda and Vaygay were debating a space-time diagram they had drawn in Kruskal-Szekeres coordinates. Ellie had no idea what they were talking about. The deceleration stage, the part of the passage that felt uphill, was still disconcerting.

This time the light at the end of the tunnel was orange.

337

They emerged at a considerable speed into the system of a contact binary, two suns touching. The outer layers of a swollen elderly red giant star were pouring onto the photosphere of a vigorous middle-aged yellow dwarf, something like the Sun. The zone of contact between the two stars was brilliant. She looked for debris rings or planets or orbiting radio observatories, but could find none. That doesn't mean very much, she told herself. These systems could have a fair number of planets and I'd never know it with this dinky long lens. She projected the double sun onto the piece of paper and photographed the image with a short-focal-length lens.

Because there were no rings, there was less scattered light in this system than around Vega; with the wide-angle lens she was able, after a bit of searching, to recognize a constellation that sufficiently resembled the Big Dipper. But she had difficulty recognizing the other constellations. Since the bright stars in the Big Dipper are a few hundred light-years from Earth, she concluded that they had not jumped more than a few hundred light-years.

She told this to Eda and asked him what he thought.

'What do I think? I think this is an Underground.'

'An Underground?'

She recalled her sensation of falling, into the depths of Hell it had seemed for a moment, just after the Machine had been activated.

'A Metro. A subway. These are the stations. The stops. Vega and this system and others. Passengers get on and off at the stops. You change trains here.'

He gestured at the contact binary, and she noticed that his hand cast two shadows, one anti-yellow and the other anti-red, like in – it was the only image that came to mind – a discotheque.

'But *we*, we cannot get off,' Eda continued. 'We are in a closed railway car. We're headed for the terminal, the end of the line.'

Drumlin had called such speculations Fantasyland, and

338

this was – so far as she knew – the first time Eda had succumbed to the temptation.

Of the Five, she was the only observational astronomer, even though her specialty was not in the optical spectrum. She felt it her responsibility to accumulate as much data as possible, in the tunnels and in the ordinary four-dimensional space-time into which they would periodically emerge. The presumptive black hole from which they exited would always be in orbit around some star or multiple-star system. They were always in pairs, always two of them sharing a similar orbit – one from which they were ejected, and another into which they fell. No two systems were closely similar. None was very like the solar system. All provided instructive astronomical insights. Not one of them exhibited anything like an artifact – a second dodecahedron, or some vast engineering project to take apart a world and reassemble it into what Xi had called a device.

At this time they emerged near a star visibly changing its brightness (she could tell from the progression of f/stops required) – perhaps it was one of the RR Lyrae stars; next was a quintuple system; then a feebly luminous brown dwarf. Some were in open space, some were embedded in nebulosity, surrounded by glowing molecular clouds.

She recalled the warning 'This will be deducted from your share in Paradise.' Nothing had been deducted from hers. Despite a conscious effort to retain a professional calm, her heart soared at this profusion of suns. She hoped that every one of them was a home to someone. Or would be one day.

But after the fourth jump she began to worry. Subjectively, and by her wristwatch, it felt something like an hour since they had 'left' Hokkaido. If this took much longer, the absence of amenities would be felt. Probably there were aspects of human physiology that could not be deduced even after attentive television viewing by a very advanced civilization.

And if the extraterrestrials were so smart, why were they putting us through so many little jumps? All right, maybe the hop from Earth used rudimentary equipment because only primitives were working one side of the tunnel. But after Vega? Why couldn't they jump us directly to wherever the dodec was going?

Each time she came barreling out of a tunnel, she was expectant. What wonders had they in store for her next? It put her in mind of a very upscale amusement park, and she found herself imagining Hadden peering down his telescope at Hokkaido the moment the Machine had been activated.

As glorious as the vistas offered by the Message makers were, and however much she enjoyed a kind of proprietary mastery of the subject as she explained some aspect of stellar evolution to the others, she was after a time disappointed. She had to work to track the feeling down. Soon she had it: The extraterrestrials were boasting. It was unseemly. It betrayed some defect of character.

As they plunged down still another tunnel, this one broader and more tortuous than the others, Lunacharsky asked Eda to guess why the subway stops were put in such unpromising star systems. 'Why not around a single star, a young star in good health and with no debris?'

'Because,' Eda replied, '– of course, I am only guessing as you ask – because all such systems are inhabited . . .'

'And they don't want the tourists scaring the natives,' Sukhavati shot back.

Eda smiled. 'Or the other way around.'

'But that's what you mean, isn't it? There's some sort of ethic of noninterference with primitive planets. They know that every now and then some of the primitives might use the subway . . .'

'And they're *pretty* sure of the primitives,' Ellie continued the thought, 'but they can't be *absolutely* sure. After all, primitives are primitive. So you let them ride only on subways that go to the sticks. The builders must be a very cautious bunch. But then why did they send us a local train and not an express?'

'Probably it's too hard to build an express tunnel,' said Xi, years of digging experience behind him. Ellie thought of the Honshu–Hokkaido Tunnel, one of the prides of civil engineering on Earth, all of fifty-one kilometers long.

A few of the turns were quite steep now. She thought about her Thunderbird, and then she thought about getting sick. She decided she would fight it as long as she could. The dodecahedron had not been equipped with airsickness bags.

Abruptly they were on a straightaway, and then the sky was full of stars. Everywhere she looked there were stars, not the paltry scattering of a few thousand still occasionally known to naked-eye observers on Earth, but a vast multitude – many almost touching their nearest neighbors it seemed – surrounding her in every direction, many of them tinted yellow or blue or red, especially red. The sky was blazing with nearby suns. She could make out an immense spiraling cloud of dust, an accretion disk apparently flowing into a black hole of staggering proportions, out of which flashes of radiation were coming like heat lightning on a summer's night. If this was the center of the Galaxy, as she suspected, it would be bathed in synchrotron radiation. She hoped the extraterrestrials had remembered how frail humans were.

And swimming into her field of view as the dodec rotated was . . . a prodigy, a wonder, a miracle. They were upon it almost before they knew it. It filled half the sky. Now they were flying over it. On its surface were hundreds, perhaps thousands, of illuminated doorways, each a different shape. Many were polygonal or circular or with an elliptical cross section, some had projecting appendages or a sequence of partly overlapping off-

341

center circles. She realized they were docking ports, thousands of different docking ports – some perhaps only meters in size, others clearly kilometers across, or larger. Every one of them, she decided, was the template of some interstellar machine like this one. Big creatures in serious machines had imposing entry ports. Little creatures, like us, had tiny ports. It was a democratic arrangement, with no hint of particularly privileged civilizations. The diversity of ports suggested few social distinctions among the sundry civilizations, but it implied a breathtaking diversity of beings and cultures. Talk about Grand Central Station! she thought.

The vision of a populated Galaxy, of a universe spilling over with life and intelligence, made her want to cry for joy.

They were approaching a yellow-lit port which, Ellie could see, was the exact template of the dodecahedron in which they were riding. She watched a nearby docking port, where something the size of the dodecahedron and shaped approximately like a starfish was gently insinuating itself onto its template. She glanced left and right, up and down, at the almost imperceptible curvature of this great Station situated at what she guessed was the center of the Milky Way. What a vindication for the human species, invited here at last! There's hope for us, she thought. There's hope!

'Well, it isn't Bridgeport.'

She said this aloud as the docking maneuver completed itself in perfect silence.

20
Grand Central Station

All things are artificial, for nature is the art of God.

> – THOMAS BROWNE
> 'On Dreams'
> *Religio Medici* (1642)

Angels need an assumed body, not for themselves, but on our account.

> – THOMAS AQUINAS
> *Summa Theologica*, I, 51, 2

The devil hath power
To assume a pleasing shape.

> – WILLIAM SHAKESPEARE
> *Hamlet*, II, ii, 628

The airlock was designed to accommodate only one person at a time. When questions of priority had come up – which nation would be first represented on the planet of another star – the Five had thrown up their hands in disgust and told the project managers that this wasn't *that* kind of mission. They had conscientiously avoided discussing the issue among themselves.

Both the interior and the exterior doors of the airlock opened simultaneously. They had given no command. Apparently, this sector of Grand Central was adequately pressurized and oxygenated.

'Well, who wants to go first?' Devi asked.

Video camera in hand, Ellie waited in line to exit, but then decided that the palm frond should be with her when she set foot on this new world. As she went to retrieve it, she heard a whoop of delight from outside, probably from Vaygay. Ellie rushed into the bright sunlight. The threshold of the airlock's exterior doorway was flush with the sand. Devi was ankle-deep in the water, playfully splashing in Xi's direction. Eda was smiling broadly.

It was a beach. Waves were lapping on the sand. The blue sky sported a few lazy cumulus clouds. There was a stand of palm trees, irregularly spaced a little back from the water's edge. A sun was in the sky. One sun. A yellow one. Just like ours, she thought. A faint aroma was in the air; cloves, perhaps, and cinnamon. It could have been a beach on Zanzibar.

So they had voyaged 30,000 light-years to walk on a beach. Could be worse, she thought. The breeze stirred, and a little whirlwind of sand was created before her. Was all this just some elaborate simulation of the Earth, perhaps reconstructed from the data returned by a routine scouting expedition millions of years earlier? Or had the five of them undertaken this epic voyage only to improve their knowledge of descriptive astronomy, and then been unceremoniously dumped into some pleasant corner of the Earth?

When she turned, she discovered that the dode-cahedron had disappeared. They had left the supercon-ducting supercomputer and its reference library as well as some of the instruments aboard. It worried them for about a minute. They were safe and they had survived a trip worth writing home about. Vaygay glanced from the frond she had struggled to bring here to the colony of palm trees along the beach, and laughed.

'Coals to Newcastle,' Devi commented.

But *her* frond was different. Perhaps they had different species here. Or maybe the local variety had been pro-duced by an inattentive manufacturer. She looked out to sea. Irresistibly brought to mind was the image of the first colonization of the Earth's land, some 400 million years ago. Wherever this was – the Indian Ocean or the center of the Galaxy – the five of them had done something unparalleled. The itinerary and destinations were entirely out of their hands, it was true. But they had crossed the ocean of interstellar space and begun what surely must be a new age in human history. She was very proud.

Xi removed his boots and rolled up to his knees the legs of the tacky insignia-laden jump suit the governments had decreed they all must wear. He ambled through the gentle surf. Devi stepped behind a palm tree and emerged sari-clad, her jump suit draped over her arm. It reminded Ellie of a Dorothy Lamour movie. Eda produced the sort of linen hat that was his visual trademark throughout the world. Ellie videotaped them in short jumpy takes. It would look, when they got home, exactly like a home movie. She joined Xi and Vaygay in the surf. The water seemed almost warm. It was a pleasant afternoon and, everything considered, a welcome change from the Hokkaido winter they had left little more than an hour before.

'Everyone has brought something symbolic,' said Vaygay, 'except me.'

'How do you mean?'

'Sukhavati and Eda bring national costumes. Xi here has brought a grain of rice.' Indeed, Xi was holding the grain in a plastic bag between thumb and forefinger. 'You have your palm frond,' Vaygay continued. 'But me, I have brought no symbols, no mementos from Earth. I'm the only real materialist in the group, and everything I've brought is in my head.'

Ellie had hung her medallion around her neck, under the jump suit. Now she loosened the collar and pulled out the pendant. Vaygay noticed, and she gave it to him to read.

'It's Plutarch, I think,' he said after a moment. 'Those were brave words the Spartans spoke. But remember, the Romans won the battle.'

From the tone of this admonition, Vaygay must have

thought the medallion a gift from der Heer. She was warmed by his disapproval of Ken – surely justified by events – and by his steadfast solicitude. She took his arm.

'I would kill for a cigarette,' he said amiably, using his arm to squeeze her hand to his side.

The five of them sat together by a little tide pool. The breaking of the surf generated a soft white noise that reminded her of Argus and her years of listening to cosmic static. The Sun was well past the zenith, over the ocean. A crab scuttled by, sidewise dexterous, its eyes swiveling on their stalks. With crabs, coconuts, and the limited provisions in their pockets, they could survive comfortably enough for some time. There were no footprints on the beach besides their own.

'We think they did almost all the work.' Vaygay was explaining his and Eda's thinking on what the five of them had experienced. 'All the project did was to make the faintest pucker in space-time, so they would have something to hook their tunnel onto. In all of that multidimensional geometry, it must be very difficult to detect a tiny pucker in space-time. Even harder to fit a nozzle onto it.'

'What are you saying? They changed the geometry of space?'

'Yes. We're saying that space is topologically non-simply connected. It's like – I know Abonneba doesn't like this analogy – it's like a flat two-dimensional surface, the smart surface, connected by some maze of tubing with some other flat two-dimensional surface, the dumb surface. The only way you can get from the smart surface to the dumb surface in a reasonable time is through the tubes. Now imagine that the people on the smart surface lower a tube with a nozzle on it. They will make a tunnel between the two surfaces, provided the dumb ones cooperate by making a little pucker on *their* surface, so the nozzle can attach itself.'

'So the smart guys send a radio message and tell the

dumb ones how to make a pucker. But if they're truly two-dimensional beings, how *could* they make a pucker on their surface?'

'By accumulating a great deal of mass in one place.' Vaygay said this tentatively.

'But that's not what we did.'

'I know. I know. Somehow the benzels did it.'

'You see,' Eda explained softly, 'if the tunnels are black holes, there are real contradictions implied. There is an interior tunnel in the exact Kerr solution of the Einstein Field Equations, but it's unstable. The slightest perturbation would seal it off and convert the tunnel into a physical singularity through which nothing can pass. I have tried to imagine a superior civilization that would control the internal structure of a collapsing star to keep the interior tunnel stable. This is very difficult. The civilization would have to monitor and stabilize the tunnel forever. It would be especially difficult with something as large as the dodecahedron falling through.'

'Even if Abonneba can discover how to keep the tunnel open, there are many other problems,' Vaygay said. 'Too many. Black holes collect problems faster than they collect matter. There are the tidal forces. We should have been torn apart in the black hole's gravitational field. We should have been stretched like people in the paintings of El Greco or the sculptures of that Italian . . . ?' He turned to Ellie to fill in the blank.

'Giacometti,' she suggested. 'He was Swiss.'

'Yes, like Giacometti. Then other problems: As measured from Earth it takes an infinite amount of time for us to pass through a black hole, and we could never, never return to Earth. Maybe this is what happened. Maybe we will never go home. Then, there should be an inferno of radiation near the singularity. This is a quantum-mechanical instability. . . .'

'And finally,' Eda continued, 'a Kerr-type tunnel can lead to grotesque causality violations. With a modest change of trajectory inside the tunnel, one could emerge

347

from the other end as early in the history of the universe as you might like – a picosecond after the Big Bang, for example. That would be a very disorderly universe.'

'Look, fellas,' she said, 'I'm no expert in General Relativity. But didn't we *see* black holes? Didn't we fall into them? Didn't we emerge out of them? Isn't a gram of observation worth a ton of theory?'

'I know, I know,' Vaygay said in mild agony. 'It has to be something else. Our understanding of physics can't be so far off. Can it?'

He addressed this last question, a little plaintively, to Eda, who only replied, 'A naturally occurring black hole can't be a tunnel; they have impassable singularities at their centers.'

With a jerry-rigged sextant and their wristwatches, they timed the angular motion of the setting Sun. It was 360 degrees in twenty-four hours, Earth standard. Before the Sun got too low on the horizon, they disassembled Ellie's camera and used the lens to start a fire. She kept the frond by her side, fearful that someone would carelessly throw it on the flames after dark. Xi proved to be an expert fire maker. He positioned them upwind and kept the fire low.

Gradually the stars came out. They were all there, the familiar constellations of Earth. She volunteered to stay up awhile tending the fire while the others slept. She wanted to see Lyra rise. After some hours, it did. The night was exceptionally clear, and Vega shone steady and brilliant. From the apparent motion of the constellations across the sky, from the southern hemisphere constellations that she could make out, and from the Big Dipper lying near the northern horizon, she deduced that they were in tropical latitudes. If all this is a simulation, she thought before falling asleep, they've gone to a great deal of trouble.

She had an odd little dream. The five of them were swimming – naked, unselfconscious, underwater – now poised lazily near a staghorn coral, now gliding into crannies that were the next moment obscured by drifting seaweed. Once she rose to the surface. A ship in the shape of a dodecahedron flew by, low above the water. The walls were transparent, and inside she could see people in dhotis and sarongs, reading newspapers and casually conversing. She dove back underwater. Where she belonged.

Although the dream seemed to go on for a long time, none of them had any difficulty breathing. They were inhaling and exhaling water. They felt no distress – indeed, they were swimming as naturally as fish. Vaygay even looked a little like a fish – a grouper, perhaps. The water must be fiercely oxygenated, she supposed. In the midst of the dream, she remembered a mouse she had once seen in a physiology laboratory, perfectly content in a flask of oxygenated water, even paddling hopefully with its little front feet. A vermiform tail streamed behind. She tried to remember how much oxygen was needed, but it was too much trouble. She was thinking less and less, she thought. That's all right. Really.

The others were now distinctly fishlike. Devi's fins were translucent. It was obscurely interesting, vaguely sensual. She hoped it would continue, so she could figure something out. But even the question she wanted to answer eluded her. Oh, to breathe warm water, she thought. What will they think of next?

Ellie awoke with a sense of disorientation so profound it bordered on vertigo. Where was she? Wisconsin, Puerto Rico, New Mexico, Wyoming, Hokkaido? Or the Strait of Malacca? Then she remembered. It was unclear, to within 30,000 light-years, where in the Milky Way Galaxy she was; probably the all-time record for disorientation, she thought. Despite the headache, Ellie laughed; and Devi, sleeping beside her, stirred. Because of the upward slope of the beach – they had reconnoitered out to a kilometer or so the previous afternoon and found not a hint of habitation – direct sunlight had not yet reached her. Ellie was recumbent on a pillow of sand. Devi, just awakening, had slept with her head on the rolled-up jump suit.

'Don't you think there's something candy-assed about a culture that needs soft pillows?' Ellie asked. 'The ones who put their heads in wooden yokes at night, that's who the smart money's on.'

Devi laughed and wished her good morning.

They could hear shouting from farther up the beach. The three men were waving and beckoning; Ellie and Devi roused themselves and joined them.

Standing upright on the sand was a door. A wooden door – with paneling and a brass doorknob. Anyway it looked like brass. The door had black-painted metal hinges and was set in two jambs, a lintel, and a threshold. No nameplate. It was in no way extraordinary. For Earth.

'Now go 'round the back,' Xi invited.

From the back, the door was not there at all. She could see Eda and Vaygay and Xi, Devi standing a little apart, and the sand continuous between the four of them and her. She moved to the side, the heels of her feet moistened by the surf, and she could make out a single dark razor-thin vertical line. She was reluctant to touch it. Returning to the back again, she satisfied herself that there were no shadows or reflections in the air before her, and then stepped through.

'Bravo.' Eda laughed. She turned around and found the closed door before her.

'What did you see?' she asked.

'A lovely woman strolling through a closed door two centimeters thick.'

Vaygay seemed to be doing well, despite the dearth of cigarettes.

'Have you tried opening the door?' she asked.

'Not yet,' Xi replied.

She stepped back again, admiring the apparition.

350

'It looks like something by – What's the name of that French surrealist?' Vaygay asked.

'René Magritte,' she answered. 'He was Belgian.'

'We're agreed, I take it, that this isn't really the Earth,' Devi proposed, her gesture encompassing ocean, beach, and sky.

'Unless we're in the Persian Gulf three thousand years ago, and there are djinns about.' Ellie laughed.

'Aren't you impressed by the care of the construction?'

'All right,' Ellie answered. 'They're very good, I'll grant them that. But what's it for? Why go to the trouble of all this detail work?'

'Maybe they just have a passion for getting things right.'

'Or maybe they're just showing off.'

'I don't see,' Devi continued, 'how they could know our doors so well. Think of how many different ways there are to make a door. How *could* they know?'

'It could be television,' Ellie responded. 'Vega has received television signals from Earth up to – let's see – 1974 programming. Clearly, they can send the interesting clips here by special delivery in no time flat. Probably there've been a lot of doors on television between 1936 and 1974. Okay,' she continued, as if this were not a change of subject, 'what do we think would happen if we opened the door and walked in?'

'If we are here to be tested,' said Xi, 'on the other side of that door is probably the Test, maybe one for each of us.'

He was ready. She wished she were.

The shadows of the nearest palms were now falling on the beach. Wordlessly they regarded one another. All four of them seemed eager to open the door and step through. She alone felt some . . . reluctance. She asked Eda if he would like to go first. We might as well put our best foot forward, she thought.

He doffed his cap, made a slight but graceful bow,

turned, and approached the door. Ellie ran to him and kissed him on both cheeks. The others embraced him also. He turned again, opened the door, entered, and disappeared into thin air, his striding foot first, his trailing hand last. With the door ajar, there had seemed to be only the continuation of beach and surf behind him. The door closed. She ran around it, but there was no trace of Eda.

Xi was next. Ellie found herself struck by how docile they all had been, instantly obliging every anonymous invitation proffered. They could have told us where they were taking us, and what all this was *for*, she thought. It could have been part of the Message, or information conveyed after the Machine was activated. They could have told us we were docking with a simulation of a beach on Earth. They could have told us to expect the door. True, as accomplished as they are, the extraterrestrials might know English imperfectly, with television as their only tutor. Their knowledge of Russian, Mandarin, Tamil, and Hausa would be even more rudimentary. But they had invented the language introduced in the Message primer. Why not use it? To retain the element of surprise?

Vaygay saw her staring at the closed door and asked if she wished to enter next.

'Thanks, Vaygay. I've been thinking. I know it's a little crazy. But it just struck me: Why do we have to jump through every hoop they hold out for us? Suppose we don't do what they ask?'

'Ellie, you are so American. For me, this is just like home. I'm used to doing what the authorities suggest – especially when I have no choice.' He smiled and turned smartly on his heel.

'Don't take any crap from the Grand Duke,' she called after him.

High above, a gull squawked. Vaygay had left the door ajar. There was still only beach beyond.

'Are you all right?' Devi asked her.

'I'm okay. Really. I just want a moment to myself. I'll be along.'

'Seriously, I'm asking as a doctor. Do you feel all right?'

'I woke up with a headache, and I think I had some very fanciful dreams. I haven't brushed my teeth or had my black coffee. I wouldn't mind reading the morning paper either. Except for all that, really I'm fine.'

'Well, that sounds all right. For that matter I have a bit of a headache, too. Take care of yourself, Ellie. Remember everything, so you'll be able to tell it to me . . . next time we meet.'

'I will,' Ellie promised.

They kissed and wished each other well. Devi stepped over the threshold and vanished. The door closed behind her. Afterward, Ellie thought she had caught a whiff of curry.

She brushed her teeth in salt water. A certain fastidious streak had always been a part of her nature. She breakfasted on coconut milk. Carefully she brushed accumulated sand off the exterior surfaces of the microcamera system and its tiny arsenal of video-cassettes on which she had recorded wonders. She washed the palm frond in the surf, as she had done the day she found it on Cocoa Beach just before the launch up to *Methuselah*.

The morning was already warm and she decided to take a swim. Her clothes carefully folded on the palm frond, she strode boldly out into the surf. Whatever else, she thought, the extraterrestrials are unlikely to find themselves aroused by the sight of a naked woman, even if she is pretty well preserved. She tried to imagine a microbiologist stirred to crimes of passion after viewing a paramecium caught *in flagrante delicto* in mitosis.

Languidly, she floated on her back, bobbing up and down, her slow rhythm in phase with the arrival of successive wave crests. She tried to imagine thousands of comparable . . . chambers, simulated worlds, whatever these were – each a meticulous copy of the nicest part of

353

someone's home planet. Thousands of them, each with sky and weather, ocean, geology, and indigenous life indistinguishable from the originals. It seemed an extravagance, although it also suggested that a satisfactory outcome was within reach. No matter what your resources, you don't manufacture a landscape on this scale for five specimens from a doomed world.

On the other hand . . . The idea of extraterrestrials as zookeepers had become something of a cliché. What if this sizable Station with its profusion of docking ports and environments was *actually* a zoo? 'See the exotic animals in their native habitats,' she imagined some snail-headed barker shouting. Tourists come from all over the Galaxy, especially during school vacations. And then when there's a test, the Stationmasters temporarily move the critters and the tourists out, sweep the beach free of footprints, and give the newly arriving primitives a half day of rest and recreation before the test ordeal begins.

Or maybe this was how they *stocked* the zoos. She thought about the animals locked away in terrestrial zoos who were said to have experienced difficulties breeding in captivity. Somersaulting in the water, she dived beneath the surface in a moment of self-consciousness. She took a few strong strokes in toward the beach, and for the second time in twenty-four hours wished that she had had a baby.

There was no one about, and not a sail on the horizon. A few seagulls were stalking the beach, apparently looking for crabs. She wished she had brought some bread to give them. After she was dry, she dressed and inspected the doorway again. It was merely waiting. She felt a continuing reluctance to enter. More than reluctance. Maybe dread.

She withdrew, keeping it in view. Beneath a palm tree, her knees drawn up under her chin, she looked out over the long sweep of white sandy beach.

After a while she got up and stretched a little. Carrying

the frond and the microcamera with one hand, she approached the door and turned the knob. It opened slightly. Through the crack she could see the whitecaps offshore. She gave it another push, and it swung open without a squeak. The beach, bland and disinterested, stared back at her. She shook her head and returned to the tree, resuming her pensive posture.

She wondered about the others. Were they now in some outlandish testing facility avidly checking away on the multiple-choice questions? Or was it an oral examination? And who were the examiners? She felt the uneasiness well up once again. Another intelligent being – independently evolved on some distant world under unearthly physical conditions and with an entirely different sequence of random genetic mutations – such a being would not resemble anyone she knew. Or even imagined. If this was a Test station, then there were Stationmasters, and the Stationmasters would be thoroughly, devastatingly nonhuman. There was something deep within her that was bothered by insects, snakes, starnosed moles. She was someone who felt a little shudder – to speak plainly, a tremor of loathing – when confronted with even slightly malformed human beings. Cripples, children with Down's syndrome, even the appearance of Parkinsonism evoked in her, against her clear intellectual resolve, a feeling of disgust, a wish to flee. Generally she had been able to contain her fear, although she wondered if she had ever hurt someone because of it. It wasn't something she thought about much; she would sense her own embarrassment and move on to another topic.

But now she worried that she would be unable even to confront – much less to win over for the human species – an extraterrestrial being. They hadn't thought to screen the Five for that. There had been no effort to determine whether they were afraid of mice or dwarfs or Martians. It had simply not occurred to the examining committees.

She wondered why they hadn't thought of it; it seemed an obvious enough point now.

It had been a mistake to send her. Perhaps when confronted with some serpent-haired galactic Station-master, she would disgrace herself – or far worse, tip the grade given to the human species, in whatever un-fathomable test was being administered, from pass to fail. She looked with both apprehension and longing at the enigmatic door, its lower boundary now under water. The tide was coming in.

There was a figure on the beach a few hundred meters away. At first she thought it was Vaygay, perhaps out of the examining room early and come to tell her the good news. But whoever it was wasn't wearing a Machine Project jump suit. Also, it seemed to be someone youn-ger, more vigorous. She reached for the long lens, and for some reason hesitated. Standing up, she shielded her eyes from the Sun. Just for a moment, it had seemed . . . It was clearly impossible. They would not take such shameless advantage of her.

But she could not help herself. She was racing toward him on the hard sand near the water's edge, her hair streaming behind her. He looked as he had in the most recent picture of him she had seen, vigorous, happy. He had a day's growth of beard. She flew into his arms, sobbing.

'Hello, Presh,' he said, his right hand stroking the back of her head.

His voice was right. She instantly remembered it. And his smell, his gait, his laugh. The way his beard abraded her cheek. All of it combined to shatter her self-possession. She could feel a massive stone seal being pried open and the first rays of light entering an ancient, almost forgotten tomb.

She swallowed and tried to gain control of herself, but seemingly inexhaustible waves of anguish poured out of her and she would weep again. He stood there patiently, reassuring her with the same look she now remembered he had given her from his post at the bottom of the staircase during her first solo journey down the big steps. More than anything else she had longed to see him again, but she had suppressed the feeling, been impatient with it, because it was so clearly impossible to fulfill. She cried for all the years between herself and him.

In her girlhood and as a young woman she would dream that he had come to her to tell her that his death had been a mistake. He was really fine. He would sweep her up into his arms. But she would pay for those brief respites with poignant reawakenings into a world in which he no longer was. Still, she had cherished those dreams and willingly paid their exorbitant tariff when the next morning she was forced to rediscover her loss and experience the agony again. Those phantom moments were all she had left of him.

And now here he was – not a dream or a ghost, but flesh and blood. Or close enough. He had called to her from the stars, and she had come.

She hugged him with all her might. She knew it was a trick, a reconstruction, a simulation, but it was flawless. For a moment she held him by the shoulders at arm's length. He was perfect. It was as if her father had these many years ago died and gone to Heaven, and finally – by this unorthodox route – she had managed to rejoin him. She sobbed and embraced him again.

It took her another minute to compose herself. If it had been Ken, say, she would have at least toyed with the idea that another dodecahedron – maybe a repaired Soviet Machine – had made a later relay from the Earth to the center of the Galaxy. But not for a moment could such a possibility be entertained for him. His remains were decaying in a cemetery by a lake.

She wiped her eyes, laughing and crying at once.

'So, what do I owe this apparition to – robotics or hypnosis?'

357

'Am I an artifact or a dream? You might ask that about anything.'

'Even today, not a week goes by when I don't think that I'd give anything – anything I had – just to spend a few minutes with my father again.'

'Well, here I am,' he said cheerfully, his hands raised, making a half turn so she could be sure that the back of him was there as well. But he was so *young*, younger surely than she. He had been only thirty-six when he died.

Maybe this was their way of calming her fears. If so, they were very . . . thoughtful. She guided him back toward her few possessions, her arm around his waist. He certainly *felt* substantial enough. If there were gear trains and integrated circuits underneath his skin, they were well hidden.

'So how are we doing?' she asked. The question was ambiguous. 'I mean –'

'I know. It took you many years from receipt of the Message to your arrival here.'

'Do you grade on speed or accuracy?'

'Neither.'

'You mean we haven't completed the Test yet?'

He did not answer.

'Well, *explain* it to me.' She said this in some distress. 'Some of us have spent years decrypting the Message and building the Machine. Aren't you going to tell me what it's all about?'

'You've become a real scrapper,' he said, as if he really were her father, as if he were comparing his last recollections of her with her present, still incompletely developed self.

He gave her hair an affectionate tousle. She remembered that from childhood also. But how could they, 30,000 light-years from Earth, know her father's affectionate gestures in long-ago and far-away Wisconsin? Suddenly she knew.

'Dreams,' she said. 'Last night, when we were all

dreaming, you were inside our heads, right? You drained everything we know.'

'We only made copies. I think everything that used to be in your head is still there. Take a look. Tell me if anything's missing.' He grinned, and went on.

'There was so much your television programs didn't tell us. Oh, we could figure out your technological level pretty well, and a lot more about you. But there's so much more to your species than that, things we couldn't possibly learn indirectly. I recognize you may feel some breach of privacy –'

'You're joking.'

'– but we have so little time.'

'You mean the Test is over? We answered all your questions while we were asleep last night? So? Did we pass or fail?'

'It isn't like that,' he said. 'It isn't like sixth grade.'

She had been in the sixth grade the year he died.

'Don't think of us as some interstellar sheriff gunning down outlaw civilizations. Think of us more as the Office of the Galactic Census. We collect information. I know you think nobody has anything to learn from you because you're technologically so backward. But there are other merits to a civilization.'

'What merits?'

'Oh, music. Lovingkindness. (I like that word.) Dreams. Humans are very good at dreaming, although you'd never know it from your television. There are cultures all over the Galaxy that trade dreams.'

'You operate an interstellar cultural exchange? That's what this is all about? You don't care if some rapacious, bloodthirsty civilization develops interstellar space-flight?'

'I said we admire lovingkindness.'

'If the Nazis had taken over the world, our world, and then developed interstellar spaceflight, wouldn't you have stepped in?'

'You'd be surprised how rarely something like that

359

happens. In the long run, the aggressive civilizations destroy themselves, almost always. It's their nature. They can't help it. In such a case, our job would be to leave them alone. To make sure that no one bothers them. To let them work out their destiny.'

'Then why didn't you leave *us* alone? I'm not complaining, mind you. I'm only curious as to how the Office of the Galactic Census works. The first thing you picked up from us was that Hitler broadcast. Why did you make contact?'

'The picture, of course, was alarming. We could tell you were in deep trouble. But the music told us something else. The Beethoven told us there was hope. Marginal cases are our specialty. We thought you could use a little help. Really, we can offer only a little. You understand. There are certain limitations imposed by causality.'

He had crouched down, running his hands through the water, and was now drying them on his pants.

'Last night, we looked inside you. All five of you. There's a lot in there: feelings, memories, instincts, learned behavior, insights, madness, dreams, loves. Love is very important. You're an interesting mix.'

'All that in one night's work?' She was taunting him a little.

'We had to hurry. We have a pretty tight schedule.'

'Why, is something about to . . .'

'No, it's just that if we don't engineer a consistent causality, it'll work itself out on its own. Then it's almost always worse.'

She had no idea what he meant.

' "Engineer a consistent causality." My dad never used to talk like that.'

'Certainly he did. Don't you remember how he spoke to you? He was a well-read man, and from when you were a little girl he – I – talked to you as an equal. Don't you remember?'

360

She remembered. She remembered. She thought of her mother in the nursing home.

'What a nice pendant,' he said, with just that air of fatherly reserve she had always imagined he would have cultivated had he lived to see her adolescence. 'Who gave it to you?'

'Oh this,' she said, fingering the medallion. 'Actually it's from somebody I don't know very well. He tested my faith. . . . He . . . But you must know all this already.'

Again the grin.

'I want to know what you think of us,' she said shortly, 'what you really think.'

He did not hesitate for a moment. 'All right. I think it's amazing that you've done as well as you have. You've got hardly any theory of social organization, astonishingly backward economic systems, no grasp of the machinery of historical prediction, and very little knowledge about yourselves. Considering how fast your world is changing, it's amazing you haven't blown yourselves to bits by now. That's why we don't want to write you off just yet. You humans have a certain talent for adaptability – at least in the short term.'

'That's the issue, isn't it?'

'That's *one* issue. You can see that, after a while, the civilizations with only short-term perspectives just aren't around. They work out their destinies also.'

She wanted to ask him how he honestly *felt* about humans. Curiosity? Compassion? No feelings whatever, just all in a day's work? In his heart of hearts – or whatever equivalent internal organs he possessed – did he think of her as she thought of . . . an ant? But she could not bring herself to raise the question. She was too much afraid of the answer.

From the intonation of his voice, from the nuances of his speech, she tried to gain some glimpse of who it was here disguised as her father. She had an enormous amount of direct experience with human beings; the

Stationmasters had less than a day's. Could she not discern something of their true nature beneath this amiable and informative facade? But she couldn't. In the content of his speech he was, of course, not her father, nor did he pretend to be. But in every other respect he was uncannily close to Theodore F. Arroway, 1924 –1960, vendor of hardware, loving husband and father. If not for a continuous effort of will, she knew she would be slobbering over this, this . . . copy. Part of her kept wanting to ask him how things had been since he had gone to Heaven. What were his views on Advent and Rapture? Was anything special in the works for the Millennium? There were human cultures that taught an afterlife of the blessed on mountaintops or in clouds, in caverns or oases, but she could not recall any in which if you were very, very good when you died you went to the beach.

'Do we have time for some questions before . . . whatever it is we have to do next?'

'Sure. One or two anyway.'

'Tell me about your transportation system.'

'I can do better than that,' he said. 'I can show you. Steady now.'

An amoeba of blackness leaked out from the zenith, obscuring Sun and blue sky.

'That's quite a trick,' she gasped.

The same sandy beach was beneath her feet. She dug her toes in. Overhead . . . was the Cosmos. They were, it seemed, high above the Milky Way Galaxy, looking down on its spiral structure and falling toward it at some impossible speed. He explained matter-of-factly, using her own familiar scientific language to describe the vast pinwheel-shaped structure. He showed her the Orion Spiral Arm, in which the Sun was, in this epoch, embedded. Interior to it, in decreasing order of mythological significance, were the Sagittarius Arm, the Norma/Scutum Arm, and the Three Kiloparsec Arm.

A network of straight lines appeared, representing the

transportation system they had used. It was like the illuminated maps in the Paris Metro. Eda had been right. Each station, she deduced, was in a star system with a low-mass double black hole. She knew the black holes couldn't have resulted from stellar collapse, from the normal evolution of massive star systems, because they were too small. Maybe they were primordial, left over from the Big Bang, captured by some unimaginable starship and towed to their designated station. Or maybe they were made from scratch. She wanted to ask about this, but the tour was pressing breathlessly onward.

There was a disk of glowing hydrogen rotating about the center of the Galaxy, and within it a ring of molecular clouds rushing outward toward the periphery of the Milky Way. He showed her the ordered motions in the giant molecular cloud complex Sagittarius B2, which had for decades been a favorite hunting ground for complex organic molecules by her radio-astronomical colleagues on Earth. Closer to the center, they encountered another giant molecular cloud, and then Sagittarius A West, an intense radio source that Ellie herself had observed at Argus.

And just adjacent, at the very center of the Galaxy, locked in a passionate gravitational embrace, was a pair of immense black holes. The mass of one of them was five million suns. Rivers of gas the size of solar systems were pouring down its maw. Two colossal – she ruminated on the limitations of the languages of Earth – two supermassive black holes are orbiting one another at the center of the Galaxy. One had been known, or at least strongly suspected. But two? Shouldn't that have shown up as a Doppler displacement of spectral lines? She imagined a sign under one of them reading ENTRANCE and under the other EXIT. At the moment, the entrance was in use; the exit was merely there.

And that was where this Station, Grand Central Station, was – just safely outside the black holes at the centre of the Galaxy. The skies were made brilliant by millions of nearby young stars; but the stars, the gas, and the dust were being eaten up by the entrance black hole.

'It goes somewhere, right?' she asked.

'Of course.'

'Can you tell me where?'

'Sure. All this stuff winds up in Cygnus A.'

Cygnus A was something she knew about. Except only for a nearby supernova remnant in Cassiopeia, it was the brightest radio source in the skies of Earth. She had calculated that in one second Cygnus A produces more energy than the Sun does in 40,000 years. The radio source was 600 million light-years away, far beyond the Milky Way, out in the realm of the galaxies. As with many extragalactic radio sources, two enormous jets of gas, fleeing apart at almost the speed of light, were making a complex web of Rankine-Hugoniot shock fronts with the thin intergalactic gas – and producing in the process a radio beacon that shone brightly over most of the universe. All the matter in this enormous structure, 500,000 light-years across, was pouring out of a tiny, almost inconspicuous point in space exactly midway between the jets.

'You're *making* Cygnus A?'

She half-remembered a summer's night in Michigan when she was a girl. She had feared she would fall into the sky.

'Oh, it's not just us. This is a . . . cooperative project of many galaxies. That's what we mainly do – engineering. Only a . . . few of us are involved with emerging civilizations.'

At each pause she had felt a kind of tingling in her head, approximately in the left parietal lobe.

'There are cooperative projects between galaxies?' she asked. 'Lots of galaxies, each with a kind of Central Administration? With hundreds of billions of stars in each galaxy. And then those administrations cooperate. To pour millions of suns into Centaurus . . . sorry, Cygnus A? The . . . Forgive me, I'm just staggered by the scale. Why would you do all this? Whatever for?'

'You mustn't think of the universe as a wilderness. It hasn't been that for billions of years,' he said. 'Think of it more as . . . cultivated.'

Again a tingling.

'But what for? What's there to cultivate?'

'The basic problem is easily stated. Now don't get scared off by the scale. You're an astronomer, after all. The problem is that the universe is expanding, and there's not enough matter in it to stop the expansion. After a while, no new galaxies, no new stars, no new planets, no newly arisen lifeforms – just the same old crowd. Everything's getting run-down. It'll be boring. So in Cygnus A we're testing out the technology to make something new. You might call it an experiment in urban renewal. It's not our only trial run. Sometime later we might want to close off a piece of the universe and prevent space from getting more and more empty as the aeons pass. Increasing the local matter density's the way to do it, of course. It's good honest work.'

Like running a hardware store in Wisconsin.

If Cygnus A was 600 million light-years away, then astronomers on Earth – or anywhere in the Milky Way for that matter – were seeing it as it had been 600 million years ago. But on Earth 600 million years ago, she knew, there had hardly been any life even in the oceans big enough to shake a stick at. They were *old*.

Six hundred million years ago, on a beach like this one . . . except no crabs, no gulls, no palm trees. She tried to imagine some microscopic plant washed ashore, securing a tremulous toehold just above the water line, while these beings were occupied with experimental galactogenesis and introductory cosmic engineering.

'You've been pouring matter into Cygnus A for the last six hundred million years?'

'Well, what you've detected by radio astronomy was just some of our early feasibility testing. We're much further along now.'

And in due course, in another few hundred million years she imagined, radio astronomers on Earth – if any – will detect substantial progress in the reconstruction of the universe around Cygnus A. She steeled herself for further revelations and vowed she would not let them intimidate her. There was a hierarchy of beings on a scale she had not imagined. But the Earth had a place, a significance in that hierarchy; they would not have gone to all this trouble for nothing.

The blackness rushed back to the zenith and was consumed; Sun and blue sky returned. The scene was the same; surf, sand, palms, Magritte door, microcamera, frond, and her . . . father.

'Those moving interstellar clouds and rings near the center of the Galaxy – aren't they due to periodic explosions around here? Isn't it dangerous to locate the Station here?'

'Episodic, not periodic. It only happens on a small scale, nothing like the sort of thing we're doing in Cygnus A. And it's manageable. We know when it's coming and we generally just hunker down. If it's really dangerous, we take the Station somewhere else for a while. This is all routine, you understand.'

'Of course. Routine. You built it all? The subways, I mean. You and those other . . . engineers from other galaxies?'

'Oh no, we haven't built any of it.'

'I've missed something. Help me understand.'

'It seems to be the same everywhere. In our case, we emerged a long time ago on many different worlds in the Milky Way. The first of us developed interstellar spaceflight, and eventually chanced on one of the transit stations. Of course, we didn't know what it was. We weren't even sure it was artificial until the first of us were brave enough to slide down.'

'Who's "we"? You mean the ancestors of your . . . race, your species?'

'No, no. We're many species from many worlds.

366

Eventually we found a large number of subways – various ages, various styles of ornamentation, and all abandoned. Most were still in good working condition. All we did was make some repairs and improvements.'

'No other artifacts? No dead cities? No records of what happened? No subway builders left?'

He shook his head.

'No industrialized, abandoned planets?'

He repeated the gesture.

'There was a Galaxy-wide civilization that picked up and left without leaving a trace – except for the stations?'

'That's more or less right. And it's the same in other galaxies also. Billions of years ago, they all went some-where. We haven't the slightest idea where.'

'But where could they go?'

He shook his head for the third time, but now very slowly.

'So then you're not . . .'

'No, we're just caretakers,' he said. 'Maybe someday they'll come back.'

'Okay, just one more,' she pleaded, holding her index finger up before her as, probably, had been her practice at age two. 'One more question.'

'All right,' he answered tolerantly. 'But we only have a few minutes left.'

She glanced at the doorway again, and suppressed a tremor as a small, almost transparent crab sidled by.

'I want to know about your myths, your religions. What fills you with awe? Or are those who make the numinous unable to feel it?'

'You make the numinous also. No, I know what you're asking. Certainly we feel it. You recognize that some of this is hard for me to communicate to you. But I'll give you an example of what you're asking for. I don't say this is it exactly, but it'll give you a . . .'

He paused momentarily and again she felt a tingle, this time in her left occipital lobe. She entertained the notion that he was rifling through her neurons. Had he missed something last night? If so, she was glad. It meant they weren't perfect.

'. . . flavor of our numinous. It concerns pi, the ratio of the circumference of a circle to its diameter. You know it well, of course, and you also know you can never come to the end of pi. There's no creature in the universe, no matter how smart, who could calculate pi to the last digit – because there is no last digit, only an infinite number of digits. Your mathematicians have made an effort to calculate it out to . . .'

Again she felt the tingle.

'. . . none of you seem to know. . . . Let's say the ten-billionth place. You won't be surprised to hear that other mathematicians have gone further. Well, eventually – let's say it's in the ten-to-the-twentieth-power place – something happens. The randomly varying digits disappear, and for an unbelievably long time there's nothing but ones and zeros.'

Idly, he was tracing a circle out on the sand with his toe. She paused a heartbeat before replying.

'And the zeros and ones finally stop? You get back to a random sequence of digits?' Seeing a faint sign of encouragement from him, she raced on. 'And the number of zeros and ones? Is it a product of prime numbers?'

'Yes, eleven of them.'

'You're telling me there's a message in eleven dimensions hidden deep inside the number pi? Someone in the universe communicates by . . . mathematics? But . . . help me, I'm really having trouble understanding you. Mathematics isn't arbitrary. I mean pi has to have the same value everywhere. How can you hide a message inside pi? It's built into the fabric of the universe.'

'Exactly.'

She stared at him.

'It's even better than that,' he continued. 'Let's assume that only in base-ten arithmetic does the sequence of zeros and ones show up, although you'd recognize that something funny's going on in any other arithmetic. Let's also assume that the beings who first made this discovery had ten fingers. You see how it looks? It's as if pi has been waiting for billions of years for ten-fingered mathematicians with fast computers to come along. You see, the Message was kind of addressed to us.'

'But this is just a metaphor, right? It's not really pi and the ten to the twentieth place? You don't actually have ten fingers.'

'Not really.' He smiled at her again.

'Well, for heaven's sake, what does the Message say?'

He paused for a moment, raised an index finger, and then pointed to the door. A small crowd of people was excitedly pouring out of it.

They were in a jovial mood, as if this were a long-delayed picnic outing. Eda was accompanying a stunning young woman in a brightly colored blouse and skirt, her hair neatly covered with the lacy *gele* favored by Moslem women in Yorubaland; he was clearly overjoyed to see her. From photographs he had shown, Ellie recognized her as Eda's wife. Sukhavati was holding hands with an earnest young man, his eyes large and soulful; she assumed it was Surindar Ghosh, Devi's long-dead medical-student husband. Xi was in animated discourse with a small vigorous man of commanding demeanor; he had drooping wispy mustaches and was garbed in a richly brocaded and beaded gown. Ellie imagined him personally overseeing the construction of the funerary model of the Middle Kingdom, shouting instructions to those who poured the mercury.

Vaygay ushered over a girl of eleven or twelve, her blond braids bobbing as she walked.

'This is my granddaughter, Nina . . . more or less. My Grand Duchess. I should have introduced you before. In Moscow.'

Ellie embraced the girl. She was relieved that Vaygay had not appeared with Meera, the ecdysiast. Ellie observed his tenderness toward Nina and decided she liked him more than ever. Over all the years she had known him, he had kept this secret place within his heart well hidden.

'I have not been a good father to her mother,' he confided. 'These days, I hardly see Nina at all.'

She looked around her. The Stationmasters had produced for each of the Five what could only be described as their deepest loves. Perhaps it was only to ease the barriers of communication with another, appallingly different species. She was glad none of them were happily chatting with an exact copy of themselves.

What if you could do this back on Earth? she wondered. What if, despite all our pretense and disguise, it was necessary to appear in public with the person we loved most of all? Imagine this a prerequisite for social discourse on Earth. It would change everything. She imagined a phalanx of members of one sex surrounding a solitary member of the other. Or chains of people. Circles. The letters 'H' or 'Q.' Lazy figure-8s. You could monitor deep affections at a glance, just by looking at the geometry – a kind of general relativity applied to social psychology. The practical difficulties of such an arrangement would be considerable, but no one would be able to lie about love.

The Caretakers were in a polite but determined hurry. There was not much time to talk. The entrance to the airlock of the dodecahedron was now visible, roughly where it had been when they first arrived. By symmetry, or perhaps because of some interdimensional conservation law, the Magritte doorway had vanished. They introduced everyone. She felt silly, in more ways than one, explaining in English to the Emperor Qin who her father was. But Xi dutifully translated, and they all solemnly shook hands as if this were their first encounter, perhaps at a suburban barbecue. Eda's wife was a considerable beauty, and Surindar Ghosh was giving her a more than casual inspection. Devi did not seem to mind;

perhaps she was merely gratified at the accuracy of the imposture.

'Where did you go when you stepped through the doorway?' Ellie softly asked her.

'Four-sixteen Maidenhall Way,' she answered.

Ellie looked at her blankly.

'London, 1973. With Surindar.'

She nodded her head in his direction. 'Before he died.'

Ellie wondered what she would have found had she crossed that threshold on the beach. Wisconsin in the late '50s, probably. She hadn't shown up on schedule, so he had come to find her. He had done that in Wisconsin more than once.

Eda had also been told about a message deep inside a transcendental number, but in his story it was not π or e, the base of natural logarithms, but a class of numbers she had never heard of. With an infinity of transcendental numbers, they would never know for sure which number to examine back on Earth.

'I hungered to stay and work on it,' he told Ellie softly, 'and I sensed they needed help – some way of thinking about the decipherment that hadn't occurred to them. But I think it's something very personal for them. They don't want to share it with others. And realistically, I suppose we just aren't smart enough to give them a hand.'

They hadn't decrypted the message in π? The Station-masters, the Caretakers, the designers of new galaxies hadn't figured out a message that had been sitting under their thumbs for a galactic rotation or two? Was the message that difficult, or were they . . . ?

'Time to go home,' her father said gently.

It was wrenching. She didn't want to go. She tried staring at the palm frond. She tried asking more questions.

'How do you mean "go home"? You mean we're going to emerge somewhere in the solar system? How will we get down to Earth?'

371

'You'll see,' he answered. 'It'll be interesting.'

He put his arm around her waist, guiding her toward the open airlock door.

It was like bedtime. You could be cute, you could ask bright questions, and maybe they'd let you stay up a little later. It used to work, at least a little.

'The Earth is linked up now, right? Both ways. If we can go home, you can come down to us in a jiffy. You know, that makes me awfully nervous. Why don't you just sever the link? We'll take it from here.'

'Sorry, Presh,' he replied, as if she had already shamelessly prolonged her eight o'clock bedtime. Was he sorry about bedtime, or about being unready to denozzle the tunnel? 'For a while at least, it'll be open only to inbound traffic,' he said. 'But we don't expect to use it.'

She liked the isolation of the Earth from Vega. She preferred a fifty-two-year-long leeway between un-acceptable behavior on Earth and the arrival of a punitive expedition. The black hole link was uncomfortable. They could arrive almost instantaneously, perhaps only in Hokkaido, perhaps anywhere on Earth. It was a transition to what Hadden had called microintervention. No matter what assurances they gave, they would watch us more closely now. No more dropping in for a casual look-see every few million years.

She explored her discomfort further. How . . . theo-logical . . . the circumstances had become. Here were beings who live in the sky, beings enormously know-ledgeable and powerful, beings concerned for our sur-vival, beings with a set of expectations about how we should behave. They disclaim such a role, but they could clearly visit reward and punishment, life and death, on the puny inhabitants of Earth. Now how is this different, she asked herself, from the old-time religion? The answer occurred to her instantly: It was a matter of evidence. In her videotapes, in the data the others had acquired, there would be hard evidence of the existence of the Station, of what went on here, of the black hole transit system.

There would be five independent, mutually corroborative stories supported by compelling physical evidence. This one was fact, not hearsay and hocus-pocus.

She turned toward him and dropped the frond. Wordlessly, he stooped and returned it to her.

'You've been very generous in answering all my questions. Can I answer any for you?'

'Thanks. You answered all our questions last night.'

'That's it? No commandments? No instructions for the provincials?'

'It doesn't work that way, Presh. You're grown up now. You're on your own.' He tilted his head, gave her that grin, and she flew into his arms, her eyes again filling with tears. It was a long embrace. Eventually, she felt him gently disengage her arms. It was time to go to bed. She imagined holding up her index finger and asking for still one more minute. But she did not want to disappoint him.

'Bye, Presh,' he said. 'Give your mother my love.'

'Take care,' she replied in a small voice. She took one last look at the seashore at the center of the Galaxy. A pair of seabirds, petrels perhaps, were suspended on some rising column of air. They remained aloft with hardly a beat of their wings. Just at the entrance to the airlock, she turned and called to him.

'What does your *Message* say? The one in pi?'

'We don't know,' he replied a little sadly, taking a few steps toward her. 'Maybe it's a kind of statistical accident. We're still working on it.'

The breeze stirred up, tousling her hair once again.

'Well, give us a call when you figure it out,' she said.

21
Causality

As flies to wanton boys are we to the gods –
They kill us for their sport.

> – WILLIAM SHAKESPEARE
> *King Lear*, IV, i, 36

Who is all-powerful should fear everything.

> – PIERRE CORNEILLE
> *Cinna* (1640), Act IV, Scene II

They were overjoyed to be back. They whooped it up, giddy with excitement. They climbed over the chairs. They hugged and patted one another on the back. All of them were close to tears. They had succeeded – but not only that, they had returned, safely negotiating all the tunnels. Abruptly, amidst a hail of static, the radio began blaring out the Machine status report. All three benzels were decelerating. The built-up electrical charge was dissipating. From the commentary, it was clear that Project had no idea of what had happened.

Ellie wondered how much time had passed. She glanced at her watch. It had been a day at least, which would bring them well into the year 2000. Appropriate enough. Oh, wait till they hear what we have to tell them, she thought. Reassuringly, she patted the compartment where the dozens of video microcassettes were stored. How the world would change when these films were released!

The space between and around the benzels had been repressurized. The airlock doors were being opened. Now there were radio inquiries about their well-being.

'We're fine!' she shouted back into her microphone. 'Let us out. You won't believe what happened to us.'

The Five emerged from the airlock happy, effusively greeting their comrades who had helped build and operate the Machine. The Japanese technicians saluted them. Project officials surged toward them.

Devi said quietly to Ellie, 'As far as I can tell, everyone's wearing exactly the same clothing they did yesterday. Look at that ghastly yellow tie on Peter Valerian.'

'Oh, he wears that old thing all the time,' Ellie replied. 'His wife gave it to him.' The clocks read 15:20. Activation had occurred close to three o'clock the previous afternoon. So they had been gone just a little over twenty-four . . .

'What day is it?' she asked. They looked at her uncomprehendingly. Something was wrong.

'Peter, for heaven's sake, what day is it?'

'How do you mean?' Valerian answered. 'It's today, Friday, December 31, 1999. It's New Year's Eve. Is that what you mean? Ellie, are you all right?'

Vaygay was telling Archangelsky to let him begin at the beginning, but only after his cigarettes were produced. Project officials and representatives of the Machine Consortium were converging around them. She saw der Heer wedging his way to her through the crowd.

'From your perspective, what happened?' she asked as finally he came within conversational range.

'Nothing. The vacuum system worked, the benzels spun up, they accumulated quite an electrical charge, they reached the prescribed speed, and then everything reversed.'

'What do you mean, "everything reversed"?'

'The benzels slowed down and the charge dissipated. The system was repressurized, the benzels stopped, and all of you came out. The whole thing took maybe twenty minutes, and we couldn't talk to you while the benzels were spinning. Did you experience anything at all?'

She laughed. 'Ken, my boy,' she said, 'have I got a story for you.'

There was a party for project personnel to celebrate Machine Activation and the momentous New Year. Ellie and her traveling companions did not attend. The television stations were full of celebrations, parades, exhibits, retrospectives, prognostications and optimistic addresses by national leaders. She caught a glimpse of remarks by the Abbot Utsumi, beatific as ever. But she could not dawdle. Project Directorate had quickly concluded, from the fragments of their adventures that the Five had time to recount, that something had gone wrong. They found themselves hustled away from the milling crowds of government and Consortium officials for a preliminary interrogation. It was thought prudent, project officials explained, for each of the Five to be questioned separately.

Der Heer and Valerian conducted her debriefing in a small conference room. There were other project officials present, including Vaygay's former student Anatoly Goldmann. She understood that Bobby Bui, who spoke Russian, was sitting in for the Americans during Vaygay's interrogation.

They listened politely, and Peter was encouraging now and again. But they had difficulty understanding the sequence of events. Much of what she related somehow worried them. Her excitement was noncontagious. It was hard for them to grasp that the dodecahedron had been gone for twenty minutes, much less a day, because the armada of instruments exterior to the benzels had filmed and recorded the event, and reported nothing extraordinary. All that had happened, Valerian explained, was that the benzels had reached their prescribed speed, several instruments of unknown purpose had the equivalent of their needles move, the benzels slowed down and stopped, and the Five emerged in a state of great excitement. He didn't exactly say 'babbling non-

376

sense,' but she could sense his concern. They treated her with deference, but she knew what they were thinking: The only function of the Machine was in twenty minutes to produce a memorable illusion, or – just possibly – to drive the Five of them mad.

She played back the video microcassettes for them, each carefully labeled: 'Vega Ring System,' for example, or 'Vega Radio (?) Facility,' 'Quintuple System,' 'Galactic Center Starscape,' and one bearing the inscription 'Beach.' She inserted them in 'play' mode one after the other. They had nothing on them. The cassettes were blank. She couldn't understand what had gone wrong. She had carefully learned the operation of the video microcamera system and had used it successfully in tests before Machine Activation. She had even done a spot check on some of the footage after they had left the Vega system. She was further devastated later when she was told that the instruments carried by the others had also somehow failed. Peter Valerian wanted to believe her, der Heer also. But it was hard for them, even with the best will in the world. The story the Five had come back with was a little, well, unexpected – and entirely unsupported by physical evidence. Also, there hadn't been enough time. They had been out of sight for only twenty minutes.

This was not the reception she had expected. But she was confident it would all sort itself out. For the moment, she was content to play the experience back in her mind and make some detailed notes. She wanted to be sure she would forget nothing.

Although a front of extremely cold air was moving in from Kamchatka, it was still unseasonably warm when late on New Year's Day, a number of unscheduled flights arrived at Sapporo International Airport. The new American Secretary of Defense, Michael Kitz, and a team of hastily gathered experts arrived in an airplane marked 'The United States of America.' Their presence was confirmed by Washington only when the story was about to break in Hokkaido. The terse press release noted that the visit was routine, that there was no crisis, no danger, and that 'nothing extraordinary has been reported at the Machine Systems Integration Facility northeast of Sapporo.' A Tu-120 had flown overnight from Moscow, carrying, among others, Stefan Baruda and Timofei Gotsridze. Doubtless neither group was delighted to spend this New Year's holiday away from their families. But the weather in Hokkaido was a pleasant surprise; it was so warm that the sculptures in Sapporo were melting, and the dodecahedron of ice had become an almost featureless small glacier, the water dripping off rounded surfaces that once had been the edges of the pentagonal surfaces.

Two days later, a severe winter storm struck, and all traffic into the Machine facility, even by four-wheel-drive vehicles, was interrupted. Some radio and all television links were severed; apparently a microwave relay tower had been blown down. During most of the new interrogations, the only communication with the outside world was by telephone. And just conceivably, Ellie thought, by dodecahedron. She was tempted to steal herself onboard and spin up the benzels. She enjoyed elaborating on this fantasy. But in fact there was no way to know whether the Machine would ever work again, at least from this side of the tunnel. He had said it would not. She allowed herself to think of the seashore again. And him. Whatever happened next, a wound deep within her was being healed. She could feel the scar tissue knitting. It had been the most expensive psychotherapy in the history of the world. And that's saying a lot, she thought.

Debriefings were given to Xi and Sukhavati by representatives of their nations. Although Nigeria played no significant role in Message acquisition or Machine construction, Eda acquiesced readily enough to a long inter-

378

view with Nigerian officials. But it was perfunctory compared with the interrogations administered to them by project personnel. Vaygay and Ellie underwent still more elaborate debriefings by the high-level teams brought from the Soviet Union and the United States for this specific purpose. At first these American and Soviet interrogations excluded foreign nationals, but after complaints were carried through the World Machine Consortium, the US and the SU relented, and the sessions were again internationalized.

Kitz was in charge of her debriefing, and considering what short notice he must have been given, he had arrived surprisingly well prepared. Valerian and der Heer put in an occasional good word for her, and every now and then asked a searching question. But it was Kitz's show.

He told her he was approaching her story skeptically but constructively, in what he hoped was the best scientific tradition. He trusted she would not mistake the directness of his questions for some personal animus. He held her only in the greatest respect. He, in turn, would not permit his judgment to be clouded by the fact that he had been against the Machine Project from the beginning. She decided to let this pathetic deception pass unchallenged, and began her story.

At first he listened closely, asked occasional questions of detail, and apologized when he interrupted. By the second day no such courtesies were in evidence.

'So the Nigerian is visited by his wife, the Indian by her dead husband, the Russian by his cute granddaughter, the Chinese by some Mongol warlord –'

'Qin was not a Mongol –'

'– and you, for crissake, you get visited by your dearly departed father, who tells you that he and his friends have been busy rebuilding the universe, for crissake. "Our Father Who art in Heaven . . ."? This is straight religion. This is straight cultural anthropology. This is straight Sigmund Freud. Don't you see that? Not only do you claim your own father came back from the dead, you actually expect us to believe that he made the universe –'

'You're distorting what –'

'Come off it, Arroway. Don't insult our intelligence. You don't present us with a shred of evidence, and you expect us to believe the biggest cock-and-bull story of all time? You know better than that. You're a smart lady. How could you figure to get away with it?'

She protested. Valerian protested also; this kind of interrogation, he said, was a waste of time. The Machine was undergoing sensitive physical tests at this moment. That was how the validity of her story could be checked. Kitz agreed the physical evidence would be important. But the nature of Arroway's story, he argued, was revealing, a means of understanding what had actually happened.

'Meeting your father in Heaven and all that, Dr Arroway, is telling, because you've been raised in the Judeo-Christian culture. You're essentially the only one of the Five from that culture, and you're the only one who meets your father. Your story is just too pat. It's not imaginative enough.'

This was worse than she had thought possible. She felt a moment of epistemological panic – as when your car is not where you parked it, or the door you locked last night is ajar in the morning.

'You think we made all this up?'

'Well, I'll tell you, Dr Arroway. When I was very young, I worked in the Cook County Prosecutor's office. When they were thinking about indicting some-body, they asked three questions.' He ticked them off on his fingers. 'Did he have the opportunity? Did he have the means? Did he have the motive?'

'To do what?'

He looked at her in disgust.

'But our watches showed that we'd been gone more than a day,' she protested.

'I don't know how I could have been so stupid,' Kitz

380

said, striking his forehead with his palm. 'You've demolished my argument. I forgot that it's impossible to set your watch ahead by a day.'

'But that implies a conspiracy. You think Xi lied? You think Eda lied? You –'

'What I think is we should move on to something more important. You know, Peter' – Kitz turned toward Valerian – 'I'm persuaded you're right. A first draft of the Materials Assessment Report will be here tomorrow morning. Let's not waste more time on . . . stories. We'll adjourn till then.'

Der Heer had said not a word through the entire afternoon's session. He offered her an uncertain grin, and she couldn't help contrasting it with her father's. Sometimes Ken's expression seemed to urge her, to implore her. But to what end she had no way of knowing; perhaps to change her story. He had remembered her recollections of her childhood, and he knew how she had grieved for her father. Clearly he was weighing the possibility that she had gone crazy. By extension, she supposed, he was also considering the likelihood that the others had gone crazy, too. Mass hysteria. Shared delusion. *Folie à cinq.*

'Well, here it is,' Kitz said. The report was about a centimeter thick. He let it fall to the table, scattering a few pencils. 'You'll want to look through it, Dr Arroway, but I can give you a quick summary. Okay?'

She nodded assent. She had heard through the grapevine that the report was highly favorable to the account the Five had given. She hoped it would put an end to the nonsense.

'The dodecahedron *apparently*' – he laid great stress on this word – 'has been exposed to a very different environment than the benzels and the supporting structures. It's *apparently* been subjected to huge tensile and compressional stresses. It's a miracle the thing didn't fall to pieces. So it's a miracle you and the others didn't fall to pieces at the same time. Also, it's *apparently* seen an intense radiation environment – there's low-level induced radioactivity, cosmic ray tracks, and so on. It's another miracle that you survived the radiation. Nothing else has been added or taken away. There's no sign of erosion or scraping on the side vertices that you claim kept bumping into the walls of the tunnels. There's not even any scoring, as there would have been if it entered the Earth's atmosphere at high velocity.'

'So doesn't that confirm our story? Michael, think about it. Tensile and compressional stresses – tidal forces – are exactly what you expect if you fall down a classical black hole. That's been known for fifty years at least. I don't know why we didn't feel it, but maybe the dodec protected us somehow. And high radiation doses from the inside of the black hole and from the environment of the Galactic Center, a known gamma ray source. There's independent evidence for black holes, and there's independent evidence for a Galactic Center. We didn't make those things up. I don't understand the absence of scraping, but that depends on the interaction of a material we've hardly studied with a material that's completely unknown. I wouldn't expect any scoring or charring, because we don't claim we entered through the Earth's atmosphere. It seems to me the evidence almost entirely confirms our story. What's the problem?'

'The problem is you people are too clever. Too clever. Look at it from the point of view of a skeptic. Step back and look at the big picture. There's a bunch of bright people in different countries who think the world is going to hell in a handbasket. They claim to receive a complex Message from space.'

'Claim?'

'Let me continue. They decrypt the Message and announce instructions on how to build a very complicated Machine at a cost of trillions of dollars. The world's in a funny condition, the religions are all shaky about the oncoming Millennium, and to everybody's surprise the

382

Machine gets built. There's one or two slight changes in personnel, and then essentially these same people –'

'It's *not* the same people. It's not Sukhavati, it's not Eda, it's not Xi, and there were –'

'Let me continue. *Essentially* these same people then get to sit down in the Machine. Because of the way the thing is designed, no one can see them and no one can talk to them after the thing is activated. So the Machine is turned on and then it turns itself off. Once it's on, you can't *make* it stop in less than twenty minutes. Okay. Twenty minutes later, these same people emerge from the Machine, all jaunty-jolly, with some bullshit story about traveling faster than light inside black holes to the center of the Galaxy and back. Now suppose you hear this story and you're just ordinarily cautious. You ask to see their evidence. Pictures, videotapes, any other data. Guess what? It's all been conveniently erased. Do they have artifacts of the superior civilization they say is at the center of the Galaxy? No. Mementos? No. A stone tablet? No. Pets? No. Nothing. The only physical evidence is some subtle damage done to the Machine. So you ask yourself, couldn't people who were so motivated and so clever arrange for what looks like tension stresses and radiation damage, especially if they could spend two trillion dollars faking the evidence?'

She gasped. She remembered the last time she had gasped. This was a truly venomous reconstruction of events. She wondered what had made it attractive to Kitz. He must, she thought, be in real distress.

'I don't think anybody's going to believe your story,' he continued. 'This is the most elaborate – and the most expensive – hoax ever perpetrated. You and your friends tried to hoodwink the President of the United States and deceive the American people, to say nothing of all the other governments on the Earth. You must really think everybody else is stupid.'

'Michael, this is madness. Tens of thousands of people worked to acquire the Message, to decode it, and to build

383

the Machine. The Message is on magnetic tapes and printouts and laserdisks in observatories all over the world. You think there's a conspiracy involving all the radio astronomers on the planet, and the aerospace and cybernetics companies, and –'

'No, you don't need a conspiracy that big. All you need is a transmitter in space that looks as if it's broadcasting from Vega. I'll tell you how I think you did it. You prepare the Message, and get somebody – somebody with an established launch capability – to put it up. Probably as an incidental part of some other mission. And into some orbit that looks like sidereal motion. Maybe there's more than one satellite. Then the transmitter turns on, and you're all ready in your handy-dandy observatory to receive the Message, make the big discovery, and tell us poor slobs what it all means.'

This was too much even for the impassive der Heer. He roused himself from a slumped position in his chair. 'Really, Mike –' he began, but Ellie cut him short.

'I wasn't responsible for most of the decoding. Lots of people were involved. Drumlin, especially. He started out as a committed skeptic, as you know. But once the data came in, Dave was entirely convinced. You didn't hear any reservations from him.'

'Oh yes, poor Dave Drumlin. The *late* Dave Drumlin. You set him up. The professor you never liked.'

Der Heer slumped still further down in his chair, and she had a sudden vision of him regaling Kitz with secondhand pillow talk. She looked at him more closely. She couldn't be sure.

'During the decrypting of the Message, you couldn't do everything. There was *so much* you had to do. So you overlooked this and you forgot that. Here's Drumlin growing old, worried about his former student eclipsing him and getting all the credit. Suddenly he sees how to be involved, how to play a central role. You appealed to his narcissism, and you hooked him. And if he hadn't

384

figured out the decryption, you would have helped him along. If worse came to worst, you would have peeled all the layers off the onion yourself.'

'You're saying that we were able to invent such a Message. Really, it's an outrageous compliment to Vaygay and me. It's also impossible. It can't be done. You ask any competent engineer if that kind of Machine – with brand-new subsidiary industries, components wholly unfamiliar on Earth – you ask if that could have been invented by a few physicists and radio astronomers on their days off. When do you imagine we had *time* to invent such a Message even if we knew how? Look how many bits of information are in it. It would have taken years.'

'You *had* years, while Argus was getting nowhere. The project was about to be closed. Drumlin, you remember, was pushing that. So just at the right moment you find the Message. Then there's no more talk about closing down your pet project. I think you and that Russian *did* cook the whole thing up in your spare time. You had years.'

'This is madness,' she said softly.

Valerian interrupted. He had known Dr Arroway well during the period in question. She had done productive scientific work. She never had the time required for so elaborate a deception. Much as he admired her, he agreed that the Message and the Machine were far beyond her ability – or indeed anybody's ability. Anybody on Earth.

But Kitz wasn't buying it. 'That's a personal judgment, Dr Valerian. There are many persons, and there can be many judgments. You're fond of Dr Arroway. I understand. I'm fond of her, too. It's understandable you would defend her. I don't take it amiss. But there's a clincher. You don't know about it yet. I'm going to tell you.'

He leaned forward, watching Ellie intently. Clearly he was interested to see how she would respond to what he was about to say.

385

'The Message stopped the moment we activated the Machine. The moment the benzels reached cruising speed. To the second. All over the world. Every radio observatory with a line-of-sight to Vega saw the same thing. We've held back telling you about it so we wouldn't distract you from your debriefing. The Message stopped in mid-bit. Now that was really foolish of you.'

'I don't know anything about it, Michael. But so what if the Message stopped? It's fulfilled its purpose. We built the Machine, and we went to . . . where they wanted us to go.'

'It puts you in a peculiar position,' he went on.

Suddenly she saw where he was headed. She hadn't expected this. He was arguing conspiracy, but she was contemplating madness. If Kitz wasn't mad, might she be? If our technology can manufacture substances that induce delusions, could a much more advanced technology induce highly detailed collective hallucinations? Just for a moment it seemed possible.

'Let's imagine it's last week,' he was saying. 'The radio waves arriving on Earth right now are supposed to have been sent from Vega twenty-six years ago. They take twenty-six years to cross space to us. But twenty-six years ago, Dr Arroway, there wasn't any Argus facility, and you were sleeping with acid-heads, and moaning about Vietnam and Watergate. You people are so smart, but you forgot the speed of light. There's no way that activating the Machine can turn the Message off until twenty-six years pass – unless in ordinary space you can send a message faster than light. And we both know that's impossible. I remember you complaining about how stupid Rankin and Joss were for not knowing you can't travel faster than light. I'm surprised you thought you could get away with this one.'

'Michael, listen. It's how we were able to get from here to there and back in no time flat. Twenty minutes, anyway. It can be acausal around a singularity. I'm not an expert on this. You should be talking to Eda or Vaygay.'

'Thank you for the suggestion,' he said. 'We already have.'

She imagined Vaygay under some comparably stern interrogation by his old adversary Archangelsky or by Baruda, the man who had proposed destroying the radio telescopes and burning the data. Probably they and Kitz saw eye to eye on the awkward matter before them. She hoped Vaygay was bearing up all right.

'You understand, Dr Arroway. I'm *sure* you do. But let me explain again. Perhaps you can show me where I missed something. Twenty-six years ago those radio waves were heading out for Earth. Now imagine them in space between Vega and here. Nobody can catch the radio waves after they've left Vega. Nobody can stop them. Even if the transmitter knew instantaneously – through the black hole, if you like – that the Machine had been activated, it would be twenty-six years before the signal stops arriving on Earth. Your Vegans couldn't have known twenty-six years ago when the Machine was going to be activated. And to the minute. You would have to send a message *back in time* to twenty-six years ago, for the Message to stop on December thirty-first, 1999. You do follow, don't you?'

'Yes, I follow. This is wholly unexplored territory. You know, it's not called a space-time continuum for nothing. If they can make tunnels through space, I suppose they can make some kind of tunnels through time. The fact that we got back a day early shows that they have at least a limited kind of time travel. So maybe as soon as we left the Station, they sent a message twenty-six years back into time to turn the transmission off. I don't know.'

'You see how convenient it is for you that the Message stops just now. If it *was* still broadcasting, we could find your little satellite, capture it, and bring back the trans-mission tape. That would be definitive evidence of a hoax. Unambiguous. But you couldn't risk that. So you're reduced to black hole mumbo-jumbo. Probably embarrassing for you.'

He looked concerned.

It was like some paranoid fantasy in which a patch-work of innocent facts are reassembled into an intricate conspiracy. The facts in this case were hardly common-place, and it made sense for the authorities to test other possible explanations. But Kitz's rendition of events was so malign that it revealed, she thought, someone truly wounded, afraid, in pain. In her mind, the likelihood that all this was a collective delusion diminished a little. But the cessation of the Message transmission – if it had happened as Kitz had said – was worrisome.

'Now, I tell myself, Dr Arroway, you scientists had the brains to figure all this out, and the motivation. But by yourselves you didn't have the means. If it wasn't the Russians who put up this satellite for you, it *could* have been any one of half a dozen other national launch authorities. But we've looked into all that. Nobody launched a free-flying satellite in the appropriate orbits. That leaves private launch capability. And the most interesting possibility that's come to our notice is a Mr S. R. Hadden. Know him?'

'Don't be ridiculous, Michael. I talked to you about Hadden before I went up to *Methuselah*.'

'Just wanted to be sure we agree on the basics. Try this on for size: You and the Russian concoct this scheme. You get Hadden to bankroll the early stages – the satellite design, the invention of the Machine, the encrypting of the Message, faking the radiation damage, all that. In return, after the Machine Project gets going, he gets to play with some of that two trillion dollars. He likes the idea. There might be enormous profit in it, and from his history, he'd love to embarrass the government. When you get stuck in decrypting the Message, when you can't find the primer, you even go to him. He tells you where to look for it. That was also careless. It would have been better if you figured it out yourself.'

388

'It's *too* careless,' offered der Heer. 'Wouldn't someone who was really perpetrating a hoax . . .'

'Ken, I'm surprised at you. You've been very credulous, you know? You're demonstrating exactly why Arroway and the others thought it would be clever to ask Hadden's advice. And to make sure we knew she'd gone to see him.'

He returned his attention to her. 'Dr Arroway, try to look at it from the standpoint of a neutral observer . . .'

Kitz pressed on, making sparkling new patterns of facts assemble themselves in the air before her, rewriting whole years of her life. She hadn't thought Kitz dumb, but she hadn't imagined him this inventive either. Perhaps he had received help. But the emotional propulsion for this fantasy came from Kitz.

He was full of expansive gestures and rhetorical flourishes. This was not merely part of his job. This interrogation, this alternative interpretation of events, had roused something passionate in him. After a moment she thought she saw what it was. The Five had come back with no immediate military applications, no political liquid capital, but only a story that was surpassing strange. And that story had certain implications. Kitz was now master of the most devastating arsenal on Earth, while the Caretakers were building galaxies. He was a lineal descendant of a progression of leaders, American and Soviet, who had devised the strategy of nuclear confrontation, while the Caretakers were an amalgam of diverse species from separate worlds working together in concert. Their very existence was an unspoken rebuke. Then consider the possibility that the tunnel could be activated from the other end, that there might be nothing he could do to prevent it. They could be here in an instant. How could Kitz defend the United States under such circumstances? His role in the decision to build the Machine – the history of which he seemed to be actively rewriting – could be interpreted by an unfriendly tribunal as dereliction of duty. And what account could Kitz give the extraterrestrials of his stewardship of the planet, he and his predecessors? Even if no avenging angels came storming out of the tunnel, if the truth of the journey got out the world would change. It was already changing. It would change much more.

Again she regarded him with sympathy. For a hundred generations, at least, the world had been run by people much worse than he. It was his misfortune to come to bat just as the rules of the game were being rewritten.

'. . . even if you believed every detail of your story,' he was saying, 'don't you think the extraterrestrials treated you badly? They take advantage of your tenderest feelings by dressing themselves up as dear old Dad. They don't tell you what they're doing, they expose all your film, destroy all your data, and don't even let you leave that stupid palm frond up there. Nothing on the manifest is missing, except for a little food, and nothing that isn't on the manifest is returned, except for a little sand. So in twenty minutes you gobbled some food and dumped a little sand out of your pockets. You come back one nanosecond or something after you leave, so to any neutral observer you never left at all.

'Now, if the extraterrestrials wanted to make it unambiguously clear you'd really gone somewhere, they would've brought you back a day later, or a week. Right? If there was nothing inside the benzels for a while, we'd be dead certain that you'd gone somewhere. If they wanted to make it easy for you, they wouldn't have turned off the Message. Right? That makes it look bad, you know. They could've figured that out. Why would they want to make it bad for you? And there's other ways they could've supported your story. They could've given you something to remember them by. They could've let you bring back your movies. Then nobody could claim all this is just a clever fake. So how come they didn't do that? How come the extraterrestrials don't confirm your story? You spent years of your life trying to find them. Don't they appreciate what you've done?

390

'Ellie, how can you be so sure your story really happened? If, as you claim, all this isn't a hoax, couldn't it be a . . . delusion? It's painful to consider, I know. Nobody wants to think they've gone a little crazy. Considering the strain you've been under, though, it's no big deal. And if the only alternative is criminal conspiracy . . . Maybe you want to carefully think this one through.'

She had already done so.

Later that day she met with Kitz alone. A bargain had in effect been proposed. She had no intention of going along with it. But Kitz was prepared for that possibility as well.

'You never liked me from the first,' he said. 'But I'm going to rise above that. We're going to do something really fair.

'We've already issued a new release saying that the Machine just didn't work when we tried to activate it. Naturally, we're trying to understand what went wrong. With all the other failures, in Wyoming and Uzbekistan, nobody is doubting this one.

'Then in a few weeks we'll announce that we're still not getting anywhere. We've done the best we could. The Machine is too expensive to keep working on. Probably we're just not smart enough to figure it out yet. Also, there's still some danger, after all. We always knew that. The Machine might blow up or something. So all in all, it's best to put the Machine Project on ice – at least for a while. It's not that we didn't try.

'Hadden and his friends would oppose it, of course, but as he's been taken from us . . .'

'He's only three hundred kilometers overhead,' she pointed out.

'Oh, haven't you heard? Sol died just around the time the Machine was activated. Funny how it happened. Sorry, I would have told you. I forgot you were . . . close to him.'

She did not know whether to believe Kitz. Hadden was in his fifties and had certainly seemed in good physical health. She would pursue this topic later.

'And what, in your fantasy, becomes of us?' she asked.

'Us? Who's "us"?'

'Us. The five of us. The ones who went aboard the Machine that you claim never worked.'

'Oh. After a little more debriefing you'll be free to leave. I don't think any of you will be foolish enough to tell this cock-and-bull story on the outside. But just to be safe, we're preparing some psychiatric dossiers on the five of you. Profiles. Low-key. You've always been a little rebellious, mad at the system – whichever system you grew up in. It's okay. It's good for people to be independent. We encourage that, especially in scientists. But the strain of the last few years has been trying – not actually disabling, but trying. Especially for Doctors Arroway and Lunacharsky. First they're involved in finding the Message, decrypting it, and convincing the governments to build the Machine. Then problems in construction, industrial sabotage, sitting through an Activation that goes nowhere . . . It's been tough. All work and no play. And scientists are highly strung anyway. If you've all become a little unhinged at the failure of the Machine, everybody will be sympathetic. Understanding. But nobody'll believe your story. Nobody. If you behave yourselves, there's no reason that the dossiers ever have to be released.

'It'll be clear that the Machine is still here. We're having a few wire service photographers in to photograph it as soon as the roads are open. We'll show them the Machine didn't go anywhere. And the crew? The crew is naturally disappointed. Maybe a little disheartened. They don't want to talk to the press just yet.

'Don't you think it's a neat plan?' He smiled. He wanted her to acknowledge the beauty of the scheme. She said nothing.

'Don't you think we're being very reasonable, after

spending two trillion dollars on that pile of shit? We could put you away for life, Arroway. But we're letting you go free. You don't even have to put up bail. I think we're behaving like gentlemen. It's the Spirit of the Millennium. It's Machindo.'

22

Gilgamesh

That it will never come again
Is what makes life so sweet.

– EMILY DICKINSON
Poem Number 1741

In this time – heralded expansively as the Dawn of a New
Age – burial in space was an expensive commonplace.
Commercially available and a competitive business, it
appealed especially to those who, in former times, would
have requested that their remains be scattered over the
county of their birth, or at least the mill town from which
they had extracted their first fortune. But now you could
arrange for your remains to circumnavigate the Earth
forever – or as close to forever as matters in the workaday
world. You need only insert a short codicil in your will.
Then – assuming, of course, that you have the Wherewithal – when you die and are cremated, your ashes are
compressed into a tiny almost toylike bier, on which is
embossed your name and your dates, a short memorial
verse, and the religious symbol of your choice (choose
one of three). Along with hundreds of similar miniature
coffins, it is then boosted up and dumped out at an
intermediate altitude, expeditiously avoiding both the
crowded corridors of geosynchronous orbit and the
disconcerting atmospheric drag of low-Earth orbit. Instead, your ashes triumphantly circle the planet of your
birth in the midst of the Van Allen radiation belts, a
proton blizzard where no satellite in its right mind would
risk going to in the first place. But ashes do not mind.

At these heights, the Earth had become enveloped in
the remains of its leading citizens, and an uninstructed

visitor from a distant world might rightly believe he had chanced upon some somber space-age necropolis. The hazardous location of this mortuary would explain the absence of memorial visits from grieving relatives.

S. R. Hadden, contemplating this image, had been appalled at what minor portions of immortality these deceased worthies had been willing to settle for. All their organic parts – brains, hearts, everything that distinguished them as a person – were atomized in their cremations. There isn't any of you *left* after cremation, he thought, just powdered bone, hardly enough even for a very advanced civilization to reconstruct you from the remains. And then, for good measure, your coffin is placed smack in the Van Allen belts, where even your ashes get slowly fried.

How much better if a few of your cells could be preserved. Real living cells, with the DNA intact. He visualized a corporation that would, for a healthy fee, freeze a little of your epithelial tissue and orbit it high – well above the Van Allen belts, maybe even higher than geosynchronous orbit. No reason to die first. Do it now, while it's on your mind. Then, at least, alien molecular biologists – or their terrestrial counterparts of the far future – could reconstruct you, clone you, more or less from scratch. You would rub your eyes, stretch, and wake up in the year ten million. Or even if nothing was done with your remains, there would still be in existence multiple copies of your genetic instructions. You would be alive *in principle*. In either case it could be said that you would live forever.

But as Hadden ruminated on the matter further, this scheme also seemed too modest. Because that wasn't *really* you, a few cells scraped off the soles of your feet. At best they could reconstruct your physical form. But that's not the same as *you*. If you were really serious, you should include family photographs, a punctiliously detailed autobiography, all the books and tapes you've enjoyed, and as much else about yourself as possible.

Favorite brands of after-shave lotion, for example, or diet cola. It was supremely egotistical, he knew, and he loved it. After all, the age has produced a sustained eschatological delirium. It was natural to think of your own end as everyone else was contemplating the demise of the species, or the planet, or the massed celestial ascent of the Elect.

You couldn't expect the extraterrestrials to know English. If they're to reconstruct you, they'd have to know your language. So you must include a kind of translation, a problem Hadden enjoyed. It was almost the obverse of the Message decryption problem.

All of this required a substantial space capsule, so substantial that you need no longer be limited to mere tissue samples. You might as well send your body whole. If you could quick-freeze yourself after death, so to say, there was a subsidiary advantage. Maybe enough of you would be in working order that whoever found you could do better than just reconstructing you. Maybe they could bring you back to life – of course, after fixing whatever it was that you had died of. If you languished a little before freezing, though – because, say, the relatives had not realized you were dead yet – prospects for revival diminished. What would really make sense, he thought, was to freeze someone just *before* death. That would make eventual resuscitation much more likely, although there was probably limited demand for this service.

But then why *just* before dying? Suppose you knew you had only a year or two to live. Wouldn't it be better to be frozen immediately, Hadden mused – before the meat goes bad? Even then – he sighed – no matter what the nature of the deteriorating illness, it might *still* be irremediable after you were revived; you would be frozen for a geological age, and then awakened only to die promptly from a melanoma or a cardiac infarction about which the extraterrestrials might know nothing.

No, he concluded, there was only one perfect realization of this idea: Someone in robust health would have to

396

be launched on a one-way journey to the stars. As an incidental benefit, you would be spared the humiliation of disease and old age. Far from the inner solar system, your equilibrium temperature would fall to only a few degrees above absolute zero. No further refrigeration would be necessary. Perpetual care provided. Free.

By this logic he came to the final step of the argument: If it requires a few years to get to the interstellar cold, you might as well stay awake for the show, and get quick-frozen only when you leave the solar system. It would also minimize overdependence on the cryogenics.

Hadden had taken every reasonable precaution against an unexpected medical problem in Earth orbit, the official account went, even to preemptive sonic disintegration of his gall and kidney stones before he ever set foot in his chateau in the sky. And then he went and died of anaphylactic shock. A bee had buzzed angrily out of a bouquet of freesias sent up on *Narnia* by an admirer. Carelessly, *Methuselah*'s capacious pharmacy had not stocked the appropriate antiserum. The insect had probably been immobilized by the low temperatures in *Narnia*'s cargo bay and was not really to blame. Its small and broken body had been sent down for examination by forensic entomologists. The irony of the billionaire felled by a bee did not escape the notice of newspaper editorials and Sunday sermons.

But in fact, this was all a deception. There had been no bee, no sting, and no death. Hadden remained in excellent health. Instead, on the stroke of the New Year, nine hours after the Machine had been activated, the rocket engines flamed on a sizable auxiliary vehicle docked to *Methuselah*. It rapidly achieved escape velocity from the Earth-Moon system. He called it *Gilgamesh*.

Hadden had spent his life amassing power and contemplating time. The more power you have, he found, the more you crave. Power and time were connected, because all men are equal in death. That is why the ancient

397

kings built monuments to themselves. But the monuments become eroded, the royal accomplishments obliterated, the very names of the kings forgotten. And, most important, they themselves were dead as doornails. No, this was more elegant, more beautiful, more satisfying. He had found a low door in the wall of time.

Had he merely announced his plans to the world, certain complications would ensue. If Hadden was frozen to four degrees Kelvin at ten billion kilometers from Earth, what exactly was his legal status? Who would control his corporations? This way was much tidier. In a minor codicil of an elaborate last will and testament, he had left his heirs and assigns a new corporation, skilled in rocket engines and cryogenics, that would eventually be called Immortality, Inc. He need never think of the matter again.

Gilgamesh was not equipped with a radio. He no longer wished to know what had happened to the Five. He wanted no more news of Earth – nothing cheering, nothing to make him disconsolate, none of the pointless tumult he had known. Only solitude, elevated thoughts . . . silence. If anything adverse should occur in the next few years, *Gilgamesh*'s cryogenics could be activated by the flip of a switch. Until then, there was a full library of his favorite music, and literature and videotapes. He would not be lonely. He had never really been much for company. Yamagishi had considered coming, but ultimately reneged; he would be lost, he said, without 'staff.' And on this journey there were insufficient inducements, as well as inadequate space, for staff. The monotony of the food and the modest scale of the amenities might be daunting to some, but Hadden knew himself to be a man with a great dream. The amenities mattered not at all.

In two years, this flying sarcophagus would fall into the gravitational potential well of Jupiter, Just outside its radiation belt, be slingshot around the planet and then flung off into interstellar space. For a day he would have a view still more spectacular than that out the window of

398

his study on *Methuselah* – the roiling multicolored clouds of Jupiter, the largest planet. If it were only a matter of the view, Hadden would have opted for Saturn and the rings. He preferred the rings. But Saturn was at least four years from Earth and that was, all things considered, taking a chance. If you're stalking immortality, you have to be very careful.

At these speeds it would take ten thousand years to travel even the distance to the nearest star. When you're frozen to four degrees above absolute zero, though, you have plenty of time. But some fine day – he was sure of it, though it be a million years from now – *Gilgamesh* would by chance enter someone else's solar system. Or his funeral bark would be intercepted in the darkness between the stars, and other beings – very advanced, very far-seeing – would take the sarcophagus aboard and know what had to be done. It had never really been attempted before. No one who ever lived on Earth had come this close.

Confident that in his end would be his beginning, he closed his eyes and folded his arms experimentally across his chest, as the engines flared again, this time more briefly, and the burnished craft was sleekly set on its long journey to the stars.

Thousands of years from now, God knows what would be happening on Earth, he thought. It was not his problem. It never really had been. But he, he would be asleep, deep-frozen, perfectly preserved, his sarcophagus hurtling through the interstellar void, surpassing the Pharaohs, besting Alexander, outshining Qin. He had contrived his own Resurrection.

23

Reprogramming

We have not followed cunningly devised fables . . . but were eyewitnesses.

— II Peter 1:16

> Look and remember. Look upon this sky;
> Look deep and deep into the sea-clean air,
> The unconfined, the terminus of prayer.
> Speak now and speak into the hallowed dome.
> What do you hear? What does the sky reply?
> The heavens are taken; this is not your home.

— Karl Jay Shapiro
Travelogue for Exiles

The telephone lines had been repaired, the roads plowed clean, and carefully selected representatives of the world's press were given a brief look at the facility. A few reporters and photographers were taken through the three matching apertures in the benzels, through the airlock, and into the dodec. There were television commentaries recorded, the reporters seated in the chairs that the Five had occupied, telling the world of the failure of this first courageous attempt to activate the Machine. Ellie and her colleagues were photographed from a distance, to show that they were alive and well, but no interviews were to be given just yet. The Machine Project was taking stock and considering its future options. The tunnel from Honshu to Hokkaido was open again, but the passageway from Earth to Vega was closed. They hadn't actually tested this proposition – Ellie wondered whether, when the Five finally left the site, the project would try to spin up the benzels again –

but she believed what she had been told: The Machine would not work again; there would be no further access to the tunnels for the beings of Earth. We could make little indentations in space-time as much as we liked; it would do us no good if no one hooked up from the other side. We had been given a glimpse, she thought, and then were left to save ourselves. If we could.

In the end, the Five were permitted to talk among themselves. She systematically bade farewell to each. No one blamed her for the blank cassettes.

'These pictures on the cassettes are recorded in magnetic domains, on tape,' Vaygay reminded her. 'A strong electrical field accumulated on the benzels, and they were, of course, moving. A time-varying electrical field makes a magnetic field. Maxwell's equations. It seems to me that's how your tapes were erased. It was not your fault.'

Vaygay's interrogation had baffled him. They had not exactly accused him but merely suggested that he was part of an anti-Soviet conspiracy involving scientists from the West.

'I tell you, Ellie, the only remaining open question is the existence of intelligent life in the Politburo.'

'And the White House. I can't believe the President would allow Kitz to get away with this. She committed herself to the project.'

'This planet is run by crazy people. Remember what they have to do to get where they are. Their perspective is so narrow, so . . . brief. A few years. In the best of them a few decades. They care only about the time they are in power.'

She thought about Cygnus A.

'But they're not sure our story is a lie. They cannot prove it. Therefore, we must convince them. In their hearts, they wonder, "Could it be true?" A few even want it to be true. But it is a risky truth. They need something close to certainty. . . . And perhaps we can provide it. We can refine gravitational theory. We can

401

make new astronomical observations to confirm what we were told – especially for the Galactic Center and Cygnus A. They're not going to stop astronomical research. Also, we can study the dodec, if they give us access. Ellie, we will change their minds.'

Difficult to do if they're all crazy, she thought to herself.

'I don't see how the governments could convince people this is a hoax,' she said.

'Really? Think of what else they've made people believe. They've persuaded us that we'll be safe if only we spend all our wealth so everybody on Earth can be killed in a moment – when the governments decide the time has come. I would think it's hard to make people believe something so foolish. No, Ellie, they're good at convincing. They need only say that the Machine doesn't work, and that we've gone a little mad.'

'I don't think we'd seem so mad if we all told our story together. But you may be right. Maybe we should try to find some evidence first. Vaygay, will you be okay when you . . . go back?'

'What can they do to me? Exile me to Gorky? I could survive that; I've had my day at the beach. . . . No, I will be safe. You and I have a mutual-security treaty, Ellie. As long as you're alive, they need me. And vice versa, of course. If the story is true, they will be glad there was a Soviet witness; eventually, they will cry it from the rooftops. And like your people, they will wonder about military and economic uses of what we saw.

'It doesn't matter what they tell us to do. All that matters is that we stay alive. Then we will tell our story – all five of us – discreetly, of course. At first only to those we trust. But those people will tell others. The story will spread. There will be no way to stop it. Sooner or later the governments will acknowledge what happened to us in the dodecahedron. And until then we are insurance policies for each other. Ellie, I am very happy about all this. It is the greatest thing that ever happened to me.'

'Give Nina a kiss for me,' she said just before he left on the night flight to Moscow.

Over breakfast, she asked Xi if he was disappointed.

'Disappointed? To go *there*' – he lifted his eyes skyward – 'to see *them*, and to be disappointed? I am an orphan of the Long March. I survived the Cultural Revolution. I was trying to grow potatoes and sugar beets for six years in the shadow of the Great Wall. Upheaval has been my whole life. I know disappointment.

'You have been to a banquet, and when you come home to your starving village you are disappointed that they do not celebrate your return? This is no disappointment. We have lost a minor skirmish. Examine the . . . disposition of forces.'

He would shortly be departing for China, where he had agreed to make no public statements about what had happened in the Machine. But he would return to supervise the dig at Xian. The tomb of Qin was waiting for him. He wanted to see how closely the Emperor resembled that simulation on the far side of the tunnels.

'Forgive me. I know this is impertinent,' she said after a while, 'but the fact that of all of us, you alone met someone who . . . In all your life, wasn't there anyone you loved?'

She wished she had phrased the question better.

'Everyone I ever loved was taken from me. Obliterated. I saw the emperors of the twentieth century come and go,' he answered. 'I longed for someone who could not be revised, or rehabilitated, or edited out. There are only a few historical figures who cannot be erased.'

He was looking at the tabletop, fingering the teaspoon. 'I devoted my life to the Revolution, and I have no regrets. But I know almost nothing of my mother and father. I have no memories of them. Your mother is still alive. You remember your father, and you found him again. Do not overlook how fortunate you are.'

★

In Devi, Ellie sensed a grief she had never before noticed. She assumed it was a reaction to the skepticism with which Project Directorate and the governments had greeted their story. But Devi shook her head.

'Whether they believe us is not very important for me. The experience itself is central. Transforming. Ellie, that really happened to us. It was *real*. The first night we were back here on Hokkaido, I dreamt that our experience was a dream, you know? But it wasn't, it wasn't.

'Yes, I'm sad. My sadness is . . . You know, I satisfied a lifelong wish up there when I found Surindar again, after all these years. He was exactly as I remembered him, exactly as I've dreamed of him. But when I saw him, when I saw so perfect a simulation, I knew: This love was precious *because* it had been snatched away, *because* I had given up so much to marry him. Nothing more. The man was a fool. Ten years with him, and we would have been divorced. Maybe only five. I was so young and foolish.'

'I'm truly sorry,' Ellie said. 'I know a little about mourning a lost love.'

'Ellie,' she replied, 'you don't understand. For the first time in my adult life, I do *not* mourn Surindar. What I mourn is the family I renounced for his sake.'

Sukhavati was returning to Bombay for a few days and then would visit her ancestral village in Tamil Nadu.

'Eventually,' she said, 'it will be easy to convince ourselves this was only an illusion. Every morning when we wake up, our experience will be more distant, more dreamlike. It would have been better for us all to stay together, to reinforce our memories. *They* understood this danger. That's why they took us to the seashore, something like our own planet, a reality we can grasp. I will not permit anyone to trivialize this experience. Remember. It really happened. It was not a dream. Ellie, don't forget.'

Eda was, considering the circumstances, very relaxed. She soon understood why. While she and Vaygay had been undergoing lengthy interrogations, he had been calculating.

'I think the tunnels are Einstein-Rosen bridges,' he said. 'General Relativity admits a class of solutions, called wormholes, similar to black holes, but with no evolutionary connection – they cannot be generated, as black holes can, by the gravitational collapse of a star. But the usual sort of wormhole, once made, expands and contracts before anything can cross through; it exerts disastrous tidal forces, and it also requires – at least as seen by an observer left behind – an infinite amount of time to get through.'

Ellie did not see how this represented much progress, and asked him to clarify. The key problem was holding the wormhole open. Eda had found a class of solutions to his field equations that suggested a new macroscopic field, a kind of tension that could be used to prevent a wormhole from contracting fully. Such a wormhole would pose none of the other problems of black holes; it would have much smaller tidal stresses, two-way access, quick transit times as measured by an exterior observer, and no devastating interior radiation field.

'I don't know whether the tunnel is stable against small perturbations,' he said. 'If not, they would have to build a very elaborate feedback system to monitor and correct the instabilities. I'm not yet sure of any of this. But at least if the tunnels can be Einstein-Rosen bridges, we can give some answer when they tell us we were hallucinating.'

Eda was eager to return to Lagos, and she could see the green ticket of Nigerian Airlines peeking out of his jacket pocket. He wondered if he could completely work through the new physics their experience had implied. But he confessed himself unsure that he would be equal to the task, especially because of what he described as his advanced age for theoretical physics. He was thirty-eight. Most of all, he told Ellie, he was desperate to be reunited with his wife and children.

She embraced Eda. She told him that she was proud to have known him.

'Why the past tense?' he asked. 'You will certainly see me again. And Ellie,' he added, almost as an after-thought, 'will you do something for me? Remember everything that happened, every detail. Write it down. And send it to me. Our experience represents experimental data. One of us may have seen some point that the others missed, something essential for a deep understanding of what happened. Send me what you write. I have asked the others to do the same.'

He waved, lifted his battered briefcase, and was ushered into the waiting project car.

They were departing for their separate nations, and it felt to Ellie as if her own family were being sundered, broken, dispersed. She too had found the experience transforming. How could she not? A demon had been exorcised. Several. And just when she felt more capable of love than she had ever been, she found herself alone.

They spirited her out of the facility by helicopter. On the long flight to Washington in the government airplane, she slept so soundly that they had to shake her awake when the White House people came aboard – just after the aircraft landed briefly on an isolated runway at Hickam Field, Hawaii.

They had made a bargain. She could go back to Argus, although no longer as director, and pursue any scientific problem she pleased. She had, if she liked, lifetime tenure.

'We're not unreasonable,' Kitz had finally said in agreeing to the compromise. 'You come back with a solid piece of evidence, something really convincing, and we'll join you in making the announcement. We'll say we asked you to keep the story quiet until we could be absolutely sure. Within reason, we'll support any re-search you want to do. If we announce the story now, though, there'll be an initial wave of enthusiasm and then

406

the skeptics will start carping. It'll embarrass you and it'll embarrass us. Much better to gather the evidence, if you can.' Perhaps the President had helped him change his mind. It was unlikely Kitz was enjoying the compromise.

But in return she must say nothing about what had happened aboard the Machine. The Five had sat down in the dodecahedron, talked among themselves, and then walked off. If she breathed a word of anything else, the spurious psychiatric profile would find its way to the media and, reluctantly, she would be dismissed.

She wondered whether they had attempted to buy Peter Valerian's silence, or Vaygay's, or Abonneba's. She couldn't see how – short of shooting the debriefing teams of five nations and the World Machine Consortium – they could hope to keep this quiet forever. It was only a matter of time. So, she concluded, they were buying time.

It surprised her how mild the threatened punishments were, but violations of the agreement, if they happened, would not come on Kitz's watch. He was shortly retiring; in a year, the Lasker Administration would be leaving office after the constitutionally mandated maximum of two terms. He had accepted a partnership in a Washington law firm known for its defense-contractor clientele.

Ellie thought Kitz would attempt something more. He seemed unworried about anything she might claim occurred at the Galactic Center. What he agonized about, she was sure, was the possibility that the tunnel was still open *to* even if not *from* the Earth. She thought the Hokkaido facility would soon be disassembled. The technicians would return to their industries and universities. What stories would they tell? Perhaps the dodecahedron would be displayed in the Science City of Tsukuba. Then, after a decent interval when the world's attention was to some extent distracted by other matters, perhaps there would be an explosion at the Machine site –

nuclear, if Kitz could contrive a plausible explanation for the event. If it was a nuclear explosion, the radiological contamination would be an excellent reason to declare the whole area a forbidden zone. It would at least isolate the site from casual observers and might just shake the nozzle loose. Probably Japanese sensibilities about nuclear weapons, even if exploded underground, would force Kitz to settle for conventional explosives. They might disguise it as one of the continuing series of Hokkaido coal-mine disasters. She doubted if any explosion – nuclear or conventional – could disengage the Earth from the tunnel.

But perhaps Kitz was imagining none of these things. Perhaps she was selling him short. After all, he too must have been influenced by Machindo. He must have a family, friends, someone he loved. He must have caught at least a whiff of it.

The next day, the President awarded her the National Medal of Freedom in a public ceremony at the White House. Logs were burning in a fireplace set in a white marble wall. The President had committed a great deal of political as well as the more usual sort of capital to the Machine Project and was determined to make the best face of it before the nation and the world. Investments in the Machine by the United States and other nations, the argument went, had paid off handsomely. New technologies, new industries were blossoming, promising at least as much benefit for ordinary people as the inventions of Thomas Edison. We had discovered that we are not alone, that intelligences more advanced than we existed out there in space. They had changed forever, the President said, our conception of who we are. Speaking for herself – but also, she thought, for most Americans – the discovery had strengthened her belief in God, now revealed to be creating life and intelligence on many worlds, a conclusion that the President was sure would be in harmony with all religions. But the greatest good granted us by the Machine, the President said, was the spirit it had brought to Earth – the increasing mutual understanding within the human community, the sense that we were all fellow passengers on a perilous journey in space and in time, the goal of a global unity of purpose that was now known all over the planet as Machindo.

The President presented Ellie to the press and the television cameras, told of her perseverance over twelve long years, her genius in detecting and decoding the Message, and her courage in going aboard the Machine. No one knew what the Machine would do. Dr Arroway had willingly risked her life. It was not Dr Arroway's fault that nothing happened when the Machine was activated. She had done as much as any human possibly could. She deserved the thanks of all Americans, and of all people everywhere on Earth. Ellie was a very private person. Despite her natural reticence, she had when the need arose shouldered the burden of explaining the Message and the Machine. Indeed, she had shown a patience with the press that she, the President, admired particularly. Dr Arroway should now be permitted some real privacy, so she could resume her scientific career. There had been press announcements, briefings, interviews with Secretary Kitz and Science Adviser der Heer. The President hoped the press would respect Dr Arroway's wish that there be no press conference. There was, however, a photo opportunity. Ellie left Washington without determining how much the President knew.

They flew her back in a small sleek jet of the Joint Military Airlift Command, and agreed to stop in Janesville on the way. Her mother was wearing her old quilted robe. Someone had put a little color on her cheeks. Ellie pressed her face into the pillow beside her mother. Beyond regaining a halting power of speech, the old woman had recovered the use of her right arm sufficiently to give Ellie a few feeble pats on her shoulder.

'Mom, I've got something to tell you. It's a great

thing. But try to be calm. I don't want to upset you. Mom . . . I saw Dad. I *saw* him. He sends you his love.'

'Yes . . .' The old woman slowly nodded. 'Was here yesterday.'

John Staughton, Ellie knew, had been to the nursing home the previous day. He had begged off accompanying Ellie today, pleading an excess of work, but it seemed possible that Staughton merely did not wish to intrude on this moment. Nevertheless, she found herself saying, with some irritation, 'No, no. I'm talking about *Dad*.'

'Tell him . . .' The old woman's speech was labored. 'Tell him, chiffon dress. Stop cleaners . . . way home from store.'

Her father evidently still ran the hardware store in her mother's universe. And Ellie's.

The long sweep of cyclone fencing now stretched uselessly from horizon to horizon, blighting the expanse of scrub desert. She was glad to be back, glad to be setting up a new, although much smaller-scale, research program.

Jack Hibbert had been appointed Acting Director of the Argus facility, and she felt unburdened of the administrative responsibilities. Because so much telescope time had been freed when the signal from Vega had ceased, there was a heady air of progress in a dozen long-languishing subdisciplines of radio astronomy. Her co-workers offered not a hint of support for Kitz's notion of a Message hoax. She wondered what der Heer and Valerian were telling their friends and colleagues about the Message and the Machine.

Ellie doubted that Kitz had breathed a word of it outside the recesses of his soon-to-be-vacated Pentagon office. She had been there once; a Navy enlisted man – sidearm in leather holster and hands clasped behind his back – had stiffly guarded the portal, in case in the warren of concentric hallways some passerby should succumb to an irrational impulse.

Willie had himself driven the Thunderbird from Wyoming, so it would be waiting for her. By agreement she could drive it only on the facility, which was large enough for ordinary joyriding. But no more West Texas landscapes, no more coney honor guards, no more mountain drives to glimpse a southern star. This was her sole regret about the seclusion. But the ranks of saluting rabbits were at any rate unavailable in winter.

At first a sizable press corps haunted the area in hopes of shouting a question at her or photographing her through a telescopic lens. But she remained resolutely isolated. The newly imported public relations staff was effective, even a little ruthless, in discouraging inquiries. After all, the President had asked for privacy for Dr Arroway.

Over the following weeks and months, the battalion of reporters dwindled to a company and then to a platoon. Now only a squad of the most steadfast remained, mostly from *The World Hologram* and other sensationalist weekly newspapers, the chiliast magazines, and a lone representative from a publication that called itself *Science and God*. No one knew what sect it belonged to, and its reporter wasn't telling.

When the stories were written, they told of twelve years of dedicated work, culminating in the momentous, triumphant decryption of the Message and followed by the construction of the Machine. At the peak of world expectation, it had, sadly, failed. The Machine had gone nowhere. Naturally Dr Arroway was disappointed, maybe, they speculated, even a little depressed.

Many editorialists commented that this pause was welcome. The pace of new discovery and the evident need for major philosophical and religious reassessments represented so heady a mix that a time of retrenchment and slow reappraisal was needed. Perhaps the Earth was not yet ready for contact with alien civilizations. Sociologists and some educators claimed that the mere existence of extraterrestrial intelligences more advanced

411

than we would require several generations to be properly assimilated. It was a body blow to human self-esteem, they said. There was enough on our plate already. In another few decades we would much better understand the principles underlying the Machine. We would see what mistake we had made, and we would laugh at how trivial an oversight had prevented it from functioning in its first full trial back in 1999.

Some religious commentators argued that the failure of the Machine was a punishment for the sin of pride, for human arrogance. Billy Jo Rankin in a nationwide television address proposed that the Message had in fact come straight from a Hell called Vega, an authoritative consolidation of his previous positions on the matter. The Message and the Machine, he said, were a latter-day Tower of Babel. Humans foolishly, tragically, had aspired to reach the Throne of God. There had been a city of fornication and blasphemy built thousands of years ago called Babylon, which God had destroyed. In our time, there was another such city with the same name. Those dedicated to the Word of God had fulfilled His purpose there as well. The Message and the Machine represented still another assault of wickedness upon the righteous and God-fearing. Here again the demonic initiatives had been forestalled – in Wyoming by a divinely inspired accident, in Godless Russia through the confounding of Communist scientists by the Divine Grace.

But despite these clear warnings of God's will, Rankin continued, humans had for a third time tried to build the Machine. God let them. Then, gently, subtly, He caused the Machine to fail, deflected the demonic intent, and once more demonstrated His care and concern for His wayward and sinful – if truth be told, His unworthy – children on Earth. It was time to learn the lessons of our sinfulness, our abominations, and, before the coming Millennium, the real Millennium that would begin on January 1, 2001, rededicate our planet and ourselves to God.

The Machines should be destroyed. Every last one of them, and all their parts. The pretense that by building a machine rather than by purifying their hearts humans could stand at the right hand of God must be expunged, root and branch, before it was too late.

In her little apartment Ellie heard Rankin out, turned off the television set and resumed her programming.

The only outside calls she was permitted were to the rest home in Janesville, Wisconsin. All incoming calls except from Janesville were screened out. Polite apologies were provided. Letters from der Heer, Valerian, from her old college friend Becky Ellenbogen, she filed unopened. There were a number of messages delivered by express mail services, and then by courier, from South Carolina, from Palmer Joss. She was much more tempted to read these, but did not. She wrote him a note that read only, 'Dear Palmer, Not yet. Ellie,' and posted it with no return address. She had no way to know if it would be delivered.

A television special on her life, made without her consent, described her as more reclusive now than Neil Armstrong, or even Greta Garbo. Ellie took it all with cheerful equanimity. She was otherwise occupied. Indeed, she was working night and day.

The prohibitions on communication with the outside world did not extend to purely scientific collaboration, and through open-channel asynchronous telenetting she and Vaygay organized a long-term research program. Among the objects to be examined were the vicinity of Sagittarius A at the center of the Galaxy, and the great extragalactic radio source, Cygnus A. The Argus telescopes were employed as part of a phased array, linked with the Soviet telescopes in Samarkand. Together, the American-Soviet array acted as if they were part of a single radio telescope the size of the Earth. Operating at a wavelength of a few centimeters, they could resolve sources of radio emission as small as the inner solar system if they were as far away as the center of the Galaxy.

413

She worried that this was not good enough, that the two orbiting black holes were considerably smaller than that. Still, a continuous monitoring program might turn up something. What they really needed, she thought, was a radio telescope launched by space vehicle to the other side of the Sun, and working in tandem with radio telescopes on Earth. Humans could thereby create a telescope effectively the size of the Earth's orbit. With it, she calculated, they could resolve something the size of the Earth at the center of the Galaxy. Or maybe the size of the Station.

She spent most of her time writing, modifying existing programs for the Cray 21, and setting down an account – as detailed as she possibly could make it – of the salient events that had been squeezed into the twenty minutes of Earthtime after they activated the Machine. Halfway through, she realized she was writing samizdat. Typewriter and carbon paper technology. She locked the original and two copies in her safe – beside a yellowing copy of the Hadden Decision – secreted the third copy behind a loose plank in the electronics bay of Telescope 49, and burned the carbon paper. It generated a black acrid smoke. In six weeks she had finished reprogramming and just as her thoughts returned to Palmer Joss, he presented himself at the Argus front gate.

His way had been cleared by a few phone calls from a special assistant to the President, with whom, of course, Joss had been acquainted for years. Even here in the Southwest with its casual sartorial codes, he wore, as always, a jacket, a white shirt, and a tie. She gave him the palm frond, thanked him for the pendant, and despite all of Kitz's admonitions to keep her delusional experience quiet, immediately told him everything.

They adopted the practice of her Soviet colleagues, who whenever anything politically unorthodox needed to be said, discovered the urgent necessity for a brisk walk. Every now and then he would stop and, a distant observer would see, lean toward her. Each time she

414

would take his arm and they would walk on.

He listened sympathetically, intelligently, indeed generously – especially for someone whose doctrines must, she thought, be challenged at their fundaments by her account . . . if he gave them any credence at all. After all his reluctance at the time the Message had first been received, at last she was showing Argus to him. He was companionable, and she found herself happy to see him. She wished she had been less preoccupied when she had seen him last, in Washington.

Apparently at random, they climbed up the narrow metal exterior stairways that straddled the base of Telescope 49. The vista of 130 radio telescopes – most of them rolling stock on their own set of railway tracks – was like nothing else on Earth. In the electronics bay she slid back the plank and retrieved a bulky envelope with Joss's name upon it. He put it in his inside breast pocket, where it made a discernible bulge.

She told him about the Sag A and Cyg A observing protocols. She told him about her computer programe.

'It's very time-consuming, even with the Cray, to calculate pi out to something like ten to the twentieth place. And we don't know that what we're looking for is *in* pi. They sort of said it wasn't. It might be *e*. It might be one of the family of transcendental numbers they told Vaygay about. It might be some altogether different number. So a simpleminded brute-force approach – just calculating fashionable transcendental numbers forever – is a waste of time. But here at Argus we have very sophisticated decryption algorithms, designed to find patterns in a signal, designed to pull out and display anything that looks nonrandom. So I rewrote the programs . . .'

From the expression on his face, she was afraid she had not been clear. She made a small swerve in the monologue.

'. . . but not to calculate the digits in a number like pi, print them out, and present them for inspection. There

415

isn't enough time for that. Instead, the program races through the digits in pi and pauses even to think about it only when there's some anomalous sequence of zeros and ones. You know what I'm saying? Something nonrandom. By chance, there'll be some zeros and ones, of course. Ten percent of the digits will be zeros, and another ten percent will be ones. On average. The more digits we race through, the longer the sequences of pure zeros and ones that we should get by accident. The program knows what's expected statistically and only pays attention to unexpectedly long sequences of zeros and ones. And it doesn't only look in base ten.'

'I don't understand. If you look at enough random numbers, won't you get any pattern you want simply by chance?'

'Sure. But you can calculate how likely that is. If you get a very complex message very early on, you know it can't be by chance. So, every day in the early hours of the morning the computer works on this problem. No data from the outside world goes in. And so far no data from the inside world comes out. It just runs through the optimum series expansion for pi and watches the digits fly. It minds its own business. Unless it finds something, it doesn't speak unless it's spoken to. It's sort of contemplating its navel.'

'I'm no mathematician, God knows. But could you give me a f'r instance?'

'Sure.' She searched in the pockets of her jump suit for a piece of paper and could find none. She thought about reaching into his inside breast pocket, retrieving the envelope she had just given him and writing on it, but decided that was too risky out here in the open. After a moment, he understood and produced a small spiral notebook.

'Thanks. Pi starts out 3.1415926 . . . You can see that the digits vary pretty randomly. Okay, a one appears twice in the first four digits, but after you keep on going for a while it averages out. Each digit – 0, 1, 2, 3, 4, 5, 6,

416

7, 8, 9 – appears almost exactly ten percent of the time when you've accumulated enough digits. Occasionally you'll get a few consecutive digits that are the same – 4444, for example – but not more than you'd expect statistically. Now, suppose you're running merrily through these digits and suddenly you find nothing but fours. Hundreds of fours all in a row. That couldn't carry any information, but it also couldn't be a statistical fluke. You could calculate the digits in pi for the age of the universe and, if the digits are random, you'd never go deep enough to get a hundred consecutive fours.'

'It's like the search you did for the Message. With these radio telescopes.'

'Yes; in both cases we were looking for a signal that's well out of the noise, something that can't be just a statistical fluke.'

'But it doesn't have to be a hundred fours – is that right? It could *speak* to us?'

'Sure. Imagine after a while we get a long sequence of just zeros and ones. Then, just as we did with the Message, we could pull a picture out, if there's one in there. You understand, it could be *anything*.'

'You mean you could decode a picture hiding in pi and it would be a mess of Hebrew letters?'

'Sure. Big black letters, carved in stone.'

He looked at her quizzically.

'Forgive me, Eleanor, but don't you think you're being a mite too . . . indirect? You don't belong to a silent order of Buddhist nuns. Why don't you just tell your story?'

'Palmer, if I had hard evidence, I'd speak up. But if I don't have any, people like Kitz will say that I'm lying. Or hallucinating. That's why that manuscript's in your inside pocket. You're going to seal it, date it, notarize it, and put it in a safety-deposit box. If anything happens to me, you can release it to the world. I give you full authority to do anything you want with it.'

'And if nothing happens to you?'

'If nothing happens to me? Then, when we find what we're looking for, that manuscript will confirm our story. If we find evidence of a double black hole at the Galactic Center, or some huge artificial construction in Cygnus A, or a message hiding inside pi, this' – she tapped him lightly on the chest – 'will be my evidence. Then I'll speak out. . . . Meantime, don't lose it.'

'I still don't understand,' he confessed. 'We know there's a mathematical order to the universe. The law of gravity and all that. How is this different? So there's order inside the digits of pi. So what?'

'No, don't you see? This *would* be different. This isn't just starting the universe out with some precise mathematical laws that determine physics and chemistry. This is a *message*. Whoever makes the universe hides messages in transcendental numbers so they'll be read fifteen billion years later when intelligent life finally evolves. I criticized you and Rankin the time we first met for not understanding this. "If God wanted us to know that he existed, why didn't he send us an unambiguous message?" I asked. Remember?'

'I remember very well. You think God is a mathematician.'

'Something like that. If what we're told is true. If this isn't a wild-goose chase. If there's a message hiding in pi and not one of the infinity of other transcendental numbers. That's a lot of ifs.'

'You're looking for Revelation in arithmetic. I know a better way.'

'Palmer, this is the *only* way. This is the only thing that would convince a skeptic. Imagine we find something. It doesn't have to be tremendously complicated. Just something more orderly than could accumulate by chance that many digits into pi. That's all we need. Then mathematicians all over the world can find exactly the same pattern or message or whatever it proves to be. Then there are no sectarian divisions. Everybody begins reading the same Scripture. No one could then argue that the key miracle in the religion was some conjurer's trick, or that later historians had falsified the record, or that it's just hysteria or delusion or a substitute parent for when we grow up. *Everyone* could be a believer.'

'You can't be sure you'll find *any*thing. You can hide here and compute till the cows come home. Or you can go out and tell your story to the world. Sooner or later you'll have to choose.'

'I'm hoping I won't have to choose, Palmer. First the physical evidence, then the public announcements. Otherwise . . . Don't you see how vulnerable we'd be? I don't mean for myself, but . . .'

He shook his head almost imperceptibly. A smile was playing at the corners of his lips. He had detected a certain irony in their circumstances.

'Why are you so eager for me to tell my story?' she asked.

Perhaps he took it for a rhetorical question. At any rate he did not respond, and she continued.

'Don't you think there's been a strange . . . reversal of our positions? Here I am, the bearer of the profound religious experience I can't prove – really, Palmer, I can barely fathom it. And here you are, the hardened skeptic trying – more successfully than I ever did – to be kind to the credulous.'

'Oh no, Eleanor,' he said, 'I'm not a skeptic. I'm a believer.'

'Are you? The story I have to tell isn't exaactly about Punishment and Reward. It's not exactly Advent and Rapture. There's not a word in it about Jesus. Part of my message is that we're not central to the purpose of the Cosmos. What happened to me makes us all seem very small.'

'It does. But it also makes God very big.'

She glanced at him for a moment and rushed on.

'You know, as the Earth races around the Sun, the powers of this world – the religious powers, the secular

419

powers – once pretended the Earth wasn't moving at all. They were in the business of being powerful. Or at least pretending to be powerful. And the truth made them feel too small. The truth frightened them; it undetermined their power. So they suppressed it. Those people found the truth dangerous. You're sure you know what believing me entails?'

'I've been searching, Eleanor. After all these years, believe me, I know the truth when I see it. Any faith that admires truth, that strives to know God, must be brave enough to accommodate the universe. I mean the *real* universe. All those light-years. All those worlds. I think of the scope of your universe, the opportunities it affords the Creator, and it takes my breath away. It's much better than bottling Him up in one small world. I never liked the idea of Earth as God's green footstool. It was too reassuring, like a children's story . . . like a tranquilizer. But your universe has *room* enough, and time enough, for the kind of God I believe in.

'I say you don't need any more proof. There are proofs enough already. Cygnus A and all that are just for the scientists. You think it'll be hard to convince ordinary people that you're telling the truth. I think it'll be easy as pie. You think your story is too peculiar, too alien. But I've heard it before. I know it well. And I bet you do too.'

He closed his eyes and, after a moment, recited:

He dreamed, and behold a ladder set up on the earth, and the top of it reached to heaven: and behold the angels of God ascending and descending on it. . . . Surely the Lord is in this place; and I knew it not. . . . This is none other but the House of God, and this is the gate of heaven.

He had been a little carried away, as if preaching to the multitudes from the pulpit of a great cathedral, and when he opened his eyes it was with a small self-deprecatory smile. They walked down a vast avenue, flanked left and right by enormous white-washed radio telescopes strain-

420

ing at the sky, and after a moment he spoke in a more conversational tone:

'Your story has been foretold. It's happened before. Somewhere inside of you, you must have known. None of your details are in the Book of Genesis. Of course not. How could they be? The Genesis account was right for the time of Jacob. Just as your witness is right for this time, for our time.

'People are going to believe you, Eleanor. Millions of them. All over the world. I know it for certain. . . .'

She shook her head, and they walked on for another moment in silence before he continued.

'All right, then. I understand. You take as much time as you have to. But if there's any way to hurry it up, do it – for my sake. We have less than a year to the Millennium.'

'I understand also. Bear with me a few more months. If we haven't found something in pi by then, I'll consider going public with what happened up there. Before January 1. Maybe Eda and the others would be willing to speak out also. Okay?'

They walked in silence back toward the Argus administration building. The sprinklers were watering the meager lawn, and they stepped around a puddle that, on this parched earth, seemed alien, out of place.

'Have you ever been married?' he asked.

'No, I never have. I guess I've been too busy.'

'Ever been in love?' The question was direct, matter-of-fact.

'Halfway, half a dozen times. But' – she glanced at the nearest telescope – 'there was always so much noise, the signal was hard to find. And you?'

'Never,' he replied flatly. There was a pause, and then he added with a faint smile, 'But I have faith.'

She decided not to pursue this ambiguity just yet, and they mounted the short flight of stairs to examine the Argus mainframe computer.

421

24

The Artist's Signature

Behold, I tell you a mystery; we shall not all sleep, but we shall all be changed.

— I Corinthians 15:51

The universe seems . . . to have been determined and ordered in accordance with number, by the forethought and the mind of the creator of all things; for the pattern was fixed, like a preliminary sketch, by the domination of number preexistent in the mind of the world-creating God.

— Nicomachus of Gerasa
Arithmetic I, 6 (ca. A.D. 100)

She rushed up the steps of the nursing home and, on the newly repainted green veranda, marked off at regular intervals by empty rocking chairs, she saw John Staughton – stooped, immobile, his arms dead weights. In his right hand he clutched a shopping bag in which Ellie could see a translucent shower cap, a flowered makeup case, and two bedroom slippers adorned with pink pom-poms.

'She's gone,' he said as his eyes focused. 'Don't go in,' he pleaded. 'Don't look at her. She would've hated for you to see her like this. You know how much pride she took in her appearance. Anyway, she's not *in* there.'

Almost reflexively, out of long practice and still unresolved resentments, Ellie was tempted to turn and enter anyway. Was she prepared, even now, to defy him as a matter of principle? What was the principle, exactly? From the havoc on his face, there was no question about the authenticity of his remorse. He had loved her mother. Maybe, she thought, he loved her more than I did, and a wave of self-reproach swept through her. Her mother had been so frail for so long that Ellie had tested, many times, how she would respond when the moment came. She remembered how beautiful her mother had been in the picture that Staughton had sent her, and suddenly, despite her rehearsals for this moment, she was wracked with sobs.

Startled by her distress, Staughton moved to comfort her. But she put up a hand, and with a visible effort regained her self-control. Even now, she could not bring herself to embrace him. They were strangers, tenuously linked by a corpse. But she had been wrong – she knew it in the depths of her being – to have blamed Staughton for her father's death.

'I have something for you,' he said as he fumbled in the shopping bag. Some of the contents circulated between top and bottom, and she could see now an imitation-leather wallet and a plastic denture case. She had to look away. At last he straightened up, flourishing a weather-beaten envelope.

'For Eleanor,' it read. Recognizing her mother's hand-writing, she moved to take it. Staughton took a startled step backward, raising the envelope in front of his face as if she had been about to strike him.

'Wait,' he said. 'Wait. I know we've never gotten along. But do me this one favor: Don't read the letter until tonight. Okay?'

In his grief, he seemed a decade older.

'Why?' she asked.

'Your favorite question. Just do me this one courtesy. Is it too much to ask?'

'You're right,' she said. 'It's not too much to ask. I'm sorry.'

He looked her directly in the eye.

'Whatever happened to you in that Machine,' he said, 'maybe it changed you.'

'I hope so, John.'

★

She called Joss and asked him if he would perform the funeral service. 'I don't have to tell you I'm not religious. But there were times when my mother was. You're the only person I can think of whom I'd want to do it, and I'm pretty sure my stepfather will approve.' He would be there on the next plane, Joss assured her.

In her hotel room, after an early dinner, she fingered the envelope, caressing every fold and scuff. It was old. Her mother must have written it years ago, carrying it around in some compartment of her purse, debating with herself whether to give it to Ellie. It did not seem newly resealed, and Ellie wondered whether Staughton had read it. Part of her hungered to open it, and part of her hung back with a kind of foreboding. She sat for a long time in the musty armchair thinking, her knees drawn up limberly against her chin.

A chime sounded, and the not quite noiseless carriage of her telefax came to life. It was linked to the Argus computer. Although it reminded her of the old days, there was no real urgency. Whatever the computer had found was not about to go away; π would not set as the Earth turned. If there was a message hiding inside π, it would wait for her forever.

She examined the envelope again, but the echo of the chime intruded. If there was content inside a transcendental number, it could only have been built into the geometry of the universe from the beginning. This new project of hers was in experimental theology. But so is all of science, she thought.

'STAND BY,' the computer printed out on the telefax screen.

She thought of her father . . . well, the simulacrum of her father . . . about the Caretakers with their network of tunnels through the Galaxy. They had witnessed and perhaps influenced the origin and development of life on millions of worlds. They were building galaxies, closing off sectors of the universe. They could manage at least a limited kind of time travel. They were gods beyond the

424

pious imaginings of almost all religions – all Western religions, anyway. But even they had their limitations. They had not built the tunnels and were unable to do so. They had not inserted the message into the transcendental number, and could not even read it. The Tunnel builders and the π inscribers were somebody else. They didn't live here any more. They had left no forwarding address. When the Tunnel builders had departed, she guessed, those who would eventually be the Caretakers had become abandoned children. Like her, like her.

She thought about Eda's hypothesis that the tunnels were wormholes, distributed at convenient intervals around innumerable stars in this and other galaxies. They resembled black holes, but they had different properties and different origins. They were not exactly massless, because she had seen them leave gravitational wakes in the orbiting debris in the Vega system. And through them beings and ships of many kinds traversed and bound up the Galaxy.

Wormholes. In the revealing jargon of theoretical physics, the universe was their apple and someone had tunneled through, riddling the interior with passageways that crisscrossed the core. For a bacillus who lived on the surface, it was a miracle. But a being standing outside the apple might be less impressed. From that perspective, the Tunnel builders were only an annoyance. But if the Tunnel builders are worms, she thought, who are we?

The Argus computer had gone deep into π, deeper than anyone on Earth, human or machine, had ever gone, although not nearly so deep as the Caretakers had ventured. This was much too soon, she thought, to be the long-undecrypted message about which Theodore Arroway had told her on the shores of that uncharted sea. Maybe this was just a gearing up, a preview of coming attractions, an encouragement to further exploration, a token so humans would not lose heart. Whatever it was, it could not possibly be the message the Caretakers were struggling with. Maybe there were easy messages and

425

hard messages, locked away in the various transcendental numbers, and the Argus computer had found the easiest. With help.

At the Station, she had learned a kind of humility, a reminder of how little the inhabitants of Earth really knew. There might, she thought, be as many categories of beings more advanced than humans as there are between us and the ants, or maybe even between us and the viruses. But it had not depressed her. Rather than a daunting resignation, it had aroused in her a swelling sense of wonder. There was so much more to aspire to now.

It was like the step from high school to college, from everything coming effortlessly to the necessity of making a sustained and disciplined effort to understand at all. In high school, she had grasped her coursework more quickly than almost anybody. In college, she had discovered many people much quicker than she. There had been the same sense of incremental difficulty and challenge when she entered graduate school, and when she became a professional astronomer. At every stage, she had found scientists more accomplished than she, and each stage had been more exciting than the last. Let the revelations roll, she thought, looking at the telefax. She was ready.

'TRANSMISSION PROBLEM. S/N<10. PLEASE STAND BY.'

She was linked to the Argus computer by a communications relay satellite called *Defcom Alpha*. Perhaps there had been an attitude-control problem, or a programming foul-up. Before she could think about it further, she found she had opened the envelope.

ARROWAY HARDWARE, the letterhead said, and sure enough, the type font was that of the old Royal her father had kept at home to do both business and personal accounts. 'June 13, 1964' was typed in the upper right-hand corner. She had been fifteen then. Her father could not have written it; he had been dead for years. A glance at the bottom of the page confirmed the neat hand of her mother.

My sweet Ellie,

Now that I'm dead, I hope you can find it in your heart to forgive me. I know I committed a sin against you, and not just you. I couldn't bear how you'd hate me if you knew the truth. That's why I didn't have the courage to tell you while I was alive. I know how much you loved Ted Arroway, and I want you to know I did, too. I still do. But he wasn't your real father. Your real father is John Staughton. I did something very wrong. I shouldn't have and I was weak, but if I hadn't you wouldn't be in the world, so please be kind when you think about me. Ted knew and he gave me forgiveness and we said we'd never tell you. But I look out the window right now and I see you in the backyard. You're sitting there thinking about stars and things that I never could understand and I'm so proud of you. You make such a point about the truth, I thought it was right that you should know this truth about yourself. Your beginning, I mean.

If John is still alive, then he's given you this letter. I know he'll do it. He's a better man than you think he is, Ellie. I was lucky to find him again. Maybe you hate him so much because something inside of you figured out the truth. But really you hate him because he isn't Theodore Arroway. I know.

There you are, still sitting out there. You haven't moved since I started this letter. You're just thinking. I hope and pray that whatever you're seeking, you'll find. Forgive me. I was only human.

Love,
Mom

Ellie had assimilated the letter in a single gulp, and immediately read it again. She had difficulty breathing. Her hands were clammy. The impostor had turned out to be the real thing. For most of her life, she had rejected her own father, without the vaguest notion of what she was doing. What strength of character he had shown during all those adolescent outbursts when she taunted him for not being her father, for having no right to tell her what to do.

The telefax chimed again, twice. It was now inviting her to press the RETURN key. But she did not have the will to go to it. It would have to wait. She thought of her Fa . . . of Theodore Arroway, and John Staughton, and her mother. They had sacrificed much for her, and she had been too self-involved even to notice. She wished Palmer were with her.

The telefax chimed once more, and the carriage moved tentatively, experimentally. She had programmed the computer to be persistent, even a little innovative, in attracting her attention if it thought it had found something in π. But she was much too busy undoing and reconstructing the mythology of her life. Her mother would have been sitting at the desk in the big bedroom upstairs, glancing out of the window as she wondered how to phrase the letter, and her eye had rested on Ellie at age fifteen, awkward, resentful, rebellious.

Her mother had given her another gift. With this letter, Ellie had cycled back and come upon herself all those years ago. She had learned so much since then. There was so much more to learn.

Above the table on which the chattering telefax sat was a mirror. In it she saw a woman neither young nor old, neither mother nor daughter. They had been right to keep the truth from her. She was not sufficiently advanced to receive that signal, much less decrypt it. She had spent her career attempting to make contact with the most remote and alien of strangers, while in her own life she had made contact with hardly anyone at all. She had been fierce in debunking the creation myths of others, and oblivious to the lie at the core of her own. She had studied the universe all her life, but had overlooked its clearest message: For small creatures such as we the vastness is bearable only through love.

The Argus computer was so persistent and inventive in its attempts to contact Eleanor Arroway that it almost conveyed an urgent personal need to share the discovery.

The anomaly showed up most starkly in Base 11 arithmetic, where it could be written out entirely as zeros and ones. Compared with what had been received from Vega, this could be at best a simple message, but its statistical significance was high. The program reassembled the digits into a square raster, an equal number across and down. The first line was an uninterrupted file of zeros, left to right. The second line showed a single numeral one, exactly in the middle, with zeros to the borders, left and right. After a few more lines, an unmistakable arc had formed, composed of ones. The simple geometrical figure had been quickly constructed, line by line, self-reflexive, rich with promise. The last line of the figure emerged, all zeros except for a single centered one. The subsequent line would be zeros only, part of the frame.

Hiding in the alternating patterns of digits, deep inside the transcendental number, was a perfect circle, its form traced out by unities in a field of noughts.

The universe was made on purpose, the circle said. In whatever galaxy you happen to find yourself, you take the circumference of a circle, divide it by its diameter, measure closely enough, and uncover a miracle — another circle, drawn kilometers downstream of the decimal point. There would be richer messages farther in. It doesn't matter what you look like, or what you're made of, or where you come from. As long as you live in this universe, and have a modest talent for mathematics, sooner or later you'll find it. It's already here. It's inside everything. You don't have to leave your planet to find it. In the fabric of space and in the nature of matter, as in a great work of art, there is, written small, the artist's signature. Standing over humans, gods, and demons, subsuming Caretakers and Tunnel builders, there is an intelligence that antedates the universe.

The circle had closed.

She found what she had been searching for.

Author's Note

Although of course I have been influenced by those I know, none of the characters herein is a close portrait of a real person. Nevertheless, this book owes much to the world SETI community – a small band of scientists from all over our small planet, working together, sometimes in the face of daunting obstacles, to listen for a signal from the skies. I would like to acknowledge a special debt of gratitude to the SETI pioneers Frank Drake, Philip Morrison, and the late I. S. Shklovskii. The search for extraterrestrial intelligence is now entering a new phase, with two major programs under way – the 8-million-channel META/Sentinel survey at Harvard University, sponsored by the Pasadena-based Planetary Society, and a still more elaborate program under the auspices of the National Aeronautics and Space Administration. My fondest hope for this book is that it will be made obsolete by the pace of real scientific discovery.

Several friends and colleagues have been kind enough to read an earlier draft and/or make detailed comments that have influenced the book's present form. I am deeply grateful to them, including Frank Drake, Pearl Druyan, Lester Grinspoon, Irving Gruber, Jon Lomberg, Philip Morrison, Nancy Palmer, Will Provine, Stuart Shapiro, Steven Soter, and Kip Thorne. Professor Thorne took the trouble to consider the galactic transportation system described herein, generating fifty lines of equations in the relevant gravitational physics. Helpful advice on content or style came from Scott Meredith, Michael Korda, John Herman, Gregory Weber, Clifton Fadiman, and the late Theodore Sturgeon. Through the many stages of the preparation of this book Shirley Arden has worked long and flawlessly; I am very grateful to her, and to Kel Arden. I thank Joshua Lederberg for first suggesting to me many years ago and perhaps playfully that a high form of intelligence might live at the center of the Milky Way Galaxy. The idea has antecedents, as all ideas do, and something similar seems to have been envisioned around 1750 by Thomas Wright, the first person to mention explicitly that the Galaxy might have a center.

This book has grown out of a treatment for a motion picture that Ann Druyan and I wrote in 1980–81. Lynda Obst and Gentry Lee facilitated that early phase. At every stage in the writing of this book I have benefited tremendously from Ann Druyan – from the earliest conceptualization of the plot and central characters to the final galley proofing. What I learned from her in the process is what I cherish most about the writing of this book.

Carl Sagan's *Cosmos*, first published in 1980, is one of the best-selling science books ever published in the English language. The accompanying Peabody and Emmy Award-winning television series was seen in 60 countries. His other books include *The Dragons of Eden*, awarded the Pulitzer Prize in 1978, *Broca's Brain*, and (with Ann Druyan) the bestseller *Comet*.

Dr Sagan was deeply involved in spacecraft exploration of the planets and in the radio search for extraterrestrial intelligence. His numerous awards include the NASA Medals for Exceptional Scientific Achievement and for Distinguished Public Service, the John F. Kennedy Astronautics Award, the Honda Prize, and the Joseph Priestley Award 'for distinguished contributions to the welfare of Mankind'. He also received the annual Awards for Public Service of the Federation of American Scientists and of Physicians for Social Responsibility.

Carl Sagan died in December 1996.